Tales of Soldiers and Civilians

Tales of Soldiers and Civilians

AMBROSE BIERCE

Edited by Donald T. Blume

ℰℯ

The Kent State University Press

KENT AND LONDON

© 2004 by The Kent State University Press, Kent, Ohio 44242

ALL RIGHTS RESERVED

Library of Congress Catalog Card Number 2003015267

ISBN 0-87338-777-5 (pbk)

ISBN 0-87338-789-9 (cloth)

Manufactured in the United States of America

08 07 06 05 04   5 4 3 2 1

Library of Congress Cataloging-in-Publication Data

Bierce, Ambrose, 1842–1914?

Tales of soldiers and civilians / Ambrose Bierce ; edited by Donald T. Blume.

p.   cm.

Includes bibliographical references.

ISBN 0-87338-789-9 (alk. paper)

ISBN 0-87338-777-5 (pbk. : alk. paper)

1. United States—History—Civil War, 1861–1865—Fiction. 2. Supernatural—Fiction.

3. Horror tales, American. 4. War stories, American. 5. Soldiers—Fiction.

I. Blume, Donald T., 1964– II. Title.

PS1097.T3 2003

813'.4—dc22   2003015267

British Library Cataloging-in-Publication data are available.

For the residents of Carcosa.

Contents

ℰℑ

Introduction

I. San Francisco, after the War

Ambrose Bierce's dedicatory preface to the 1892 collection of nineteen short stories entitled *Tales of Soldiers and Civilians* identifies the volume as "its author's main and best ambition." Readers taking this sentiment to heart are on their way to comprehending that the book, published in San Francisco in 1892,[1] was not merely a collection of nineteen loosely connected short stories awkwardly divided into two unmatched parts, but an artfully crafted masterwork offered up as an idiosyncratic writer's literary counterpoint to the popular novels and novelists of the late nineteenth century.

Culturally, politically, and economically, San Francisco in the 1880s and 1890s was the West Coast's answer—the West Coast's only answer—to all the cities east of the Rocky Mountains. In 1890, with its population rapidly approaching three hundred thousand, San Francisco was the eighth most populous city in the United States; moreover, the aggregate wealth moving through the city's businesses and ports was exceeded only by that of New York City. Understandably, popular wisdom in San Francisco during this era vociferously held that San Francisco was in all things the greatest city in the greatest state in the greatest nation on the face of the earth. While such sentiments were prevalent elsewhere in the nation during the latter decades of the nineteenth century, the residents of San Francisco had a more solid foundation for their pride. Perched on the edge of the continent and looking westward across the vast expanse of the Pacific with its islands, nations, and seas of economic opportunity, San Francisco imbibed its postwar draught of nationalism with brimming chasers of Imperialism and Manifest Destiny. The state of mind that this heady mixture produced was definitively jingoistic, and thus there should be no surprise that it was San Francisco that saw the rise of William Randolph Hearst, the nation's second newspaper magnate after Joseph Pulitzer, whose personal ambitions led to several failed presidential bids and the creation of a legendary media empire.

When Hearst, having recently graduated from Harvard, took over the reins of the *San Francisco Examiner*, his first newspaper, in the spring of 1887, his first act of note was to acquire the services of Ambrose Bierce, then the city's most famous journalist. Bierce, as both a veteran of the Civil War and a journalist, knew and understood long before most of his contemporaries that the nation's increasingly jingoistic mood of the 1880s and 1890s was a logical outgrowth of the Civil War. Bierce recognized that many veterans, far from being exhausted by the terrible conflict they had survived, were eager to soldier on. He perceived that after laying down their firearms, many if not most of the veterans had immediately and eagerly rearmed themselves: the vast majority were content to verbally revisit old battles over dinner tables and at bars; others, laying claim to battlefield glories real or imagined, ran for political office or sought in diverse ways to profit professionally from their war service. By the 1880s, this war of words had grown so hot and heavy that an experienced war veteran like Bierce could have made a career as a journalist simply by focusing on it alone.

Crucially, Bierce realized that what he satirically called the "late lamented rebellion" or the "late lukewarmness" was in demonstrable ways a more significant part of the lives of the nation's civilian population in the 1880s and 1890s than it had been during its original incarnation. From his prominent vantage point in San Francisco, Bierce had recognized since the early 1880s that veterans and noncombatants alike were glorifying war to an alarming degree. Presciently, Bierce comprehended that this process, if unchecked, would inevitably lead the nation into a similarly horrible and potentially even more foolish effusion of blood. It was against this postwar, San Francisco–based backdrop of inchoate imperialistic nationalism that Bierce wrote his "Soldiers" tales.

Of course, by the late 1880s, when Bierce began to write the bulk of the tales that comprise his 1892 collection, he had been a civilian for over twenty years. Thus, the "Civilians" tales that comprise the second seemingly dichotomous half of that collection in fact constitute an apt counterpoint to the preceding war stories: Bierce's overarching intent was no less than to explore the complex interconnections between soldiers and civilians. Stated more figuratively, Bierce recognized in *Tales of Soldiers and Civilians* that war and peace together comprise a counterpoint harmony.

II. The Author of "Prattle"

During the 1880s and 1890s, the residents of the San Francisco area were intimately familiar with Bierce through his famous and infamous, usually satirical, and always thought-provoking weekly "Prattle" column. Beginning in the latter half of the 1870s, the column, an outgrowth of the "Town Crier" column Bierce had taken over at the *San Francisco News Letter and California Advertiser*, was published successively in the San Francisco–based *Argonaut*, *Wasp*, and *Examiner* papers for over two decades. As may be imagined, the scope and quality of Bierce's writings in "Prattle" make a brief and accurate general description somewhat elusive but worth pursuing. A typical column might contain entries about the ravages of mad dogs, the misbehavior of socially climbing men and women, and the collusion between nonexistent ghosts and predatory spiritualists, and yet it could just as easily focus on the actions of corrupt politicians and businessmen, or on a strange-but-true tale of an average citizen then making the rounds in the local press. As a critic of contemporary culture, Bierce directed his ire at murderers of all stripes, bad minor poets, local cranks, world-renowned novelists and writers, local artists, medical quacks, famous actors and actresses, potential and actual supervisors of asylums for the insane or blind, dog lovers, and sundry other subjects. By the standards of his day and ours, Bierce's journalism was often brilliantly insightful, viciously libelous, petty, and grand, frequently in the space of a single paragraph. Bierce could calmly eviscerate an aspiring local poet in a single sentence and have done with him or her forever, and yet he could also pour forth over a span of many weeks a seemingly endless stream of vituperative paragraphs about the unnatural horrors of oleomargarine. Nothing and nobody were safe from censorious criticism in "Prattle," which in effect and in sum was a public journal of Bierce's private thoughts.

Considered collectively, then, "Prattle" is a complex tapestry. Many of its themes and subjects surface repeatedly and consistently over the years and give the column a recognizable underlying pattern, but other topics are like random threads surfacing once or twice or a dozen times, then disappearing perhaps forever, perhaps to await a later year or season. "Prattle," in short, presents Bierce's idiosyncratic and therefore occasionally distorted view of reality: in individual "Prattle" columns little things often assume for a paragraph or two or ten immense significance, even as reputedly great events are deliberately paled into insignificance via probing inquiries or curt dismissals. Through such means Bierce quite deliberately attempted to train his regular readers to think like himself. Thus, if Bierce lavished attention on a subject and rendered it significant, or if he argued that a seemingly burning issue or ascendant human figure was a thing of the moment destined for oblivion, readers either agreed or fell by Bierce's intellectual wayside.

Ironically, critics who have belittled Bierce for skewering countless no-bodies even while praising him both for taking on "rail rogues" like Leland Stanford and Collis Huntington and for criticizing prejudice directed against San Francisco's Chinese immigrants and Jews simply have not understood Bierce's method: his criticism carried the weight it did in large part because it was not constrained to traditionally significant issues. Indeed, it was because Bierce took up his editorial pen in early 1883 and decried in "Prattle" the all-too-readily perceived evils of that time's oleomargarine and the obviously inflated literary claims of local poets and writers every bit as loudly and per-sistently as he decried the more obscure evils of the railroad barons, corrupt politicians, and famous authors that readers of "Prattle" were inclined to value his stands against these more prominent figures. In effect, Bierce's low criti-cism enabled the success of his more ambitious criticism by encouraging read-ers to place a high degree of trust in his critical judgment (oleomargarine of the day was typically made from animal byproducts of at best dubious prov-enance). It was across this wide-ranging journalistic backdrop that Bierce wrote the nineteen "Soldiers" and "Civilians" tales he would eventually pub-lish together and yet divided as *Tales of Soldiers and Civilians.*

III. THE HETERODOX LITERARY CRITIC

Much of Bierce's literary criticism that found its way into "Prattle" verges on what some might today judge contrary or perverse. In fact, Bierce's critical perspective is more properly termed *heterodox:* he had an abiding interest in attacking orthodoxies wherever he encountered them. The two most ortho-dox and prominent writers Bierce most dramatically attacked during this pe-riod remain prominent today: Henry James and W. D. Howells. While he criticized many writers, Bierce's anathematic criticisms of James and Howells are particularly telling and need to be examined; still, before considering them, we need to understand the intellectual origins of his critical stance.

Unlike his near contemporaries and acquaintances Bret Harte and Samuel Clemens, who opportunistically first founded their reputations in the San Francisco literary marketplace and then quickly and permanently abandoned San Francisco in search of further fame and fortune in the East, Bierce ulti-mately followed a much different course even though he initially intended to follow the same trail. Arriving in San Francisco in the fall of 1866, he quickly carved out the solid beginnings of a journalistic career in the city, and then, after auspiciously marrying on Christmas Day in 1871, the following spring he traveled to England with his bride, Mary Ellen, or Mollie. In England, Bierce and his wife quickly made a home for themselves and the first and then the second of their children. In the spring of 1875, while Bierce continued to write, Mollie Bierce returned to California with the two children for what was planned to be a temporary visit; however, when she relayed to her husband the news that she was pregnant with the couple's third child, the plan changed and Bierce returned to San Francisco in the fall of 1875. And thus San Francisco recovered one of its rising literary stars.

By the early 1880s, when he accepted the position of editor at the San Francisco–based *Wasp*, Bierce's star was ascendant and bright. In a very real sense, Bierce had become and would remain for the better part of two decades the most important critical voice in San Francisco. While his criticism cut a wide swath through culture in all its manifestations, when he was in the proper critical mood Bierce saw himself as the West's answer to W. D. Howells. In other words, Bierce may have been only an occasional literary critic, but when he was that literary critic he commanded a wide audience. In particular, San Francisco's aspiring writers, whose ranks eventually included Frank Norris and Jack London, if they ignored Bierce's oracular pronouncements, did so at their peril. (Norris and London apparently listened.)

When he did utter them, Bierce's pronouncements tended to be thunderous. Nine years prior to the publication of *Tales of Soldiers and Civilians*, but only shortly after that book's first story, "A Holy Terror," appeared in the *Wasp* on December 23, 1882, Bierce attacked what he saw as the overblown literary reputations of Henry James and W. D. Howells. Writing in his *Wasp*-based "Prattle" column on February 17, 1883, Bierce poured out a stream of critical ink that smoked and burned with righteous indignation:

> I have not seen the current number of the *London Quarterly Review*, but the *Bulletin* of Saturday last reprinted from it some coldly just criticism of the literary work of Messrs. W. D. Howells and Henry James, Jr. These two eminent triflers and cameo-cutters-in-chief to Her Littleness the Bostonese small virgin, have for some years been the acknowledged leaders of American literature. Their measureless, meaningless and unimaginative novels, destitute of plot, destitute of purpose, destitute of art, are staple subjects of discussion in coteries of the "cultured." One may not have read Homer, Goethe or Hugo, but let him look to himself if he have not studied James. One may venture to fall ill of Scott, but woe betide the luckless wight unwell of too much Howells. For there shall arise a soft-eyed Creature of the Craze and slay him in the midst of tumultuous applause.
>
> Hawthorne, Bryant, Emerson, Longfellow—these are dead and damned. Whittier, Lowell, Holmes—they speak to averted understandings. These

noble names of a golden age amongst whose palaces and temples we moved unaware gleam dim and spectral in the enchanted moondawn of their successors. While yet the sky is all ablaze with crimson glories of the day that is done, the orb of the new dispensation unveils her fat and foolish face and looks over the hills like a man with a lantern. Outlined against her disc in transient silhouette, behold the figures of this brace of nobodies, complacently enamored of their own invirility and poring like sponges the vocal incense of a valleyful of idiots.

> The conscious swains, rejoicing in the sight,
> Eye the blue vault and bless the useful light,

But I venture to tell them it is all moonshine—that this new literature is the offspring of mental incapacity wet-nursed by a conspiracy. The American literature that is in vogue at any one time is the literature of the magazines, the form and direction being given by the *Atlantic Monthly*, whose editor may easily be a fool, but *ex officio* he is an Olympian deity. Our magazines are the advertising circulars of the book-publishers who own them. Their function is to "puff" the books which first appeared as serials in their pages. In their pages their writers "puff" one another. In the *Atlantic*, for example, the editor, T. B. Aldrich (a nerveless, colorless jellyfish of literature) will have a long laudatory review of W. D. Howells. A few months later W. D. Howells will have a long laudatory review of Henry James, Jr. Later, Henry James, Jr., will come to the fore with a long laudatory review of T. B. Aldrich, and the circle is complete. Three dwarfs have towered above the heads of their fellow men by standing on one another's shoulders in turn.

The public does not "drop on to" this thrifty game; even the press is deluded by it. The *Atlantic* has played it boldly with marked cards since its foundation. *Harper* was quick to emulate, and *The Century* has been taken into full fellowship. There is no kind of cheating that this trinity of literary blacklegs do not practice: their play understands itself all the time. Ladies and gentlemen of culture, you have the distinguished honor of assisting at it as victims of it. Men and women of cultivation are otherwise engaged at another table.

Out of all this are evolved literary reputations. Men of letters manufacture one another. The two finest products of the mill are James and Howells. Neither can think and the latter cannot write. He can not write at all. The other day, in fulfillment of a promise, I took a random page of this man's work and in twenty minutes had marked forty solecisms—instances of the use of words without a sense of their importance or a knowledge of their meaning—the substitution of a word that he did not want for a word that he did not think of. Confusion of thought leads to obscurity of expression. Without words there is no thought, only feeling, emotion. Words are the mechanism of thought. The master knows his machine, and precision is nine parts of style. This Howells thinks into the hopper and the mangled thought comes out all over his cranky apparatus in gobs and splashes of expression. His loose locutions resemble the clean-cut rhetoric of a master as the ropy riddances of a cowfrog resemble the polished and definite productions of a lady linnet.[2]

This representative salvo of thought was deliberately confrontational. As the editor and chief contributor to the *Wasp*, which at the time had a weekly circulation of nearly thirteen thousand copies, Bierce had ample reason in February of 1883 to think himself more than the equal of Howells as a writer and thinker, nor did he cater, as he felt James did, to the cramped literary tastes of shriveled Boston virgins who preferred their novels to be "meaningless and unimaginative" and worse.

IV. A Novel of His Own

In fact, while Bierce considered the popular and critically acclaimed novels of his day to be aesthetically moribund, he did not hold all novelists and novels in disesteem. For example, Bierce consistently praised two men, Victor Hugo and Leo Tolstoy, whose greatest works had, as Bierce was well aware, appeared prior to 1880. Rather than catering to the debased literary tastes of the American public by writing novels after the fashion of Howells and James and their ilk, Bierce, when he decided to make his definitive literary mark, elected to follow a different course. And so, upon taking up his position at the *Examiner*, he most visibly focused his creative talent on the short story or prose tale. As might be expected, this interest in the prose tale, coupled with Bierce's well-known distaste for contemporary novelists and novels, has long caused Bierce to be rather dismissively viewed as an imitator or lesser literary descendant of Edgar Allan Poe, particularly where his horror and ghost stories are concerned. In part because of this oversimplification, Bierce's "main and best ambition" has, in terms of its presence in the literary anthologies, been rendered down by scholars and critics seeking to identify the "best" or "most important" products of Bierce's pen into three short stories: "An Occurrence at Owl Creek Bridge," "Chickamauga, and "The Man and the Snake." At least in part as a result, Bierce has been relegated to a minor place in American letters, merely, one might argue, because he failed to write a novel.[3]

For his part, Bierce did not limit his own highest praise to one or two short stories, but to a book containing nineteen. This distinction is significant as *Tales of Soldiers and Civilians* was almost certainly conceived of by Bierce as his rebuttal to or version of the late-nineteenth-century American novel and thus the book, if we are to be fair to Bierce's vision, must be understood as a single work.

Apart from the work itself, perhaps the most authoritative evidence that can be cited in support of the claim that *Tales of Soldiers and Civilians* was conceived of by Bierce as a kind of novel is found in Walter Neale's 1929 biography of Bierce (*Life of Ambrose Bierce*, New York: Neale). In his study, Neale, a close friend of Bierce during the last decade of the author's life, reproduced a conversation he had had with Bierce about novels. In it, Neale, apparently wholly oblivious to the ironic implications of what he was writing down for posterity, recorded that Bierce described a novel as "a collection of short stories, rather loosely connected usually, and frequently so disconnected as to be unintelligible" (376). This cryptic definition seems to have been tailored by Bierce with *Tales of Soldiers and Civilians* in mind: he certainly knew at this time in his life and career that his artfully assembled collection of nineteen tales had proven largely unintelligible to most readers, and, unlike most late-nineteenth-century novels (but not wholly unlike many earlier picaresque novels), Bierce's book was in point of fact a collection of short stories. Bierce's definition is, as is typical with Bierce, open to divergent interpretations. Some may choose, as Neale did, to view it as a typical example of Bierce's well-known cynical attitude toward novels; that said, it is important to note that Neale, who has been fairly described by critics as Bierce's Boswell, was not always fully aware of Bierce's elaborate machinations and Bierce thus had the ability to employ Neale as an unwitting medium capable of relaying important information to posterity.

Neale, in addition to being Bierce's friend and biographer, is in fact the publisher responsible for producing *The Collected Works of Ambrose Bierce*, which appeared in twelve volumes between 1909 and 1912. For rather obvious reasons, the volumes have long been critically regarded as the repository of Bierce's definitive works. Planned and produced late in Bierce's life, the volumes have furthermore been widely taken to be the product of an aging author's desire to gratify a misplaced sense of his own importance. In point of fact, an examination of Bierce's correspondence with Neale and Silas O. Howes, another close friend, reveals that Neale and not Bierce was the driving force behind this seemingly self-serving project. A "fan" of Bierce, Neale was personally responsible for the grandiose scope of the endeavor—including the midproduction expansion of the project from ten to twelve volumes. Ironically, even though he personally selected what went into the twelve volumes, Bierce privately agreed with the contemporary critics who were condemning the earlier volumes for being overly voluminous long before the project was completed. Tellingly, however, Bierce's letters reveal that he was practically hamstrung by Neale's insistence that each volume contain four hundred pages of material. This requirement for four-hundred-page volumes is of particular relevance to the present critical reputation of *Tales of Soldiers and Civilians*—a reputation that rests largely on the bloated and greatly altered twenty-six-tale collection that resulted at least in part from Neale's requirement.

The degree to which Bierce found Neale's imposition of a four-hundred-page volume length irksome is worth considering in more detail, but it should be noted first that the surviving correspondence suggests that Bierce never tried to republish his original nineteen-story volume of 1892 which had already been displaced in the marketplace by a revised, reordered, and expanded 1898 volume issued by Putnam's. Instead, Bierce seems to have regarded the successful completion of his entire *Collected Works* as taking precedence over the prior literary claims of individual volumes. Because of this change in authorial intention, the second volume of that project, *In the Midst of Life (Tales of Soldiers and Civilians)* never seems to have been regarded by Bierce as a volume that merited special treatment. Thus it was that in the spring of 1908 Bierce quickly prepared the volume and sent it off for Neale's approval. Having apparently already added at least one story, "A Resumed Identity," to this second volume, Bierce complained somewhat resentfully in a June 24, 1908, letter to Neale about the latter's request for even more material. Neale, believing 100,000 words were required to produce volumes of four hundred pages, had previously sent word counts of the first two volumes as part of his plea. According to Neale's estimates, Bierce's planned *Ashes of the Beacon* contained 77,630 words and *In the Midst of Life (Tales of Soldiers and Civilians)* 87,453. Bierce disagreed with Neale's math, but more significantly objected to the effect additions would have on both *In The Midst of Life (Tales of Soldiers and Civilians)* and *Can Such Things Be?* the third volume of the project:

> As to the stories ("In the Midst of Life") I cannot bring that book up to 100,000 without taking from Vol. III, as planned now; and then for Vol. III I should have to take from another volume stories of a different kind. In short, to make 100,000 would break up all my present plans, entail more new writing than I could do in the year of the contract, and produce a less coherent result.
>
> I figure that 87,453 words will make 400 pages of nearly 220 words each. (This takes no account of the possible "introduction.") That it seems to me is enough.

However, I'm adding some stories that I thought I had lost to Vol. III ("Can Such Things Be?") and hope to have the book ready for you when you come. Then we will see how much *that* will contain, and know what to do in the matter of the *story* volumes.

I assure you it has been no light labor to plan this thing as far as I've got, getting in all that I want in, and not having to use what I *don't* want in order to fill out spaces unprovided for. The dam [*sic*] stuff is not elastic; it's hard to make it *fit* into the volumes.

Although the "possible 'introduction'" for the second volume never materialized, Bierce's frustrated references to "this thing" and the "stuff" it was being formed from suggests that he viewed the eventual completion of his *Collected Works* as the main thrust of all his labor. Similarly, despite his expressed desire to retain his right to select the contents of his volumes, this letter reveals he was not above tampering with the aesthetic integrity of individual volumes in order to move the project toward completion.

On July 20, 1909, Bierce informed Neale of a last-minute change in the contents of the two volumes. In his letter, Bierce explained that the proofs of *In the Midst of Life* would "go to Hamilton's shop" the following morning and that he had included a table of contents on which he had "marked . . . three (3) stories to be taken out and put into Vol. III." In the remainder of the paragraph Bierce revealed the details:

> Hope it does not give too much trouble—I had to consider the matter of suitableness for that volume, as fixed by its title. I have not marked these stories for transference, in the proofs, thinking it will be better for you to give the order. They are, as you will see, "A Tough Tussle," "A Resumed Identity," and "The Damned Thing."

Despite this assertion that he has had to consider the "suitableness" of the three tales for inclusion in *Can Such Things Be?* the evidence in the correspondence record reveals that Bierce quickly acknowledged erring in his removal of "A Tough Tussle" from *In The Midst of Life (Tales of Soldiers and Civilians)*. Not long after the second volume of his *Collected Works* appeared in print, Bierce, in a letter to Howes dated November 11, 1909, responding to his friend's criticism of the new volume, was unable to explain why the story had migrated to *Can Such Things Be?* Reconstructing Howes's criticism from Bierce's extant reply of November 11, 1909, Howes had observed that Bierce's decision to remove "A Tough Tussle" from the collection and place it into *Can Such Things Be?* was a mistake. Tellingly, Bierce did not disagree in his reply, but instead graciously and quickly conceded Howes's point: "why I took out the 'Tough Tussle' from Vol. II and put it into Vol. III I don't now remember. By its character it belongs in the former."

In his haste to cut and paste together the pages needed to bring his various volumes in closer to the required four hundred pages, Bierce had perhaps forgotten that the story's apparent uncanny elements (which if truly supernatural made the tale more appropriate for inclusion in *Can Such Things Be?*) were in fact carefully accounted for by wholly rational explanations. Similarly, this desire to find material suitable for inclusion in *Can Such Things Be?* can account for the removal of "The Middle Toe of the Right Foot," "Haïta, the Shepherd," and "An Inhabitant of Carcosa" from the 1909 collection. Ironically, this proposed explanation calls into question several of Bierce's additions to the 1909 collection, as the stories Bierce added include "The Famous Gilson Bequest," which concludes with the appearance of Gilson's ghost, and "The Eyes of the Panther," which features a woman whose eyes have the uncanny ability to mimic a panther's.

Ultimately, it seems that the final form of the *Collected Works* version of *In the Midst of Life (Tales of Soldiers and Civilians)* was more heavily influenced by matters of expediency than of literary art. Nevertheless, generations of critics have persisted in erroneously equating this last authoritative volume of "Soldiers" and "Civilians" tales with Bierce's best edition. While Neale and many critics may have shared this misapprehension, Bierce knew differently: his best edition was his first, *Tales of Soldiers and Civilians*. Of course, if true this would seem to provide all the more incentive for Bierce to have republished his original collection and redeem his contemporary critical reputation, but in 1909 Bierce was not particularly concerned with his contemporary reputation.

V. An Elaborate Deception

In Neale's biography of Bierce, we can see just how remote the 1892 collection had become during the last years of Bierce's life. After quoting extensively from an essay about Bierce by Bierce's late friend the critic Percival Pollard, Neale, noting Pollard's description of the original *Tales of Soldiers and Civilians*, observed that he had been "unable to identify 'the thin little volume' comprising nineteen stories" that Pollard had singled out for high praise. Pollard's description concluded with a line that should have revealed much: "In this book of his, on which his fame must largely rest, there were but nineteen stories." From this statement Neale concluded that Pollard was in all probability referring to a mutilated, pirated edition (282). Compounding his error, Neale wrote, "Evidently, Pollard did not intend to imply that the nineteen stories to which he refers were selected by him for special mention from many others" (283). Ironically but understandably, given his friend's emotional and financial interest in the *Collected Works* project, Bierce seems never to have told Neale that his 1892 collection had a special significance.

While the reasons already considered help explain why Bierce allowed the nineteen stories of his 1892 collection to swell to twenty-two in 1898 and then twenty-six in his 1909 collection, it is equally important to realize that Bierce, who had long believed that the critical reputations of authors were subject to posthumous revision, had concluded that his literary reputation would benefit more from a remote and thorough posthumous reevaluation than it could from a last-minute flurry of positive but ephemeral publicity. Of course, it may seem that Bierce could have more easily facilitated a positive posthumous critical reappraisal by insisting that Neale allow him to reconstruct his 1892 collection, but Bierce quite possibly felt the literary mystery he was creating would better serve his ultimate goal. Hinting at the true state of things concerning his 1909 collection, in a letter of November 1, 1909, to his friend Howes, Bierce opined, "You'll see that it is more and less than 'In the Midst of Life' [of 1898] and that book's predecessor, 'Tales of Soldiers and Civilians.'" The words "more" and "less" in Bierce's sentence are somewhat confusing. Although the story count grew from nineteen to twenty-two in the 1898 collection, and to a final twenty-six in the 1909 collection, in reality the 1909 collection was less one "Soldiers" story ("A Tough Tussle") and three "Civilians" stories ("The Middle Toe of the Right Foot," "Haïta, the Shepherd," and "An Inhabitant of Carcosa") that had been present in the original 1892 collection. Thus, the twenty-six stories in the 1909 collection include six more "Soldiers" tales and five more "Civilians" tales that were not present in the original collection. Finally, the word "less" in Bierce's description also probably reflects Bierce's tacit admission that the 1909 collection was less aesthetically satisfying than his earlier collections, and the use of the term "predecessor" accurately conveys how Bierce viewed his earlier books: they were dead and buried, rightly the property of posthumous critics.

As if deliberately included to facilitate those posthumous critics, evidence of Bierce's continued preference for his original title and his original collection remains visible in the opening pages of the 1909 volume. Thus he retained the original *Tales of Soldiers and Civilians* title in parentheses following the title imposed on the 1892 English edition of his collection by Chatto and Windus; moreover, he restored the preface of the original collection: "Denied existence by the chief publishing houses of the country, this book owes itself to Mr. E. L. G. STEELE, merchant, of this city. In attesting Mr. STEELE's faith in his judgment and his friend, it will serve its author's main and best ambition." Because the 1892 and 1909 collections are so obviously different in content, the restoration of this preface goes beyond mere convention. Beneath its seeming conventionality, the restored preface allowed Bierce to subtly point his literary finger back to the work that remained his "main and best ambition." Indeed, the original preface does not directly identify the 1892 book as that "main and best ambition." Instead, Bierce cryptically claims the book "will serve its author's main and best ambition" by affirming or verifying "Mr. Steele's faith in his judgment and his friend." Ultimately this is merely a roundabout way of saying that the book will serve to prove the merits of the book.

The scenario sketched out in the preceding paragraphs may seem overly devious, but skeptics should reserve their judgment: the convoluted intricacies of this plot can be traced much further. To a certain extent, the strange nature of Bierce's treatment of the book stems from the rejection of the original collection by Putnam's. At some point after this house objected to the inclusion of the "Civilians" material, Bierce, knowing what he was about and undoubtedly incensed at the colossal stupidity of professional East Coast editors, enlisted the financial backing of his friend E. L. G. Steele, a local San Francisco businessman, and brought out the book on his own terms. As far as Bierce was concerned, the plot only thickened when the London-based house that secured the English rights to the book took it upon itself to reorder the volume's contents and issue it under their own preferred title, *In The Midst of Life*. Biographers and critics have long been aware that Bierce initially reacted to these developments with what can be fairly termed outrage. But, typically, these same biographers and critics have interpreted Bierce's use of title supplied by Chatto and Windus for the 1898 and 1909 collections as evidence that he eventually realized the superior merits of this title. In fact, even in public Bierce never fully reconciled himself to the title given his collection by Chatto and Windus: in both the 1898 and 1909 collections he retained his original title as a subtitle. While some could argue (as Bierce himself did in his 1898 preface) that the original title was retained in this capacity to avoid misleading potential purchasers of the collection, by the time the 1909 collection appeared this concern no longer existed: the volume was specifically identified as part of a collected edition of Bierce's works. Nevertheless, Bierce pointedly both retained his original title in parentheses, and restored the original collection's dedicatory preface to E. L. G. Steele.

Critics have long brought their own biases to bear when interpreting Bierce's regard for the title given his book by Chatto and Windus. To date, the most detailed defense of the title forced on Ambrose Bierce's book has been that of Mary Grenander in her essay "Ambrose Bierce and *In The Midst of Life*."[4] Grenander, not aware of certain *Examiner*-based evidence, argued that Bierce had finally come around to accepting and endorsing the title of the English edition—"a stroke of genius Bierce was slow to appreciate"—by the time his 1898 collection went to press (331, 325). Aware that Bierce had reacted with extreme dismay to the title when he had first become aware of it, Grenander attempted to explain Bierce's reaction: "Possibly he did not recognize its source as the burial service in the Anglican Book of Common Prayer, for the unstated part is what reverberates in the reader's mind: 'In the midst of life we are in death'" (325). In fact, several "Prattle" entries make it abundantly clear that Bierce was quite familiar with the phrase. A *Wasp*-based "Prattle" passage of February 3, 1882, provides a suitable example:

> My brethren and sisters, the pretext of my discourse will be found in the Book of Jehosaphat, seventeenth chapter and fourth verse: "And they laid him out." Now, my fellow travelers to the bar of eternity, there are various kinds of laying out. Firstly, there is the laying out of a town. . . . Secondly, you poor weak worms and miserable sinners (Brother Fitch will please remain seated) there is the lay-out of a gambler. . . . Thirdly, my beloved lambs, there is the layung [*sic*] out of a corpse—and that is the sort that the inspired writer had in mind. "And they that laid him out." Think of it— "they laid him out!"
>
> Brethren and sisters it is awful. "In the midst of life we are in death." Man cometh up as a flower—a lily of the valley, as it were—and first thing he knows he is cut down—and they lay him out. It was but yesterday, my friends, that Brother Langerman was abroad in the land. He held his head high and his elbows out; he was conspicuously to the fore. But the ways of Providence are not as man's ways—and they laid him out. The seals were broken from the vials of wrath—and they laid him out. In the twinkling of an eye he was changed—for they laid him out. And now, brethren, may the blessings of common sense, the communion and fellowship of the *Wasp*, rest and abide with this congregation forever *and* ever, amen.

Clearly, Bierce was no stranger to the words Chatto and Windus attached to his collection of tales. Furthermore, one main objection Bierce would have had to the title is revealed in the "Prattle" passage: the phrase in question, which appears in the "Order for the Burial of the Dead" in the English *Book of Common Prayer*, has an obvious and inescapable Christian connotation.

Similarly, Grenander's assertion that the preface to Bierce's 1898 edition of *In the Midst of Life* provides "some indication that he was beginning to recognize the merit of Chatto's [title]" is equally suspect, especially when we note that a decade later Bierce recycled the preface of the original collection in his 1909 volume (329). In fact, Bierce's disregard for the English title had not diminished over the years if an *Examiner* article of February 21, 1897, can be trusted. Despite the passage of five full years since the publication of his 1892 collection, Bierce, writing in "Ambrose Bierce on Writer Folk," does not evince a great deal of sympathy for the title's supposed merits:

> An animated discussion is "on" in London over a mischance that has befallen one Albert Sutro, who made, for Messrs. Henry, publishers, a translation of Maeterlinck's "Seven Princesses." The translation, as sent in, had the approval of Maeterlinck himself, but it lacked that of Messrs. Henry, it seems; for when the book appeared the text had been so altered that the translator hardly recognized it, his own name being about the only familiar thing in the scheme of words. It is perhaps natural that he should "rise to remark" and his "language is plain." He will learn patience by and by, and might profit by my own humble example. Messrs. Chatto & Windus, of London, bought the English copyright of a book of mine, and not only "cut it about" to suit themselves, but actually substituted for my title a title of their own. If their rascality had been balked at that point they would have been sick. It was not: I have recently learned from Baron Tauchnitz, who published it at Leipzig (and whom I had always supposed to have "pirated" it) that he paid Chatto & Windus for the continental rights— which they did not own! Tauchnitz supposed that he was paying me. The book not being copyrighted in Germany—he did not really owe me anything; so it is a matter between him and the gentlemen who fleeced him. The matter is mentioned here merely to show that there are two kinds of publishers: one tries to pay an honorarium to an author whom he does not owe; the other intercepts and pockets it.

At this late date, then, Bierce had not yet accepted the merits of the title kindly supplied by the English publisher. Moreover, he provided indirect evidence of where his true allegiance rested by quoting from Bret Harte's poem "Plain Language from Truthful James," a brief poem about the deceptive nature of an apparently inexperienced Chinese card player that effectively put Harte on the literary map. Given the context of the article, Bierce's decision to quote Harte in this particular instance is especially appropriate since another of Harte's works, the well-known *Tales of the Argonauts*, a collection of stories about California's Gold Rush era first published in 1875, provided inspiration for at least two of Bierce's tales ("A Holy Terror" and "An Heiress from Redhorse"), and Bierce quite probably was thinking of this book when he composed the original title of his collection, *Tales of Soldiers and Civilians*. For that matter, the title *Tales of Soldiers and Civilians* appears to descend not only from Harte's *Tales of the Argonauts*, but also from such classic American short story collections as Poe's *Tales of the Grotesque and Arabesque* and Hawthorne's *Twice-Told Tales*.[5] It therefore seems reasonable to conclude that Bierce chose his title with these men and their important contributions to American literature and the genre of the prose tale in mind.

During the 1880s and early 1890s, Bierce knew that short stories or tales written in the English language were first and foremost an American genre, despite inroads then being made by the British, including, for example, the publication of Rudyard Kipling's *Plain Tales from the Hills* in 1887. Thus, the evidence suggests that Bierce thought carefully and deeply about his original title and pretentiously chose it with these prestigious American predecessors in mind. In any event, given the internal and interrelated complexity of the stories contained under the title, the unvoiced but apparent critical assumption that Bierce, with little or no forethought, attached a simplistic title to his collection in order to fulfill that requirement of bookmaking is patently ludicrous.

Of course, despite his initial outrage, Bierce retained the English title in his 1898 and 1909 editions, suggesting that he had come to accept the merits of the title. As we have seen, Grenander argues that the preface of the 1898 edition contains additional evidence of this shift. Ironically, with a shift in perspective, the 1898 preface can be viewed in an entirely different light:

> In reissuing this book, with considerable alterations and additions, it has been thought expedient, for uniformity, to give it the title under which it was published in London and Leipzig. The merely descriptive name of the original American edition (published by the late E. L. G. Steele) is retained as a sub-title in order to prevent misunderstandings by purchasers—if the book be so fortunate as to have any.

Certainly, for individuals impressed by the readily apparent "literary" heft of the London-derived title or for a publisher like Putnam's that had after all rejected Bierce's original collection, this preface may well seem to support the conclusion that Bierce has recognized the imposed title's merits. Still, it is quite easy to extract a different meaning from the preface than the one Grenander identified. Even on its surface, Bierce's vague assertion that "it has been thought expedient" to adopt the English title is hardly a rousing endorsement of it. Who in fact had this expedient thought? Bierce or a faceless editor? If we assume the latter, then Bierce's labeling of his original title as being "merely descriptive" is easily read as Bierce's own cynical restatement of an argument proffered against his preferred original title by that same editor. In this light, the preface to the 1898 edition suggests that Bierce was at the time both far from happy about the imposed title, and exacting a subtle measure of revenge on those parties responsible for its continued existence. Even more tellingly, Bierce's inclusion in parentheses of the 1892 volume's publisher, "the late E. L. G. Steele," effectively but slyly belies the apparent sentiments of the previous lines: if his apparent disregard for the original collection's title had been sincere it is unlikely that Bierce would have identified his late friend by name and so tarnish his reputation by inference.

Ultimately, the available evidence suggests that Bierce maintained, even after seeing his 1909 collection into print, a high regard for the original *Tales of Soldiers and Civilians* of 1892. Furthermore, the fact that Bierce appears to have encrypted this regard into both the 1909 volume's title and dedication, and variously into his communications with Howes and Neale, suggests that Bierce knew there was much more to the original 1892 volume than met the untutored eye.

VI. A NOVEL OF TWO PARTS

The complete story of how the 1892 volume took shape is far beyond the scope of this introduction, but a few of the highlights should be addressed. On July 21, 1889, Bierce in his *Examiner*-based "Prattle" made a brief and seemingly almost optimistic reference to "the American novel of the future" which he hoped would consist of two parts, "one part labeled 'For Ladies,' the other 'For Gents.'" Indirectly, this "Prattle" column provides evidence that Bierce's eventual production of a book divided into two sections was a carefully considered endeavor:

> Mrs. Florence Finch Kelley has published a book of fiction with the warning sub-title—adapted from the English of Edmund Yates: "A Story for Men and Women."[6] That is honest of Mrs. Kelley, and I commend her forethought to Mesdames Ella Wheeler Wilcox, Laura Daintry, Amelia Rives Chanler, and Edgar Saltus. Mrs. Gertrude Atherton also might advantageously adopt the frank rattlesnake practice. I am not without a hope that the American novel of the future will be printed in two parts separated by a blank leaf, one part labeled "For Ladies," the other "For Gents."

Since Bierce in this passage is suggesting that such a division of subject matter would allow readers to avoid material best left to the opposite sex, he is essentially proposing that books should be produced with two distinct readerships in mind: this proposal is doubly realized in *Tales of Soldiers and Civilians* wherein nineteen stories, many with carefully hidden subtexts, are divided into the two separate categories identified by the title of the collection. Of course, the especially useful nature of this "Prattle" passage is that it helps to explain why Bierce did divide his book into two juxtaposed sections, a decision that was largely responsible for his initial failure to place the book with Putnam's, which had specifically objected to Bierce's inclusion of the "Civilians" stories.[7] In this light, Bierce's determination to divide the book into these two sections must be viewed as especially significant: for example, by the late spring of 1891 or earlier, when he began preparing the text of *Tales of Soldiers and Civilians*, Bierce had nearly enough war-related writings—between his fictional war stories and his biographical war sketches—to produce a straightforward collection of war stories of the same length. Alternatively, by the simple expedient of writing a few more war tales between July 1889 and May 1891, Bierce could have easily filled his 1892 book exclusively with fictional war stories. Later editors, working with all of Bierce's war stories, have taken this latter approach, but Bierce, despite two later opportunities which yielded the 1898 and 1909 collections, never did. Viewed collectively, these points suggest that Bierce, in electing to divide his book into "Soldiers" and "Civilians" sections, was not simply throwing the two groups of stories together for reasons of expediency.

Returning to the question of the intended audience of *Tales of Soldiers and Civilians*, it appears that with regard to each group of stories Bierce had two distinct kinds of readers in mind: the informed and the uninformed. Thus a familiar story like "An Occurrence at Owl Creek Bridge" is interpreted by most modern readers in the way Bierce envisioned ignorant readers would in his day: they envision Peyton Farquhar's hallucination as a thing of an instant that flashes through his dying brain. Bierce and other "students of hanging" such as regular readers of the *Examiner* knew Farquhar was potentially able to enjoy his hallucination at a more leisurely pace. Again, at the most basic level, readers would have been able to see many of the stories as examples of how individuals can succumb to or be manipulated by irrational emotions—such as the excess of fear that kills the protagonist of "The Man and the Snake" when he is confronted by a stuffed snake. On the other hand, some stories, like "Haïta, the Shepherd," contain such artfully hidden subtexts that few readers have ever realized these subtexts exist. Thus, while "Haïta, the Shepherd" appears to be an allegorical tale about the fleeting nature of human happiness, it in fact conceals an autobiographically inspired message about the inability of men to find happiness in marriage due to the cruel and irrational fickleness of women.

It is possible to show that most of the nineteen stories included in the 1892 collection are infused with complicated subtexts. Furthermore, it is ascertainable that Bierce, after publishing most of the tales in the milieu of the *Examiner* (which served him well as an enormously rich and complicated host), carefully ordered the tales in each of the two subsections. And, finally, it is apparent that Bierce went so far as to deliberately craft concluding tales for both of these divisions, including "An Heiress from Redhorse," a story that, in part because Bierce's later collections displaced it into the interior of the "Civilians" section of his book, has long been regarded as one of Bierce's weaker tales. In fact, "An Heiress from Redhorse" was Bierce's brilliantly crafted conclusion to the 1892 collection. Typically readers think "An Heiress from Redhorse" (retitled "A Lady from Redhorse" in the 1898 and 1909 collections) tells a happy tale about a somewhat foolish heiress, but this reading reflects only the semblance of reality. In fact, the tale serves as the collection's deliberately false but conventionally fitting "happy ending" which Bierce ostensibly provided for the novel-reading, uncritical public he disdained. The heiress's true fate is somewhat different and turns on the answer to the question as to why a handsome man would want to marry a newly rich old maid.

Today, when reading *Tales of Soldiers and Civilians*, we may not be ready to account it a traditional novel, but it is certainly time to recognize that this highly idiosyncratic collection of nineteen loosely connected tales divided into two sections is truly the sum of all its parts. And when the critical dust stirred up by that reconsideration finally settles, *Tales of Soldiers and Civilians* may well be recognized as a masterpiece of nineteenth-century American literature.

A Note on the Appendix

Following the text of this edition is an appendix containing a selection of related readings extracted from the *Wasp*, the *San Francisco News Letter and California Advertiser*, and the *Examiner*. Grouped under the tales they are most closely connected to and arranged chronologically, these selections reproduce much of the thematically related background material available to Bierce's original readers. Readers of the present edition should find the selections helpful in more fully understanding the stories.

Textual Note

In preparing the text of this new edition I have carefully considered and drawn from the available authoritative texts of the nineteen stories. The text before you, while consisting entirely of Bierce's words, is thus an eclectic one informed by my judgment. In sum, my first and guiding principle in assembling this edition has been to always strive to realize the work that Bierce envisioned and attempted to realize in his 1892 book. Because that envisioned work, as I understand it, is at times closer in spirit to the original texts of the individual stories than even their close successors in the 1892 incarnation of *Tales of Soldiers and Civilians*, I have occasionally avoided adopting seemingly straightforward authoritative emendations made during the preparation of the 1892 and later editions because they appear to depart from the original spirit of that work. Backing up this admittedly rather ethereal-sounding claim, my exhaustive study of the individual tales that comprise *Tales of Soldiers and Civilians* and its successor collections, *Ambrose Bierce's Civilians and Soldiers in Context: A Critical Study*, also published by the Kent State University Press, allows me to factually demonstrate that many of Bierce's revisions to individual tales made during his preparation of the 1892, 1898, and 1909 volumes are flawed. Thus, although a comprehensive list of emendations is not provided for this edition, the critical study documents the problematic textual issues surrounding the stories and collections.

For my primary copytext I have used the paste-up copytext of the 1892 collection. This copytext, bearing galley divisions, consists of copies of the original newspaper-based publications of the stories cut into column form and glued onto separate pages which were then hand-corrected by Bierce. A collation of this copytext with the published 1892 collection revealed that many additional changes, authoritative and otherwise, were introduced presumably at the galley or page-proof stage. While no galleys or page proofs appear to have survived, a note on page 105 of the copytext in Bierce's hand stating "proofs to this point" suggests that Bierce was able to compare the copytext to the page proofs before the book went to press. The 1892 collection, *Tales of Soldiers and Civilians*, despite two later authoritative books descending from it, is in its entirety the best version of the work to appear during Bierce's lifetime. As my critical study explains, the 1898 and 1909 volumes, although they contain some valuable authoritative emendations, are heavily flawed texts that must be understood in light of the circumstances of their respective publications.

Using Bierce's original paste-up copytext for his 1892 book as the copytext for this present volume allows for the correction of numerous "accidental" emendations introduced as Bierce's paste-up copytext was set into fresh type. In particular, the original paste-up copytext is free from the profusion of commas that were inserted into sentences as the 1892 book was typeset. Bierce detested this practice of "close punctuation," the insertion of what he deemed superfluous commas into sentences. While he did make substantial efforts to undo these changes during his preparation of the stories for inclusion in the *Collected Works* volumes, Bierce's letters to his publisher reveal that he remained unhappy with the final outcome.

Again seeking to follow Bierce's intentions, many more colons appear in this edition than in the 1892 and later collections. As a journalist, Bierce had a penchant for didacticism, and in his short stories many sentences were originally written with an eye to their didactic impact: colons were frequently employed by Bierce to encourage readers to follow his trains of thought. When the stories were set into type for the 1892 edition many of these colons were silently and often awkwardly converted into semicolons. Although Bierce appears to have accepted them, these changes did not originate with him: while he carefully edited the punctuation of the 1892 edition's paste-up copytext, there is only one instance where he changed a colon to a semicolon—it appears in the first sentence of the second paragraph of "An Occurrence at Owl Creek Bridge."

A third punctuation mark, the exclamation point, is also of more than passing interest. During his editing of the 1892 copytext, Bierce changed seven periods to exclamation points while replacing one exclamation point with a question mark. At the galley or proof stage more apparently authoritative emendations were introduced. Discounting excised or added passages, sixteen additional exclamation marks appeared while twenty were removed. A few further additions and deletions (occasionally effecting prior deletions or additions) occurred during the preparations of the 1898 and 1909 versions of the stories. Because many of the additions that first appear in the published 1892 collection seem arbitrary, in this edition I have adopted the usage pattern found in the revised paste-up copytext for the 1892 edition as a starting point and have then accepted such of the later additions and deletions as do not seem inconsistent with Bierce's original intentions. In particular, this edition rejects twelve of the sixteen exclamation points added to the 1892 collection after the paste-up editing stage while it retains eleven of the excised marks.

In regard to a range of other typesetting matters, including Bierce's spelling idiosyncrasies and his use of italics and accent marks, I have typically adopted the forms present in Bierce's as-emended 1892 edition's copytext, and thus "centre" and "lustre" appear in the present edition as "center" and "luster." Conversely, on the copytext Bierce emended "reconnoiter" to "reconnoitre," and he retained the variant "theatre," in a reference to a "drop-scene" on a stage. Thus the present edition retains both these spellings. Where two or more variants are found in the 1892 copytext—as with the typography of the word "débris"—I have typically adopted the most frequent usage. In situations where proper nouns are employed—as in various references to "Fate" and "Hell," or in dialogue containing direct references to military officers by title alone—I have regularized Bierce's original and usual capitalization patterns. Finally, this present edition retains a range of Bierce's idiosyncratic typographical preferences. Citing several examples, in this edition the word "today" is always hyphenated "to-day," the exclamation "Oh!" is rendered "O!" and "aeolian" appears twice as "Æolian."

A wide range of "substantive" problems were confronted during the preparation of this edition. While a complete accounting is impractical, an overview of the problems encountered and a range of examples should allow readers some insight into the decisions that resulted in the present text. Most obviously, this new edition includes only the nineteen stories assembled by Bierce in his original 1892 collection, *Tales of Soldiers and Civilians*. As the rationale for holding this original collection in higher esteem than its successors has been put forward elsewhere, this most obvious difference can be glossed over in deference to other problems.

In the preparation of this edition, for each story six physical texts were considered: the original newspaper text, the edited paste-up copytext to the 1892 text, the 1892 text, the 1898 text, the edited copytext to the 1909 text, and the 1909 text. Collations of the texts yielded much information about Bierce's editing practices, and in particular collating the 1892 stories with their paste-up copytexts allowed the recovery of many changes introduced at the galley/proof stage. Consideration of the various texts and collations reveals that while substantive changes were introduced at each opportunity, the vast majority of substantive changes were effected by Bierce during his preparation of the 1892 collection. For example, during his preparation of the 1892 book Bierce heavily revised several of the stories in an apparent attempt to better fit them into the collection. While Bierce made some substantive changes during his preparation of the 1898 collection, in general his editing of this edition appears to have been cursory (the fairly numerous typographical errors in this edition suggest that he was significantly less involved with its production than he was with that of the 1892 collection or the stories he prepared for the two relevant volumes of his *Collected Works*). This conclusion is borne out by the 1898 collection's most egregious departure from the original collection: the appending of stories to the ends of both the "Soldiers" and "Civilians" sections. Finally, it is clear that the nineteen stories that appear spread out through two of the 1909 volumes, with a few exceptions, were primarily edited with an eye for grammatical or stylistic issues. This focus presumably was partly the result of Bierce's publication, early in 1909, of *Write It Right*, a pithy grammatical guide he was quite proud of.

Although seemingly straightforward, the above account touches on several problems encountered in preparing this edition. First, several of Bierce's most ambitious editing efforts during the preparation of his 1892 collection introduced troubling textual problems. In effect, his attempts to revise stories written many months or years earlier often did more harm than good. A particularly good example of this is found in the revised versions of "The Horseman in the Sky" which appear in the 1892 and later collections. In editing this story Bierce attempted to dramatically alter the protagonist's fate.

Originally, Carter Druse, the young Union soldier who kills his Confederate father in carrying out his military duty, is rendered obviously insane by his actions. In the revised story Carter Druse appears to be sane in the aftermath of his act of patricide. Unfortunately, in addition to arguably weakening the thematic impact of the story, the revisions Bierce incorporated into the story, which he renamed "A Horseman in the Sky," created a series of often subtle problems involving other elements of the story. The solution in this present edition was to restore the original text.

Another class of changes that presents difficulties involves material added by Bierce in order to clarify aspects of his stories. With some frequency these additions appear awkwardly heavy-handed—as when he added to a concluding line of "Killed at Resaca" the descriptive phrase "this detestable creature" in a superfluous effort to clarify how readers were to regard a woman who is indirectly likened to a venomous snake in the immediately succeeding line. Noting this particular gloss helps to explain why Bierce's editing efforts occasionally went astray. Since many of the nineteen stories have artfully constructed plots that function on two different levels for two different groups of readers, which we can denote the informed and the uninformed, changes introduced in order to simplify the reading experiences of uninformed readers often negatively impact the reading experiences of the informed. For another illustration, we can consider one pithy passage found in "A Holy Terror."

A story of greed-inspired grave desecration, sundry immoralities, and dramatic deaths, "A Holy Terror" was originally published by Bierce in the December 23, 1882, Christmas issue of the *Wasp*. On the 1892 copytext, while editing a section of the story in which the protagonist is standing in a re-opened grave before the upright coffin of a woman identified as "Scarry," Bierce introduced several troubling changes. Originally Bierce had written that, "Along the outer edges of the coffin, at long intervals, were rust-eaten heads of ornamental screws. This frail example of the undertaker's art had been put into the grave the wrong side up!" Bierce altered the passage to read, "Along the outer edges of the coffin, at long intervals, were rust-eaten heads of nails. This frail product of the carpenter's art had been put into the grave the wrong side up!" A cursory consideration suggests that these changes are of little consequence, but the changes have hidden repercussions. To begin, at the most practical level the change from "ornamental screws" to "heads of nails" is problematic: as the coffin is standing on end in an open grave that is only indifferently illuminated by moonlight, the observation of rusted nail heads seems to be asking a bit much of anyone's powers of observation. More important, the original choice of "screws" is potentially a deliberate pun on the mysterious dead woman's occupation. In the same way, the original reference to the "frail example of the undertaker's art" is almost certainly a veiled reference to the dead woman's earlier history as a member of the "frail sister-hood." In other words, these and other emendations to the 1892 copytext suggest that Bierce had forgotten just how artful the original version of the story was. Similarly interesting problematic changes surface again and again in many of the nineteen stories.

Yet another emendation introduced in the copytext of the 1909 version of "A Holy Terror" can serve as an example of one more type of authoritative change that requires a subjective analysis when an eclectic text is being prepared. Thus, on the copytext for "A Holy Terror" Bierce rejected the perfectly serviceable but clearly more colorful "spittoon" in favor of the more polished and literary "cuspidor." Many of the changes Bierce introduced during his various editing efforts sought the same end. The cumulative effect should be obvious: as the emendations accumulate the texts become more rigid and pretentious. As I trace this class of changes to Bierce's rather stilted editorial aesthetic—an aesthetic that was particularly to the fore in the aftermath of the publication of *Write It Right*—rather than his artistic impulse, where such authoritative revisions exist, I have frequently rejected them.

Soldiers

A Horseman in the Sky.

I.

One sunny afternoon in the autumn of the year 1861 a soldier lay in a clump of laurel by the side of a road in Western Virginia. He lay at full length upon his stomach, his feet resting upon the toes, his head upon the left forearm. His extended right hand loosely grasped his rifle. But for the somewhat methodical disposition of his limbs and a slight rhythmic movement of the cartridge-box at the back of his belt he might have been thought to be dead. He was asleep at his post of duty. But if detected he would be dead shortly afterward, death being the just and legal penalty of his crime.

The clump of laurel in which the criminal lay was in an angle of the road which, after ascending southward a steep acclivity to that point turned sharply to the west, running along the summit for perhaps one hundred yards. There it turned southward again and went zig-zagging downward through the forest. At the salient of that second angle was a large flat rock, jutting out from the ridge to the northward, overlooking the deep valley from which the road ascended. The rock capped a high cliff: a stone dropped from its outer edge would have fallen sheer downward one thousand feet to the tops of the pines. The angle where the soldier lay was on another spur of the same cliff. Had he been awake he would have commanded a view, not only of the short arm of the road and the jutting rock but of the entire profile of the cliff below it. It might well have made him giddy to look.

The country was wooded everywhere except at the bottom of the valley to the northward, where there was a small natural meadow, through which flowed a stream scarcely visible from the valley's rim. This open ground looked hardly larger than an ordinary dooryard, but was really several acres in extent. Its green was more vivid than that of the enclosing forest. Away beyond it rose a line of giant cliffs similar to those upon which we are supposed to stand in our survey of the savage scene, and through which the road had somehow made its climb to the summit. The configuration of the valley, indeed, was such that from our point of observation it seemed entirely shut in, and one could not but have wondered how the road which found a way out of it had found a way into it, and whence came and whither went the waters of the stream that parted the meadow more than a thousand feet below.

No country is so wild and difficult but men will make it a theater of war: concealed in the forest at the bottom of that military rat-trap, in which half a hundred men in possession of the exits might have starved an army to submission, lay five regiments of Federal infantry. They had marched all the previous day and night and were resting. At nightfall they would take to the road again, climb to the place where their unfaithful sentinel now slept, and descending the other slope of the ridge fall upon a camp of the enemy at about midnight. Their hope was to surprise him, for the road led to the rear of his camp. In case of failure their position would be perilous in the extreme; and fail they surely would should accident or vigilance apprise him of the movement.

II.

The sleeping sentinel in the clump of laurel was a young Virginian named Carter Druse. He was the son of wealthy parents—an only child—and had known such ease and cultivation and high living as wealth and taste were able to command in the mountain country of Western Virginia. His home was but a few miles from where he now lay. One morning he had risen from the breakfast table and said, quietly but gravely: "Father, a Union regiment has arrived at Grafton. I am going to join it."

The father lifted his leonine head, looked at the son a moment in silence and replied: "Go, Carter, and, whatever may happen, I hope that you will do what you conceive to be your duty. Virginia must get on without you. Should we both live to the end of the war we will speak further of the matter. Your mother, as the physician has informed you, is in a most critical condition; at the best she cannot be with us longer than a few weeks, but that time is precious. It would be better not to disturb her."

So Carter Druse, bowing reverently to his father, who returned the salute with a stately courtesy that masked a breaking heart, left the home of his childhood to go soldiering. By conscience and courage, by deeds of devotion and daring, he soon commended himself to his fellows and his officers; and it was to these qualities and to some knowledge of the country that he owed his selection for his present perilous duty at the extreme outpost. Nevertheless fatigue had been stronger than resolution and he had fallen asleep. What good or bad angel came in a dream to rouse him from his state of crime who shall say? Without a movement, without a sound, in the profound silence and the languor of the late afternoon, some invisible messenger of Fate touched with unsealing finger the eyes of his consciousness—whispered into the ear of his spirit the mysterious awakening word which no human lips have ever spoken, no human memory ever has recalled. He quietly raised his forehead from his arm and looked between the masking stems of the laurels, instinctively closing his right hand about the stock of his rifle.

His first feeling was a keen artistic delight. On a colossal pedestal, the cliff, motionless at the extreme edge of the capping rock and sharply outlined against the sky, was an equestrian statue of impressive dignity. The figure of the man sat the figure of the horse, straight and soldierly but with the repose of a Grecian god carved in the marble which limits the suggestion of activity. The gray costume harmonized with its aerial background; the metal of accouterment and caparison was softened and subdued by the shadow; the animal's skin had no points of high light. A carbine strikingly foreshortened lay across the pommel of the saddle, kept in place by the right hand grasping it at the "grip"; the left hand, holding the bridle rein, was invisible. In silhouette against the sky the profile of the horse was cut with the sharpness of a cameo; it looked across the heights of air to the confronting cliffs beyond. The face of the rider, turned slightly to the left, showed only an outline of temple and beard; he was looking downward to the bottom of the valley. Magnified by its lift against the sky and by the soldier's testifying sense of the formidableness of a near enemy the group appeared of heroic, almost colossal, size.

For an instant Druse had a strange half-defined feeling that he had slept to the end of the war and was looking upon a noble work of art reared upon that commanding eminence to commemorate the deeds of an heroic past of which he had been an inglorious part. The feeling was dispelled by a slight movement of the group; the horse, without moving its feet, had drawn its body slightly backward from the verge; the man remained immobile as before. Broad awake and keenly alive to the significance of the situation, Druse now brought the butt of his rifle against his cheek by cautiously pushing the barrel forward through the bushes, cocked the piece and glancing through the sights covered a vital spot of the horseman's breast. A touch upon the trigger and all would have been well with Carter Druse. At that instant the horseman turned his head and looked in the direction of his concealed foeman—seemed to look into his very face, into his eyes—into his brave, compassionate heart.

Is it, then, so terrible to kill an enemy in war?—an enemy who has surprised a secret vital to the safety of oneself and comrades?—an enemy more formidable for his knowledge than all his army for its numbers? Carter Druse grew deathly pale; he shook in every limb, turned faint and saw the statuesque group before him as black figures, rising, falling, moving unsteadily in arcs of circles in a fiery sky. His hand fell away from his weapon, his head slowly dropped until his face rested on the leaves in which he lay. This courageous gentleman and hardy soldier was near swooning from intensity of emotion.

It was not for long: in another moment his face was raised from earth; his hands resumed their places on the rifle; his forefinger sought the trigger. Mind, heart and eyes were clear, conscience and reason sound. He could not hope to capture that enemy; to alarm him would but send him dashing to his camp with his fatal news. The duty of the soldier was plain: the man must be shot dead from ambush—without warning, without a moment's spiritual preparation, with never so much as an unspoken prayer, he must be sent to his account. But no—there is a hope; he may have discovered nothing—perhaps he is but admiring the sublimity of the landscape. If permitted he may turn and ride carelessly away in the direction whence he came. Surely it will be possible to judge at the instant of his withdrawing whether he knows. It may well be that his fixity of attention—Druse turned his head and looked below, through the deeps of air downward, as from the surface to the bottom of a translucent sea. He saw creeping across the green meadow a sinuous line of figures of men and horses—some foolish commander was permitting the soldiers of his escort to water their beasts in the open, in plain view from a dozen summits!

Druse withdrew his eyes from the valley and fixed them again upon the group of man and horse in the sky, and again it was through the sights of his rifle. He was calm now. His teeth were firmly but not rigidly closed; his nerves were as tranquil as a sleeping babe's—not a tremor affected any muscle of his body: his breathing, until suspended in the act of taking aim, was regular and slow. Duty had silenced conscience; the spirit had said to the body: "Peace, be still." He fired.

III.

At this moment an officer of the Federal force, who in a spirit of adventure or in quest of knowledge had left the hidden *bivouac* in the valley and climbing the slope had made his way to the lower edge of a small open space near the foot of the cliff, was considering what he had to gain by pushing his exploration further. At a distance of a quarter-mile before him, but apparently at a stone's throw, rose from its fringe of pines the gigantic face of rock, towering to so great a height above him that it made him giddy to look up to where its edge cut a sharp, rugged line against the sky. It presented a clean, vertical profile against a background of blue sky to a point half of the way down, and of distant hills hardly less blue thence to the tops of the trees at its base.

Lifting his eyes to the dizzy altitude of its summit the officer saw an astonishing sight—a man on horseback riding down into the valley through the air!

Straight upright sat the rider, in military fashion, with a firm seat in the saddle, a strong clutch upon the rein to hold his charger from too impetuous a plunge. From his bare head his long hair streamed upward, waving like a plume. His right hand was concealed in the cloud of the horse's lifted mane. The animal's body was as level as if every hoof-stroke encountered the resistant earth. Its motions were those of a wild gallop, but even as the officer looked they ceased, with all the legs thrown sharply forward as in the act of alighting from a leap. But this was a flight!

Filled with amazement and terror by this apparition of a horseman in the sky—half-believing himself the chosen scribe of some new Apocalypse, the officer was overcome by the intensity of his emotions; his legs failed him and he fell. Almost at the same instant he heard a crashing sound in the trees—a sound that died without an echo, and all was still.

The officer rose to his feet trembling. The familiar sensation of an abraded shin recalled his dazed faculties. Pulling himself together he ran rapidly obliquely away from the cliff to a point a half-mile from its foot; thereabout he expected to find his man; and thereabout he naturally failed. In the fleeting instant of his vision his imagination had been so wrought upon by the apparent grace and ease and intention of the marvelous performance, that it did not occur to him that the line of march of aerial cavalry is directly downward, and that he could find the objects of his search at the very foot of the cliff. A half-hour later he returned to camp.

This officer was a wise man: he knew better than to tell an incredible truth. He said nothing of what he had seen. But when the commander asked him if in his scout he had learned anything of advantage to the expedition he answered:

"Yes, sir; there is no road leading down into this valley from the southward."

The commander, knowing better, smiled.

IV.

After firing his shot private Carter Druse reloaded his rifle and resumed his watch. Ten minutes had hardly passed when a Federal sergeant crept cautiously to him on hands and knees. Druse neither turned his head nor looked at him, but lay without motion or sign of recognition.

"Did you fire?" the sergeant whispered.

"Yes."

"At what?"

"A horse. It was standing on yonder rock—pretty far out. You see it is no longer there. I am a great marksman; you know I once shot a match with the Devil in Hell and beat him."

The sergeant was shocked and startled. He looked searchingly at Druse. The man's face was white; his eyes were restless and glittered with a strange, uncanny light. The sergeant, still on hands and knees, involuntarily backed a little away from him.

"See here, Druse," he said after a moment's silence, "it's no use making a mystery. I order you to report. Was there anybody—anybody at all—except the horse?"

"Do you mean the horse which had wings?"

"Well, yes, if that's the kind of horse you shot. Was there any one else?"

"Yes."

"Who?"

"My father."

The sergeant rose to his feet and walked rapidly down the road toward the valley.

An Occurrence at Owl Creek Bridge.

I.

A man stood upon a railroad bridge in Northern Alabama, looking down into the swift waters twenty feet below. The man's hands were behind his back; the wrists bound with a cord. A rope loosely encircled his neck. It was attached to a stout cross-timber above his head and the slack fell to the level of his knees. Some loose boards laid upon the sleepers supporting the metals of the railway supplied a footing for him and his executioners—two private soldiers of the Federal army, directed by a sergeant who in civil life may have been a deputy sheriff. At a short remove upon the same temporary platform was an officer in the uniform of his rank, armed. He was a captain. A sentinel at each end of the bridge stood with his rifle in the position known as "support," that is to say, vertical in front of the left shoulder, the hammer resting on the forearm thrown straight across the chest—a formal and unnatural position, enforcing an erect carriage of the body. It did not appear to be the duty of these two men to know what was occurring at the center of the bridge; they merely blockaded the two ends of the foot-plank which traversed it.

Beyond one of the sentinels nobody was in sight; the railroad ran straight away into a forest for a hundred yards, then, curving, was lost to view. Doubtless there was an outpost further along. The other bank of the stream was open ground—a gentle acclivity crowned with a stockade of vertical tree trunks, loopholed for rifles, with a single embrasure through which protruded the muzzle of a brass cannon commanding the bridge. Midway of the slope between bridge and fort were the spectators—a single company of infantry in line, at "parade rest": the butts of the rifles on the ground, the barrels inclining slightly backward against the right shoulder, the hands crossed upon the stock. A lieutenant stood at the right of the line, the point of his sword upon the ground, his left hand resting upon his right. Excepting the group of four at the center of the bridge not a man moved. The company faced the bridge, staring stonily, motionless. The sentinels, facing the banks of the stream, might have been statues to adorn the bridge. The captain stood with folded arms, silent, observing the work of his subordinates but making no sign. Death is a dignitary who when he comes announced is to be received with formal manifestations of respect, even by those most familiar with him. In the code of military etiquette silence and fixity are forms of deference.

The man who was engaged in being hanged was apparently about thirty-five years of age. He was a civilian, if one might judge from his dress, which was that of a planter. His features were good—a straight nose, firm mouth, broad forehead from which his long dark hair was combed straight back, falling behind his ears to the collar of his well-fitting frock-coat. He wore a mustache and pointed beard but no whiskers; his eyes were large and dark-gray and had a kindly expression which one would hardly have expected in one whose neck was in the hemp. Evidently this was no vulgar assassin. The liberal military code makes provision for hanging many kinds of people, and gentlemen are not excluded.

The preparations being complete the two private soldiers stepped aside and each drew away the plank upon which he had been standing. The sergeant turned to the captain, saluted and placed himself immediately behind that officer, who in turn moved apart one pace. These movements left the condemned man and the sergeant standing on the two ends of the same plank, which spanned three of the cross-ties of the bridge. The end upon which the civilian stood almost, but not quite, reached a fourth. This plank had been held in place by the weight of the captain; it was now held by that of the sergeant. At a signal from the former the latter would step aside, the plank would tilt and the condemned man go down between two ties. The arrangement commended itself to his judgment as simple and effective. His face had not been covered nor his eyes bandaged. He looked a moment at his "unsteadfast footing," then let his gaze wander to the swirling water of the stream racing madly beneath his feet. A piece of dancing driftwood caught his attention and his eyes followed it down the current. How slowly it appeared to move! What a sluggish stream!

He closed his eyes in order to fix his last thoughts upon his wife and children. The water, touched to gold by the early sun, the brooding mists under the banks at some distance down the stream, the fort, the soldiers, the piece of drift—all had distracted him. And now he became conscious of a new disturbance. Striking through the thought of his dear ones was a sound which he could neither ignore nor understand, a sharp, distinct, metallic percussion like the stroke of a blacksmith's hammer upon the anvil; it had the same ringing quality. He wondered what it was, and whether immeasurably distant or near by—it seemed both. Its recurrence was regular, but as slow as the tolling of a death knell. He awaited each stroke with impatience and—he knew not why—apprehension. The intervals of silence grew progressively longer: the delays became maddening. With their greater infrequency the sounds increased in strength and sharpness. They hurt his ear like the thrust of a knife: he feared he would shriek. What he heard was the ticking of his watch.

He unclosed his eyes and saw again the water below him. "If I could free my hands," he thought, "I might throw off the noose and spring into the stream. By diving I could evade the bullets and, swimming vigorously, reach the bank, take to the woods and get away home. My home, thank God, is as yet outside them: my wife and little ones are still beyond the invader's farthest advance."

As these thoughts, which have here to be set down in words, were flashed into the doomed man's brain rather than evolved from it the captain nodded to the sergeant. The sergeant stepped aside.

II.

Peyton Farquhar was a well-to-do planter, of an old and highly respected Alabama family. Being a slave owner and like other slave owners a politician he was naturally an original secessionist and ardently devoted to the Southern cause. Circumstances of an imperious nature which it is unnecessary to relate here had prevented him from taking service with the gallant army that had fought the disastrous campaigns ending with the fall of Corinth, and he chafed under the inglorious restraint, longing for the release of his energies, the larger life of the soldier, the opportunity for distinction. That opportunity, he felt, would come, as it comes to all in war-time. Meanwhile he did what he could. No service was too humble for him to perform in aid of the South, no adventure too perilous for him to undertake if consistent with the character of a civilian who was at heart a soldier and who in good faith and without too much qualification assented to at least a part of the frankly villainous dictum that all is fair in love and war.

One evening while Farquhar and his wife were sitting on a rustic bench near the entrance to his grounds, a gray-clad soldier rode up to the gate and asked for a drink of water. Mrs. Farquhar was only too happy to serve him with her own white hands. While she was gone to fetch the water her husband approached the dusty horseman and inquired eagerly for news from the front.

"The Yanks are repairing the railroads," said the man, "and are getting ready for another advance. They have reached the Owl Creek bridge, put it in order and built a stockade on the other bank. The commandant has issued an order which is posted everywhere, declaring that any civilian caught interfering with the railroad, its bridges, tunnels or trains will be summarily hanged. I saw the orders."

"How far is it to the Owl Creek bridge?" Farquhar asked.

"About thirty miles."

" Is there no force on this side the creek?"

"Only a picket post half a mile out, on the railroad, and a single sentinel at this end of the bridge."

"Suppose a man—a civilian and student of hanging—should elude the picket post and perhaps get the better of the sentinel," said Farquhar, smiling, "what could he accomplish?"

The soldier reflected. "I was there a month ago," he replied. "I observed that the flood of last winter had lodged a great quantity of driftwood against the wooden pier at this end of the bridge. It is now dry and would burn like tow."

The lady had now brought the water, which the soldier drank. He thanked her ceremoniously, bowed to her husband and rode away. An hour later, after nightfall, he repassed the plantation, going northward in the direction from which he had come. He was a Federal scout.

III.

As Peyton Farquhar fell straight downward through the bridge he lost consciousness and was as one already dead. From this state he was awakened— ages later, it seemed to him—by the pain of a sharp pressure upon his throat, followed by a sense of suffocation. Keen, poignant agonies seemed to shoot from his neck downward through every fiber of his body and limbs. These pains appeared to flash along well-defined lines of ramification and to beat with an inconceivably rapid periodicity. They seemed like streams of pulsating fire heating him to an intolerable temperature. As to his head, he was conscious of nothing but a feeling of fullness—of congestion. These sensations were unaccompanied by thought. The intellectual part of his nature was already effaced: he had power only to feel, and feeling was torment. He was conscious of motion. Encompassed in a luminous cloud, of which he was now merely the fiery heart, without material substance, he swung through unthinkable arcs of oscillation, like a vast pendulum. Then all at once, with terrible suddenness the light about him shot upward with the noise of a loud plash; a frightful roaring was in his ears and all was cold and dark. The power of thought was restored; he knew that the rope had broken and he had fallen into the stream. There was no additional strangulation: the noose about his neck was already suffocating him and kept the water from his lungs. To die of hanging at the bottom of a river!—the idea seemed to him ludicrous. He opened his eyes in the blackness and saw above him a gleam of light, but how distant, how inaccessible! He was still sinking, for the light became dimmer and dimmer until it was a mere shimmer. Then it began to grow and brighten and he knew that he was rising toward the surface—knew it with reluctance, for he was now very comfortable. "To be hanged and drowned," he thought, "that is not so bad; but I do not wish to be shot. No; I will not be shot: that is not fair."

He was not conscious of an effort, but a sharp pain in his wrists apprised him that he was trying to free his hands. He gave the struggle his attention, as an idler might observe the feat of a juggler, without interest in the outcome. What splendid effort!—what magnificent, what superhuman strength! Ah, that was a fine endeavor! Bravo! The cord fell away; his arms parted and floated upward, the hands dimly seen on each side in the growing light. He watched them with a new interest as first one and then the other pounced upon the noose at his neck. They tore it away and thrust it fiercely aside, its undulations resembling those of a water-snake. "Put it back, put it back!" He thought he shouted these words to his hands, for the undoing of the noose had been succeeded by the direst pang that he had yet experienced. His neck ached horribly, his brain was on fire; his heart, which had been fluttering faintly, gave a great leap, trying to force itself out at his mouth. His whole body was racked and wrenched with an insupportable anguish! But his disobedient hands gave no heed to the command. They beat the water vigorously with quick downward strokes, forcing him to the surface. He felt his head emerge; his eyes were blinded by the sunlight; his chest expanded convulsively and with a supreme and crowning agony his lungs engulfed a great draught of air, which instantly he expelled in a shriek!

He was now in full possession of his physical senses. They were, indeed, preternaturally keen and alert. Something in the awful disturbance of his organic system had so exalted and refined them that they made record of things never before perceived. He felt the ripples upon his face and heard their separate sounds as they struck. He looked at the forest on the bank of the stream, saw the individual trees, the leaves and the veining of each leaf— saw the very insects upon them: the locusts, the brilliant-bodied flies, the gray spiders stretching their webs from twig to twig. He noted the prismatic colors in all the dewdrops upon a million blades of grass. The humming of the gnats that danced above the eddies of the stream, the beating of the dragon flies' wings, the strokes of the water-spiders' legs, like oars which had lifted their boat—all these made audible music. A fish slid along beneath his eyes and he heard the rush of its body parting the water.

He had come to the surface facing down the stream; in a moment the visible world seemed to wheel slowly round, himself the pivotal point, and he saw the bridge, the fort, the soldiers. Upon the bridge, the captain, the sergeant, the two privates, his executioners. They were in silhouette against the blue sky. They shouted and gesticulated, pointing at him; the captain had drawn his pistol, but did not fire; the others were unarmed. Their movements were grotesque and horrible; their forms gigantic.

Suddenly something struck the water smartly within a few inches of his head, spattering his face with spray. A sharp report followed, and he saw one of the sentinels with his rifle at his shoulder, a light cloud of blue smoke rising from the muzzle. The man in the water saw the eye of the man on the bridge gazing into his own through the sights of the rifle. He observed that it was a gray eye and remembered having read that gray eyes were keenest and that all famous marksmen had them. Nevertheless, this one had missed.

A counter-swirl had caught Farquhar and turned him half-round: he was again looking into the forest on the bank opposite the fort. The sound of a clear, high voice in a monotonous sing-song now rang out behind him and came across the water with a distinctness that pierced and subdued all other sounds, even the beating of the ripples in his ears. Although no soldier, he had frequented camps enough to know the dread significance of that deliberate, drawling, aspirated chant: the lieutenant on shore was taking a part in the morning's work. How coldly and pitilessly—with what an even, calm intonation, presaging and enforcing tranquillity in the men—with what accurately measured intervals fell those cruel words:

"Attention, company . . . Shoulder arms . . . Ready . . . Aim . . . Fire."

Farquhar dived—dived as deeply as he could. The water roared in his ears like the voice of Niagara, yet he heard the dulled thunder of the volley, and rising again toward the surface met shining bits of metal, singularly flattened, oscillating slowly downward. Some of them touched him on the face and hands, then fell away, continuing their descent. One lodged between his collar and neck; it was uncomfortably warm and he snatched it out.

As he rose to the surface, gasping for breath, he saw that he had been a long time under water: he was perceptibly farther down-stream—nearer to safety. The soldiers had almost finished reloading: the metal ramrods flashed all at once in the sunshine as they were drawn from the barrels, turned in the air and thrust into their sockets. The two sentinels fired independently and ineffectually.

The hunted man saw all this over his shoulder; he was now swimming vigorously with the current. His brain was as energetic as his arms and legs: he thought with the rapidity of lightning.

"The officer," he reasoned, "will not make that martinet's error a second time. It is as easy to dodge a volley as a single shot. He has probably already given the command to fire at will. God help me, I cannot dodge them all!"

An appalling plash within two yards of him, followed by a loud rushing sound, *diminuendo,* which seemed to travel back through the air to the fort and died in an explosion which stirred the very river to its deeps! A rising sheet of water, which curved over him, fell down upon him, blinded him, strangled him! The cannon had taken a hand in the game. As he shook his head free from the commotion of the smitten water he heard the deflected shot humming through the air ahead, and in an instant it was cracking and smashing the branches in the forest beyond.

"They will not do that again," he thought: "the next time they will use a charge of grape. I must keep my eye upon the gun; the smoke will apprise me—the report arrives too late: it lags behind the missile. It is a good gun."

Suddenly he felt himself whirled round and round—spinning like a top. The water, the banks, the forest, the now distant bridge, fort and men—all were commingled and blurred. Objects were represented by their colors only: circular horizontal streaks of color—that was all he saw. He had been caught in a vortex and was being whirled on with a velocity of advance and gyration that made him giddy and sick. In a few moments he was flung upon the gravel at the foot of the left bank of the stream—the southern bank—and behind a projecting point which concealed him from his enemies. The sudden arrest of his motion, the abrasion of one of his hands on the gravel, restored him and he wept with delight. He dug his fingers into the sand, threw it over himself in handfuls and audibly blessed it. It looked like gold, like diamonds, rubies, emeralds: he could think of nothing beautiful which it did not resemble. The trees upon the bank were giant garden plants—he noted a definitive order in their arrangement, inhaled the fragrance of their blooms. A strange, roseate light shone through the spaces among their trunks and the wind made in their branches the music of Æolian harps. He had no wish to perfect his escape; was content to remain in that enchanting spot until re-taken.

A whizz and rattle of grapeshot among the branches high above his head roused him from his dream. The baffled cannoneer had fired him a random farewell. He sprang to his feet, rushed up the sloping bank and plunged into the forest.

All that day he traveled, laying his course by the rounding sun. The forest seemed interminable; nowhere did he discover a break in it, not even a woodman's road. He had not known that he lived in so wild a region. There was something uncanny in the revelation.

By nightfall he was fatigued, footsore, famishing. The thought of his wife and children urged him on. At last he found a road which led him in what he knew to be the right direction. It was as wide and straight as a city street, yet it seemed untraveled. No fields bordered it; no dwelling anywhere. Not so much as the barking of a dog suggested human habitation. The black bodies of the great trees formed a straight wall on both sides, terminating on the horizon in a point, like a diagram in a lesson in perspective. Overhead, as he looked up through this rift in the wood, shone great golden stars looking unfamiliar and grouped in strange constellations. He was sure they were arranged in some order which had a secret and malign significance. The wood on either side was full of singular noises, among which—once, twice and again—he distinctly heard whispers in an unknown tongue.

His neck was in pain and lifting his hand to it he found it horribly swollen. He knew that it had a circle of black where the rope had bruised it. His eyes felt congested: he could no longer close them. His tongue was swollen with thirst; he relieved its fever by thrusting it forward from between his teeth into the cool air. How softly the turf had carpeted the untraveled avenue! He could no longer feel the roadway beneath his feet!

Doubtless, despite his suffering he fell asleep while walking, for now he sees another scene—perhaps he has merely recovered from a delirium. He stands at the gate of his own home. All is as he left it and all bright and beautiful in the morning sunshine. He must have traveled the entire night. As he pushes open the gate and passes up the wide white walk he sees a flutter of female garments: his wife, looking fresh and cool and sweet, steps down from the veranda to meet him. At the bottom of the steps she stands waiting, with a smile of ineffable joy, an attitude of matchless grace and dignity. Ah, how beautiful she is! He springs forward with extended arms. As he is about to clasp her he feels a stunning blow upon the back of the neck; a blinding white light blazes all about him with a sound like the shock of a cannon— then all is darkness and silence.

Peyton Farquhar was dead: his body, with a broken neck, swung gently from side to side beneath the timbers of the Owl Creek bridge.

Chickamauga.

One sunny Autumn afternoon a child strayed away from its rude home in a small field and entered a forest unobserved. It was happy in a new sense of freedom from control—happy in the opportunity of exploration and adventure; for this child's spirit, in bodies of its ancestors, had for thousands of years been trained to memorable feats of discovery and conquest—victorious in battles whose critical moments were centuries, whose victors' camps were great cities of hewn stone. From the cradle of its race it had conquered its way through two continents and passing a great sea had penetrated a third, there to be born to war and dominance as a heritage.

The child was a boy aged about six years; the son of a poor planter. In his younger manhood the father had been a soldier; had fought against naked savages and followed the flag of his country into the capital of a civilized race to the far South. In the peaceful life of a planter the warrior-fire survived; once kindled it is never extinguished. The man loved military books and pictures and the boy had understood enough to make himself a wooden sword, though even the eye of his father would hardly have known it for what it was. This weapon he now bore bravely, as became the son of an heroic race, and pausing now and again in the sunny spaces of the forest assumed, with some exaggeration, the postures of aggression and defense that he had been taught by the engraver's art. Made reckless by the ease with which he overcame invisible foes attempting to stay his advance, he committed the common enough military error of pushing the pursuit to a dangerous extreme, until he found himself upon the margin of a wide but shallow brook, whose rapid waters barred his direct advance against the flying foe who had crossed with illogical ease. But the intrepid victor was not to be baffled: the spirit of the race which had passed the great sea burned unconquerable in that small breast and would not be denied. Finding a place where some bowlders in the bed of the stream lay but a step or a leap apart, he made his way across and fell again upon the rear-guard of his imaginary foe, putting all to the sword.

Now that the battle had been won, prudence required that he withdraw to his base of operations. Alas! like many a mightier conqueror, and like one, the mightiest, he could not

> curb the lust for war,
> Nor learn that tempted Fate will leave the loftiest star.

Advancing from the bank of the creek he suddenly found himself confronted with a new and more formidable enemy: in the path that he was following, bolt upright, with ears erect and paws suspended before it, sat a rabbit. With a startled cry the child turned and fled, he knew not in what direction, calling with inarticulate cries for his mother, weeping, stumbling, his tender skin cruelly torn by brambles, his little heart beating hard with terror—breathless, blind with tears—lost in the forest! Then, for more than an hour, he wandered with aimless feet through the tangled under-growth, till at last, overcome with fatigue, he lay down in a narrow space between two rocks within a few yards of the stream and still grasping his toy sword, no longer a weapon but a companion, sobbed himself to sleep. The wood-birds sang merrily above his head, the squirrels, whisking their bravery of tail, ran barking from tree to tree, unconscious of the pity of it, and somewhere far away was a strange, muffled thunder, as if the partridges were drumming in celebration of Nature's victory over the son of her immemorial enslavers. And back at the little plantation, where white men and black were hastily searching the fields and hedgerows in alarm, a mother's heart was breaking for her missing child.

Hours passed, and then the little sleeper rose to his feet. The chill of the evening was in his limbs, the fear of the gloom in his heart. But he had rested, and he no longer wept. With some blind instinct which impelled to action he struggled through the undergrowth about him and came to a more open ground—on his right the brook, to the left a gentle acclivity studded with infrequent trees; over all, the gathering gloom of twilight. A thin ghostly mist rose along the water. It frightened and repelled him; instead of recrossing, in the direction whence he had come, he turned his back upon it and went forward toward the dark inclosing wood. Suddenly he saw before him a strange moving object, which he took to be some large animal—a dog, a pig—he could not name it; perhaps it was a bear. He had seen pictures of bears, but knew of nothing to their discredit and had vaguely wished to meet one. But something in form or movement of this object—something in the awkwardness of its approach—told him that it was not a bear, and curiosity was stayed by fear. He stood still and as it came slowly on gained courage every moment, for he saw that at least it had not the long, menacing ears of the rabbit. Possibly his impressionable mind was half conscious of something familiar in its shambling, awkward gait. Before it had approached near enough to resolve his doubts he saw that it was followed by another—and another. To right and to left were many more: the whole open space about him was alive with them—all moving toward the brook.

They were men. They crept upon their hands and knees. They used their hands only, dragging their legs. They used their knees only, their arms hanging uselessly at their sides. They strove to rise to their feet, but fell prone in the attempt. They did nothing naturally, and nothing alike, save only to advance foot by foot in the same direction. Singly, in pairs and in little groups, they came on through the gloom, some halting now and again while others crept slowly past them, then resuming their movement. They came by dozens and by hundreds: as far on either hand as one could see in the deepening gloom they extended and the black wood behind them appeared to be inexhaustible. The very ground seemed in motion toward the creek. Occasionally one who had paused did not again go on, but lay motionless. He was dead. Some, pausing, made strange gestures with their hands; erected their arms and lowered them again; clasped their heads; spread their palms upward, as men are sometimes seen to do in public prayer.

Not all of this did the child note; it is what would have been noted by an older observer; he saw little but that these were men, yet crept like babes. Being men, they were not terrible, though some of them were unfamiliarly clad. He moved among them freely, going from one to another and peering into their faces with childish curiosity. All their faces were singularly white and many were streaked and gouted with red. Something in this—something too, perhaps, in their grotesque attitudes and movements—reminded him of the painted clown whom he had seen last summer in the circus, and he laughed as he watched them. But on and ever on they crept, these maimed and bleeding men, as heedless as he of the dramatic contrast between his laughter and their own ghastly gravity. To him it was a merry spectacle. He had seen his father's negroes creep upon their hands and knees for his amusement—had ridden them so, fancying them his horses. He now approached one of these crawling figures from behind and with an agile movement mounted it astride. The man sank upon his breast, recovered, flung the small boy fiercely to the ground as an unbroken colt might have done, then turned upon him a face that lacked a lower jaw—from the upper teeth to the throat was a great red gap fringed with hanging shreds of flesh and splinters of bone. The unnatural prominence of nose, the absence of chin, the fierce eyes, gave this man the appearance of a great bird of prey crimsoned in throat and breast by the blood of its quarry.

The man rose to his knees, the child to his feet. The man shook his fist at the child; the child, terrified at last, ran to a tree near by, got upon the farther side of it and took a more serious view of the situation. And so the uncanny multitude dragged itself slowly and painfully along in hideous pantomime—moved forward down the slope like a swarm of great black beetles, with never a sound of going—in silence profound, absolute.

Instead of darkening, the haunted landscape began to brighten. Through the belt of trees beyond the brook shone a strange red light, the trunks and branches of the trees making a black lacework against it. It struck the creeping figures and gave them monstrous shadows which caricatured their movements on the lit grass. It fell upon their faces, touching their whiteness with a ruddy tinge, accentuating the stains with which so many of them were freaked and maculated. It sparkled on buttons and bits of metal in their clothing. Instinctively the child turned toward the growing splendor and moved down the slope with his horrible companions; in a few moments had passed the foremost of the throng—not much of a feat considering his advantages. He placed himself in the lead, his wooden sword still in hand, and solemnly directed the march, conforming his pace to theirs and occasionally turning as if to see that his forces did not straggle. Surely such a leader never before had such a following.

Scattered about upon the ground now slowly narrowing by the encroachment of this awful march to water, were certain articles to which, in the leader's mind, were coupled no significant associations: an occasional blanket, tightly rolled lengthwise, doubled and the ends bound together with a string; a heavy knapsack here, and there a broken musket—such things, in short, as are found in the rear of retreating troops: the "spoor" of men flying from their hunters. Everywhere near the creek, which here had a margin of lowland, the earth was trodden into mud by the feet of men and horses. An observer of better experience in the use of his eyes would have noticed that these footprints pointed in both directions: the ground had been twice passed over—in advance and in retreat. A few hours before, these desperately stricken men, with their more fortunate and now distant comrades, had penetrated the forest in thousands. Their successive battalions, breaking into swarms and reforming in lines, had passed the child on every side—had almost trodden on him as he slept. The rustle and murmur of their march had not awakened him. Almost within a stone's throw of where he lay they had fought a battle: but all unheard by him were the roar of the musketry, the shock of cannon, "the thunder of the captains and the shouting." He had slept through it all, grasping his little wooden sword with perhaps a tighter clutch in unconscious sympathy with his martial environment, but as heedless of the grandeur of the struggle as the dead who died to make the glory.

The fire beyond the belt of woods on the farther side of the creek, reflected to earth from the canopy of its own smoke, was now suffusing the whole landscape. It transformed the sinuous line of mist to the vapor of gold. The water gleamed with dashes of red, and red, too, were many of the stones protruding above the surface. But that was blood; the less desperately wounded had stained them in crossing. On them, too, the child now crossed with eager steps: he was going to the fire. As he stood upon the farther bank he turned about to look at the companions of his march. The advance was arriving at the creek. The stronger had already drawn themselves to the brink and plunged their faces in the flood. Three or four who lay without motion appeared to have no heads. At this the child's eyes expanded with wonder: even his hospitable understanding could not accept a phenomenon implying such vitality as that. After slaking their thirst these men had not the strength to back away from the water, nor to keep their heads above it. They were drowned. In rear of these, the open spaces of the forest showed the leader as many formless figures of his grim command as at first; but not nearly so many were in motion. He waved his cap for their encouragement and smilingly pointed with his weapon in the direction of the guiding light—a pillar of fire to this strange exodus.

Confident of the fidelity of his forces, he now entered the belt of woods, passed through it easily in the red illumination, climbed a fence, ran across a field, turning now and again to coquet with his responsive shadow, and so approached the blazing ruin of a dwelling. Desolation everywhere. In all the wide glare not a living thing was visible. He cared nothing for that; the spectacle pleased, and he danced with glee in imitation of the wavering flames. He ran about, collecting fuel, but every object that he found was too heavy for him to cast in from the distance to which the heat limited his approach. In despair he flung in his sword—a surrender to the superior forces of nature. His military career was at an end.

Shifting his position, his eyes fell upon some outbuildings which had an oddly familiar appearance, as if he had dreamed of them. He stood considering them with wonder, when suddenly the entire plantation, with its enclosing forest, seemed to turn as if upon a pivot. His little world swung half around; the points of the compass were reversed. He recognized the blazing building as his own home!

For a moment he stood stupefied by the power of the revelation; then ran with aimless feet, making a half circuit of the ruin. There, conspicuous in the light of the conflagration, lay the dead body of a woman—the white face turned upward, the hands thrown out and clutched full of grass, the clothing deranged, the long dark hair in tangles and full of clotted blood. The greater part of the forehead was torn away and from the jagged hole the brain protruded, overflowing the temple, a frothy mass of gray, crowned with clusters of crimson bubbles. The work of a shell.

The child moved his little hands, making wild, uncertain gestures. He uttered a series of inarticulate and indescribable cries—something between the chattering of an ape and the gobbling of a turkey—a startling, soulless, unholy sound—the language of a devil. The child was a deaf mute.

Then he stood motionless, with quivering lips, looking down upon the wreck.

A Son of the Gods.

A Study in the Historical Present Tense.

A breezy day and a sunny landscape. An open country to your right and left and forward; behind, a wood. In the edge of this wood, facing the open but not venturing into it, long lines of troops, halted. The wood is alive with them, and full of confused noises—the occasional rattle of wheels, as a battery of artillery gets into position to cover the advance; the hum and a murmur of the soldiers, talking; a sound of innumerable feet in the dry leaves that strew the interspaces among the trees; hoarse commands of officers. Detached groups of horsemen are well in front—not altogether exposed—many of them intently regarding the crest of a hill a mile away in the direction of the interrupted advance. For this powerful army, moving in battle order through a forest, has met with a formidable obstacle—the open country. The crest of that gentle hill a mile away has a sinister look: it says, Beware! Along it runs a stone wall extending to left and right a great distance. Behind the wall is a hedge; behind the hedge are seen the tops of trees in rather straggling order. Behind the trees—what? It is necessary to know.

Yesterday, and for many days and nights previously, we had been fighting somewhere: always there was cannonading, with occasional keen rattlings of musketry, mingled with cheers, our own or the enemy's, we seldom knew, attesting some temporary advantage. This morning at daybreak the enemy was gone. We have moved forward across his earthworks, across which we had so often vainly attempted to move before, through the débris of his abandoned camps, among the graves of his fallen, into the woods beyond.

How curiously we regarded everything! how odd it all seemed! Nothing appeared quite familiar; the most commonplace objects—an old saddle, a splintered wheel, a forgotten canteen—everything related something of the mysterious personality of those strange men who had been killing us. The soldier never becomes wholly familiar with the conception of his foes as men like himself: he cannot divest himself of the feeling that they are another order of beings, differently conditioned, in an environment not altogether of the earth. The smallest vestiges of them rivet his attention and engage his interest. He thinks of them as inaccessible; and catching an unexpected glimpse of them, they appear farther away, and therefore larger, than they really are—like objects in a fog. He is somewhat in awe of them.

From the edge of the wood leading up the acclivity are the tracks of horses and wheels—the wheels of cannon. The yellow grass is beaten down by the feet of infantry. Clearly they have passed this way in thousands; they have not withdrawn by the country roads. This is significant—it is the difference between retiring and retreating.

That group of horsemen is our commander, his staff and escort. He is facing the distant crest, holding his field-glass against his eyes with both hands, his elbows needlessly elevated; it is a fashion: it seems to dignify the act; we are all addicted to it. Suddenly he lowers the glass and says a few words to those about him. Two or three aides detach themselves from the group and canter away into the woods, along the lines in each direction. We did not hear his words but we know them: "Tell General X. to send forward the skirmish line." Those of us who have been out of place resume our positions; the men resting at ease straighten themselves and the ranks are re-formed without a command. Some of us staff officers dismount and look at our saddle girths; those already on the ground remount.

Galloping rapidly along in the edge of the open ground comes a young officer on a snow-white horse. His saddle-blanket is scarlet. What a fool! No one who has ever been in action but remembers how naturally every rifle turns toward the man on a white horse; no one but has observed how a bit of red enrages the bull of battle. That such colors are fashionable in military life must be accepted as the most astonishing of all the phenomena of human vanity. They would seem to have been devised to increase the death rate.

This young officer is in full uniform, as if on parade. He is all agleam with bullion—a blue-and-gold edition of the Poetry of War. A wave of derisive laughter runs abreast of him all along the line. But how handsome he is! with what careless grace he sits his horse!

He reins up within a respectful distance of the corps commander and salutes. The old soldier nods familiarly; he evidently knows him. A brief colloquy between them is going on; the young man seems to be preferring some request which the elder one is indisposed to grant. Let us ride a little nearer. Ah! too late—it is ended. The young officer salutes again, wheels his horse and rides straight toward the crest of the hill. He is deathly pale.

A thin line of skirmishers, the men deployed at three paces or so apart, now pushes from the wood into the open. The commander speaks to his bugler, who claps his instrument to his lips.

Tra-la-la! Tra-la-la! The skirmishers halt in their tracks.

Meantime the young horseman has advanced a hundred yards. He is riding at a walk, straight up the long slope, with never a turn of the head. Ah! How beautiful he is!—how glorious! Gods! what would we not give to be in his place—with his soul! He does not draw his saber: his right hand hangs easily at his side. The breeze catches the plume in his hat and flutters it smartly. The sunshine rests upon his shoulder straps, lovingly, like a visible benediction. Straight on he rides. Ten thousand pairs of eyes are fixed upon him with an intensity that he can hardly fail to feel; ten thousand hearts keep quick time to the inaudible hoof beats of his snowy steed. He is not alone—he draws all souls after him: we are but "dead men all." But we remember that we laughed. On and on, straight for the hedge-lined wall, he rides. Not a look backward. O, if he would but turn—if he could but see the love, the adoration, the atonement!

Not a word is spoken: the populous depths of the forest still murmur with their unseen and unseeing swarm, but all along the fringe there is silence absolute. The burly commander is an equestrian statue of himself. The mounted staff officers, their field-glasses up, are motionless all. The line of battle in the edge of the wood stands at a new kind of "attention," each man in the attitude in which he was caught by the consciousness of what is going on. All these hardened and impenitent man-killers, to whom death in its awfulest forms is a fact familiar to their every-day observation—who sleep on hills trembling with the thunder of great guns, dine in the midst of streaming missiles and play at cards among the dead faces of their dearest friends—all are watching with suspended breath and beating hearts the outcome of an act involving the life of one man. Such is the magnetism of courage and devotion.

If now you should turn your head you would see a simultaneous movement among the spectators—a start, as if it had received an electric shock—and looking forward again to the now distant horseman you would see that he has in that instant altered his direction and is riding at an angle to his former course. The spectators suppose the sudden deflection to be caused by a shot, perhaps a wound; but take this field-glass and you will observe that he is riding towards a break in the wall and hedge. He means, if not killed, to ride through and overlook the country beyond.

You are not to forget the nature of this man's act; it is not permitted to you to think of it as an instance of bravado, nor, on the other hand, a needless sacrifice of self. If the enemy occupies the hill, he is in force on that ridge. The investigator will encounter nothing less than a line of battle; there is no need of pickets, videttes, skirmishers, to give warning of our approach; the attacking lines will be visible, conspicuous, exposed to an artillery fire that will shave the ground, the moment they break from cover; and for half the distance to a sheet of rifle bullets in which nothing can live. In short, if the

enemy is there it would be madness to attack him in front: he must be ma-
neuvered out by the immemorial plan of threatening his line of communication, as necessary to his existence as to the diver at the bottom of the sea his
air tube. But how ascertain if the enemy is there? There is but one way:
somebody must go and see. The natural and customary thing to do is to send
forward a line of skirmishers. But in this case they will answer in the affirma-
tive with all their lives; the enemy, crouching in double ranks behind the
stone wall and in cover of the hedge, will wait until it is possible to count each
assailant's teeth. At the first volley a half of the questioning line will fall, the
other half before it can accomplish the predestined retreat. What a price to
pay for gratified curiosity! At what a dear rate an army must sometimes pur-
chase knowledge! "Let me pay all," says this gallant man—this military Christ!

There is no hope except the hope against hope that the crest is clear. True,
he might prefer capture to death: so long as he advances the line will not
fire—why should it? He can safely ride into the hostile ranks and become a
prisoner of war. But this would defeat his object. It would not answer our
question; it is necessary either that he return unharmed or be shot to death
before our eyes. Only so shall we know how to act. If captured—why, that
might have been done by a half dozen stragglers.

Now begins an extraordinary contest of intellect between a man and an
army. Our horseman, now within a quarter of a mile of the crest, suddenly
wheels to the left and gallops in a direction parallel to it. He has caught sight
of his antagonist: he knows all. Some slight advantage of ground has enabled
him to overlook a part of the line. If he were here he could tell us in words.
But that is now hopeless; he must make the best use of the few minutes of life
remaining to him, by compelling the enemy himself to tell us as much and as
plainly as possible—which, naturally, that discreet power is reluctant to do.
Not a rifleman in those crouching ranks, not a cannoneer at those masked
and shotted guns, but knows the needs of the situation, the imperative duty
of forbearance. Besides, there has been time enough to forbid them all to
fire. True, a single rifle shot might drop him and be no great disclosure. But
firing is infectious—and see how rapidly he moves, with never a pause except
as he whirls his horse about to take a new direction, never directly backward
toward us, never directly forward toward his executioners. All this is visible
through the glass: it seems occurring within pistol shot; we see all but the
enemy, whose presence, whose thoughts, whose motives we infer. To the
unaided eye there is nothing but a black figure on a white horse, tracing slow
zigzags against the slope of a distant hill—so slow they seem almost to creep.

Now—the glass again—he has tired of his failure, or sees his error, or has
gone mad: he is dashing directly forward at the wall, as if to take it at a leap,
hedge and all! One moment only and he wheels right about and is speeding

like the wind straight down the slope—toward his friends, toward his death! Instantly the wall is topped with a fierce roll of smoke for a distance of hundreds of yards to right and left. This is as instantly dissipated by the wind, and before the rattle of the rifles reaches us he is down. No, he recovers his seat; he has but pulled his horse upon its haunches. They are up and away. A tremendous cheer bursts from our ranks, relieving the insupportable tension of our feelings. And the horse and its rider? Yes, they are up and away. Away, indeed—they are making directly to our left, parallel to the now steadily blazing and smoking wall. The rattle of the musketry is continuous, and every bullet's target is that courageous heart.

Suddenly a great bank of white smoke pushes upward from behind the wall. Another and another—a dozen roll up before the thunder of the explosions and the humming of the missiles reach our ears and the missiles themselves come bounding through clouds of dust into our covert, knocking over here and there a man and causing a temporary distraction, a passing thought of self.

The dust drifts away. Incredible!—that enchanted horse and rider have passed a ravine and are climbing another slope to unveil another conspiracy of silence, to thwart the will of another armed host. Another moment and that crest too is in eruption. The horse rears and strikes the air with its forefeet. They are down at last. But look again—the man has detached himself from the dead animal. He stands erect, motionless, holding his saber in his right hand straight above his head. His face is to the enemy. Now he lowers his hand to a level with his face, moves it outward, the blade of the saber describing a downward curve. It is a sign to the enemy, to us, to the world, to posterity. It is a hero's salute to Death and History!

Again the spell is broken: our men attempt to cheer. They are choking with emotion—they utter hoarse discordant cries. They clutch their weapons and press tumultuously forward into the open. The skirmishers, without orders, against orders, are going forward at a keen run, like hounds unleashed. Our cannon speak and the enemy's now open in full chorus; to right and left as far as we can see, the distant crest, seeming now so near, erects its towers of cloud and the great round shot pitch roaring down among our moving masses. Flag after flag of ours emerges from the wood, line after line sweeps forth, catching the sunlight on its burnished arms. The rear battalions alone are in obedience: they preserve their proper distance from the insurgent front.

The commander has not moved. He now removes his field-glass from his eyes and glances to right and left. He sees the human current flowing on either side of him and his huddled escort, like tide waves parted by a rock. Not a sign of feeling in his face: he is thinking. Again he directs his eyes forward; they slowly traverse that malign and awful crest. He addresses a calm word to his bugler.

Tra-la-la! Tra-la-la! The injunction has an imperiousness which enforces it. It is repeated by all the bugles of all the subordinate commanders: the sharp metallic notes assert themselves above the hum of the advance and penetrate the sound of the cannon. To halt is to withdraw. The colors move slowly back; the lines face about and sullenly follow, bearing their wounded; the skirmishers return, gathering up the dead.

Ah, those many, many needless dead! That great soul whose beautiful body is lying over yonder, so conspicuous against the sere hillside—could it not have been spared the bitter consciousness of a vain devotion? Would *one* exception have marred too much the pitiless consistency of the divine, eternal plan?

One of the Missing.

Early in the morning of July 3, 1864, Jerome Searing, a private soldier of General Sherman's army, then confronting the enemy at and about Kenesaw Mountain, Georgia, turned his back upon a small group of officers with whom he had been talking in low tones, stepped across a light line of earthworks, and disappeared in a forest. None of the men in line behind the works had said a word to him, nor had he so much as nodded to them in passing, but all who saw understood that this brave man had been intrusted with some perilous duty. Jerome Searing, though a private, did not serve in the ranks: he was detailed for service at division headquarters, being borne upon the rolls as an "orderly." Orderly is a word covering a multitude of duties. An orderly may be a messenger, a clerk, an officer's servant—anything. He may perform services for which no provision is made in orders and army regulations; their nature may depend upon his aptitude, upon favor, upon accident. Private Searing, an incomparable marksman, young—it is surprising how young we all were in those days—hardy, intelligent and insensible to fear, was a scout. The general commanding his division was not content to obey orders blindly without knowing what was in his front, even when his command was not on detached service but formed a fraction of the line of the army; nor was he satisfied to receive his knowledge of his *vis-a-vis* through the customary channels: he wanted to know more than he was apprised of by the corps commander and the collisions of pickets and skirmishers. Hence Jerome Searing—with his extraordinary daring, his woodcraft, his sharp eyes and truthful tongue. On this occasion his instructions were simple: to get as near the enemy's lines as possible and learn all that he could.

In a few moments he had arrived at the picket-line, the men on duty there lying in groups of from two to four behind little banks of earth scooped out of the slight depression in which they lay, their rifles protruding from the green boughs with which they had masked their small defenses. The forest extended without a break toward the front, so solemn and silent that only by an effort of the imagination could it be conceived as populous with armed men alert and vigilant—a forest formidable with possibilities of battle. Pausing a moment in one of these rifle-pits to apprise the men of his intention Searing crept stealthily forward on his hands and knees and was soon lost to view in a dense thicket of underbrush.

"That is the last of him," said one of the men; "I wish I had his rifle: the Johnnies will hurt some of us with it."

Searing crept on, taking advantage of every accident of ground and growth to give himself better cover. His eyes penetrated everywhere, his ears took note of every sound. He stilled his breathing, and at the cracking of a twig beneath his knee stopped his progress and hugged the earth. It was slow work but not tedious: the danger made it exciting, but by no physical sign was the excitement manifest. His pulse was as regular, his nerves were as steady, as if he were trying to trap a sparrow.

"It seems a long time," he thought, "but I cannot have come very far: I am still alive."

He smiled at his own method of estimating distance, and crept forward. A moment later he suddenly flattened himself upon the earth and lay motionless, minute after minute. Through a narrow opening in the bushes he had caught sight of a small mound of yellow clay—one of the enemy's rifle-pits. After some little time he cautiously raised his head, inch by inch, then his body upon his hands spread out on each side of him—all the while intently regarding the hillock of clay. In another moment he was upon his feet, rifle in hand, striding rapidly forward with little attempt at concealment. He had rightly interpreted the signs, whatever they were: the enemy was gone.

To assure himself beyond a doubt before going back to report upon so important a matter, Searing pushed forward across the line of abandoned pits, running from cover to cover in the more open forest, his eyes vigilant to discover possible stragglers. He came to the edge of a plantation—one of those forlorn, deserted homesteads of the last years of the war, upgrown to brambles, ugly with broken fences and desolate with vacant buildings having blank apertures in place of doors and windows. After a keen reconnaissance from the safe seclusion of a clump of young pines Searing ran lightly across a field and through an orchard to a small structure which stood apart from the other farm buildings on a slight elevation. This he thought would enable him to overlook a large scope of country in the direction that he supposed the enemy to have taken in withdrawing. This building, which had originally consisted of a single room elevated upon four posts about ten feet high was now little more than a roof; the floor had fallen away, the joists and planks loosely piled on the ground below or resting on one end at various angles, not wholly torn from their fastenings above. The supporting posts were themselves no longer vertical. It looked as if the whole edifice would go down at the touch of a finger.

Concealing himself in the débris of joists and flooring Searing looked across the open ground between his point of view and a spur of Kenesaw Mountain, a half-mile away. A road leading up and across this spur was crowded with troops—the rear-guard of the retiring enemy.

Searing had now learned all that he could hope to know. It was his duty to return to his own command with all possible speed and report his discovery. But the gray column of Confederates toiling up the mountain road was singularly tempting. His rifle—an ordinary "Springfield," but fitted with a globe sight and hair-trigger—would easily send its ounce and a quarter of lead hissing into their midst. That would probably not affect the duration and result of the war, but it is the business of a soldier to kill. It is also his pleasure if he is a good soldier. Searing cocked his rifle and "set" the trigger.

But it was decreed from the beginning of time that Private Searing was not to murder anybody that bright summer morning, nor was the Confederate retreat to be announced by him. For countless ages events had been so matching themselves together in that wondrous mosaic to some parts of which, dimly discernible, we give the name of history, that the acts which he had in will would have marred the harmony of the pattern. Some twenty-five years previously, the Power charged with the execution of the work according to the design had provided against that mischance by causing the birth of a certain male child in a little village at the foot of the Carpathian Mountains, had carefully reared it, supervised its education, directed its desires into a military channel, and in due time made it a sergeant of artillery. By the concurrence of an infinite number of favoring influences and their preponderance over an infinite number of opposing ones, this sergeant of artillery had been made to commit a breach of discipline and fly from his native country to avoid punishment. He had been directed to New Orleans (instead of New York), where a recruiting officer awaited him on the wharf. He was enlisted and promoted, and things were so ordered that he now commanded a Confederate battery some three miles along the line from where Jerome Searing, the Federal scout, stood cocking his rifle. Nothing had been neglected—at every step in the progress of both these men's lives, and in the lives of their ancestors and contemporaries, and of the lives of the contemporaries of their ancestors—the right thing had been done to bring about the desired result; had anything in all this vast concatenation been overlooked, Private Searing might have fired on the retreating Confederates that morning, and would perhaps have missed. As it fell out, a captain of artillery, having nothing better to do while awaiting his turn to pull out and be off, amused himself by sighting a field-piece obliquely to his right at what he took to be some Federal officers on the crest of a hill and discharged it. The shot flew high of its mark.

As Jerome Searing drew back the hammer of his rifle and with his eyes upon the distant Confederates considered where he could plant his shot with the best hope of making a widow or an orphan or a childless mother—perhaps all three: for Private Searing, although he had repeatedly refused promotion, was not without a certain kind of ambition—he heard a rushing sound in the air, like that made by the wings of a great bird swooping down upon its prey. More quickly than he could apprehend the gradation, it increased to a hoarse and horrible roar as the missile that made it sprang at him out of the sky, striking with a deafening impact one of the posts supporting the confusion of timbers above him, smashing it into matchwood and bringing down the crazy edifice with a loud clatter, in clouds of blinding dust!

Lieutenant Adrian Searing, in command of the picket-guard on that part of the line through which his brother Jerome had passed on his mission, sat with attentive ears in his breastwork behind the line. Not the faintest sound escaped him: the cry of a bird, the barking of a squirrel, the noise of the wind among the pines—all were anxiously noted by his overstrained sense. Suddenly, directly in front of his line, he heard a faint, confused rumble, like the clatter of a falling building translated by distance. At the same moment an officer approached him on foot from the rear and saluted.

"Lieutenant," said the aide, "the colonel directs that you move forward your line and feel the enemy if you find him. If not, continue the advance until directed to halt. There is reason to think that the enemy has retired."

The lieutenant nodded and said nothing; the other officer retired. In a moment the men, apprised of their duty by the non-commissioned officers in low tones, had deployed from their rifle-pits and were moving forward in skirmishing order, with set teeth and beating hearts. The lieutenant mechanically looked at his watch. Six o'clock and eighteen minutes.

When Jerome Searing recovered consciousness he did not at once understand what had occurred. It was, indeed, some time before he opened his eyes. For a while he believed that he had died and been buried, and he tried to recall some portions of the burial service. He thought that his wife was kneeling upon his grave, adding her weight to that of the earth upon his breast. The two of them, widow and earth, had crushed his coffin. Unless the children should persuade her to go home, he would not much longer be able to breathe. He felt a sense of wrong. "I cannot speak to her," he thought; "the dead have no voice; and if I open my eyes I shall get them full of earth."

He opened his eyes—a great expanse of blue sky, rising from a fringe of the tops of trees. In the foreground, shutting out some of the trees, a high, dun mound, angular in outline and crossed by an intricate, patternless system of straight lines; in the center a bright ring of metal—the whole an immeasurable distance away—a distance so inconceivably great that it fatigued him, and he closed his eyes. The moment he did so he was conscious of an insufferable light. A sound was in his ears like the low, rhythmic thunder of a distant sea breaking in successive waves upon the beach, and out of this noise, seeming a part of it, or possibly coming from beyond it, and intermingled with its ceaseless undertone, came the articulate words: "Jerome Searing, you are caught like a rat in a trap—in a trap, trap, trap."

Suddenly there fell a great silence, a black darkness, an infinite tranquillity, and Jerome Searing, perfectly conscious of his rathood and well assured of the trap that he was in—remembering all and nowise alarmed, again opened his eyes to reconnoitre, to note the strength of his enemy, to plan his defense.

He was caught in a reclining posture, his back firmly supported by a solid beam. Another lay across his breast, but he had been able to shrink a little away from it so that it no longer oppressed him, though it was immovable. A brace joining it at an angle had wedged him against a pile of boards on his left, fastening the arm on that side. His legs, slightly parted and straight along the ground, were covered upward to the knees with a mass of débris which towered above his narrow horizon. His head was as rigidly fixed as in a vice: he could move his eyes, his chin—no more. Only his right arm was partly free. "You must help us out of this," he said to it. But he could not get it from under the heavy timber athwart his chest, nor move it outward more than six inches at the elbow.

Searing was not seriously injured, nor did he suffer pain. A smart rap on the head from a flying fragment of the splintered post, incurred simultaneously with the frightfully sudden shock to the nervous system, had momentarily dazed him. His term of unconsciousness, including the period of recovery, during which he had had the strange fancies, had probably not exceeded a few seconds, for the dust of the wreck had not wholly cleared away as he began an intelligent survey of the situation.

With his partly free right hand he now tried to get hold of the beam, which lay across, but not quite against, his breast. In no way could he do so. He was unable to depress the shoulder so as to push the elbow beyond that edge of the timber which was nearest his knees; failing in that, he could not raise the forearm and hand to grasp the beam. The brace that made an angle with it downward and backward prevented him from doing anything in that direction, and between it and his body the space was not half as wide as the length of his forearm. Obviously he could not get his hand under the beam nor over it; he could not, in fact, touch it at all. Having demonstrated his inability, he desisted, and began to think whether he could reach any of the débris piled upon his legs.

In surveying the mass with a view to determining that point his attention was arrested by what seemed to be a ring of shining metal immediately in front of his eyes. It appeared to him at first to surround some perfectly black substance, and it was somewhat more than a half-inch in diameter. It suddenly occurred to his mind that the blackness was simply shadow and that the ring was in fact the muzzle of his rifle protruding from the pile of débris. He was not long in satisfying himself that this was so—if it was a satisfaction. By closing either eye he could look a little way along the barrel—to the point where it was hidden by the rubbish that held it. He could see the one side, with the corresponding eye, at apparently the same angle as the other side with the other eye. Looking with the right eye, the weapon seemed to be directed at a point to the left of his head, and *vice versa*. He was unable to see the upper surface of the barrel, but could see the under surface of the stock at a slight angle. The piece was, in fact, aimed at the exact center of his forehead.

In the perception of this circumstance, in the recollection that just previously to the mischance of which this uncomfortable situation was the result he had cocked the gun and set the trigger so that a touch would discharge it, Private Searing was affected with a feeling of uneasiness. But that was as far as possible from fear: he was a brave man, somewhat familiar with the aspect of rifles from that point of view, and of cannon, too; and now he recalled, with something like amusement, an incident of his experience at the storming of Missionary Ridge, where, walking up to one of the enemy's embrasures from which he had seen a heavy gun throw charge after charge of grape among the assailants he had thought for a moment that the piece had been withdrawn: he could see nothing in the opening but a brazen circle. What that was he had understood just in time to step aside as it pitched another peck of iron down that swarming slope. To face firearms is one of the commonest incidents in a soldier's life—firearms, too, with malevolent eyes blazing behind them. That is what a soldier is for. Still, Private Searing did not altogether relish the situation, and turned away his eyes.

After groping, aimless, with his right hand for a time he made an ineffectual attempt to release his left. Then he tried to disengage his head, the fixity of which was the more annoying from his ignorance of what held it. Next he tried to free his feet, but while exerting the powerful muscles of his legs for that purpose it occurred to him that a disturbance of the rubbish which held them might discharge the rifle; how it could have endured what had already befallen it he could not understand, although memory assisted him with several instances in point. One in particular he recalled, in which in a moment of mental abstraction he had clubbed his rifle and beaten out another gentleman's brains, observing afterward that the weapon which he had been diligently swinging by the muzzle was loaded, capped, and at full cock—a knowledge of which circumstance would doubtless have cheered his antagonist to longer endurance. He had always smiled in recalling that blunder of his "green and salad days" as a soldier, but now he did not smile. He turned his eyes again to the muzzle of the rifle and for a moment fancied that it had moved: it seemed somewhat nearer.

Again he looked away. The tops of the distant trees beyond the bounds of the plantation interested him: he had not before observed how light and feathery they seemed, nor how darkly blue the sky was, even among their branches where they somewhat paled it with their green; above him it appeared almost black. "It will be uncomfortably hot here," he thought, "as the day advances. I wonder which way I am looking."

Judging by such shadows as he could see, he decided that his face was due north; he would at least not have the sun in his eyes, and north—well, that was toward his wife and children.

"Bah!" he exclaimed aloud, "what have they to do with it?"

He closed his eyes. "As I can't get out I may as well go to sleep. The Rebels are gone and some of our fellows are sure to stray out here foraging. They'll find me."

But he did not sleep. Gradually he became sensible of a pain in the forehead—a dull ache, hardly perceptible at first, but growing more and more uncomfortable. He opened his eyes and it was gone—closed them and it returned. "The devil!" he said, irrelevantly, and stared again at the sky. He heard the singing of birds, the strange metallic note of the meadow lark, suggesting the clash of vibrant blades. He fell into pleasant memories of his childhood; played again with his brother and sister; raced across the fields, shouting to alarm the sedentary larks; entered the somber forest beyond and with timid steps followed the faint path to Ghost Rock, standing at last with audible heart-throbs before the Dead Man's Cave and seeking to penetrate its awful mystery. For the first time he observed that the opening of the haunted cavern was encircled by a ring of metal. Then all else vanished and left him gazing into the barrel of his rifle as before. But whereas before it had seemed nearer, it now seemed an inconceivable distance away, and all the more sinister for that. He cried out and, startled by something in his own voice—the note of fear—lied to himself in denial: "If I don't sing out I might stay here till I die."

He now made no further attempt to evade the menacing stare of the gun-barrel. If he turned away his eyes an instant it was to look for assistance (although he could not see the ground on either side the ruin), and he permitted them to return, obedient to the imperative fascination. If he closed them it was from weariness, and instantly the poignant pain in his forehead—the prophecy and menace of the bullet—forced him to reopen them.

The tension of nerve and brain was too severe; nature came to his relief with intervals of unconsciousness. Reviving from one of these he became sensible of a sharp, smarting pain in his right hand, and when he worked his fingers together, or rubbed his palm with them, he could feel that they were wet and slippery. He could not see the hand, but he knew the sensation: it was running blood. In his delirium he had beaten it against the jagged fragments of the wreck, had clutched it full of splinters. He resolved that he would meet his fate more manly. He was a plain, common soldier, had no religion and not much philosophy: he could not die like a hero, with great and wise last words, even if there were some one to hear them, but he could die "game," and he would. But if he only could know when to expect the shot!

Some rats which had probably inhabited the shed came sneaking and scampering about. One of them mounted the pile of débris that held the rifle; another followed, and another. Searing regarded them at first with indifference, then with friendly interest; then, as the thought flashed into his bewildered mind that they might touch the trigger of his rifle, he screamed at them to go away. "It is no business of yours," he cried.

The creatures left; they would return later, attack his face, gnaw away his nose, cut his throat—he knew that, but he hoped by that time to be dead.

Nothing could now unfix his gaze from the little ring of metal with its black interior. The pain in his forehead was fierce and constant. He felt it gradually penetrating the brain more and more deeply, until at last its progress was arrested by the wood at the back of his head. It grew momentarily more insufferable; he began wantonly beating his lacerated hand against the splinters again to counteract that horrible ache. It seemed to throb with a slow, regular recurrence, each pulsation sharper than the preceding, and some times he cried out, thinking he felt the fatal bullet. No thoughts of home, of wife and children, of country, of glory. The whole record of memory was effaced. The world had passed away—not a vestige remained. Here in this confusion of timbers and boards is the sole universe. Here is immortality in time—each pain an everlasting life. The throbs tick off eternities.

Jerome Searing, the man of courage, the formidable enemy, the strong, resolute warrior, was as pale as a ghost. His jaw was fallen; his eyes protruded; he trembled in every fiber; a cold sweat bathed his entire body; he screamed with fear. He was not insane—he was terrified.

In groping about with his torn and bleeding hand he seized at last a strip of board, and, pulling, felt it give way. It lay parallel with his body, and by bending his elbow as much as the contracted space would permit, he could draw it a few inches at a time. Finally it was altogether loosened from the wreckage covering his legs; he could lift it clear of the ground its whole length. A great hope came into his mind: perhaps he could work it upward, that is to say backward, far enough to lift the end and push aside the rifle; or, if that were too tightly wedged, so hold the strip of board as to deflect the bullet. With this object he passed it backward inch by inch, hardly daring to breathe lest that act somehow defeat his intent, and more than ever unable to remove his eyes from the rifle, which might perhaps now hasten to improve its waning opportunity. Something at least had been gained: in the occupation of his mind in this attempt at self-defense he was less sensible of the pain in his head and had ceased to scream. But he was still dreadfully frightened and his teeth rattled like castanets.

The strip of board ceased to move to the suasion of his hand. He tugged at it with all his strength, changed the direction of its length all he could, but it had met some extended obstruction behind him, and the end in front was still too far away to clear the pile of débris and reach the muzzle of the gun. It extended, indeed, nearly as far as the trigger-guard, which, uncovered by the rubbish, he could imperfectly see with his right eye. He tried to break the strip with his hand, but had no leverage. Perceiving his defeat, all his terror returned, augmented tenfold. The black aperture of the rifle appeared to threaten a sharper and more imminent death in punishment for his rebellion. The track of the bullet through his head ached with an intenser anguish. He began to tremble again.

Suddenly he became composed. His tremor subsided. He clenched his teeth and drew down his eyebrows. He had not exhausted his means of defense: a new design had shaped itself in his mind—another plan of battle. Raising the front end of the strip of board he carefully pushed it forward through the wreckage at the side of the rifle until it pressed against the trigger-guard. Then he moved the end slowly outward until he could feel that it had cleared it; then, closing his eyes, thrust it against the trigger with all his strength. There was no explosion: the rifle had been discharged as it dropped from his hand when the building fell. But Jerome Searing was dead.

A line of Federal skirmishers sweeps across the plantation toward the mountain. They pass on both sides of the wrecked building, observing nothing. At a short distance in their rear comes their commander, Lieutenant Adrian Searing. He casts his eyes curiously upon the ruin and sees a dead body half-buried in boards and timbers. It is so covered with dust that its clothing is Confederate gray. Its face is yellowish white; the cheeks are fallen in; the temple sunken, too, with sharp ridges about them, making the forehead forbiddingly narrow; the upper lip, slightly lifted, shows the white teeth, rigidly clenched. The hair is heavy with moisture, the face as wet as the dewy grass all about. From his point of view the officer does not observe the rifle: the man was apparently killed by the fall of the building.

"Dead a week," said the officer, curtly, moving on, mechanically pulling out his watch as if to verify his estimate of time. Six o'clock and forty minutes.

Killed at Resaca.

The best soldier of our staff was Lieutenant Herman Brayle, one of the two aides-de-camp. I don't remember where the general picked him up; from some Ohio regiment, I think. None of us had previously known him, and it would have been strange if we had, for no two of us came from the same State, nor even from adjoining States. The general seemed to think that a position on his staff was a distinction that should be so judiciously conferred as not to beget any sectional jealousies and imperil the integrity of that portion of the Union which was still an integer. He would not even choose them from his own command, but by some jugglery at department headquarters obtained them from other brigades. Under such circumstances a man's services had to be very distinguished indeed to be heard of by his family and the friends of his youth; and "the speaking-trump of fame" was a trifle hoarse from loquacity, anyhow.

Lieutenant Brayle was more than six feet in height and of splendid proportions, with the light hair and gray-blue eyes which men similarly gifted usually find associated with a high order of courage. As he was commonly in full uniform, especially in action, when most officers are content to be less flamboyantly attired, he was a very striking and conspicuous figure. As to the rest, he had a gentleman's manners, a scholar's head and a lion's heart. His age was about thirty.

We all soon came to like Brayle as much as we admired him, and it was with sincere concern that in the engagement at Stone's River—our first action after he joined us—we observed that he had one most objectionable and unsoldierly quality: he was vain of his courage. During all the vicissitudes and mutations of that hideous encounter, whether our troops were fighting in the open cotton fields, in the cedar thickets or behind the railway embankment, he did not once take cover, except when sternly commanded to do so by the general, who usually had other things to think of than the lives of his staff officers—or those of his men, for that matter.

In every subsequent engagement while Brayle was with us it was the same way. He would sit his horse like an equestrian statue, in a storm of bullets and grape, in the most exposed places—wherever, in fact, duty, requiring him to go, permitted him to remain—when, without trouble and with distinct advantage to his reputation for common sense, he might have been in such security as is possible on a battle field in the brief intervals of personal inaction.

On foot, from necessity or in deference to his dismounted commander or associates, his conduct was the same. He would stand like a rock in the open when officers and men alike had taken to cover. While men older in service and years, higher in rank and of unquestionable intrepidity, were loyally preserving behind the crest of a hill lives infinitely precious to their country, this fellow would stand, equally idle, on the ridge, facing in the direction of the sharpest fire.

When battles are going on in open ground it frequently occurs that the opposing lines, confronting one another within a stone's throw for hours, hug the earth as closely as if they loved it. The line officers in their proper places flatten themselves no less, and the field officers, their horses all killed or sent to the rear, crouch beneath the infernal canopy of hissing lead and screaming iron without a thought of personal dignity.

In such circumstances the life of a staff officer of a brigade is distinctly "not a happy one," mainly because of its precarious tenure and the unnerving alternations of emotion to which he is exposed. From a position of that comparative security from which a civilian would ascribe his escape to a "miracle," he may be dispatched with an order to some commander of a prone regiment in the front line—a person for the moment inconspicuous and not always easy to locate without a deal of search among men somewhat preoccupied, and in a din amid which question and answer alike must be imparted in the sign language. It is customary in such cases to duck the head and scuttle away on a keen run, an object of lively interest to some thousands of admiring marksmen. In returning—well, it is not customary to return.

Brayle's practice was different. He would consign his horse to the care of an orderly—he loved his horse—and walk quietly away on his perilous errand with never a stoop of the back, his splendid figure, accentuated by his uniform, holding the eye with a strange fascination. We watched him with suspended breath, our hearts in our mouths. On one occasion of this kind, indeed, one of our number, an impetuous stammerer, was so possessed by his emotion that he shouted at me:

"I'll b-b-bet you t-two d-d-dollars they d-drop him b-b'fore he g-gets to that d-d-ditch!"

I did not accept the brutal wager; I thought they would. Let me do justice to a brave man's memory: in all these needless exposures of life there was no visible bravado nor subsequent narration. In the few instances when some of us had ventured to remonstrate Brayle had smiled pleasantly and made some light reply, which, however, had not encouraged a further pursuit of the subject. Once he said:

"Captain, if ever I come to grief by forgetting your advice I hope my last moments will be cheered by the sound of your beloved voice breathing into my ear the blessed words 'I told you so.'"

We laughed at the captain—just why, we could probably not have explained—and that afternoon, when he was shot to rags from an ambuscade Brayle remained by the body for some time, adjusting the limbs with needless care—there in the middle of a road swept by gusts of grape and canister. It is easy to condemn this kind of thing, and not very difficult to refrain from imitation, but it is impossible not to respect, and Brayle was liked none the less for the weakness which had so heroic an expression. We wished he were not a fool, but he went on that way to the end, sometimes hard hit, but always returning to duty as good as new.

Of course, it came at last; he who defies the law of probabilities challenges an adversary that is never beaten. It was at Resaca, in Georgia, during the movement that resulted in the capture of Atlanta. In front of our brigade the enemy's line of earthworks ran through open fields along a slight crest. At each end of this open ground we were close up to him in the woods, but the clear ground we could not hope to occupy until night, when darkness would enable us to burrow like moles and throw up earth. At this point our line was a quarter-mile away in the edge of a wood. Roughly, we formed a semicircle, the enemy's fortified line being the chord of the arc.

"Lieutenant, go tell Colonel Ward to work up as close as he can get cover, and not to waste much ammunition in unnecessary firing. You may leave your horse."

When the general gave this direction we were in the fringe of the forest, near the right extremity of the arc. Colonel Ward was at the left. The suggestion to leave the horse obviously enough meant that Brayle was to take the longer line, through the woods and among the men. Indeed, the suggestion was needless; to go by the short route meant absolutely certain failure to deliver the message. Before anybody could interpose, Brayle had cantered lightly into the field and the enemy's works were in crackling conflagration.

"Stop that damned fool!" shouted the general.

A private of the escort, with more ambition than brains, sprang forward to obey, and within ten yards left himself dead on the field of honor.

Brayle was beyond recall, galloping easily along parallel to the enemy and less than two hundred yards distant. He was a picture to see! His hat had been blown or shot from his head, and his long blond hair rose and fell with the motion of his horse. He sat erect in the saddle, holding the reins lightly in his left hand, his right hanging carelessly at his side. An occasional glimpse of his handsome profile as he turned his head one way or the other proved that the interest which he took in what was going on was natural and without affectation.

The picture was intensely dramatic, but in no degree theatrical. Successive scores of rifles spat at him viciously as he came within range, and our own line in the edge of the timber broke out in visible and audible defense. No longer regardful of themselves or their orders, our fellows sprang to their feet and swarming into the open sent broad sheets of bullets against the blazing crest of the offending works, which poured an answering fire into their unprotected groups with deadly effect. The artillery on both sides joined the battle, punctuating the rattle and roar with deep earth-shaking explosions and tearing the air with storms of screaming grape, which from the enemy's side splintered the trees and spattered them with blood, and from ours defiled the smoke of his arms with banks and clouds of dust from his parapet.

My attention had been for a moment drawn to the general combat, but now, glancing down the unobscured avenue between these two thunder-clouds, I saw Brayle, the cause of the carnage. Invisible now from either side, and equally doomed by friend and foe, he stood in the shot-swept space, motionless, his face toward the enemy. At some little distance lay his horse. I instantly divined the cause of his inaction.

As topographical engineer I had early in the day made a hasty examination of the ground, and now remembered that at that point was a deep and sinuous gully, crossing half the field from the enemy's line, its general course at right angles to it. From where we were it was invisible, and Brayle had evidently not known of it. Clearly, it was impassable. Its salient angles would have afforded him absolute security if he had chosen to be satisfied with the miracle already wrought in his favor. He could not go forward, he would not turn back; he stood awaiting death. It did not keep him long waiting.

By some mysterious coincidence, almost instantaneously, as he fell, the firing ceased, a few desultory shots at long intervals serving rather to accentuate than break the silence. It was as if both sides had suddenly repented of their profitless crime. Four stretcher-bearers following a sergeant with a white flag soon afterward moved unmolested into the field and made straight for Brayle's body. Several Confederate officers and men came out to meet them, and with uncovered heads assisted them to take up their sacred burden. As it was borne toward us we heard beyond the hostile works fifes and a muffled drum—a dirge. A generous enemy honored the fallen brave.

Amongst the dead man's effects was a soiled Russia-leather pocket-book. In the distribution of mementoes of our friend, which the general as administrator decreed, this fell to me.

A year after the close of the war, on my way to California, I opened and idly inspected it. Out of an overlooked compartment fell a letter without envelope or address. It was in a woman's handwriting, and began with words of endearment, but no name.

It had the following date line: "San Francisco, Cal., July 9, 1862." The signature was "Darling," in marks of quotation. Incidentally, in the body of the text, the writer's full name was given—which I must be pardoned for not disclosing: the lady is living.

The letter showed evidence of cultivation and good breeding, but it was an ordinary love-letter, if a love-letter can be ordinary. There was not much in it, but there was something. It was this:

"Mr. Winters, whom I shall always hate for it, has been telling that at some battle in Virginia, where he got his hurt, you were seen crouching behind a tree. I think he wants to injure you in my regard, which he knows the story would do if I believed it. I could bear to hear of my soldier lover's death, but not of his cowardice."

These were the words which on that sunny afternoon, in a distant region, had slain a hundred men. Is woman weak?

One evening I called on the writer of that letter to return it to her. I intended also to tell her what she had done—but not that she did it. I found her in an elegantly furnished dwelling on Rincon Hill. She was beautiful, well-bred—in a word, charming.

"You knew Lieutenant Herman Brayle," I said, rather abruptly. "You know, doubtless, that he fell in battle. Among his effects was found this letter from you. My errand here is to place it in your hands."

She mechanically took the letter, glanced through it with deepening color, and then, looking at me with a smile, said:

"It is very good of you, though I am sure it was hardly worth while." She started suddenly and changed color. "This stain," she said, "is it—surely it is not—"

"Madam," I said, "pardon me, but that is the blood of the truest and bravest heart that ever beat."

She hastily flung the letter on the blazing coals. "Uh! I cannot bear the sight of blood!" she said. "How did he die?"

I had involuntarily risen and now stood partly behind her. As she asked the question she turned her face about and slightly upward. The light of the burning letter was reflected in her eyes and touched her cheek with a tinge of crimson like the stain upon the letter. I had never seen anything so beautiful.

"He was bitten by a snake," I replied.

The Affair at Coulter's Notch.

"Do you think, Colonel, that your brave Coulter would like to put one of his guns in here?" the general asked.

He was apparently not altogether serious; it certainly did not seem a place where any artillerist, however brave, would like to put a gun. The colonel thought that possibly his division commander meant good-humoredly to intimate that Captain Coulter's courage had been too highly extolled in a recent conversation between them.

"General," he replied warmly, "Coulter would like to put a gun anywhere within reach of those people"—with a motion of his hand in the direction of the enemy.

"It is the only place," said the general. He was serious, then.

The place was a depression, a "notch," in the sharp crest of a hill. It was a pass, and through it ran a turnpike which, reaching this highest point in its course by a sinuous ascent through a thin forest, made a similar, though less steep, descent toward the enemy. For a mile to the left and a mile to the right the ridge, though occupied by Federal infantry lying close behind the sharp crest and appearing as if held in place by atmospheric pressure, was inaccessible to artillery. There was no place but the bottom of the notch, and that was barely wide enough for the roadbed. From the Confederate side this point was commanded by an entire battery posted on a slightly lower elevation beyond a creek, and a mile away. All the guns but one were masked by the trees of an orchard; that one—it seemed a bit of impudence—was directly in front of a rather grandiose building, the planter's dwelling. The gun was safe enough in its exposure: the rifles of that day would not carry a mile without such an elevation as made the fire, in a military sense, harmless: it might kill here and there but could not dislodge. Coulter's Notch—it came to be called so—was not, that pleasant summer afternoon, a place where one would "like to put a gun."

Three or four dead horses lay there, sprawling in the road, three or four dead men in a trim row at one side of it and a little back down the hill. All but one were cavalrymen belonging to the Federal advance. One was a quartermaster: the general commanding the division and the colonel commanding the brigade, with their staffs and escorts, had ridden into the Notch to have a look at the enemy's guns—which had straightway obscured themselves in towering clouds of smoke. It was hardly profitable to be curious about guns which had the trick of the cuttlefish and the season of observation had been brief. At its conclusion—a short remove backward from where it began—occurred the conversation already partly reported. "It is the only place," the general repeated, thoughtfully, "to get at them."

The colonel looked at him gravely. "There is room for only one gun, General—one against six."

"That is true—for only one at a time," said the commander with something like, yet not altogether like, a smile. "But then, your brave Coulter!—a whole battery in himself."

The tone of irony was now unmistakable. It angered the colonel, but he did not know what to say. The spirit of military subordination is not favorable to retort, nor even deprecation.

At this moment a young officer of artillery came riding slowly up the road attended by his bugler. It was Captain Coulter. He could not have been more than twenty-three years of age. He was of medium height, but very slender and lithe, sitting his horse with something of the air of a civilian. In face he was of a type singularly unlike the men about him: thin, high-nosed, gray-eyed, with a slight blonde mustache, and long, rather straggling hair of the same color. There was an apparent negligence in his attire. His cap was worn with the visor a trifle askew; his coat was buttoned only at the sword-belt, showing a considerable expanse of white shirt, tolerably clean for that stage of the campaign. But the negligence was all in his dress and bearing; in his face was a look of intense interest in his surroundings. His gray eyes, which seemed occasionally to strike right and left across the landscape, like search-lights, were for the most part fixed upon the sky beyond the Notch; until he should arrive at the summit of the road, there was nothing else in that direction to see. As he came opposite his division and brigade commanders at the roadside he saluted mechanically and was about to pass on. The colonel signed to him to halt.

"Captain Coulter," he said, "the enemy has a battery of six pieces over there on the next ridge. If I rightly understand the general he directs that you bring up a gun and engage them."

There was a blank silence: the general looked stolidly at a distant regiment swarming slowly up the hill through rough undergrowth, like a torn and draggled cloud of blue smoke; the captain appeared not to have observed him. Presently the captain spoke, slowly and with apparent effort:

"On the next ridge, did you say, sir? Are the guns near the house?"

"Ah, you have been over this road before. Directly *at* the house."

"And it is—necessary—to engage them? The order is imperative?"

His voice was husky and broken. He was visibly paler. The colonel was astonished and mortified. He stole a glance at the commander. In that set, immobile face was no sign; it was as hard as bronze. A moment later the general rode away, followed by his staff and escort. The colonel, humiliated and indignant, was about to order Captain Coulter in arrest, when the latter spoke a few words in a low tone to his bugler, saluted, and rode straight forward into the Notch, where, shortly, at the summit of the road, his field-glass at his eyes, he showed against the sky, he and his horse, sharply defined and motionless as an equestrian statue. The bugler had dashed down the road in the opposite direction at headlong speed and disappeared behind a wood. Presently his bugle was heard singing in the cedars, and in an incredibly short time a single gun with its caisson, each drawn by six horses, and manned by its full complement of gunners came bounding and banging up the grade in a storm of dust, unlimbered under cover and was run forward by hand to the fatal crest among the dead horses. A gesture of the captain's arm, some strangely agile movements of the men in loading, and almost before the troops along the way had ceased to hear the rattle of the wheels a great white cloud sprang forward down the declivity, and with a deafening report the affair at Coulter's Notch had begun.

It is not intended to relate in detail the progress and incidents of that ghastly contest—a contest without vicissitudes, its alternations only different degrees of despair. Almost at the instant when Captain Coulter's gun blew its challenging cloud six answering clouds rolled upward from among the trees about the plantation house, a deep multiple report roared back like a broken echo, and thenceforth to the end the Federal cannoneers fought their hopeless battle in an atmosphere of living iron whose thoughts were lightnings and whose deeds were death.

Unwilling to see the efforts which he could not aid and the slaughter which he could not stay, the colonel had ascended the ridge at a point a quarter of a mile to the left, whence the Notch, itself invisible but pushing up successive masses of smoke, seemed the crater of a volcano in thundering eruption. With his glass he watched the enemy's guns, noting as he could the effects of Coulter's fire—if Coulter still lived to direct it. He saw that the Federal gunners, ignoring the enemy's pieces whose position could be determined by their smoke only, gave their whole attention to the one which maintained its place in the open—the lawn in front of the house, with which it was accurately in line. Over and about that hardy piece the shells exploded at intervals of a few seconds. Some exploded in the house, as could be seen by thin ascensions of smoke from the breached roof. Figures of prostrate men and horses were plainly visible.

"If our fellows are doing such good work with a single gun," said the colonel to an aide who happened to be nearest, "they must be suffering like the devil from six. Go down and present the commander of that piece with my congratulations on the accuracy of his fire."

Turning to his adjutant-general he said, "Did you observe Coulter's damned reluctance to obey orders?"

"Yes, sir, I did."

"Well, say nothing about it, please. I don't think the general will care to make any accusations. He will probably have enough to do in explaining his own connection with this uncommon way of amusing the rear-guard of a retreating enemy."

"Colonel," said the adjutant-general, "I don't know that I ought to say anything, but there is something wrong in all this. Do you happen to know that Captain Coulter is from the South?"

"No; *was* he, indeed?"

"I heard that last summer the division which the general then commanded was in the vicinity of Coulter's home—camped there for weeks and—"

"Listen!" said the colonel, interrupting with an upward gesture. "Do you hear *that?*"

"That" was the silence of the Federal gun. The staff, the orderlies, the lines of infantry behind the crest—all had "heard," and were looking curiously in the direction of the crater, whence no smoke now ascended except desultory cloudlets from the enemy's shells. Then came the blare of a bugle, a faint rattle of wheels; a minute later the sharp reports recommenced with double activity. The demolished gun had been replaced with a sound one.

"Yes," said the adjutant-general, resuming his narrative, "the general made the acquaintance of Coulter's family. There was trouble—I don't know the exact nature of it—something about Coulter's wife. She is a red-hot Secessionist, as they all are, except Coulter himself, but she is a good wife and high-bred lady. There was a complaint to army headquarters. The general was transferred to this division. It is odd that Coulter's battery should afterward have been assigned to it."

The colonel had risen from the rock upon which they had been sitting. His eyes were blazing with a generous indignation.

"See here, Morrison," said he, looking his gossiping staff officer straight in the face, "did you get that story from a gentleman or a liar?"

"I don't want to say how I got it, Colonel, unless it is necessary"—he was blushing a trifle—"but I'll stake my life upon its truth in the main."

The colonel turned toward a small knot of officers some distance away. "Lieutenant Williams!" he shouted.

One of the officers detached himself from the group, and coming forward saluted, saying: "Pardon me, Colonel, I thought you had been informed. Williams is dead down there by the gun. What can I do, sir?"

Lieutenant Williams was the aide who had had the pleasure of conveying to the officer in charge of the gun his brigade commander's congratulations.

"Go," said the colonel, "and direct the withdrawal of that gun instantly. Hold! I'll go myself."

He strode down the declivity toward the rear of the Notch at a break-neck pace, over rocks and through brambles, followed by his little retinue in tumultuous disorder. At the foot of the declivity they mounted their waiting animals and took to the road at a lively trot round a bend and into the Notch. The spectacle which they encountered there was appalling.

Within that defile, barely broad enough for a single gun, were piled the wrecks of no fewer than four—they had noted the silencing of only the last one disabled—there had been a lack of men to replace it quickly. The débris lay on both sides of the road: the men had managed to keep an open way between, through which the fifth piece was now firing. The men?—they looked like demons of the Pit! All were hatless, all stripped to the waist, their reeking skins black with blotches of powder and spattered with gouts of blood. They worked like madmen, with rammer and cartridge, lever and lanyard. They set their swollen shoulders and bleeding hands against the wheels at each recoil and heaved the heavy gun back to its place. There were no commands; in that awful environment of whooping shot, exploding shells, shrieking fragments of iron and flying splinters of wood, none could have been heard. Officers, if officers there were, were indistinguishable: all worked together—each while he lasted—governed by the eye. When the gun was sponged it was loaded; when loaded aimed and fired. There was no clashing: the duty of the instant was obvious. When one fell another, looking a trifle cleaner, seemed to rise from the earth in the dead man's tracks to fall in his turn.

With the ruined guns lay the ruined men—alongside the wreckage, under it and atop of it; and back down the road—a ghastly procession!—crept on hands and knees such of the wounded as were able to move. The colonel—he had compassionately sent his cavalcade to the right about—had to ride over those who were entirely dead in order not to crush those who were partly alive. Into that Hell he tranquilly held his way, rode up alongside the gun, and in the obscurity of the last discharge tapped upon the cheek the man holding the rammer—who straightway fell, thinking himself killed. A fiend seven times damned sprang out of the smoke to take his place, but paused and gazed up at the mounted officer with an unearthly regard, his teeth flashing between his black lips, his eyes, fierce and expanded, burning like coals beneath his bloody brow. The colonel made an authoritative gesture and pointed to the rear. The fiend bowed in token of obedience. It was Captain Coulter.

Simultaneously with the colonel's arresting sign silence fell upon the whole field of action. The procession of missiles no longer streamed into that defile of death: the enemy also had ceased firing. His army had been gone for hours, and the commander of his rear-guard, who had held his position perilously long in hope to silence the Federal fire, at that strange moment had silenced his own. "I was not aware of the breadth of my authority," thought the colonel, facetiously, riding forward to the crest to see what had really happened.

An hour later his brigade was in bivouac on the enemy's ground, and its idlers were examining, with something of awe, as the faithful inspect a saint's relics, a score of straddling dead horses and three disabled guns, all spiked. The fallen men had been carried away; their torn and broken bodies would have given too great satisfaction.

Naturally, the colonel established himself and his military family in the plantation house. It was somewhat shattered, but it was better than the open air. The furniture was greatly deranged and broken. The walls and ceilings were knocked away here and there, and there was a lingering odor of powder smoke everywhere. The beds, the closets of women's clothing, the cupboards were not greatly damaged. The new tenants for a night made themselves comfortable, and the practical effacement of Coulter's battery supplied them with an interesting topic.

During supper that evening an orderly of the escort showed himself into the dining-room and asked permission to speak to the colonel.

"What is it, Barbour?" said that officer, pleasantly, having overheard the request.

"Colonel, there is something wrong in the cellar; I don't know what— somebody there. I was down there rummaging about."

"I will go down and see," said a staff officer, rising.

"So will I," the colonel said; "let the others remain. Lead on, orderly."

They took a candle from the table and descended the cellar stairs, the orderly in visible trepidation. The candle made but a feeble light, but presently, as they advanced, its narrow circle of illumination revealed a human figure seated on the ground against the blank stone wall which they were skirting, its knees elevated, its head bowed sharply forward. The face, which should have been seen in profile, was invisible, for the man was bent so far forward that his long hair concealed it; and, strange to relate, the beard, of a much darker hue, fell in a great tangled mass and lay along the ground at his feet. They involuntarily paused; then the colonel, taking the candle from the orderly's shaking hand, approached the man and attentively considered him.

The long dark beard was the hair of a woman—dead. The dead woman clasped in her arms a dead babe. Both were clasped in the arms of the man, pressed against his breast, against his lips. There was blood in the hair of the woman; there was blood in the hair of the man. A yard away lay an infant's foot. It was near an irregular depression in the beaten earth which formed the cellar's floor—a fresh excavation with a convex bit of iron, having jagged edges, visible in one of the sides. The colonel held the light as high as he could. The floor of the room above was broken through, the splinters pointing at all angles downward. "This casemate is not bomb-proof," said the colonel gravely; it did not occur to him that his summing up of the matter had any levity in it.

They stood about the group awhile in silence; the staff officer was thinking of his unfinished supper, the orderly of what might possibly be in one of the casks on the other side of the cellar. Suddenly the man whom they had thought dead raised his head and gazed tranquilly into their faces. His complexion was coal black; the cheeks were apparently tattooed in irregular sinuous lines from the eyes downward. The lips, too, were white, like those of a stage negro. There was blood upon his forehead.

The staff officer drew back a pace, the orderly two paces.

"What are you doing here, my man?" said the colonel, unmoved.

"This house belongs to me, sir," was the reply, civilly delivered.

"To you? Ah, I see. And these?"

"My wife and child. Colonel, I am Captain Coulter."

A Tough Tussle.

One night in the autumn of 1861 a man sat alone in the heart of the forest in Western Virginia. The region was then, and still is, one of the wildest on the continent—the Cheat Mountain country. There was no lack of people close at hand, however; within a mile of where the man sat was the now silent camp of a whole Federal brigade. Somewhere about—it might be still nearer—was a force of the enemy, the numbers unknown. It was this uncertainty as to its numbers and position that accounted for the man's presence in that lonely spot: he was a young officer of a Federal infantry regiment and his business there was to guard his sleeping comrades in the camp against a surprise. He was in command of a detachment of men constituting a picket guard. These men he had stationed just at nightfall in an irregular line, determined by the nature of the ground, several hundred yards in front of where he now sat. The line ran through the forest, among the rocks and laurel thickets, the men fifteen or twenty paces apart, all in concealment and under injunction of strict silence and unremitting vigilance. In four hours, if nothing occurred, they would be relieved by a fresh detachment from the reserve now resting in care of its captain some distance away to the left and rear. Before stationing his men the young officer of whom we are speaking had pointed out to his two sergeants the spot at which he would be found if it should be necessary to consult him, or if his presence at the front line should be required.

It was a quiet enough spot—the fork of an old wood-road, on the two branches of which, prolonging themselves deviously forward in the dim moon-light, the sergeants were themselves stationed, a few paces in rear of the line. If driven sharply back by a sudden onset of the enemy—and pickets are not expected to make a stand after firing—the men would come into the con-verging roads and naturally following them to their point of intersection could be rallied and "formed." In his small way the young lieutenant was some-thing of a strategist; if Napoleon had planned as intelligently at Waterloo he would have won the battle and been overthrown later.

Second Lieutenant Brainerd Byring was a brave and efficient officer, young and comparatively inexperienced as he was in the business of killing his fellow-men. He had enlisted in the very first days of the war as a private, with no military knowledge whatever, had been made first sergeant of his company on account of his education and engaging manner, and had been lucky enough to lose his captain by a Confederate bullet; in the resulting promotions he had gained a commission. He had been in several engagements, such as they were—at Philippi, Rich Mountain, Carrick's Ford and Greenbrier—and had borne himself with such gallantry as not to attract the attention of his superior officers. The exhilaration of battle was agreeable to him, but the sight of the dead, with their clay faces, blank eyes and stiff bodies, which when not unnaturally shrunken were unnaturally swollen, had always intolerably affected him. He felt toward them a kind of reasonless antipathy that was something more than the physical and spiritual repugnance common to us all. Doubtless this feeling was due to his unusually acute sensibilities—his keen sense of the beautiful which these hideous things outraged. Whatever may have been the cause, he could not look upon a dead body without a loathing which had in it an element of resentment. What others have respected as the dignity of death had to him no existence—was altogether unthinkable. Death was a thing to be hated. It was not picturesque, it had no tender and solemn side—a dismal thing, hideous in all its manifestations and suggestions. Lieutenant Byring was a braver man than anybody knew, for nobody knew his horror of that which he was ever ready to encounter.

Having posted his men, instructed his sergeants and retired to his station, he seated himself on a log and with senses all alert began his vigil. For greater ease he loosened his sword-belt and taking his heavy revolver from his holster laid it on the log beside him. He felt very comfortable, though he hardly gave the fact a thought, so intently did he listen for any sound from the front which might have a menacing significance—a shout, a shot or the footfall of one of his sergeants coming to apprise him of something worth knowing. From the vast, invisible ocean of moonlight overhead fell, here and there, a slender, broken stream that seemed to plash against the intercepting branches and trickle to earth, forming small, white pools among the clumps of laurel. But these leaks were few and served only to accentuate the blackness of his environment, which his imagination found it easy to people with all manner of unfamiliar shapes, menacing, uncanny or merely grotesque.

He to whom the portentous conspiracy of night and solitude and silence in the heart of a great forest is not an unknown experience needs not to be told what another world it all is—how even the most commonplace and familiar objects take on another character. The trees group themselves differently: they draw closer together, as if in fear. The very silence has another quality than the silence of the day. And it is full of half-heard whispers— whispers that startle—ghosts of sounds long dead. There are living sounds, too, such as are never heard under other conditions: notes of strange night-birds, the cries of small animals in sudden encounters with stealthy foes or in their dreams. A rustling in the dead leaves—it may be the leap of a wood-rat, it may be the footfall of a panther. What caused the breaking of that twig?— what the low, alarmed twittering in that bushful of birds? There are sounds without a name, forms without substance, translations in space of objects which have not been seen to move, movements wherein nothing is observed to change its place. Ah, children of the sunlight and the gaslight, how little you know of the world in which you live.

Surrounded at a little distance by armed and watchful friends, Byring felt utterly alone. Yielding himself to the solemn and mysterious spirit of the time and place, he had forgotten the nature of his connection with the visible and audible aspects and phases of the night. The forest was boundless; men and the habitations of men did not exist. The universe was one primeval mystery of darkness, without form and void, himself the sole, dumb questioner of its eternal secret. Absorbed in thoughts born of this mood, he suffered the time to slip away unnoted. Meantime the infrequent patches of white light lying amongst the undergrowth had undergone changes of size, form and place. In one of them near by, just at the roadside, his eye fell upon an object that he had not previously observed. It was almost before his face as he sat; he could have sworn that it had not before been there. It was partly covered in shadow, but he could see that it was a human figure. Instinctively he adjusted the clasp of his sword-belt and laid hold of his pistol—again he was in a world of war, by occupation an assassin.

The figure did not move. Rising, pistol in hand, he approached. The figure lay upon its back, its upper part in shadow, but standing above it and looking down upon the face, he saw that it was a dead body. He shuddered and turned from it with a feeling of sickness and disgust, resumed his seat upon the log and, forgetting military prudence, struck a match and lit a cigar. In the sudden blackness that followed the extinction of the flame he felt a sense of relief: he could no longer see the object of his aversion. Nevertheless he kept his eyes set in that direction until it appeared again with growing distinctness. It seemed to have moved a trifle nearer.

"Damn the thing!" he muttered. "What does it want?"

It did not appear to be in need of anything but a soul.

Byring turned away his eyes and began humming a tune, but he broke off in the middle of a bar and looked at the dead man. Its presence annoyed him, though he could hardly have had a quieter neighbor. He was conscious, too, of a vague, indefinable feeling that was new to him. It was not fear but rather a sense of the supernatural—in which he did not at all believe.

"I have inherited it," he said to himself. "I suppose it will require a thousand years—perhaps ten thousand—for humanity to outgrow this feeling. Where and when did it originate? Away back, probably, in what is called the cradle of the human race—the plains of Central Asia. What we inherit as a superstition our barbarous ancestors must have held as a reasonable conviction. Doubtless they believed themselves justified by facts whose nature we cannot even conjecture in thinking a dead body a malign thing endowed with some strange power of mischief—with perhaps a will and purpose to exert it. Possibly they had some awful form of religion of which that was one of the chief doctrines, sedulously taught by their priesthood, just as ours teach the immortality of the soul. As the Aryans moved westward to and through the Caucasus passes and spread over Europe new conditions of life must have resulted in the formulation of new religions. The old belief in the malevolence of the dead body was lost from the creeds and even perished from tradition, but it left its heritage of terror, which is transmitted from generation to generation—is as much a part of us as our blood and bones."

In following out his thought he had forgotten that which suggested it; but now his eye fell again upon the corpse. The shadow had now altogether uncovered it. He saw the sharp profile, the chin in the air, the whole face a ghastly white in the moonlight. The clothing was gray, the uniform of a Confederate soldier. The coat and waistcoat unbuttoned, had fallen away on each side, exposing the white shirt. The chest seemed unnaturally prominent, but the abdomen had sunk in, leaving a sharp projection at the line of the lower ribs. The arms were extended, the left knee was thrust upward. The whole posture impressed Byring as having been studied with a view to the horrible.

"Bah!" he exclaimed; "he was an actor—he knows how to be dead."

He drew away his eyes, directing them resolutely along one of the roads leading to the front, and resumed his philosophizing where he had left off.

"It may be that our Central Asian ancestors had not the custom of burial. In that case it is easy to understand their fear of the dead, who really were a menace and an evil. They bred pestilences. Children were taught to avoid the places where they lay, and to run away if by inadvertence they came near a corpse. I think, indeed, I'd better go away from this chap."

He half rose to do so, then remembered that he had told his men in front and the officer in the rear who was to relieve him that he could at any time be found at that spot. It was a matter of pride, too. If he abandoned his post he feared they would think he feared the corpse. He was no coward and he was not going to incur anybody's ridicule. So he again seated himself, and to prove his courage looked boldly at the body. The right arm—the one farthest from him—was now in shadow. He could barely see the hand which, he had before observed, lay at the root of a clump of laurel. There had been no change, a fact which gave him a certain comfort, he could not have said why. He did not at once remove his eyes: that which we do not wish to see has a strange fascination, sometimes irresistible. Of the woman who covers her face with her hands and looks between the fingers let it be said that the wits have dealt with her not altogether justly.

Byring suddenly became conscious of a pain in his right hand. He withdrew his eyes from his enemy and looked at it. He was grasping the hilt of his drawn sword so tightly that it hurt him. He observed, too, that he was leaning forward in a strained attitude—crouching like a gladiator ready to spring at the throat of an antagonist. His teeth were clenched and he was breathing hard. This matter was soon set right, and as his muscles relaxed and he drew a long breath he felt keenly enough the ludicrousness of the incident. It affected him to laughter. Heavens! what sound was that?—what mindless devil was uttering an unholy glee in mockery of human merriment? He sprang to his feet and looked about him, not recognizing his own laugh.

He could no longer conceal from himself the horrible fact of his cowardice: he was thoroughly frightened! He would have run from the spot, but his legs refused their office; they gave way beneath him and he sat again upon the log, violently trembling. His face was wet, his whole body bathed in a chill perspiration. He could not even cry out. Distinctly he heard behind him a stealthy tread, as of some wild animal, and dared not look over his shoulder. Had the soulless living joined forces with the soulless dead?—was it an animal? Ah, if he could but be assured of that! But by no effort of will could he now unfix his gaze from the face of the dead man.

I repeat that Lieutenant Byring was a brave and intelligent man. But what would you have? Shall a man cope, single-handed, with so monstrous an alliance as that of night and solitude and silence and the dead?—while an incalculable host of his own ancestors shriek into the ear of his spirit their coward counsel, sing their doleful death-songs in his heart and disarm his very blood of all its iron? The odds are too great—courage was not made for such rough use as that.

One sole conviction now had the man in possession: that the body had moved. It lay nearer to the edge of its plot of light—there could be no doubt of it. It had also moved its arms, for, look, they are both in the shadow! A breath of cold air struck Byring full in the face; the branches of trees above him stirred and moaned. A strongly defined shadow passed across the face of the dead, left it luminous, passed back upon it and left it half obscured. The horrible thing was visibly moving! At that moment a single shot rang out upon the picket line—a lonelier and louder, though more distant shot than ever had been heard by mortal ear! It broke the spell of that enchanted man; it slew the silence and the solitude, dispersed the hindering host from Central Asia and released his modern manhood. With a cry like that of some great bird pouncing upon its prey he sprang forward, hot-hearted for action!

Shot after shot now came from the front. There were shoutings and confusion, hoof-beats and desultory cheers. Away to the rear of the sleeping camp was a singing of bugles and a grumble of drums. Pushing through the thickets on either side the roads came the Federal pickets, in full retreat, firing backward at random as they ran. A straggling group that had followed back one of the roads, as instructed, suddenly sprang away into the bushes as half a hundred horsemen thundered by them, striking wildly with their sabers as they passed. At headlong speed these mounted madmen shot past the spot where Byring had sat and vanished round an angle of the road, shouting and firing their pistols. A moment later there was a crash of musketry, followed by dropping shots—they had encountered the reserve guard in line; and back they came in dire confusion, with here and there an empty saddle and many a maddened horse, bullet-stung, snorting and plunging with pain. It was all over—"an affair of outposts."

The line was re-established with fresh men, the roll called, the stragglers were reformed. The Federal commander with a part of his staff, imperfectly clad, appeared upon the scene, asked a few questions, looked exceedingly wise and retired. After standing at arms for an hour the brigade in camp "swore a prayer or two" and went to bed.

Early the next morning a fatigue party commanded by a captain and accompanied by a surgeon searched the ground for dead and wounded. At the fork of the road a little to one side they found two bodies lying close together—that of a Federal officer and that of a Confederate private. The officer had died of a sword-thrust through the heart, but not, apparently, until he had inflicted upon his enemy no fewer than five dreadful wounds. The dead officer lay on his face in a pool of blood, the weapon still in his breast. They turned him on his back and the surgeon removed it.

"Gad!" said the captain—"it is Byring!"—adding, with a glance at the other, "They had a tough tussle."

The surgeon was examining the sword. It was that of a line officer of Federal infantry—exactly like the one worn by the captain. The only other weapon discovered was an undischarged revolver in the dead officer's belt.

The surgeon laid down the sword and approached the other body. It was frightfully gashed and stabbed, but there was no blood. He took hold of the left foot and tried to straighten the leg. In the effort the body was displaced. The dead do not wish to be moved when comfortable—it protested with a faint, sickening odor. Where it had lain were a few maggots, manifesting an imbecile activity.

The surgeon looked at the captain. The captain looked at the surgeon.

The Coup de Grâce.

The fighting had been hard and continuous—that was attested by all the senses. The very taste of battle was in the air. All was now over; it remained only to succor the wounded and bury the dead—to "tidy up a bit," as the humorist of a burying squad put it. A good deal of "tidying up" was required. As far as one could see through the forest, among the splintered trees, lay wrecks of men and horses. Among them moved the stretcher-bearers, gathering and carrying away the few who showed signs of life. Most of the wounded had died of exposure while the right to minister to their wants was in dispute. It is an army regulation that the wounded must wait: the best way to care for them is to win the battle. It must be confessed that victory is a distinct advantage to a man requiring attention, but many do not live to avail themselves of it.

The dead were collected in groups of a dozen or a score and laid side by side in rows while the trenches were dug to receive them. Some, found at too great a distance from these rallying points, were buried where they lay. There was little attempt at identification, though in most cases the burying parties being detailed to glean the same ground which they had assisted to reap the names of the victorious dead were known and listed. The enemy's fallen had to be content with counting. But of that they got enough; many of them were counted several times, and the total, as given in the official report of the victorious commander, denoted rather a hope than a result.

At some little distance from the spot where one of the burying parties had established its "bivouac of the dead," a man in the uniform of a Federal officer stood leaning against a tree. From his feet upward to his neck his attitude was that of weariness reposing; but he turned his head uneasily from side to side; his mind was apparently not at rest. He was perhaps uncertain in which direction to go; he was not likely to remain long where he was, for already the level rays of the setting sun struggled redly through the open spaces of the wood and the weary soldiers were quitting their task for the day. He would hardly make a night of it alone there among the dead. Nine men in ten whom

58

you meet after a battle inquire the way to some fraction of the army—as if any one could know. Doubtless this officer was lost. After resting himself a moment he would presumably follow one of the retiring burial squads.

When all were gone he walked straight away into the forest toward the red west, its light staining his face like blood. The air of confidence with which he now strode along showed that he was on familiar ground; he had recovered his bearings. The dead on his right and on his left were unregarded as he passed; an occasional low moan from some sorely-stricken wretch whom the relief parties had not reached, and who would have to pass a comfortless night beneath the stars with his thirst to keep him company, was equally unheeded. What, indeed, could the officer have done, being no surgeon and having no water?

At the head of a shallow ravine, a mere depression of the ground, lay a small group of bodies. He saw, and swerving suddenly from his course walked rapidly toward them. Scanning each one sharply as he passed, he stopped at last above one which lay at a slight remove from the others, near a clump of small trees. He looked at it narrowly, the crimson light suffusing it and fringing its confused outlines with fire. It seemed to stir. He stooped and laid his hand upon its face. It screamed.

The officer was Captain Downing Madwell, of a Massachusetts regiment of infantry, a daring and intelligent soldier, an honorable man.

In the regiment were two brothers named Halcrow—Caffal and Creede Halcrow. Caffal Halcrow was a sergeant in Captain Madwell's company, and these two men, the sergeant and the captain, were devoted friends. In so far as disparity of rank, difference in duties and considerations of military discipline would permit they were commonly together. They had indeed grown up together from childhood. A habit of the heart is not easily broken off. Caffal Halcrow had nothing military in his taste or disposition, but the thought of separation from his friend was disagreeable; he enlisted in the company in which Madwell was second lieutenant. Each had taken two steps upward in rank, but between the highest non-commissioned and the lowest commissioned officer the social gulf is deep and wide, and the old relation was maintained with difficulty and a difference.

Creede Halcrow, the brother of Caffal, was the major of the regiment—a cynical, saturnine man, between whom and Captain Madwell there was a natural antipathy which circumstances had nourished and strengthened to an active animosity. But for the restraining influence of their mutual relation to Caffal these two patriots would doubtless have endeavored to deprive their country of each other's services.

At the opening of the battle that morning the regiment was performing outpost duty a mile away from the main army. It had been attacked and nearly surrounded in the forest, but stubbornly held its ground. During a lull in the fighting, Major Halcrow came to Captain Madwell. The two exchanged formal salutes, and the major said: "Captain, the colonel directs that you push your company to the head of this ravine and hold your place there until recalled. I need hardly apprise you of the dangerous character of the movement, but if you wish, you can, I suppose, turn over the command to your first lieutenant. I was not, however, directed to authorize the substitution; it is merely a suggestion of my own, unofficially made."

To this deadly insult Captain Madwell coolly replied:

"Sir, I invite you to accompany the movement. A mounted officer would be a conspicuous mark, and I have long held the opinion that it would be better if you were dead."

The art of repartee was cultivated in military circles as early as 1863.

A half hour later Captain Madwell's company was driven from its position at the head of the ravine, with a loss of one-third its number. Among the fallen was Sergeant Halcrow. The regiment was soon afterward forced back to the main line, and at the close of the battle was miles away. The captain was now standing at the side of his subordinate and friend.

Sergeant Halcrow was mortally hurt. His clothing was deranged; it seemed to have been violently torn apart, exposing the abdomen. Some of the buttons of his jacket had been pulled off and lay on the ground beside him and fragments of his other garments were strewn about. His leather belt was parted and had apparently been dragged from beneath him as he lay. There had been no very great effusion of blood. The only visible wound was a wide, ragged opening in the abdomen. It was defiled with earth and dead leaves. Protruding from it was a lacerated end of the small intestine. In all his experience Captain Madwell had not seen a wound like this. He could neither conjecture how it was made nor explain the attendant circumstances—the strangely torn clothing, the parted belt, the besmirching of the white skin. He knelt and made a closer examination. When he rose to his feet he turned his eyes in various directions as if looking for an enemy. Fifty yards away, on the crest of a low, thinly-wooded hill, he saw several dark objects moving about among the fallen men—a herd of swine. One stood with its back to him, its shoulders sharply elevated. Its fore-feet were upon a human body, its head was depressed and invisible. The bristly ridge of its chine showed black against the red west. Captain Madwell drew away his eyes and fixed them again upon the thing which had been his friend.

The man who had suffered these monstrous mutilations was alive. At intervals he moved his limbs; he moaned at every breath. He stared blankly into the face of his friend and if touched screamed. In his giant agony he had torn up the ground on which he lay; his clenched hands were full of leaves and twigs and earth. Articulate speech was beyond his power: it was impossible to know if he were sensible to anything but pain. The expression of his face was an appeal; his eyes were full of prayer. For what? There was no misreading that look: the captain had too frequently seen it in eyes of those whose lips had still the power to beg for death. Consciously or unconsciously, this writhing fragment of humanity—this type and example of acute sensation—this handiwork of man and beast—this humble unheroic Prometheus was imploring everything, all, the whole non-ego, for the boon of oblivion. To the earth and the sky alike—to the trees—to the man—to whatever took form in sense or consciousness, this incarnate suffering addressed its piteous plea.

For what, indeed?—For that which we accord to even the meanest creature without sense to demand it, denying it only to the wretched of our own race. For the blessed release—the rite of uttermost compassion—the *coup de grâce*.

Captain Madwell spoke the name of his friend. He repeated it over and over without effect until emotion choked his utterance. His tears plashed upon the livid face beneath his own and blinded himself. He saw nothing but a blurred and moving object, but the moans were more distinct than ever, interrupted at briefer intervals by sharper shrieks. He turned away, struck his hand upon his forehead and strode from the spot. The swine, catching sight of him, threw up their crimson muzzles, regarding him suspiciously a second, and then with a gruff concerted grunt raced away out of sight. A horse, its foreleg splintered horribly by a cannon-shot, lifted its head sidewise from the ground and neighed piteously. Madwell stepped forward, drew his revolver and shot the poor beast between the eyes, narrowly observing its death struggle, which, contrary to his expectation, was violent and long; but at last it lay still. The tense muscles of its lips, which had uncovered the teeth in a horrible grin, relaxed; the sharp, clean-cut profile took on a look of profound peace and rest.

Along the distant thinly-wooded crest to westward the fringe of sunset fire had now nearly burned itself out. The light upon the trunks of the trees had faded to a tender gray; the shadows were in their tops, like great dark birds aperch. The night was coming and there were miles of haunted forest between Captain Madwell and camp. Yet he stood there at the side of the dead animal, apparently lost to all sense of his surroundings. His eyes were bent upon the earth at his feet; his left hand hung loosely at his side, his right still held the pistol. Suddenly he lifted his face, turned it toward his dying friend and walked rapidly back to his side. He knelt upon one knee, cocked the weapon, placed the muzzle against the man's forehead, turned away his eyes and pulled the trigger. There was no report. He had used his last cartridge for the horse.

The sufferer moaned and his lips moved convulsively. The froth that ran from them had a tinge of blood.

Captain Madwell rose to his feet and drew his sword from the scabbard. He passed the fingers of his left hand along the edge from hilt to point. He held it out straight before him, as if to test his nerves. There was no visible tremor of the blade; the ray of bleak skylight that it reflected was steady and true. He stooped and with his left hand tore away the dying man's shirt; rose and placed the point of the sword just over the heart. This time he did not withdraw his eyes. Grasping the hilt with both hands he thrust downward with all his strength and weight. The blade sank into the man's body—through his body into the earth; Captain Madwell came near falling forward upon his work. The dying man drew up his knees and at the same time threw his right arm across his breast and grasped the steel so tightly that the knuckles of the hand visibly whitened. By a violent but vain effort to withdraw the blade the wound was enlarged; a rill of blood escaped, running sinuously down into the deranged clothing. At that moment three men stepped silently forward from behind the clump of young trees which concealed their approach. Two were hospital attendants and carried a stretcher.

The third was Major Creede Halcrow.

Parker Adderson, Philosopher and Wit.

"Prisoner, what is your name?"

"As I am to lose it at daylight to-morrow morning it is hardly worth concealing. Parker Adderson."

"Your rank?"

"A somewhat humble one: commissioned officers are too precious to be risked in the perilous business of a spy. I am a sergeant."

"Of what regiment?"

"You must excuse me; if I answered that it might, for anything I know, give you an idea of whose forces are in your front. Such knowledge as that is what I came into your lines to obtain, not to impart."

"You are not without wit."

"If you have the patience to wait you will find me dull enough to-morrow."

"How do you know that you are to die to-morrow morning."

"Among spies captured by night that is the custom. It is one of the nice observances of the profession."

The general so far laid aside the dignity appropriate to a Confederate officer of high rank and wide renown as to smile. But no one in his power and out of his favor would have drawn any happy augury from that outward and visible sign of approval. It was neither genial nor infectious: it did not communicate itself to the other persons exposed to it—the caught spy who had provoked it and the armed guard who had brought him into the tent and now stood a little apart, watching his prisoner in the yellow candlelight. It was no part of that warrior's duty to smile; he had been detailed for another purpose. The conversation was resumed; it was in fact a trial for a capital offense.

"You admit then that you are a spy—that you came into my camp disguised as you are, in the uniform of a Confederate soldier, to obtain information secretly regarding the numbers and disposition of my troops."

"Regarding, particularly, their numbers. Their disposition I already knew. It is most unamiable."

The general smiled again; the guard with a severer sense of his responsibility accentuated the austerity of his expression and stood a trifle more erect than before. Twirling his gray slouch hat round and round upon his forefinger, the spy took a leisurely survey of his surroundings. They were simple enough. The tent was a common "wall tent," about eight feet by ten in dimensions, lighted by a single tallow candle stuck into the haft of a bayonet, which was itself stuck into a pine table, at which the general sat, now busily writing and apparently forgetful of his unwilling guest. An old rag carpet covered the earthen floor; an older leather-trunk, a second chair and a roll of blankets were about all else that the tent contained: in General Clavering's command Confederate simplicity and penury of "pomp and circumstance" had attained their highest development. On a large nail driven into the tent pole at the entrance was suspended a sword-belt supporting a long saber, a pistol in its holster and, absurdly enough, a bowie-knife. Of the last it was the general's habit to explain that it was a cherished souvenir of the blameless days when he was a civilian.

It was a stormy night. The rain cascaded upon the canvas in torrents, with the dull drum-like sound familiar to dwellers in tents. As the whooping blasts charged upon it the frail structure shook and swayed and strained at its confining stakes and ropes.

The general finished writing, folded the half-sheet of paper and spoke to the soldier guarding Adderson: "Here, Tassman, take that to the adjutant-general; then return."

"And the prisoner, General?" said the soldier, saluting, with an inquiring glance in the direction of that unfortunate.

"Do as I said," replied the officer, curtly.

The soldier took the note, saluted again and ducked himself out of the tent. General Clavering turned his handsome, clean-cut face toward the Federal spy, looked him in the eyes, not unkindly, and said: "It is a bad night, my man."

"For me, yes."

"Do you guess what I have written?"

"Something worth reading, I dare say. And—perhaps it is my vanity—I venture to suppose that I am mentioned in it."

"Yes; it is a memorandum for an order to be read to the troops at *reveille* concerning your execution. Also some notes for the guidance of the provost-marshal in arranging the details of that event."

"I hope, General, the spectacle will be intelligently arranged, for I shall attend it myself."

"Have you any arrangements of your own that you wish to make? Do you wish to see a chaplain, for example?"

"I could hardly secure a longer rest for myself by depriving him of some of his."

"Good God, man! do you mean to go to your death with nothing but jokes upon your lips? Do you know that this is a serious matter?"

"How can I know that? I have never been dead in all my life. I have heard that death is a serious matter, but never from any of those who have experienced it. I suspect, too, that they know as little about it as we."

The general was silent for a moment: the man interested, perhaps amused him—a type not previously encountered.

"Death," he said, "is at least a loss—a loss of such happiness as we have, and of opportunities for more."

"A loss of which we will never be conscious can be borne with composure and therefore expected without apprehension. You must have observed, General, that of all the dead men with whom it is your soldierly pleasure to strew your path none shows signs of regret."

"If the being dead is not a regrettable condition, yet the becoming so—the act of dying—appears to be distinctly disagreeable to one who has not lost the power to feel."

"Pain is disagreeable, no doubt. I never suffer it without more or less discomfort. But he who lives longest is most exposed to it. What you call dying is simply the last pain—there is really no such thing as dying. Suppose, for illustration, that I attempt to escape. You lift the revolver that you are courteously concealing in your lap below the edge of the table and—"

The general blushed like a girl, then laughed softly, disclosing his brilliant teeth, made a slight inclination of his handsome head and said nothing. The spy continued: "You fire, but in the haste and confusion of the moment your aim has been taken badly and I have in my stomach what I did not swallow. I fall, but am not dead. After a half hour of agony I *am* dead. But at any given instant of that half hour I was either alive or dead. There is no transition period. The pain was possibly equal to that produced by an attack of gout, which we regard with apprehension but not with horror. We are unreasonable: the fact that a certain case of pain has death as its outcome makes it neither more nor less severe. To-morrow morning you will cause me to be hanged. It is not known if hanging is painful, but this I know: that while conscious I shall be living and when dead unconscious. Nature appears to have ordered the matter quite in my interest—the way that I should have ordered it myself. It is so simple," he added with a smile, "that it seems hardly worth while to be hanged at all."

At the finish of his remarks there was a long silence. The general sat impassive, looking into the man's face, but apparently not attentive to what had been said. It was as if his eyes had mounted guard over the prisoner while his mind concerned itself with other matters. Presently he drew a long, deep breath, shuddered, as one awakened from a dreadful dream, and exclaimed almost inaudibly: "Death is horrible!"—this man of death.

"It was horrible to our savage ancestors," said the spy, gravely, "because they had not enough intelligence to dissociate the idea of consciousness from the idea of the physical forms in which it is manifested—just as an even lower order of intelligence, that of the monkey, for example, may be unable to imagine a house without inhabitants, and seeing a ruined hut fancies a suffering occupant. To us it is horrible because we have inherited the tendency to think it so, accounting for the notion by wild and fanciful theories of another world—as names of places give rise to legends explaining them and reasonless conduct to philosophies in justification. You can hang me, General, but there your power of evil ends: you cannot condemn me to heaven."

The general appeared not to have heard: the spy's talk had merely turned his thoughts into an unfamiliar channel, but there they pursued their will independently to conclusions of their own. The storm had ceased, and something of the solemn spirit of the night had imparted itself to his reflections, giving them the somber tinge of a supernatural dread. Perhaps there was an element of prescience in it. "I should not like to die," he said—"not to-night."

He was interrupted—if, indeed, he had intended to speak further—by the entrance of an officer of his staff, Captain Hasterlick, the provost-marshal. This recalled him to himself; the absent look passed away from his face and he smiled.

"Captain," he said, acknowledging the officer's salute, "this man is a Yankee spy captured inside our lines with incriminating papers on him. He has confessed. How is the weather?"

"The storm is over, sir, and the moon shining."

"Good: take a file of men, conduct him at once to the parade ground and shoot him."

A sharp cry broke from the spy's lips. He threw himself forward, thrust out his neck, expanded his eyes, clenched his hands.

"Good God!" he cried, hoarsely, almost inarticulately; "you do not mean that! You, forget—I am not to die until morning."

"I have said nothing of morning," replied the general, coldly; "that was an assumption of your own. You die now."

"But, General, I beg—I implore you to remember: I am to hang! It will take some time to erect the gallows—two hours—an hour. Spies are hanged; I have rights under military law. For Heaven's sake, General, consider how short—"

"Captain, observe my directions."

The officer drew his sword and fixing his eyes upon the prisoner pointed silently to the opening of the tent. The prisoner, deathly pale, hesitated; the officer grasped him by the collar and pushed him gently forward. As he approached the tent pole the frantic man sprang to it and with cat-like agility seized the handle of the bowie-knife, plucked the weapon from the scabbard and thrusting the captain aside leaped upon the general with the fury of a madman, hurling him to the ground and falling headlong upon him as he lay. The table was overturned, the candle extinguished and they fought blindly in the darkness. The provost-marshal sprang to the assistance of his superior officer and was himself prostrated upon the struggling forms. Curses and inarticulate cries of rage and pain came from the welter of limbs and bodies; the tent came down upon them and beneath its hampering and enveloping folds the struggle went on. Private Tassman, returning from his errand and dimly conjecturing the situation, threw down his rifle and laying hold of the flouncing canvas at random vainly tried to drag it off the men under it; and the sentinel who paced up and down in front, not daring to leave his beat though the skies should fall, discharged his piece. The report alarmed the camp: drums beat the long roll and bugles sounded the assembly, bringing swarms of half-clad men into the moonlight, dressing as they ran and falling into line at the sharp commands of their officers. This was well: being in line the men were under control; they stood at arms while the general's staff and the men of his escort brought order out of confusion by dragging aside the fallen tent and pulling apart the breathless and bleeding actors in that strange contention.

Breathless, indeed, was one: the captain was dead, the handle of the bowie-knife protruding from his throat and pressed back beneath his chin until the end had caught in the angle of the jaw and the hand that delivered the blow had been unable to remove the weapon. In the dead man's hand was his sword, clenched with a grip that defied the strength of the living. Its blade was streaked with red to the hilt.

Lifted to his feet, the general sank back to the earth with a moan and fainted. Besides his bruises he had two sword-thrusts—one through the thigh, the other through the shoulder.

The spy had suffered the least damage. Apart from a broken right arm, his wounds were such only as might have been incurred in an ordinary combat with nature's weapons. But he was dazed and seemed hardly to know what had occurred. He shrank away from those attending him, cowered upon the ground and uttered unintelligible remonstrances. His face, swollen by blows and stained with gouts of blood, nevertheless showed white beneath his disheveled hair—as white as that of a corpse.

"The man is not insane," said the surgeon in reply to a question; "he is suffering from fright. Who and what is he?"

Private Tassman began to explain. It was the opportunity of his life; he omitted nothing that could in any way accentuate the importance of his own relation to the night's events. When he had finished his story and was ready to begin it again nobody gave him any attention.

The general had now recovered consciousness. He raised himself upon his elbow, looked about him, and, seeing the spy crouching by a camp-fire, guarded, said, simply:

"Take that man to the parade ground and shoot him."

"The general's mind wanders," said an officer standing near.

"His mind does *not* wander," the adjutant-general said. "I have a memorandum from him about this business: he had given that same order to Hasterlick,"—with a motion of the hand toward the dead provost-marshal—"and, by God! it shall be executed."

Ten minutes later Sergeant Parker Adderson of the Federal army, philosopher and wit, kneeling in the moonlight and begging incoherently for his life, was shot to death by twenty men. As the volley rang out upon the keen air of the winter midnight General Clavering opened his big blue eyes, smiled pleasantly upon those about him and said: "How silent it all is."

The surgeon looked at the adjutant-general gravely and significantly. The patient's eyes slowly closed and thus he lay for a few moments; then smiling again, he said, faintly: "I suppose this must be death," and so passed away.

Civilians

A Watcher by the Dead.

I.

In an upper room of an unoccupied dwelling in that part of San Francisco known as North Beach lay the body of a man in a coffin. The hour was near nine in the evening; the room was dimly lighted by a single candle. Although the weather was warm, the two windows, contrary to the custom which gives the dead plenty of air, were closed and the blinds drawn down. The furniture of the room consisted of but three pieces: an arm-chair, a small reading-stand, supporting the candle, and a long kitchen table, supporting the body of the man covered from head to foot with a sheet. All these, including the body, seemed to have been recently brought in, for an observer, had there been one, would have seen that all were free from dust; whereas everything else in the room was pretty thickly coated with it, and there were cobwebs in the angles of the walls.

Under the sheet the outlines of the body could be traced, even the features, these having that unnaturally sharp definition which seems to belong to faces of the dead, but is really characteristic of those only that have been wasted by disease. From the silence of the room one would rightly have inferred that it was not in the front of the house, facing a street. It really faced nothing but a high breast of rock, the rear of the building being set into a hill.

As a neighboring church clock was striking nine with a deliberation which seemed to imply such an indolence to the flight of time that one could hardly help wondering why it took the trouble to strike at all, the single door of the room was opened and a man entered, advancing toward the coffin. As he did so the door closed, apparently of its own volition; there was a grating, as of a key turned with difficulty, and the snap of the lock bolt as it shot into its socket. A sound of retiring footsteps in the passage outside ensued, and the man was to all appearance a prisoner. Advancing to the table, he stood a moment looking down at the body; then with a slight shrug of the shoulders walked over to one of the windows and hoisted the blind. The darkness outside was absolute, the panes were covered with dust, but by wiping this away he could see that the window was fortified with strong iron bars crossing it within a few inches of the glass and imbedded in the masonry on each side. He examined the other window. It was the same. He manifested no great curiosity in the matter; did not even so much as raise the sash. If he was a prisoner he was apparently a tractable one. Having completed his examination of the room, he seated himself in the arm-chair, took a book from his pocket, drew the stand with its candle alongside and began to read.

The man was young—not more than thirty—dark in complexion, smooth-shaven, with brown hair. His face was thin and high-nosed, with a broad forehead and a "firmness" of the chin and jaw which is said by those having it to denote resolution. The eyes were gray and steadfast, not moving except with definitive purpose. They were now for the greater part of the time fixed upon his book, but he occasionally withdrew them and turned them to the body on the table, not, apparently, from any dismal fascination which under such circumstances it might be supposed to exercise upon even a courageous person, nor with a conscious rebellion against the contrary influence which might dominate a timid one. He looked at it as if in his reading he had come upon something recalling him to a sense of his surroundings. Clearly this watcher by the dead was discharging his trust with intelligence and composure, as became him.

After reading for perhaps a half-hour he seemed to come to the end of a chapter and quietly laid away the book. He then rose and taking the reading-stand from the floor carried it into a corner of the room near one of the windows, lifted the candle from it and returned to the empty fireplace before which he had been sitting.

A moment later he walked over to the body on the table, lifted the sheet and turned it back from the head, exposing a mass of dark hair and a thin face-cloth, beneath which the features showed with even sharper definition than before. Shading his eyes by interposing, his free hand between them and the candle, he stood looking at his motionless companion with a serious and tranquil regard. Satisfied with his inspection he pulled the sheet over the face again and returning to his chair took some matches off the candlestick, put them in the side pocket of his sack-coat and sat down. He then lifted the candle from its socket and looked at it critically, as if calculating how long it would last. It was barely two inches long: in another hour he would be in darkness! He replaced it in the candlestick and blew it out.

In a physician's office in Kearny street three men sat about a table, drinking punch and smoking. It was late in the evening, almost midnight indeed, and there had been no lack of punch. The eldest of the three, Dr. Helberson, was the host—it was in his rooms they sat. He was about thirty years of age; the others were even younger; all were physicians.

"The superstitious awe with which the living regard the dead," said Dr. Helberson, "is hereditary and incurable. One need no more be ashamed of it than of the act that he inherits, for example, an incapacity for mathematics, or a tendency to lie."

The others laughed. "Oughtn't a man to be ashamed to be a liar?" asked the youngest of the three, who was in fact a medical student not yet graduated.

"My dear, Harper, I said nothing about that. The tendency to lie is one thing; lying is another."

"But do you think," said the third man, "that this superstitious feeling, this fear of the dead, reasonless as we know it to be, is universal? I am myself not conscious of it."

"Oh, but it is 'in your system,' for all that," replied Helberson; "it needs only the right conditions—what Shakespeare calls the 'confederate season'—to manifest itself in some very disagreeable way that will open your eyes. Physicians and soldiers are of course more nearly free from it than others."

"Physicians and soldiers!—why don't you add hangmen and headsmen? Let us have in all the assassin classes."

"No, my dear Mancher; the juries will not let the public executioners acquire sufficient familiarity with death to be altogether unmoved by it."

Young Harper, who had been helping himself to a fresh cigar at the sideboard, resumed his seat. "What would you consider conditions under which any man of woman born would become insupportably conscious of his share of our common weakness in this regard?" he asked, rather verbosely.

"Well, I should say that if a man were locked up all night with a corpse—alone—in a dark room—of a vacant house—with no bed-covers to pull over his head—and lived through it without going altogether mad, he might justly boast himself not of woman born, nor yet, like Macduff, a product of Cæsarean section."

"I thought you never would finish piling up conditions," said Harper, "but I know a man who is neither a physician nor a soldier who will accept them all for any stake you like to name."

"Who is he?"

"His name is Jarette—a stranger in California: comes from my town in New York. I haven't any money to back him, but he will back himself with loads of it."

"How do you know that?"

"He would rather bet than eat. As for fear—I dare say he thinks it some cutaneous disorder, or possibly a particular kind of religious heresy."

"What does he look like?" Helberson was evidently becoming interested.

"Like Mancher, here—might be his twin brother."

"I accept the challenge," said Helberson, promptly.

"Awfully obliged to you for the compliment, I'm sure," drawled Mancher, who was growing sleepy. "Can't I get into this?"

"Not against me," Helberson said. "I don't want *your* money."

"All right," said Mancher; "I'll be the corpse."

The others laughed.

The outcome of this crazy conversation we have seen.

III.

In extinguishing his meagre allowance of candle Mr. Jarette's object was to preserve it against some unforeseen need. He may have thought, too, or half thought, that the darkness would be no worse at one time than another, and if the situation became insupportable it would be better to have a means of relief, or even release. At any rate it was wise to have a little reserve of light, even if only to enable him to look at his watch.

No sooner had he blown out the candle and set it on the floor at his side than he settled himself comfortably in the arm-chair, leaned back and closed his eyes, hoping and expecting to sleep. In this he was disappointed: he had never in his life felt less sleepy, and in a few minutes he gave up the attempt. But what could he do? He could not go groping about in the absolute darkness at the risk of bruising himself—at the risk, too, of blundering against the table and rudely disturbing the dead. We all recognize their right to lie at rest, with immunity from all that is harsh and violent. Jarette almost succeeded in making himself believe that considerations of this kind restrained him from risking the collision and fixed him to the chair.

While thinking of this matter he fancied that he heard a faint sound in the direction of the table—what kind of sound he could hardly have explained. He did not turn his head. Why should he—in the darkness? But he listened—why should he not? And listening he grew giddy and grasped the arms of the chair for support. There was a strange ringing in his ears; his head seemed bursting; his chest was oppressed by the constriction of his clothing. He wondered why it was so, and whether these were symptoms of fear. Then, with a long and strong expiration his chest appeared to collapse, and with the great gasp with which he refilled his exhausted lungs the vertigo left him and he knew that so intently had he listened that he had held his breath almost to suffocation. The revelation was vexatious: he rose, pushed away the chair with his foot and strode to the center of the room. But one does not stride far in darkness: he began to grope, and finding the wall followed it to an angle, turned, followed it past the two windows and there in another corner came into violent contact with the reading-stand, overturning it. It made a clatter which startled him. He was annoyed. "How the devil could I have forgotten where it was?" he muttered, and groped his way along the third wall to the fireplace. "I must put things to rights," said Mr. Jarette, feeling the floor for the candle.

Having recovered that, he lighted it and instantly turned his eyes to the table, where, naturally, nothing had undergone any change. The reading-stand lay unobserved upon the floor; he had forgotten to "put it to rights." He looked all about the room, dispersing the deeper shadows by movements of the candle in his hand, and crossing over to the door tried it by turning and pulling the knob with all his strength. It did not yield and this seemed to afford him a certain satisfaction; indeed, he secured it more firmly by a bolt which he had not before observed. Returning to his chair, he looked at his watch: it was half-past nine. With a start of surprise he held the watch at his ear. It had not stopped. The candle was now visibly shorter. He again extinguished it, placing it on the floor at his side as before.

Mr. Jarette was not at his ease: he was distinctly dissatisfied with his surroundings, and with himself for being so. "What have I to fear?" he thought. "This is ridiculous and disgraceful; I will not be so great a fool." But courage does not come of saying, "I will be courageous," nor of recognizing its appropriateness to the occasion. The more Jarette condemned himself the more reason he gave himself for condemnation; the greater the number of variations which he played upon the simple theme of the harmlessness of the dead, the more horrible grew the discord of his emotions. "What!" he cried aloud in the anguish of his spirit, "what! shall I, who have not a shade of superstition in my nature—I, who have no belief in immortality—I, who *know* (and never more clearly than now) that the after-life is the dream of a desire— shall I lose at once my bet, my honor and my self-respect, perhaps my reason, because certain savage ancestors dwelling in caves and burrows conceived the monstrous notion that the dead walk by night?—that—" Distinctly, unmistakably, Mr. Jarette heard behind him a light, soft sound of footfalls, deliberate, regular and successively nearer.

IV.

Just before daybreak the next morning Dr. Helberson and his young friend Harper were driving slowly through the streets of North Beach in the doctor's coupé.

"Have you still the confidence of youth in the courage—or stolidity—of your friend?" said the elder man. "Do you believe that I have lost this wager?"

"I *know* you have," replied the other, with enfeebling emphasis.

"Well, upon my soul, I hope so."

It was spoken earnestly, almost solemnly. There was a silence for a few moments.

"Harper," the doctor resumed, looking very serious in the shifting half-lights that entered the carriage as they passed the street lamps, "I don't feel altogether comfortable about this business. If your friend had not irritated me by the contemptuous manner in which he treated my doubt of his endurance—a purely physical quality—and by the cool incivility of his suggestion that the corpse be that of a physician I should not have gone on with it. If anything should happen we are ruined, as I fear we deserve to be."

"What can happen? Even if the matter should be taking a serious turn, of which I am not at all afraid, Mancher has only to resurrect himself and explain matters. With a genuine 'subject' from the dissecting-room, or one of your late patients, it might be different."

Dr. Mancher, then, had been as good as his promise: he was the "corpse."

Dr. Helberson was silent for a long time, as the carriage at a snail's pace crept along the same street it had traveled two or three times already. Presently he spoke: "Well, let us hope that Mancher, if he has had to rise from the dead, has been discreet about it. A mistake in that might make matters worse instead of better."

"Yes," said Harper, "Jarette might kill him. But, Doctor"—looking at his watch as the carriage passed a gas lamp—"it is nearly four o'clock at last."

A moment later the two had quitted the vehicle and were walking briskly toward the long unoccupied house belonging to the doctor, in which they had immured Mr. Jarette in virtual but not literal accordance with the terms of the mad wager. As they neared it they met a man running. "Can you tell me," he cried, suddenly checking his speed, "where I can find a doctor?"

"What's the matter?" Helberson asked, non-committal.

"Go and see for yourself," said the man, resuming his running.

They hastened on. Arrived at the house, they saw several persons entering in haste and excitement. In some of the dwellings near by and across the way the chamber windows were thrown up, showing a protrusion of heads. All heads were asking questions, none heeding the questions of the others. A few of the windows with closed blinds were illuminated; the inmates of those rooms were dressing to come down. Exactly opposite the door of the house which they sought a street lamp threw a yellow, insufficient light upon the scene, seeming to say that it could disclose a good deal more if it wished. Harper, who was now deathly pale, paused at the door and laid a hand upon his companion's arm. "It is all up with us, Doctor," he said in extreme agitation, which contrasted strangely with his free and easy words, "the game has gone against us all. Let's not go in there; I'm for lying low."

"I'm a physician," said Dr. Helberson, calmly; "there may be need of one."

They mounted the doorsteps and were about to enter. The door was open; the street lamp opposite lighted the passage into which it opened. It was full of men. Some had ascended the stairs at the farther end and, denied admittance above, waited for better fortune. All were talking, none listening. Suddenly on the upper landing there was a great commotion: a man had sprung out a door and was breaking away from those endeavoring to detain him. Down through the mass of affrighted idlers he came, pushing them aside, flattening them against the wall on one side or compelling them to cling by the rail on the other, clutching them by the throat, striking them savagely, thrusting them back down the stairs and walking over the fallen. His clothing was in disorder, he was without a hat. His eyes, wild and restless, had in them something more terrifying than his apparently superhuman strength. His face, smooth-shaven, was bloodless, his hair snow-white.

As the crowd at the foot of the stairs, having more freedom, fell away to let him pass Harper sprang forward. "Jarette! Jarette!" he cried.

Dr. Helberson seized Harper by the collar and dragged him back. The man looked into their faces without seeming to see them and sprang through the door, down the steps, into the street and away. A stout policeman, who had had inferior success in conquering his way down the stairway, followed a moment later and started in pursuit, all the heads in the windows—those of women and children now—screaming in guidance.

The stairway being now partly cleared, most of the crowd having rushed down to the street to observe the flight and pursuit, Dr. Helberson mounted to the landing, followed by Harper. At a door in the upper passage an officer denied them admittance. "We are physicians," said the doctor, and they passed in. The room was full of men, dimly seen crowded about a table. The newcomers edged their way forward and looked over the shoulders of those in the front rank. Upon the table, the lower limbs covered with a sheet, lay the body of a man, brilliantly illuminated by the beam of a bull's-eye lantern held by a policeman standing at the feet. The others, excepting those near the head—the officer himself—all were in darkness. The face of the body showed yellow, repulsive, horrible! The eyes were partly open and upturned and the jaw fallen; traces of froth defiled the lips, the chin, the cheeks. A tall man, evidently a physician, bent over the body with his hand thrust under the shirt front. He withdrew it and placed two fingers in the open mouth. "This man has been about two hours dead," said he. "It is a case for the coroner."

He drew a card from his pocket, handed it to the officer and made his way toward the door.

"Clear the room—out, all!" said the officer sharply, and the body disappeared as if it had been snatched away, as he shifted the lantern and flashed its beam of light here and there against the faces of the crowd. The effect was amazing: the men, blinded, confused, almost terrified, made a tumultuous rush for the door, pushing, crowding and tumbling over one another as they fled like the hosts of Night before the shafts of Apollo. Upon the struggling, trampling mass the officer poured his power without pity and without cessation. Caught in the current, Helberson and Harper were swept out of the room and cascaded down the stairs into the street.

"Good God, Doctor! did I not tell you that Jarette would kill him?" said Harper, as soon as they were clear of the crowd.

"I believe you did," replied the other without apparent emotion.

They walked on in silence, block after block. Against the graying east the dwellings of our hill tribes showed in silhouette. The familiar milk wagon was already astir in the streets; the baker's man would soon come upon the scene; the newspaper carrier was abroad in the land.

"It strikes me, youngster," said Helberson, "that you and I have been having too much of the morning air lately. It is unwholesome; we need a change. What do you say to a tour in Europe?"

"When?"

"I'm not particular; I should suppose that 4 o'clock this afternoon would be early enough."

"I'll meet you at the boat," said Harper.

V.

Seven years afterward these two men sat upon a bench in Madison Square, New York, in familiar conversation. Another man, who had been observing them for some time, himself unobserved, approached and, courteously lifting his hat from locks as white as snow, said: "I beg your pardon, gentlemen, but when you have killed a man by coming to life it is best to change clothes with him, and at the first opportunity make a break for liberty."

Helberson and Harper exchanged significant glances. They were apparently amused. The former then looked the stranger kindly in the eye, and replied: "That has always been my plan. I entirely agree with you as to its advant——"

He stopped suddenly and grew deathly pale. He stared at the man, open-mouthed; he trembled visibly.

"Ah!" said the stranger, "I see that you are indisposed, doctor. If you cannot treat yourself Dr. Harper can do something for you, I am sure."

"Who the devil are you?" said Harper bluntly.

The stranger came nearer and bending toward them said in a whisper: "I call myself Jarette sometimes, but I don't mind telling you, for old friendship, that I am Dr. William Mancher."

The revelation brought both men to their feet. "Mancher!" they cried in a breath; and Helberson added: "It is true by God!"

"Yes," said the stranger, smiling vaguely; "It is true enough no doubt."

He hesitated and seemed to be trying to recall something—then began humming a popular air. He had apparently forgotten their presence.

"Look here, Mancher," said the elder of the two, "tell us just what occurred that night—to Jarette, you know."

"Oh, yes, about Jarette," said the other, brightening. "It's odd I should have neglected to tell you—I tell it so often. You see I knew by overhearing him talking to himself that he was pretty badly frightened. So I couldn't resist the temptation—I couldn't, really. That was all right, though certainly I did not think he would take it so seriously—I did not, truly. And afterward—well, it was a tough job changing places with him, and then—damn you! you didn't let me out!"

Nothing could exceed the ferocity with which these last words were delivered. Both men stepped back in alarm.

"We?—why—why," Helberson stammered, losing his self-possession utterly, "we had nothing to do with it."

"Didn't I say you were Doctors Hell-born and Sharper?" inquired the lunatic, laughing.

"My name is Helberson, yes, and this gentleman is Mr. Harper," replied the former, reassured. "But we are not physicians now: we are—well, hang it, old man, we are gamblers."

And that was the truth.

"A very good profession—very good, indeed; and, by the way, I hope Sharper here paid over Jarette's money like an honest stakeholder. A very good and honorable profession," he repeated, thoughtfully, moving carelessly away; "but I stick to the old one. I am Chief Medical Officer of the Bloomington Asylum: it is my duty to cure the Superintendent."

The Man and the Snake.

It is of veritabyll report, and attested of soe many that there be nowe of wyse and learned none to gaynsaye it, that ye serpents hys eye hath a magnetick propertie that who soe falleth into its svasion is drawn forwards in despyte of his wille, and perisheth miserabyll by ye creature hys byte.

Stretched at ease upon a sofa, in gown and slippers, Harker Brayton smiled as he read the foregoing sentence in old Morryster's *Marvells of Science*. "The only marvel in the matter," he said to himself, "is that the wise and learned in Morryster's day should have believed such nonsense as is rejected by most of even the ignorant in ours."

A train of reflections followed—for Brayton was a man of thought—and he unconsciously lowered his book without altering the direction of his eyes. As soon as the volume had gone below the line of sight, something in an obscure corner of the room recalled his attention to his surroundings. What he saw, in the shadow under his bed, was two small points of light, apparently about an inch apart. They might have been reflections of the gas-jet above him, in metal nail heads; he gave them but little thought and resumed his reading. A moment later something—some impulse which it did not occur to him to analyze—impelled him to lower the book again and seek for what he saw before. The points of light were still there. They seemed to have become brighter than before, shining with a greenish luster that he had not at first observed. He thought, too, that they had moved a trifle—were somewhat nearer. They were still too much in shadow, however, to reveal their nature and origin to an indolent attention, and again he resumed his reading. Suddenly something in the text suggested a thought that made him start and drop the book for the third time to the side of the sofa, whence, escaping from his hand, it fell sprawling to the floor, back upward. Brayton, half-risen, was staring intently into the obscurity beneath the bed where the points of light shone with, it seemed to him, an added fire. His attention was now fully aroused, his gaze eager and imperative. It disclosed, almost directly under the foot rail of the bed, the coils of a large serpent—the points of light were its eyes! Its horrible head, thrust flatly forth from the innermost coil and resting upon the outermost, was directed straight toward him, the definition of the wide, brutal jaw and the idiot-like forehead serving to show the direction of its malevolent gaze. The eyes were no longer merely luminous points: they looked into his own with a meaning, a malign significance.

II.

A snake in a bedroom of a modern city dwelling of the better sort is, happily, not so common a phenomenon as to make explanation altogether needless. Harker Brayton, a bachelor of thirty-five, a scholar, idler and something of an athlete, rich, popular and of sound health, had returned to San Francisco from all manner of remote and unfamiliar countries. His tastes, always a trifle luxurious, had taken on an added exuberance from long privation; and the resources of even the Castle Hotel being inadequate to their perfect gratification, he had gladly accepted the hospitality of his friend Dr. Druring, the distinguished scientist. Dr. Druring's house, a large old-fashioned one in what was now an obscure quarter of the city, had an outer and visible aspect of proud reserve. It plainly would not associate with the contiguous elements of its altered environment, and appeared to have developed some of the eccentricities which come of isolation. One of these was a "wing," conspicuously irrelevant in point of architecture, and no less rebellious in the matter of purpose; for it was a combination of laboratory, menagerie and museum. It was here that the doctor indulged the scientific side of his nature in the study of such forms of animal life as engaged his interest and comforted his taste—which, it must be confessed, ran rather to the lower forms. For one of the higher types nimbly and sweetly to recommend itself unto his gentle senses it had at least to retain certain rudimentary characteristics allying it to such "dragons of the prime" as toads and snakes. His scientific sympathies were distinctly reptilian; he loved nature's vulgarians and described himself as the Zola of zoology. His wife and daughters not having the advantage to share his enlightened curiosity regarding the works and ways of our ill-starred fellow creatures, were with needless austerity excluded from what he called the Snakery and doomed to companionship with their own kind, though to soften the rigors of their lot he had permitted them out of his great wealth to outdo the reptiles in the gorgeousness of their surroundings and to shine with a superior splendor.

Architecturally and in point of "furnishing" the Snakery had a severe simplicity befitting the humble circumstances of its occupants, many of whom, indeed, could not safely have been intrusted with the liberty which is necessary to the full enjoyment of luxury, for they had the troublesome peculiarity of being alive. In their own apartments, however, they were under as little personal restraint as was compatible with their protection from the baneful habit of swallowing one another; and as Brayton had thoughtfully been apprised it was more than a tradition that some of them had at divers times been found in parts of the premises where it would have embarrassed them to explain their presence. Despite the Snakery and its uncanny associations—to which, indeed, he gave little attention—Brayton found life at the Druring mansion very much to his mind.

III.

Beyond a smart shock of surprise and a shudder of mere loathing Mr. Brayton was not greatly affected. His first thought was to ring the call bell and bring a servant; but although the bell cord dangled within easy reach he made no movement toward it; it had occurred to his mind that the act might subject him to the suspicion of fear, which he certainly did not feel. He was more keenly conscious of the incongruous nature of the situation than affected by its perils; it was revolting but absurd.

The reptile was of a species with which Brayton was unfamiliar. Its length he could only conjecture; the body at the largest visible part seemed about as thick as his forearm. In what way was it dangerous—if in any way? Was it venomous? Was it a constrictor? His knowledge of nature's danger signals did not enable him to say; he had never deciphered the code.

If not dangerous the creature was at least offensive. It was *de trop*—"matter out of place"—an impertinence. The gem was unworthy of the setting. Even the barbarous taste of our time and country, which had loaded the walls of the room with pictures, the floor with furniture and the furniture with bric-a-brac, had not quite fitted the place for this bit of the savage life of the jungle. Besides—insupportable thought!—the exhalations of its breath mingled with the atmosphere which he himself was breathing!

These thoughts shaped themselves with greater or less definition in Brayton's consciousness before he made the least movement in precaution. He had not even withdrawn his eyes from those of the serpent. Now, however, he had "made up his mind" what to do: he flattered himself that thought had ripened to action. Passively submitting himself to the stress of a thousand sets of opposing influences, and recognizing the instant predominance of one set over the others, he gave the process the customary names consideration and decision. It is thus that we are wise and unwise. It is thus that the withered leaf in an autumn breeze shows greater or less intelligence than its fellows, falling upon the land or upon the lake. The secret of human action is an open one: something contracts our muscles. Does it matter if we give to the preparatory molecular changes the name of Will?

Brayton rose to his feet and prepared to back softly away from the snake, without disturbing it if possible, and through the door. Men retire so from the presence of the great, for greatness is power and power is a menace. He knew that he could walk backward without obstruction and find the door without error. Should the monster follow, the taste which had plastered the walls with paintings had consistently supplied a rack of murderous Oriental weapons from which he could snatch one to suit the occasion. In the meantime the snake's eyes burned with a more pitiless malevolence than before.

Brayton lifted his right foot free of the floor to step backward. That moment he felt a strong aversion to doing so.

"I am accounted brave," he murmured; "is bravery, then, no more than pride? Because there are none to witness the shame shall I retreat?"

He was steadying himself with his right hand upon the back of a chair, his foot suspended.

"Nonsense!" he said aloud; "I am not so great a coward as to fear to seem to myself afraid."

He lifted the foot a little higher by slightly bending the knee and thrust it sharply to the floor—an inch or two in front of the other! He could not think how that occurred. A trial with the left foot had the same result; it was again in advance of the right. The hand upon the chair back was grasping it; the arm was straight, reaching somewhat backward. One might have seen that he was reluctant to lose his hold. The snake's malignant head was still thrust forth from the inner coil as before, the neck level. It had not moved, but its eyes were now electric sparks, radiating an infinity of luminous needles.

The man had an ashy pallor. Again he took a step forward, and another, partly dragging the chair, which when finally released fell upon the floor with a crash. The man groaned; the snake made neither sound nor motion, but its eyes were two dazzling suns. The reptile itself was wholly concealed by them. They gave off enlarging rings of rich and vivid colors, which at their greatest expansion successively vanished like soap-bubbles; they seemed to approach his very face, and anon were an immeasurable distance away. He heard, somewhere, the continuous throbbing of a great drum, with desultory bursts of far music, inconceivably sweet, like the tones of an Æolian harp. He knew it for the sunrise melody of Memnon's statue, and thought he stood in the Nileside reeds, hearing with exalted sense that immortal anthem through the silence of the centuries.

The music ceased; rather it became by insensible degrees the distant roll of a retreating thunderstorm. A landscape, glittering with sun and rain, stretched before him, arched with a vivid rainbow framing in its giant curve a hundred visible cities. In the middle distance a vast serpent, wearing a crown, reared its head out of its voluminous convolutions and looked at him with his dead mother's eyes. Suddenly this enchanting landscape seemed to rise swiftly upward like the drop scene at a theatre, and vanished in a blank. Something struck him a hard blow upon the face and breast. He had fallen to the floor; the blood ran from his broken nose and his bruised lips. For a moment he was dazed and stunned, and lay with closed eyes, his face against the floor. In a few moments he had recovered, and then realized that his fall, by withdrawing his eyes, had broken the spell that held him. He felt that now, by keeping his gaze averted, he would be able to retreat. But the thought of the serpent within a few feet of his head, yet unseen—perhaps in the very act of springing upon him and throwing its coils about his throat—was too horrible. He lifted his head, stared again into those baleful eyes and was again in bondage.

The snake had not moved and appeared somewhat to have lost its power upon the imagination; the gorgeous illusions of a few moments before were not repeated. Beneath that flat and brainless brow its black beady eyes simply glittered as at first with an expression unspeakably malignant. It was as if the creature, knowing its triumph assured, had determined to practice no more alluring wiles.

Now ensued a fearful scene. The man, prone upon the floor, within a yard of his enemy, raised the upper part of his body upon his elbows, his head thrown back, his legs extended to their full length. His face was white between its gouts of blood; his eyes were strained open to their uttermost expansion. There was froth upon his lips; it dropped off in flakes. Strong convulsions ran through his body, making almost serpentine undulations. He bent himself at the waist, shifting his legs from side to side. And every movement left him a little nearer to the snake. He thrust his hands forward to brace himself back, yet constantly advanced upon his elbows.

IV.

Dr. Druring and his wife sat in the library. The scientist was in rare good humor.

"I have just obtained by exchange with another collector," he said, "a splendid specimen of the *ophiophagus*."

"And what may that be?" the lady inquired with a somewhat languid interest.

"Why, bless my soul, what profound ignorance! My dear, a man who ascertains after marriage that his wife does not know Greek is entitled to a divorce. The *ophiophagus* is a snake that eats other snakes."

"I hope it will eat all yours," she said, absently shifting the lamp. "But how does it get the other snakes? By charming them, I suppose."

"That is just like you, dear," said the doctor, with an affectation of petulance. "You know how irritating to me is any allusion to that vulgar superstition about the snake's power of fascination."

The conversation was interrupted by a mighty cry which rang through the silent house like the voice of a demon shouting in a tomb! Again and yet again it sounded, with terrible distinctness. They sprang to their feet, the man confused, the lady pale and speechless with fright. Almost before the echoes of the last cry had died away the doctor was out of the room, springing up the staircase two steps at a time. In the corridor in front of Brayton's chamber he met some servants who had come from the upper floor. Together they rushed at the door, without knocking. It was unfastened and gave way. Brayton lay upon his stomach on the floor, dead. His head and arms were partly concealed under the foot rail of the bed. They pulled the body away, turning it upon the back. The face was defiled with blood and froth, the eyes were wide open, staring—a dreadful sight!

"Died in a fit," said the scientist, bending his knee and placing his hand upon the heart. While in that position he chanced to look under the bed. "Good God!" he added, "how did this thing get in here?"

He reached under the bed, pulled out the snake and flung it, still coiled, to the center of the room, whence with a harsh, shuffling sound it slid across the polished floor till stopped by the wall, where it lay without motion. It was a stuffed snake; its eyes were two shoe buttons.

A Holy Terror.

There was an entire lack of interest in the latest arrival at Hurdy-Gurdy. He was not even christened with the picturesquely descriptive nickname which is so frequently a mining camp's word of welcome to the new-comer. In almost any other camp thereabout this circumstance would of itself have secured him some such appellation as "The White-headed Conundrum," or "No Sarvey"—an expression naively supposed to suggest to quick intelligences the Spanish *quién sabe*. He came without provoking a ripple of concern upon the social surface of Hurdy-Gurdy—a place which to the general Californian contempt of men's personal antecedents superadded a local indifference of its own. The time was long past when it was of any importance who came there, or if anybody came. No one was living at Hurdy-Gurdy.

Two years before, the camp had boasted a stirring population of two or three thousand males and not fewer than a dozen females. A majority of the former had done a few weeks' earnest work in demonstrating, to the disgust of the latter, the singularly mendacious character of the person whose ingenious tales of rich gold deposits had lured them thither—work, by the way, in which there was as little mental satisfaction as pecuniary profit; for a bullet from the pistol of a public-spirited citizen had put that imaginative gentleman beyond the reach of aspersion on the third day of the camp's existence. Still, his fiction had a certain foundation in fact, and many had lingered a considerable time in and about Hurdy-Gurdy, though now all had been long gone.

But they had left ample evidence of their sojourn. From the point where Injun Creek falls into the Rio San Juan Smith, up along both banks of the former into the cañon whence it emerges, extended a double row of forlorn shanties that seemed about to fall upon one another's neck to bewail their desolation; while about an equal number appeared to have straggled up the slope on either hand and perched themselves upon commanding eminences, whence they craned forward to get a good view of the affecting scene. Most of these habitations were emaciated as by famine to the condition of mere skeletons, about which clung unlovely tatters of what might have been skin, but was really canvas. The little valley itself, torn and gashed by pick and shovel, was unhandsome with long, bending lines of decaying flume resting here and there upon the summits of sharp ridges, and stilting awkwardly across the interspaces upon unhewn poles. The whole place presented that raw and forbidding aspect of arrested development which is a new country's substitute for the solemn grace of ruin wrought by time. Whenever there remained a patch of the original soil a rank overgrowth of weeds and brambles had spread upon the scene, and from its dank, unwholesome shades the visitor curious in such matters might have obtained numberless souvenirs of the camp's former glory—fellowless boots mantled with green mold and plethoric of rotting leaves; an occasional old felt hat; desultory remnants of a flannel shirt; sardine boxes inhumanly mutilated and a surprising profusion of black bottles distributed with a truly catholic impartiality, everywhere.

II.

But the man who had now rediscovered Hurdy-Gurdy was evidently not curious as to its archæology. Nor, as he looked about him upon the dismal evidences of wasted work and broken hopes, their dispiriting significance accentuated by the ironical pomp of a cheap gilding by the rising sun, did he supplement his sighs of weariness by one of sensibility. He simply removed from the back of his tired burro a miner's outfit a trifle larger than the animal itself, picketed that creature and selecting a hatchet from his kit moved off at once across the dry bed of Injun Creek to the top of a low, gravelly hill beyond.

Stepping across a prostrate fence of brush and boards he picked up one of the latter, split it into five parts and sharpened them at one end. He then began a kind of search, occasionally stooping to examine something with close attention. At last his patient scrutiny appeared to be rewarded with success, for he suddenly erected his figure to its full height, made a gesture of satisfaction, pronounced the word "Scarry" and at once strode away with long, equal steps, which he counted, then stopped and drove one of his stakes into the earth. He then looked carefully about him, measured off a number of paces over a singularly uneven ground and hammered in another. Pacing off twice the distance at a right angle to his former course he drove down a third, and repeating the process sank home the fourth, and then a fifth. This he split at the top and in the cleft inserted an old letter envelope covered with an intricate system of pencil tracks. In short, he staked off a hill claim in strict accordance with the local mining laws of Hurdy-Gurdy and put up the customary notice.

It is necessary to explain that one of the adjuncts to Hurdy-Gurdy—one to which that metropolis became afterward itself an adjunct—was a cemetery. In the first week of the camp's existence this had thoughtfully been laid out by a committee of citizens; the day after had been signalized by a debate between two members of the committee, with reference to a more eligible site; and on the third day the necropolis was inaugurated by a double funeral. As the camp had waned the cemetery had waxed; and long before the ultimate inhabitant, victorious alike over the insidious malaria and the forthright revolver, had turned the tail of his pack-ass upon Injun Creek the outlying settlement had become a populous if not popular suburb. And now, when the town was fallen into the sere and yellow leaf of an unlovely senility, the graveyard—though somewhat marred by time and circumstance, and not altogether exempt from innovations in grammar and experiments in orthography, to say nothing of the devastating coyote—answered the humble needs of its denizens with reasonable completeness. It comprised a generous two acres of ground, which with commendable thrift but needless care had been selected for its mineral unworth, contained two or three skeleton trees (one of which had a stout lateral branch from which a weather-wasted rope still significantly dangled), half a hundred gravelly mounds, a score of rude headboards displaying the literary peculiarities above mentioned and a struggling colony of prickly pears. Altogether, God's Location, as with characteristic reverence it had been called, could justly boast of an indubitably superior quality of desolation. It was in the most thickly settled portion of this interesting demesne that Mr. Jefferson Doman staked off his claim. If in the prosecution of his design he should deem it expedient to remove any of the dead they would have the right to be suitably re-interred.

III.

This Mr. Jefferson Doman was from Elizabethtown, New Jersey, where six years before he had left his heart in the keeping of a golden-haired, demure-mannered young woman named Mary Matthews, as collateral security for his return to claim her hand.

"I just *know* you'll never get back alive—you never do succeed in anything," was the remark which illustrated Miss Matthews' notion of what constituted success and, inferentially, her view of the nature of encouragement. She added: "If you don't, I'll go to California too. I can put the coins in little bags as you dig them out."

This characteristically feminine theory of auriferous deposits did not commend itself to the masculine intelligence: it was Mr. Doman's belief that gold was found in a liquid condition. He deprecated her intent with considerable enthusiasm, suppressed her sobs with a light hand upon her mouth, laughed in her eyes as he kissed away her tears, and with a cheerful "Ta-ta" went to California to labor for her through the long, loveless years with a strong heart, an alert hope and a steadfast fidelity that never for a moment forgot what it was about. In the meantime Miss Matthews had granted a monopoly of her humble talent for sacking up coins to Mr. Jo Seeman, of New York, gambler, by whom it was better appreciated than her commanding genius for unsacking and bestowing them upon his local rivals. Of this latter aptitude, indeed, he manifested his disapproval by an act which secured him the position of clerk of the prison laundry at Sing Sing, and for her the *sobriquet* of "Split-faced Moll." At about this time she wrote to Mr. Doman a touching letter of renunciation, inclosing her photograph to prove that she had no longer a right to indulge the dream of becoming Mrs. Doman, and recounting so graphically her fall from a horse that the staid bronco upon which Mr. Doman had ridden into Red Dog to get the letter made vicarious atonement under the spur all the way back to camp. The letter failed in a signal way to accomplish its object; the fidelity which had before been to Mr. Doman a matter of love and duty was thenceforth a matter of honor also; and the photograph, showing the once pretty face hideously disfigured as by the slash of a knife, was duly installed in his affections and its more comely predecessor treated with contumelious neglect. On being apprised of this, Miss Matthews, it is only fair to say, appeared less surprised than from the apparently low estimate of Mr. Doman's generosity which the tone of her former letter attested one would naturally have expected her to be. Soon after, however, her letters grew infrequent, and then ceased altogether.

But Mr. Doman had another correspondent, Mr. Barney Bree, of Hurdy-Gurdy, formerly of Red Dog. This gentleman, although a notable figure among miners, was not a miner. His knowledge of mining consisted mainly in a marvelous command of its slang, to which he made copious contributions, enriching its vocabulary with a wealth of extraordinary phrases more remarkable for their aptness than their refinement, and which impressed the unlearned "tenderfoot" with a lively sense of the profundity of their inventor's acquirements. When not entertaining a circle of admiring auditors from San Francisco or the East, he could commonly be found pursuing the comparatively obscure industry of sweeping out the various dance-houses and purifying the spittoons.

Barney had apparently but two passions in life—love of Jefferson Doman, who had once been of some service to him, and love of whisky, which certainly had not. He had been among the first in the rush to Hurdy-Gurdy, but had not prospered, and had sunk by degrees to the position of grave digger. This was not a vocation, but Barney in a desultory way turned his trembling hand to it whenever some local misunderstanding at the card table and his own partial recovery from a prolonged debauch occurred coincidently in point of time. One day Mr. Doman received at Red Dog a letter with the simple postmark, "Hurdy, Cal."; and being occupied with another matter, carelessly thrust it into a chink of his cabin for future perusal. Some two years later it was accidentally dislodged and he read it. It ran as follows:

"HURDY, June 6.

"FRIEND JEFF.—I've hit her hard in the bone-yard. She's blind and lousy. I'm on the divvy—that's me, and mum's my lay till you toot.

"Yours,   BARNEY.

"P.S.—I've clayed her with Scarry."

With some knowledge of the general mining-camp *argot* and of Mr. Bree's private system for the communication of ideas Mr. Doman had no difficulty in understanding by this uncommon epistle that Barney while performing his duty as grave digger had uncovered a quartz ledge with no outcroppings; that it was visibly rich in free gold; that, moved by considerations of friendship, he was willing to accept Mr. Doman as a partner and pending that gentleman's declared will in the matter, would discreetly keep the discovery a secret. From the postscript it was plainly inferable that in order to conceal the treasure, he had buried above it the mortal part of a person named Scarry.

From subsequent events, as related to Mr. Doman at Red Dog it would appear that before taking this precaution Mr. Bree must have had the thrift to remove a modest competency of the gold; at any rate, it was about that time that he entered upon that memorable series of potations and treatings which is still one of the cherished traditions of the San Juan Smith country, and is spoken of with respect as far away as Ghost Rock and Lone Hand. At its conclusion some former citizens of Hurdy-Gurdy, for whom he had performed the last kindly office at the cemetery, made room for him among them, and he rested well.

IV.

Having finished staking off his claim Mr. Doman walked back to the center of it and stood again at the spot where his search among the graves had expired in the exclamation "Scarry." He bent again over the headboard which bore that name and as if to reinforce the senses of sight and hearing ran his forefinger along the rudely carved letters, and re-erecting himself appended orally to the simple inscription the shockingly forthright epitaph, "She was a holy terror!"

Had Mr. Doman been required to make these words good with proof—as considering their somewhat censorious character he doubtless should have been—he would have found himself embarrassed by the absence of reputable witnesses, and hearsay evidence would have been the best he could command. At the time when Scarry had been prevalent in the mining camps thereabout— when, as the editor of the *Hurdy Herald* would have phrased it, she was "in the plenitude of her power," Mr. Doman's fortunes had been at a low ebb, and he had led the vagrantly laborious life of a prospector. His time had been mostly spent in the mountains, now with one companion, now with another. It was from the admiring recitals of these casual partners, fresh from the various camps, that his judgment of Scarry had been made up; himself had never had the doubtful advantage of her acquaintance and the precarious distinction of her favor. And when, finally, on the termination of her perverse career at Hurdy-Gurdy, he had read in a chance copy of the *Herald* her column-long obituary (written by the local humorist of that lively sheet in the highest style of his art), Doman had paid to her memory and to her historiographer's genius the tribute of a smile and chivalrously forgotten her. Standing now at the grave-side of this mountain Messalina he recalled the leading events of her turbulent career, as he had heard them celebrated at his various camp-fires, and perhaps with an unconscious attempt at self-justification repeated that she was a holy terror, and sank his pick into her grave up to the handle. At that moment a raven, which had silently settled upon a branch of the blasted tree above his head, solemnly snapped its beak and uttered its mind about the matter with an approving croak.

Pursuing his discovery of free gold with great zeal, which he probably credited to his conscience as a gravedigger, Mr. Barney Bree had made an unusually deep sepulcher, and it was near sunset before Mr. Doman, laboring with the leisurely deliberation of one who has a "dead sure thing" and no fear of an adverse claimant's enforcement of a prior right, reached the coffin and uncovered it. When he had done so he was confronted by a difficulty for which he had made no provision; the coffin—a mere flat shell of not very well-preserved redwood boards, apparently—had no handles, and it filled the entire bottom of the excavation. The best he could do without violating the decent sanctities of the situation was to make the excavation sufficiently longer to enable him to stand at the head of the casket and getting his powerful hands underneath erect it upon its narrower end; and this he proceeded to do. The approach of night quickened his efforts. He had no thought of abandoning his task at this stage to resume it on the morrow under more advantageous conditions. The feverish stimulation of cupidity and the fascination of terror held him to his dismal work with an iron authority. He no longer idled, but wrought with a terrible zeal. His head uncovered, his outer garments discarded, his shirt opened at the neck and thrown back from his breast, down which ran sinuous rills of perspiration, this hardy and impenitent gold-getter and grave-robber toiled with a giant energy that almost dignified the character of his horrible purpose; and when the sun fringes had burned themselves out along the crest line of the western hills, and the full moon had climbed out of the shadows that lay along the purple plain, he had erected the coffin upon its foot, where it stood propped against the end of the open grave like a colossal note of admiration marking an emotion appropriate to the tragic situation. Then, as the man, standing up to his neck in the earth at the opposite extreme of the excavation, looked at the coffin upon which the moonlight now fell with a full illumination he was thrilled with a sudden terror to observe upon it the startling apparition of a dark human head—the shadow of his own. For a moment this simple and natural circumstance unnerved him. The noise of his labored breathing frightened him, and he tried to still it, but his bursting lungs would not be denied. Then, laughing half audibly and wholly without spirit, he began making movements of the head from side to side, in order to compel the apparition to repeat them. He found a comforting reassurance in asserting his command over his own shadow. He was temporizing; making, with unconscious prudence, a dilatory opposition to an impending catastrophe. He felt that invisible forces of evil were closing in upon him, and he parleyed for time with the inevitable.

He now observed in succession several extraordinary circumstances. The surface of the coffin upon which his eyes were fastened was not flat; it presented two distinct ridges, one longitudinal, the other transverse. Where these intersected at the widest part there was a corroded metallic plate that reflected the moonlight with a dismal luster. Along the outer edges of the coffin, at long intervals, were rust-eaten heads of ornamental screws. This frail example of the undertaker's art had been put into the grave the wrong side up!

Perhaps it was one of the humors of the camp—a practical manifestation of the facetious spirit that had found literary expression in the topsy-turvy obituary notice from the pen of Hurdy-Gurdy's great humorist. Perhaps it had some occult personal signification impenetrable to understandings uninstructed in local traditions. A more charitable hypothesis is that it was owing to a misadventure on the part of Mr. Barney Bree, who, making the interment unassisted, either by choice for the conservation of his golden secret, or through public apathy, had committed a blunder which he was afterward unable or unconcerned to rectify. However it had come about, poor Scarry had indubitably been put into the earth face downward.

When terror and absurdity make alliance, the effect is frightful: this strong-hearted and daring man, this hardy night worker among the dead, this defiant antagonist of darkness and desolation, succumbed to a ridiculous surprise. He was smitten with a thrilling chill—shivered, and shook his massive shoulders as if to throw off an icy hand. He no longer breathed, and the blood in his veins, unable to abate its impetus, surged hotly beneath his cold skin. Unleavened with oxygen, it mounted to his head and congested his brain. His physical functions had gone over to the enemy; his very heart was arrayed against him. He did not move; he could not have cried out. He needed but a coffin to be dead—as dead as the death that confronted him with only the length of an open grave and the thickness of a rotting plank between.

Then, one by one, his senses returned; the tide of terror that had overwhelmed his faculties began to recede. But with the return of his senses he became singularly unconscious of the object of his fear. He saw the moonlight gilding the coffin, but no longer the coffin that it gilded. Raising his eyes and turning his head, he noted, curiously and with surprise, the black branches of the dead tree, and tried to estimate the length of the weather-worn rope that dangled from its ghostly hand. The monotonous howling of distant wolves, sharply punctuated by the barking of a coyote, affected him as something he had heard years ago in a dream. An owl flapped awkwardly above him on noiseless wings, and he tried to forecast the direction of its flight when it should encounter the cliff that reared its illuminated front a mile away. His hearing took account of a gopher's stealthy tread in the shadow of the cactus. He was intensely observant; his senses were all alert; but he saw not the coffin. As one can gaze at the sun until it looks black and then vanishes, so his mind, having exhausted its capacities of dread, was no longer conscious of the separate existence of anything dreadful. The Assassin was cloaking the sword.

It was during this lull in the battle that he became sensible of a faint, sickening odor. At first he thought it was that of a rattlesnake, and involuntarily tried to look about his feet. They were nearly invisible in the gloom of the grave. A hoarse, gurgling sound, like the death-rattle in a human throat, seemed to come out of the sky, and a moment later a great, black, angular shadow, like the same sound made visible, dropped curving from the topmost branch of the spectral tree, fluttered for an instant before his face and sailed fiercely away into the mist along the creek. It was the raven. The incident recalled him to a sense of the situation, and again his eyes sought the upright coffin, now illuminated by the moon for half its length. He saw the gleam of the metallic plate and tried without moving to decipher the inscription. Then he fell to speculating upon what was behind it. His creative imagination presented him a vivid picture. The planks no longer seemed an obstacle to his vision and he saw the livid corpse of the dead woman, standing in grave-clothes, and staring vacantly at him with lidless, shrunken eyes. The lower jaw was fallen, the upper lip drawn away from the uncovered teeth. He could make out a mottled pattern on the hollow cheeks—the maculations of decay. By some mysterious process his mind reverted for the first time that day to the photograph of Mary Matthews. He contrasted its blonde beauty with the forbidding aspect of this dead face—the most lovely object that he knew with the most hideous that he could conceive.

The Assassin now advanced and displaying the blade laid it against the victim's throat. That is to say, the man became at first dimly, then definitely, aware of an impressive coincidence—a relation—a parallel, between the face on the card and the name on the head-board. The one was disfigured, the other described a disfiguration. The thought took hold of him and shook him. It transformed the face that his imagination had created behind the coffin lid; the contrast became a resemblance; the resemblance grew to identity. Remembering the many descriptions of Scarry's personal appearance that he had heard from the gossips of his camp-fire he tried with imperfect success to recall the exact nature of the disfiguration that had given the woman her ugly name; and what was lacking in his memory fancy supplied, stamping it with the validity of conviction. In the maddening attempt to recall such scraps of the woman's history as he had heard, the muscles of his arms and hands were strained to a painful tension, as by an effort to lift a great weight. His body writhed and twisted with the exertion. The tendons of his neck stood out as tense as whip-cords, and his breath came in short, sharp gasps. The catastrophe could not be much longer delayed, or the agony of anticipation would leave nothing to be done by the *coup de grâce* of verification. The scarred face behind the lid would slay him through the wood.

A movement of the coffin diverted his thoughts. It came forward to within a foot of his face, growing visibly larger as it approached. The rusted metallic plate, with an inscription illegible in the moonlight, looked him steadily in the eye. Determined not to shrink, he tried to brace his shoulders more firmly against the end of the excavation, and nearly fell backward in the attempt. There was nothing to support him; he had unconsciously moved upon his enemy, clutching the heavy knife that he had drawn from his belt. The coffin had not advanced and he smiled to think it could not retreat. Lifting his knife he struck the heavy hilt against the metal plate with all his power. There was a sharp, ringing percussion, and with a dull clatter the whole decayed coffin-lid broke in pieces and came away, falling about his feet. The quick and the dead were face to face—the frenzied, shrieking man—the woman standing tranquil in her silences. She was a holy terror.

V.

Some months later a party of ladies and gentlemen belonging to the highest social circles of San Francisco passed through Hurdy-Gurdy on their way to the Yosemite Valley by a new trail. They halted there for dinner and pending its preparation explored the desolate camp. One of the party had been at Hurdy-Gurdy in the days of its glory. He had, indeed, been one of its prominent citizens; and it used to be said that more money passed over his faro table in any one night than over those of all his competitors in a week; but being now a millionaire engaged in greater enterprises, he did not deem these early successes of sufficient importance to merit the distinction of remark. His invalid wife, a lady famous in San Francisco for the costly nature of her entertainments and her exacting rigor with regard to the social position and antecedents of those who attended them, accompanied the expedition. During their stroll among the abandoned shanties of the abandoned camp Mr. Porfer directed the attention of his wife and friends to a dead tree on a low hill beyond Injun Creek.

"As I told you," he said, "I passed through this camp in 1852, and was told that no fewer than five men had been hanged here by vigilantes at various times, and all on that tree. If I am not mistaken, a rope is dangling from it yet. Let us go over and see the place."

Mr. Porfer did not add that the rope in question was perhaps the very one from whose fatal embrace his own neck had once had an escape so narrow that an hour's delay in taking himself out of that region would have spanned it.

Proceeding leisurely down the creek to a convenient crossing, the party came upon the cleanly-picked skeleton of an animal which Mr. Porfer after due examination pronounced to be that of an ass. The distinguishing ears were gone, but much of the inedible head had been spared by the beasts and birds, and the stout bridle of horsehair was intact, as was the riata of similar material connecting it with a picket pin still firmly sunken in the earth. The wooden and metallic elements of a miner's kit lay near by. The customary remarks were made, cynical on the part of the gentlemen, sentimental and refined by the lady. A little later they stood by the tree in the cemetery and Mr. Porfer sufficiently unbent from his dignity to place himself beneath the rotten rope and confidently lay a coil of it about his neck, somewhat, it appeared, to his own satisfaction, but greatly to the horror of his wife, to whose sensibilities the performance gave a smart shock.

An exclamation from one of the party gathered them all about an open grave, at the bottom of which they saw a confused mass of human bones and the broken remnants of a coffin. Coyotes and buzzards had performed the last sad rites for pretty much all else. Two skulls were visible and in order to investigate this somewhat unusual redundancy one of the younger gentle-men had the hardihood to spring into the grave and hand them up to another before Mrs. Porfer could indicate her marked disapproval of so shocking an act, which, nevertheless, she did with considerable feeling and in very choice words. Pursuing his search among the dismal débris at the bottom of the grave the young gentleman next handed up a rusted coffin-plate with an inscription which with difficulty Mr. Porfer deciphered and read aloud with an earnest and not altogether unsuccessful attempt at the dramatic effect which he deemed befitting to the occasion and his rhetorical abilities:

JANE JARVIS.
Born in San Francisco—Died in Hurdy-Gurdy,
Aged 47.
Hell's full of such.

In deference to the piety of the reader and the nerves of Mrs. Porfer's fastidious sisterhood of both sexes, let us not touch upon the painful impression produced by this uncommon inscription, further than to say that the elocutionary powers of Mr. Porfer had never before met with such spontaneous and overwhelming recognition.

The next morsel that rewarded the ghoul in the grave was a long tangle of coal-black hair defiled with clay; but this was such an anticlimax that it received little attention. Suddenly, with a short exclamation and a gesture of excitement, the young man unearthed a fragment of grayish rock, and after a hurried inspection handed it up to Mr. Porfer. As the sunlight fell upon it, it glittered with a yellow luster: it was thickly studded with gleaming points. Mr. Porfer snatched it, bent his head over it a moment and threw it lightly away with the simple remark:

"Iron pyrites—fool's gold."

The young man in the discovery shaft was a trifle disconcerted, apparently.

Meanwhile Mrs. Porfer, unable longer to endure the disagreeable business, had walked back to the tree and seated herself at its root. While rearranging a tress of golden hair which had slipped from its confinement she was attracted by what appeared to be and really was the fragment of an old coat. Looking about to assure herself that so unladylike an act was not observed, she thrust her jeweled hand into the exposed pocket and drew out a moldy pocket-book. Its contents were as follows:

One bundle of letters, post-marked Elizabethtown, New Jersey.

One circle of blonde hair tied with a ribbon.

One photograph of a beautiful girl.

One ditto of same, singularly disfigured.

One name on back of photograph—"Jefferson Doman."

A few moments later a group of anxious gentlemen surrounded Mrs. Porfer as she sat motionless at the foot of the tree, her head dropped forward, her fingers clutching a crushed photograph. Her husband raised her head, exposing a face ghastly white, except the long, deforming cicatrice familiar to all her friends—which no art could ever hide, and which now traversed the pallor of her countenance, a visible curse.

Mary Matthews Porfer had the bad luck to be dead.

The Suitable Surroundings.

The Night.

One midsummer night a farmer's boy living about ten miles from the city of Cincinnati was following a bridle path through a dense and dark forest. He had been searching for some missing cows and at nightfall found himself a long way from home and in a part of the country with which he was but partly familiar. But he was a stouthearted lad, and knowing his general direction from his home, he plunged into the forest without hesitation, guided by the stars. Coming into the bridle path and observing that it ran in the right direction he followed it.

The night was clear, but in the woods it was exceedingly dark. It was more by the sense of touch than by that of sight that the lad kept the path. He could not, indeed, very easily go astray; the undergrowth on both sides was so thick as to be almost impenetrable. He had gone into the forest a mile or more when he was surprised to see a feeble gleam of light shining through the foliage skirting the path on his left. The sight of it startled him and set his heart beating audibly.

"The old Breede house is somewhere about here," he said to himself. "This must be a continuation of the path which we reach it by from our side. Ugh! what should a light be doing there? I don't like it."

Nevertheless he pushed on. A moment later and he had emerged from the forest into a small open space, mostly upgrown to brambles. There were remnants of a rotting fence. A few yards from the trail, in the middle of the "clearing," was the house from which the light came through an unglazed window. The window had once contained glass, but that and its supporting frame had long ago yielded to missiles flung by hands of venturesome boys to attest alike their courage and their hostility to the supernatural; for the Breede house bore the evil reputation of being "haunted." Possibly it was not, but even the hardiest skeptic could not deny that it was deserted—which in rural regions is much the same thing.

Looking at the mysterious dim light shining from the ruined window the boy remembered with apprehension that his own hand had assisted at the destruction. His penitence was of course poignant in proportion to its tardiness and inefficacy. He half expected to be set upon by all the unworldly and bodiless malevolences whom he had outraged by assisting to break alike their windows and their peace. Yet this stubborn lad, shaking in every limb, would not retreat. The blood in his veins was strong and rich with the iron of the frontiersman: he was but two removes from the generation that had subdued the Indian. He started to pass the house.

As he was going by he looked in at the blank window space and saw a strange and terrifying sight—the figure of a man seated in the center of the room, at a table upon which lay some loose sheets of paper. The elbows rested on the table, the hands supporting the head, which was uncovered. On each side the fingers were pushed into the hair. The face showed pale in the light of a single candle a little to one side. The flame illuminated that side of the face; the other was in deep shadow. The man's eyes were fixed upon the blank window space with a stare in which an older and cooler observer might have discerned something of apprehension, but which seemed to the lad altogether soulless. He believed the man to be dead.

The situation was horrible, but not without its fascination. The boy stopped to note it all. He endeavored to still the beating of his heart by holding his breath until half suffocated. He was weak, faint, trembling; he could feel the deathly whiteness of his face. Nevertheless he set his teeth and resolutely advanced to the house. He had no conscious intention—it was the mere courage of terror. He thrust his white face forward into the illuminated opening. At that instant a strange harsh cry, a shriek, broke upon the silence of the night—the note of a screech owl. The man sprang to his feet, overturning the table and extinguishing the candle. The boy took to his heels.

The Day Before.

"Good morning, Colston—I am in luck, it seems. You have often said that my commendation of your literary work was mere civility; and here you find me absorbed—actually merged—in your latest story in the *Messenger*. Nothing less shocking than your touch upon my shoulder would have roused me to consciousness."

"The proof is stronger than you seem to know," replied the man addressed: "so keen is your eagerness to read my story that you are willing to renounce selfish considerations and forego all the pleasure that you could get from it."

"I don't understand you," said the other, folding the newspaper that he held and putting it in his pocket. "You writers are a queer lot anyhow. Come, tell me what I have done or omitted in this matter. In what way does the pleasure that I get, or might get, from your work depend on *me?*"

"In many ways. Let me ask you how you would enjoy your dinner if you took it in this street car. Suppose the phonograph so perfected as to be able to give you an entire opera—singing, orchestration and all. Do you think you would get much pleasure out of it if you turned it on at your office during business hours? Do you really care for a serenade by Schubert when you hear it fiddled by an untimely Italian on a morning ferryboat? Are you always cocked and primed for admiration? Do you keep every mood on tap, ready to any demand? Let me remind you, sir, that the story which you have done me the honor to begin as a means of oblivion to the discomfort of this street car is a ghost story!"

"Well?"

"Well! Has the reader no duties corresponding to his privileges? You have paid five cents for that newspaper. It is yours. You have the right to read it when and where you will. Much of what is in it is neither helped nor harmed by time and place and mood; some of it actually requires to be read at once—while it is fizzing. But my story is not of that character. It is not 'the very latest advices' from Ghostland. You are not expected to keep yourself *au courant* with what is going on in the realm of spooks. The stuff will keep until you have leisure to put yourself into the frame of mind appropriate to the sentiment of the piece—which I respectfully submit that you cannot do in a street car, even if you are the only passenger. The solitude is not of the right sort. An author has rights which the reader is bound to respect."

"For specific example?"

"The right to the reader's undivided attention. To deny him that is immoral. To make him share your attention with the rattle of a street car, the moving panorama of the crowds on the sidewalks and the buildings beyond—with any of the thousands of distractions which make our customary environment—is to treat him with gross injustice. By God, it is infamous!"

The speaker had risen to his feet and was steadying himself by one of the straps hanging from the roof of the car. The other man looked up at him in sudden astonishment, wondering how so trivial a grievance could seem to justify so strong language. He saw that his friend's face was uncommonly pale and that his eyes glowed like living coals.

"You know what I mean," continued the writer, impetuously crowding his words—"you know what I mean, Marsh. My stuff in this morning's *Messenger* is plainly sub-headed 'A Ghost Story.' That is ample notice to all: every honorable reader will understand it as prescribing by implication the conditions under which the work is to be read."

The man addressed as Marsh winced a trifle; then asked with a smile: "What conditions? You know I'm only a plain business man who cannot be supposed to understand such things. How, when, where should I read your ghost story?"

"In solitude—at night—by the light of a candle. There are certain emotions which a writer can easily enough excite—such as compassion or merriment. I can move you to tears or laughter under almost any circumstances. But for my ghost story to be effective you must be made to feel fear—at least a strong sense of the supernatural—and that is a different matter. I have a right to expect that if you read me at all you will give me a chance; that you will make yourself accessible to the emotion which I try to inspire."

The car had now arrived at its terminus and stopped. The trip just completed was its first for the day and the conversation of the two early passengers had not been interrupted. The streets were yet silent and desolate; the house tops were just touched by the rising sun. As they stepped from the car and walked away together Marsh narrowly eyed his companion, who was reported, like most men of uncommon literary ability, to be addicted to various destructive vices. That is the revenge which dull minds take upon bright ones in resentment of their superiority. Mr. Colston was known as a man of genius. There are honest souls who believe that genius is a mode of excess. It was known that Colston did not drink liquor, but many said that he ate opium. Something in his appearance that morning—a certain wildness of the eyes, an unusual pallor, a thickness and rapidity of speech were taken by Mr. Marsh to confirm the report. Nevertheless he had not the self-denial to abandon a subject which he found interesting, however it might excite his friend.

"Do you mean to say," he began, "that if I take the trouble to observe your directions—place myself in the condition which you demand: solitude, night and a tallow candle—you can with your ghastliest work give me an uncomfortable sense of the supernatural, as you call it? Can you accelerate my pulse, make me start at sudden noises, send a nervous chill along my spine and cause my hair to rise?"

Colston turned suddenly and looked him squarely in the eyes as they walked. "You would not dare—you have not the courage," he said. He emphasized the words with a contemptuous gesture. "You are brave enough to read me in a street car; but—in a deserted house—alone—in the forest—at night! Bah! I have a manuscript in my pocket that would kill you."

Marsh was angry. He knew himself a man of courage and the words stung him. "If you know such a place," he said, "take me there to-night and leave me your story and a candle. Call for me when I've had time enough to read it and I'll tell you the entire plot and—kick you out of the place."

That is how it occurred that the farmer's boy, looking in at an unglazed window of the Breede house, saw a man sitting in the light of a candle.

The Day After.

Late in the afternoon of the next day three men and a boy approached the Breede house from that point of the compass toward which the boy had fled the preceding night. They were in high spirits apparently: they talked loudly and laughed. They made facetious and good-humored ironical remarks to the boy about his adventure, which evidently they did not believe in. The boy accepted their raillery with seriousness, making no reply. He had a sense of the fitness of things and knew that one who professes to have seen a dead man rise from his seat and blow out a candle is not a credible witness.

Arrived at the house and finding the door bolted on the inside, the party of investigators entered without further ceremony than breaking it down. Leading out of the passage into which this door opened was another on the right and one on the left. These two doors also were fastened, and were broken in. They entered at random the one on the left first. It was vacant. In the room on the right—the one which had the blank front window—was the dead body of a man.

It lay partly on one side, with the forearm beneath it, the cheek on the floor. The eyes were wide open; the stare was not an agreeable thing to encounter. The lower jaw had fallen; a little pool of saliva had collected beneath the mouth. An overthrown table, a partly burned candle, a chair and some paper with writing on it were all else that the room contained. The men looked at the body, touching the face in turn. The boy gravely stood at the head, assuming a look of ownership. It was the proudest moment of his life. One of the men said to him: "You're a good 'un"—a remark which was received by the two others with nods of acquiescence. It was Skepticism apologizing to Truth. Then one of the men took from the floor the sheets of manuscript and stepped to the window, for already the evening shadows were gloaming the forest. The song of the whip-poor-will was heard in the distance and a monstrous beetle sped by the window on roaring wings and thundered away out of hearing.

The Manuscript.

"Before committing the act which, rightly or wrongly, I have resolved on and appearing before my Maker for judgment, I, James R. Colston, deem it my duty as a journalist to make a statement to the public. My name is, I believe, tolerably well known to the people as a writer of tragic tales, but the somberest imagination never conceived anything so gloomy as my own life and history. Not in incident: my history has been destitute of adventure and action. But my mental career has been lurid with experiences such as kill and damn. I shall not recount them here—some of them are written and ready for publication elsewhere. The object of these few lines is to explain to whomsoever may be interested that my death is voluntary—my own act. I shall die at ten o'clock in the evening on the fifteenth of July—a significant anniversary to me, for it was on that day and at that hour that my friend in time and eternity, Charles Breede, performed his vow to me by the same act which his fidelity to our pledge now entails upon me: he took his life in his little house in the Copeton woods. There was the customary verdict of 'temporary insanity.' Had I testified at that inquest—had I told all I knew they would have called *me* mad!

"I have still a week of life in which to arrange my worldly affairs and prepare for the great change. It is enough, for I have but few affairs and it is now four years since death became an imperative obligation.

"I shall bear this writing on my body: the finder will please hand it to the coroner.

"JAMES R. COLSTON.

"P.S.—Willard Marsh, on this the fatal 15th day of July I hand you this manuscript, sealed, to be opened and read under the conditions agreed upon, and at the place which I designate. I forego my intention to keep it on my body to explain the manner of my death, which is not important. It will serve to explain the manner of yours. I am to call for you during the night to receive assurance that you have read the manuscript. You know me well enough to expect me. But, my friend, it *will be after 10 o'clock*. May God have mercy on our souls!

"J. R. C."

Before the man who was reading this manuscript had finished one of the others had picked up the candle and lighted it. When the reader had done he quietly thrust the paper against the flame and despite the protestations of the others held it until it was burnt to ashes. At the inquest nothing could elicit an intelligible account of what the paper contained. The man who did this, and who placidly endured a severe reprimand from the coroner, was a son-in-law of the late Charles Breede.

From the "Times."

"Yesterday the Commissioners of Lunacy committed to the Asylum Mr. James R. Colston, a writer of some local reputation, connected with the *Messenger*. It will be remembered that on the evening of the 15th inst. Mr. Colston was given into custody by one of his fellow-lodgers in the Baine House, who had observed him acting very suspiciously: baring his throat and whetting a razor—occasionally trying its edge by actually cutting through the skin of his arm, etc.

On being handed over to the police the unfortunate man made a desperate resistance and has ever since been so violent that it has been necessary to keep him in a strait-jacket. It is thought that his malady is due to grief and excitement caused by the recent mysterious death of his friend Willard Marsh."

An Inhabitant of Carcosa.

For there be divers sorts of death—some wherein the body remaineth; and in some it vanisheth quite away with the spirit. This commonly occureth only in solitude (such is God's will) and, none seeing the end, we say the man is lost, or gone on a long journey—which indeed he hath; but sometimes it hath happened in sight of many, as abundant testimony sheweth. In one kind of death the spirit also dieth, and this it hath been known to do while yet the body was in vigor for many years. Sometimes, as is veritably attested, it dieth with the body, but after a season it is raised up again in that place that the body did decay.—*Brayconne's Meditations*

Pondering upon these words of my favorite author, and questioning their full meaning, as one who having an intimation yet doubts if there be not something behind other than that which he has discerned, I noted not whither I had strayed until a sudden chill wind striking my face revived in me a sense of my surroundings. I observed with astonishment that everything seemed unfamiliar. On every side of me stretched a bleak and desolate expanse of plain, covered with a tall overgrowth of sear grass, which rustled and whistled in the autumn wind with Heaven knows what mysterious and uncanny suggestion. Protruded at long intervals above it, stood strangely shaped and sombre colored rocks, which seemed, somehow, to have an understanding with one another and to exchange looks of uncomfortable significance, as if they had reared their heads to watch the issue of some foreseen event. A few blasted trees here and there appeared as leaders in this malevolent conspiracy of silent expectation.

The day, I thought, must be far advanced, though the sun was invisible; and although sensible that the air was raw and chill my consciousness of that fact was rather mental than physical—I had no feeling of discomfort. Over all the dismal landscape a canopy of low, lead-colored clouds hung like a visible curse. In all this there were a menace and a portent—a hint of crime, an intimation of doom. Bird, beast or insect there was none. The wind sighed in the bare branches of the dead trees and the gray grass bent to whisper its dread secret to the earth; but no other sound or motion broke the awful repose of that dismal place.

I observed in the herbage a number of weather-worn stones, evidently shaped with tools. They were broken, covered with moss and half sunken in the earth. Some lay prostrate, some leaned at various angles, none were vertical. They were obviously headstones of graves, though the graves themselves no longer existed as either mounds or depressions—the years had leveled all. Scattered here and there, more massive blocks showed where some pompous mausoleum or ambitious monument had once flung its feeble defiance at oblivion. So old seemed these relics—these vestiges of vanity and memorials of affection and piety—so battered and worn and stained—so neglected, deserted, forgotten the place, that I could not help thinking myself the discoverer of the burial ground of a pre-historic race of men—a nation whose very name was long extinct.

Filled with these reflections, I was for some time heedless of the sequence of my own experiences, but soon I thought, "How came I hither?" A moment's thought seemed to make this all clear and explain at the same time, though in a disquieting way, the singularly weird character with which my fancy had invested all that I saw and heard. I was ill: I remembered now how I had been prostrated by a sudden fever, and how my family had told me that in my periods of delirium I had constantly cried out for liberty and air, and had been held in bed to prevent my escape out-of-doors. Now I had eluded the vigilance of my attendants and had wandered hither to—to where? I could not conjecture. Clearly I was at a considerable distance from the city where I dwelt—the ancient and famous city of Carcosa.

No signs of human life were anywhere visible nor audible; no rising smoke—no watchdog's bark, nor lowing of cattle, no shouts of children at play—nothing but this dismal burial-place with its air of mystery and dread, due to my own disordered brain. Was I not becoming again delirious, there beyond human aid? Was it not indeed *all* an illusion of my madness? I called aloud the names of my wife and sons—reached out my hands in search of theirs, even as I walked among the crumbling stones and in the withered grass.

A noise behind me caused me to turn about. A wild animal, a lynx, was approaching. The thought came to me: "If I break down here in the desert—if the fever returns and I fail, this beast will be at my throat." I sprang toward it, shouting. It trotted tranquilly by within a hand's breadth of me and disappeared behind a rock.

A moment later a man's head appeared to rise out of the ground a short distance away—he was ascending the far slope of a low hill whose crest was hardly to be distinguished from the general level. His whole figure soon came into view against the background of gray cloud. He was half naked, half clad in skins. His hair was unkempt, his beard long and ragged. In one hand he carried a bow and arrow; the other held a blazing torch with a long trail of black smoke. He walked slowly and with caution, as if he feared falling into some open grave concealed by the tall grass. This strange apparition surprised but did not alarm, and taking such a course as to intercept him I met him almost face to face, accosting him with the familiar salutation, "God keep you."

He gave no heed, nor did he arrest his pace.

"Good stranger," I continued, "I am ill and lost. Direct me, I beseech you, to Carcosa."

The man broke into a barbarous chant in an unknown tongue, passing on and away.

An owl on the branch of a decayed tree hooted dismally and was answered by another in the distance. Looking upward I saw through a sudden rift in the clouds Aldebaran and the Hyades!

Amazed at this revelation, I seated myself at the root of a great tree, seriously to consider what it were best to do. That I was mad I could no longer doubt, yet recognized a ground of doubt in the conviction. Of fever I had no trace. I counted my pulse beats: they were slow and regular. I had, withal, a sense of exhilaration and vigor altogether unknown to me—a feeling of mental and physical exaltation. My senses seemed all alert—I could feel the air as a ponderous substance; I could hear the silence.

A great root of the giant tree against whose bole I leaned as I sat held enclosed in its grasp a slab of granite, a portion of which protruded into a recess formed by another root. The stone was thus partly protected from the weather, though greatly decomposed. Its edges were worn round, its corners eaten away, its faces deeply furrowed and scaled. Glittering particles of mica were visible in the earth beneath it—the vestiges of its decomposition. This stone had apparently marked the grave out of which the tree had sprung ages ago. Its exacting roots had robbed the grave and made the stone a prisoner.

A sudden wind pushed some dry leaves and twigs from the uppermost face of the stone; I saw the low-relief letters of an inscription and bent to read it: "In memoriam"—God in Heaven! *my* name in full!—the date of *my* birth!—the date of *my* death!

A level shaft of rosy light illuminated the whole side of the tree as I sprang to my feet in terror. The sun was rising in the east. I stood between the tree and its broad red disk—no shadow darkened the trunk! A chorus of howling wolves saluted the dawn. I saw them sitting on their haunches, singly and in groups, on the summits of irregular mounds and tumuli, filling a half of my desert prospect and extending to the horizon—the ancient and famous city of Carcosa.

———————————

Such are the facts imparted to the medium Bayrolles by the spirit Hoseib Alar Robardin.

The Boarded Window.

In 1830, a few miles back from what is now the great city of Cincinnati, lay an immense and almost unbroken forest. The whole region was sparsely settled by people of the frontier—restless souls who no sooner had hewn fairly habitable homes out of the wilderness and attained to that degree of prosperity which to-day we should call indigence than impelled by some mysterious impulse of their nature they abandoned all and pushed further westward to encounter new perils and privations in the effort to regain comforts which they had voluntarily renounced. Many of them had already forsaken that region for the remoter settlements, but among those remaining was one who had been of those first arriving. He lived alone in a house of logs surrounded on all sides by the great forest of whose gloom and silence he seemed a part, for no one had ever known him to smile nor speak a needless word. His simple wants were supplied by the sale or barter of skins of wild animals in the river town; for not a thing did he grow upon the land which if needful he might have claimed by right of undisturbed possession. There were evidences of "improvement"—a few acres of ground immediately about the house had once been cleared of its trees, the decayed stumps of which were half concealed by the new growth that had been suffered to repair the ravage wrought by the ax. Apparently the man's zeal for agriculture had burned with a failing flame, expiring in penitential ashes.

The little log house with its chimney of sticks, its roof of warping clapboards weighted with traversing poles and its chinking of clay had a single door and, directly opposite, a window. The latter, however, was boarded up—nobody could remember a time when it was not. And none knew why it was so closed; certainly not because of the occupant's dislike of light and air, for on those rare occasions when a hunter had passed that lonely spot, the recluse had commonly been seen sunning himself on his doorstep if Heaven had provided sunshine for his need. I fancy there are few persons living to-day who ever knew the secret of that window, but I am one, as in due time you shall see.

The man's name was said to be Murlock. He was apparently seventy years old, actually about fifty. Something besides years had had a hand in his aging. His hair and long full beard were white, his gray lusterless eyes sunken, his face singularly seamed with wrinkles which appeared to belong to two intersecting systems. In figure he was tall and spare with a stoop of the shoulders—a burden bearer. I never saw him: these particulars I learned from my grandfather, from whom also I got the man's story when I was a lad. He had known him when living near by in that early day.

One day Murlock was found in his cabin, dead. It was not a time and place for coroners and newspapers, and I suppose it was agreed that he had died from natural causes or I should have been told, and should remember. I know only that with what was probably a sense of the fitness of things the body was buried near the cabin alongside the grave of his wife, who had preceded him by so many years that local tradition had retained hardly a hint of her existence. That closes the final chapter of this true story—excepting, indeed, the circumstance that many years afterward, in company with an equally intrepid spirit, I penetrated to the place and ventured near enough to the ruined cabin to throw a stone against it, and ran away to avoid the ghost which every well-informed boy thereabout knew haunted the spot. As this record grows naturally out of my personal relation to what it records, that circumstance, as a part of the relation, has a certain relevancy. But there is an earlier chapter—that supplied by my grandfather.

When Murlock built his cabin and began laying sturdily about with his ax to hew out a farm—the rifle meanwhile his means of support—he was young, strong and full of hope. In that Eastern country whence he came he had married, as was the fashion, a young woman in all ways worthy of his honest devotion, who shared the dangers and privations of his lot with a willing spirit and light heart. There is no known record of her name; of her charms of mind and person tradition is silent and the doubter is at liberty to entertain his doubt; but God forbid that I should share it! Of their affection and happiness there is assurance abundant in every added day of the man's widowed life; for what but the magnetism of a blessed memory could have chained that venturesome spirit to a lot like that?

One day Murlock returned from gunning in a distant part of the forest to find his wife prostrate with fever and delirious. There was no physician within miles, no neighbor; nor was she in a condition to be left to summon help. So he set about the task of nursing her back to health; but at the end of the third day she passed into a comatose state and so died, with never a gleam of returning reason.

From what we know of a nature like his we may venture to sketch in some of the details of the outline picture drawn by my grandfather. When convinced that she was dead Murlock had sense enough to remember that the dead must be prepared for burial. In performance of this sacred duty he blundered now and again: did certain things incorrectly; and others, which he did correctly, were done over and over. His occasional failures to accomplish some simple and ordinary act filled him with astonishment, like that of a drunken man who wonders at the suspension of familiar natural laws. He was surprised, too, that he did not weep—surprised and a little ashamed: surely it is unkind not to weep for the dead. "To-morrow," he said aloud, "I shall have to make the coffin and dig the grave; and then I shall miss her, when she is no longer in sight, but now—she is dead, of course, but it is all right—it *must* be all right, somehow. Things cannot be as bad as they seem."

He stood over the body in the fading light, adjusting the hair and putting the finishing touches to the simple toilet; doing all mechanically, with soulless care. And still through his consciousness ran an undersense of conviction that all was right—that he should have her again as before and everything explained. He had had no experience in grief; his capacity had not been enlarged by use. His heart could not contain it all, nor his imagination rightly conceive it. He did not know he was so hard hit; that knowledge would come later, and never go. Grief is an artist of powers as various as the characters of the instruments upon which he plays his dirges for the dead, evoking from some the sharpest, shrillest notes, from others the low, grave chords that throb recurrent like the slow beating of a distant drum. Some natures it startles; some it stupefies. To one it comes like the stroke of an arrow, stinging all the sensibilities to a keener life; to another as the blow of a bludgeon, which in crushing benumbs. We may conceive Murlock to have been that way affected, for (and here we are upon surer ground than that of conjecture) no sooner had he finished his pious work than, sinking into a chair by the side of the table upon which the body lay, and noting how white the profile showed in the deepening gloom, he laid his arms upon the table's edge and dropped his face into them, tearless yet and unutterably weary. At that moment came in through the open window a long wailing sound like the cry of a lost child in the far deeps of the darkening wood! But the man did not move. Again and nearer than before sounded that unearthly cry upon his failing sense. Perhaps it was a wild beast. Perhaps it was a dream. For Murlock was asleep.

Some hours later, as it afterward appeared, this unfaithful watcher awoke and raising his head from his arms intently listened—he knew not why. There in the black darkness by the side of his dead, recalling all without a shock, he strained his eyes to see—he knew not what. His senses were all alert; his breath was suspended; his blood had stilled its tides as if to assist the silence. Who—what had waked him, and where was it?

Suddenly the table shook beneath his arms, and at the same moment he heard, or fancied that he heard, a light soft step—another—sounds as of bare feet upon the floor!

He was terrified beyond the power to cry out or move. Perforce he waited—waited there in the darkness through centuries of such dread as one may know yet live to tell. He tried vainly to speak the dead woman's name, vainly to stretch forth his hand across the table to learn if she were there. His throat was powerless, his arms and hands were like lead. Then occurred something most frightful. Some heavy body seemed hurled against the table with an impetus that pushed it against his breast so sharply as nearly to overthrow him, and at the same instant he heard and felt the fall of something upon the floor with so violent a thump that the whole house was shaken by the impact. Then ensued a scuffling and a confusion of sounds impossible to describe. Murlock had risen to his feet. Fear had by excess forfeited control of his faculties. He flung his hands upon the table. Nothing was there!

There is a point at which terror may turn to madness—and madness incites to action. With no definite intent—from no motive but the wayward impulse of a madman—Murlock sprang to the wall and with a little groping seized his loaded rifle and without aim discharged it. By the flash which lit up the room with a vivid illumination he saw an enormous panther dragging the dead woman toward the window, its teeth fixed in her throat! Then there were darkness blacker than before, and silence; and when he returned to consciousness the sun was high and the woods vocal with songs of birds.

The body lay near the window, where the beast had left it when frightened away by the flash and report of the rifle. The clothing was deranged, the long hair in disorder, the limbs lay anyhow. From the throat, dreadfully lacerated, had issued a pool of blood not yet entirely coagulated. The ribbon with which he had bound the wrists was broken; the hands were tightly clenched. Between the teeth was a fragment of the animal's ear.

The Middle Toe of the Right Foot.

I.

It is well known that the old Manton house is haunted. In all the rural district near about, and even in the town of Marshall, a mile away, not one person of unbiased mind entertains a doubt of it: incredulity is confined to those opinionated persons who will be called "cranks" as soon as the useful word shall have penetrated the intellectual demesne of the Marshall *Advance*. The evidence that the house is haunted is of two kinds: the testimony of disinterested witnesses who have had ocular proof, and that of the house itself. The former may be disregarded and ruled out on any of the various grounds of objection which may be urged against it by the ingenious; but facts within the observation of all are fundamental and controlling.

In the first place, the Manton house has been unoccupied by mortals for more than ten years, and with its outbuildings is slowly falling into decay—a circumstance which in itself the judicious will hardly venture to ignore. It stands a little way off the loneliest reach of the Marshall and Harriston road, in an opening which was once a farm and is still disfigured with strips of rotting fence half covered with brambles and overrunning a stony and sterile soil long unacquainted with the plow. The house itself is in tolerably good condition, though badly weather-stained and in dire need of attention from the glazier, the smaller male population of the region having attested in the manner of its kind its disapproval of dwellings without dwellers. The house is two stories in height, nearly square, its front pierced by a single doorway flanked on each side by a window boarded up to the very top. Corresponding windows above, not protected, serve to admit light and rain to the rooms of the upper floor. Grass and weeds grow pretty rankly all about, and a few shade trees, somewhat the worse for wind and leaning all in one direction, seem to be making a concerted effort to run away. In short, as the Marshall town humorist explained in the columns of the *Advance*, "the proposition that the Manton house is badly haunted is the only logical conclusion from the premises." The fact that in this dwelling Mr. Manton thought it expedient one night some ten years ago to rise and cut the throats of his wife and two small children, removing at once to another part of the country, has no doubt done its share in directing public attention to the fitness of the place for supernatural phenomena.

To this house one summer evening came four men in a wagon. Three of them promptly alighted, and the one who had been driving hitched the team to the only remaining post of what had been a fence. The fourth remained seated in the wagon. "Come," said one of his companions, approaching him, while the others moved away in the direction of the dwelling—"this is the place."

The man addressed was deathly pale and trembled visibly. "By God!" he said harshly, "this is a trick, and it looks as if you were in it."

"Perhaps I am," the other said, looking him straight in the face and speaking in a tone which had something of contempt in it. "You will remember, however, that the choice of place was with your own assent left to the other side. Of course if you are afraid of spooks—"

"I am afraid of nothing," the man interrupted with another oath and sprang to the ground. The two then joined the others at the door, which one of them had already opened with some difficulty, caused by rust of lock and hinge. All entered. Inside it was dark, but the man who had unlocked the door produced a candle and matches and made a light. He then unlocked a door on their right as they stood in the passage. This gave them entrance to a large square room that the candle but dimly lighted. The floor had a thick carpeting of dust, which partly muffled their footfalls. Cobwebs were in the angles of the walls and depended from the ceiling like strips of rotting lace, making undulatory movements in the disturbed air. The room had two windows in adjoining sides, but from neither could anything be seen except the rough inner surfaces of boards a few inches from the glass. There was no fireplace, no furniture; there was nothing. Besides the cobwebs and the dust, the four men were the only objects there which were not a part of the architecture. Strange enough they looked in the yellow light of the candle. The one who had so reluctantly alighted was especially "spectacular"—he might have been called sensational. He was of middle age, heavily built, deep chested and broad shouldered. Looking at his figure one would have said that he had a giant's strength; at his features, that he would use it like a giant. He was clean shaven, his hair rather closely cropped and gray. His low forehead was seamed with wrinkles above the eyes, and over the nose these became vertical. The heavy black brows followed the same law, saved from meeting only by an upward turn at what would otherwise have been the point of contact. Deeply sunken beneath these, glowed in the obscure light a pair of eyes of uncertain color, but obviously enough too small. There was something forbidding in their expression, which was not bettered by the cruel mouth and wide jaw. The nose was well enough, as noses go; one does not expect much of noses. All that was sinister in the man's face seemed accentuated by an unnatural pallor—he appeared altogether bloodless.

The appearance of the other men was sufficiently commonplace: they were such persons as one meets and forgets that he met. All were younger than the man described, between whom and the eldest of the others, who stood apart, there was apparently no kindly feeling. They avoided looking at one another.

"Gentlemen," said the man holding the candle and keys, "I believe everything is right. Are you ready, Mr. Rosser?"

The man standing apart from the group bowed and smiled.

"And you, Mr. Grossmith?"

The heavy man bowed and scowled.

"You will please remove your outer clothing."

Their hats, coats, waistcoats and neckwear were soon removed and thrown outside the door, in the passage. The man with the candle now nodded, and the fourth man—he who had urged Mr. Grossmith to leave the wagon—produced from the pocket of his overcoat two long, murderous-looking bowie-knives, which he drew from the scabbards.

"They are exactly alike," he said, presenting one to each of the two principals—for by this time the dullest observer would have understood the nature of this meeting. It was to be a duel to the death.

Each combatant took a knife, examined it critically near the candle and tested the strength of blade and handle across his lifted knee. Their persons were then searched in turn, each by the second of the other.

"If it is agreeable to you, Mr. Grossmith, said the man holding the light, "you will place yourself in that corner."

He indicated the angle of the room farthest from the door, to which Grossmith retired, his second parting from him with a grasp of the hand which had nothing of cordiality in it. In the angle nearest the door Mr. Rosser stationed himself, and after a whispered consultation his second left him, joining the other near the door. At that moment the candle was suddenly extinguished, leaving all in profound darkness. This may have been done by a draught from the opened door; whatever the cause, the effect was appalling!

"Gentlemen," said a voice which sounded strangely unfamiliar in the altered condition affecting the relations of the senses, "gentlemen, you will not move until you hear the closing of the outer door."

A sound of trampling ensued, the closing of the inner door and its locking; and finally the outer one closed with a concussion which shook the entire building. Instantly—audible without and within—a strange wild shriek resounded through the vacant upper chambers, and a startled owl, dashing clumsily out of one of the blank windows, flew away through the night to the nearest wood.

A few minutes afterward a belated farmer's boy met a wagon which was being driven furiously toward the town of Marshall. He declared that behind the two figures on the front seat stood a third with its hands upon the bowed shoulders of the others, who appeared to struggle vainly to free themselves from its grasp. This figure, unlike the others, was clad in white, and had undoubtedly boarded the wagon as it passed the haunted house. As the lad could boast a considerable former experience with the supernatural thereabout his word had the weight justly due to the testimony of an expert. The story eventually appeared in the *Advance*, with some slight literary embellishments and a concluding intimation that the gentlemen referred to would be allowed the use of the paper's columns for their version of the night's adventure. But the privilege remained without a claimant.

II.

The events which led up to this "duel in the dark" were simple enough. One evening three young men of the town of Marshall were sitting in a quiet corner of the porch of the village hotel, smoking and discussing such matters as three educated young men of a Missouri village would naturally find interesting. Their names were King, Sancher and Rosser. At a little distance, within easy hearing but taking no part in the conversation, sat a fourth. He was a stranger to the others. They merely knew that on his arrival by the stage coach that afternoon he had written in the hotel register the name Robert Grossmith. He had not been observed to speak to any one except the hotel clerk. He seemed, indeed, singularly fond of his own company—or, as the *personnel* of the *Advance* expressed it, "grossly addicted to evil associations." But then it should be said in justice to the stranger that the *personnel* was himself of a too convivial disposition fairly to judge one differently gifted, and had, moreover, experienced a slight rebuff in an effort at an "interview."

"I hate any kind of deformity in a woman," said King, "whether natural or—or acquired. I have a theory that any physical defect has its correlative mental and moral defect."

"I infer, then," said Rosser, gravely, "that a lady lacking the moral advantage of a nose would find the struggle to become Mrs. King an arduous enterprise."

"Of course you may put it that way," was the reply; "but, seriously, I once threw over a most charming girl on learning quite accidentally that she had suffered amputation of a toe. My conduct was brutal if you like, but if I had married that girl I should have been miserable and should have made her so."

"Whereas," said Sancher, with a light laugh, "by marrying a gentleman of more liberal views she escaped with a cut throat."

"Ah, you know to whom I refer. Yes, she married Manton, but I don't know about his liberality: I'm not sure but he cut her throat because he discovered that she lacked that excellent thing in woman, the middle toe of the right foot."

"Look at that chap!" said Rosser in a low voice, his eyes fixed upon the stranger.

That person was obviously listening intently to the conversation.

"Damn his impudence!" whispered King—"what ought we to do?"

"That's an easy one," Rosser replied, rising. "Sir," he continued, addressing the stranger, "I think it would be better if you would remove your chair to the other end of the veranda. The presence of gentlemen is evidently an unfamiliar situation to you."

The man sprang to his feet and strode forward with clenched hands, his face white with rage. All were now standing. Sancher stepped between the belligerents.

"You are hasty and unjust," he said to Rosser; "this gentleman has done nothing to deserve such language."

But Rosser would not withdraw a word. By the custom of the country and the time there could be but one outcome to the quarrel.

"I demand the satisfaction due a gentleman," said the stranger, who had become more calm. "I have not an acquaintance in this region. Perhaps you, sir," bowing to Sancher, "will be kind enough to represent me in this matter."

Sancher accepted the trust—somewhat reluctantly it must be confessed, for the man's appearance and manner were not at all to his liking. King, who during the colloquy had hardly removed his eyes from the stranger's face and had not spoken a word, consented with a nod to act for Rosser, and the upshot of it was that the principals having retired a meeting was arranged for the next evening. The nature of the arrangements has been already disclosed. The duel with knives in a dark room was once a commoner feature of Southwestern life than it is likely to be again. How thin a veneering of "chivalry" covered the essential brutality of the code under which such encounters were possible we shall see.

III.

In the blaze of a midsummer noonday the old Manton house was hardly true to its traditions. It was of the earth, earthy. The sunshine caressed it warmly and affectionately, with evident unconsciousness of its bad reputation. The grass greening all the expanse in its front seemed to grow, not rankly, but with a natural and joyous exuberance, and the weeds blossomed quite like plants. Full of charming lights and shadows and populous with pleasant-voiced birds, the neglected shade trees no longer struggled to run away, but bent reverently beneath their burdens of sun and song. Even in the glassless upper windows was an expression of peace and contentment, due to the light within. Over the stony fields the visible heat danced with a lively tremor incompatible with the gravity which is an attribute of the supernatural.

Such was the aspect under which the place presented itself to Sheriff Adams and two other men who had come out from Marshall to look at it. One of these men was Mr. King, the sheriff's deputy; the other, whose name was Brewer, was a brother of the late Mrs. Manton. Under a law of the State of Missouri relating to property which has been for a certain period abandoned by an owner whose residence cannot be ascertained the sheriff was legal custodian of the Manton farm and appurtenances thereunto belonging. His present visit was in mere perfunctory compliance with some order of a court in which Mr. Brewer had an action to get possession of the property as heir to his deceased sister. By a mere coincidence the visit was made on the day after the night that Deputy King had unlocked the house for another and very different purpose. His presence now was not of his own choosing: he had been ordered to accompany his superior and at the moment could think of nothing more prudent than simulated alacrity in obedience. He had intended going anyhow—but in other company.

Carelessly unlocking the front door, the sheriff was surprised to see lying on the floor of the passage into which it opened a confused heap of men's apparel. Examination showed it to consist of two hats and the same number of coats, waistcoats and scarves, all in a remarkably good state of preservation, albeit somewhat defiled by the dust in which they lay. Mr. Brewer was equally astonished, but Mr. King's emotion is not of record. With a new and lively interest in his own actions the sheriff now unlatched and pushed open a door on the right and the three entered. The room was apparently vacant—no: as their eyes became accustomed to the dimmer light something was visible in the farthest angle of the wall. It was a human figure—that of a man crouching close in the corner. Something in the attitude made the intruders halt when they had barely passed the threshold—halt and hold their breath. The figure more and more clearly defined itself. The man was upon one knee, his back in the angle of the wall, his shoulders elevated to the level of his ears, his hands before his face, palms outward, the fingers spread and crooked like claws. The white face turned upward on the retracted neck had an expression of unutterable fright, the mouth half open, the eyes incredibly expanded. He was stone dead—dead of terror! Yet, with the exception of a bowie-knife which had evidently fallen from his own hand, not another object was in the room.

In the thick dust which covered the floor were some confused footprints near the door and along the wall through which it opened. Along one of the adjoining walls, too, past the boarded-up windows, was the trail made by the man himself in reaching his corner. Instinctively in approaching the body the three men now followed that trail. The sheriff grasped one of the outthrown arms; it was as rigid as iron, and the application of a gentle force rocked the entire body without altering the relation of its parts. Brewer, pale with horror, gazed intently into the distorted face. "God of mercy!" he suddenly cried, "it is Manton!"

"You are right," said King, with an evident attempt at calmness: "I knew Manton. He wore a full beard and his hair long, but this is he."

He might have added: "I recognized him when he challenged Rosser. I told Rosser and Sancher who he was before we played him this horrible trick. When Rosser left this dark room at our heels, forgetting his clothes in the excitement, and driving away with us in his undershirt—all through the discreditable proceedings we knew whom we were dealing with, murderer and coward that he was!"

But nothing of this did Mr. King say. With his better light he was trying to penetrate the mystery of the man's death. That he had not once moved from the corner where he had been stationed; that his posture was that of neither attack nor defense; that he had dropped his weapon; that he had obviously perished of sheer terror of something that he *saw*—these were circumstances which Mr. King's disturbed intelligence could not rightly comprehend.

Groping in intellectual darkness for a clew to his maze of doubt, his gaze, directed mechanically downward in the way of one who ponders momentous matters, fell upon something which, there in the light of day and in the presence of living companions struck him with an invincible terror. In the dust of years that lay thick upon the floor—leading from the door by which they had entered, straight across the room to within a yard of Manton's crouching corpse—were three parallel lines of footprints—light but definite impressions of bare feet, the outer ones those of small children, the inner a woman's. From the point at which they ended they did not return: they pointed all one way. Brewer, who had observed them at the same moment, was leaning forward in an attitude of rapt attention, horribly pale.

"Look at that!" he cried, pointing with both hands at the nearest print of the woman's right foot, where she had apparently stopped and stood. "The middle toe is missing—it was Gertrude!"

Gertrude was the late Mrs. Manton, sister to Mr. Brewer.

Haïta, the Shepherd.

In the heart of Haïta the illusions of learning and experience had not supplanted those of youth. His thoughts were pure and pleasant, for his life was simple and his soul devoid of ambition. He rose with the sun and went forth to pray at the shrine of Hastur, the god of shepherds, who heard and was pleased. After performance of this pious rite Haïta unbarred the gate of the fold and with a cheerful mind drove his flock afield, eating his morning meal of curds and oat cake as he went, occasionally pausing to add a few berries, cold with dew, or to drink of the waters that came away from the hills to join the stream in the middle of the valley and be borne along with it, he knew not whither.

During the long summer day, as his sheep cropped the good grass which the gods had made to grow for them, or lay with their fore-legs doubled under their breasts and chewed the cud, Haïta, reclining in the shadow of a tree or sitting upon a rock, played so sweet music upon his reed pipe that sometimes from the corner of his eye he got accidental glimpses of the minor sylvan deities leaning forward out of the copse to hear; but if he looked at them directly they vanished. From this—for he must be thinking if he would not turn into one of his own sheep—he drew the solemn inference that happiness may come if not sought, but if looked for will never be seen; for next to the favor of Hastur, who never disclosed himself, Haïta most valued the friendly interest of his neighbors, the shy immortals of the wood and stream. At nightfall he drove his flock back to the fold, saw that the gate was secure and retired to his cave for refreshment and for dreams.

So passed his life, one day like another, save when the storms uttered the wrath of an offended god. Then Haïta cowered in his cave, his face hidden in his hands, and prayed that he alone might be punished for his sins and the world saved from destruction. Sometimes when there was a great rain, and the stream came out of its banks, compelling him to urge his terrified flock to the uplands, he interceded for the people in the great cities which he had been told lay in the plain beyond the two blue hills which formed a gateway of his valley.

"It is kind of thee, O Hastur," so he prayed, "to give me mountains so near to my dwelling and my fold that I and my sheep can escape the angry torrents; but the rest of the world thou must thyself deliver in some way that I know not of, or I will no longer worship thee."

And Hastur, knowing that Haïta was a youth who kept his word, spared the cities and turned the waters into the sea.

So he had lived since he could remember. He could not rightly conceive any other mode of existence. The holy hermit who lived at the head of the valley, a full hour's journey away, from whom he had heard the tale of the great cities where dwelt people—poor souls!—who had no sheep, gave him no knowledge of that early time when, so he reasoned, he must have been small and helpless like a lamb.

It was through thinking on these mysteries and marvels and on that horrible change to silence and decay which he felt sure must sometime come to him as he had seen it come to so many of his flock—as it came to all living things except the birds—that Haïta first became conscious how miserable was his lot.

"It is necessary," he said, "that I know whence and how I came; for how can one perform his duties unless able to judge what they are by the way in which he was intrusted with them? And what contentment can I have when I know not how long it is to last? Perhaps before another sun I may be changed, and then what will become of the sheep? What, indeed, will have become of me?"

Pondering these things Haïta became melancholy and morose. He no longer spoke cheerfully to his flock, nor ran with alacrity to the shrine of Hastur. In every breeze he heard whispers of malign deities whose existence he now first observed. Every cloud was a portent signifying disaster, and the darkness was full of new terrors. His reed pipe when applied to his lips gave out no melody but a dismal wail; the sylvan and riparian intelligences no longer thronged the thicket-side to listen, but fled from the sound, as he knew by the stirred leaves and bent flowers. He relaxed his vigilance and many of his sheep strayed away into the hills and were lost. Those that remained became lean and ill for lack of good pasturage, for he would not seek it for them, but conducted them day after day to the same spot through mere abstraction while puzzling about life and death—of immortality he knew nothing.

One day while indulging in the gloomiest reflections he suddenly sprang from the rock upon which he sat, and with a determined gesture of the right hand exclaimed: "I will no longer be a suppliant for knowledge which the gods withhold. Let them look to it that they do me no wrong. I will do my duty as best I can and if I err upon their own heads be it!"

Suddenly, as he spoke, a great brightness fell about him, causing him to look upward, thinking the sun had burst through a rift in the clouds; but there were no clouds. Hardly more than an arm's length away stood a beautiful maiden. So beautiful she was that the flowers about her feet folded their petals in despair and bent their heads in token of submission; so sweet her look that the humming birds thronged her eyes, thrusting their thirsty bills almost into them, and the wild bees were about her lips. And such was her radiance that the shadows of all objects lay divergent from her feet, turning as she moved.

Haïta was entranced. Rising, he knelt before her in adoration and she laid her hand upon his head.

"Come," she said in a voice which had the music of all the bells of his flock—"come, thou art not to worship me, who am no goddess, but if thou art truthful and dutiful I will abide with thee."

Haïta seized her hand and, stammering his joy and gratitude, arose, and hand in hand they stood and smiled in one another's eyes. He gazed upon her with reverence and rapture. He said: "I pray thee, lovely maid, tell me thy name and whence and why thou comest."

At this she laid a warning finger on her lip and began to withdraw. Her beauty underwent a visible alteration that made him shudder, he knew not why, for still she was beautiful. The landscape was darkened by a giant shadow sweeping across the valley with the speed of a vulture. In the obscurity the maiden's figure grew dim and indistinct and her voice seemed to come from a distance as she said in a tone of sorrowful reproach: "Presumptuous and ungrateful man! must I then so soon leave thee? Would nothing do but thou must at once break the Eternal Compact?"

Inexpressibly grieved, Haïta fell upon his knees and implored her to remain—rose and sought her in the deepening darkness—ran in circles, calling to her aloud; but all in vain. She was no longer visible, but out of the gloom he heard her voice saying: "Nay, thou shalt not have me by seeking. Go to thy duty, faithless shepherd, or we never meet again."

Night had fallen; the wolves were howling in the hills and the terrified sheep crowding about Haïta's feet. In the demands of the hour he forgot his disappointment, drove his sheep to the fold and repairing to the place of worship poured out his heart in gratitude to Hastur for permitting him to save his flock, then retired to his cave and slept.

When Haïta woke the sun was high and shone in at his cave, illuminating it with a great glory. And there, beside him, sat the maiden! She smiled upon him with a smile that seemed the visible music of his pipe of reeds. He dared not speak, fearing to offend her as before, for he knew not what he could venture to say.

"Because," she said, "thou didst thy duty by the flock, and didst not forget to thank Hastur for staying the wolves of the night, I am come to thee again. Wilt thou have me for a companion?"

"Who would not have thee forever?" replied Haïta. "O! never again leave me until—until I—change and become silent and motionless."

Haïta had no word for death.

"I wish, indeed," he continued, "that thou wert of my own sex, that we might wrestle and run races and so never tire of being together."

At these words the maiden arose and passed out of the cave, and Haïta, springing from his couch of fragrant boughs to overtake and detain her, observed to his astonishment that the rain was falling and the stream in the middle of the valley had come out of its banks. The sheep were bleating in terror, for the rising waters had invaded their fold. And there was danger for the unknown cities of the distant plain.

It was many days before Haïta saw the maiden again. One day he was returning from the head of the valley, where he had gone with ewe's milk and oat cake and berries for the holy hermit, who was too old and feeble to provide himself with food.

"Poor old man!" he said aloud as he trudged along homeward. "I will return to-morrow and bear him on my back to my own dwelling, where I can care for him. Doubtless it is for this that Hastur has reared me all these years and gives me health and strength."

As he spoke, the maiden, clad in glittering garments, met him in the path with a smile which took away his breath.

"I am come again," she said, "to dwell with thee if thou wilt now have me, for none else will. Thou mayest have learned wisdom and art willing to take me as I am, nor care to know."

Haïta threw himself at her feet. "Beautiful being," he cried, "if thou wilt but deign to accept all the devotion of my heart and soul—after Hastur be served—it is yours forever. But alas! thou art capricious and wayward. Before to-morrow's sun I may lose thee again. Promise, I beseech thee, that however in my ignorance I may offend, thou wilt forgive and remain always with me."

Scarcely had he finished speaking when a troop of wolves sprang out of the hills and came racing toward him with crimson mouths and fiery eyes. The maiden again vanished and he turned and fled for his life. Nor did he stop until he was in the cot of the holy hermit, whence he had set out. Hastily barring the door against the wolves he cast himself upon the ground and wept.

"My son," said the hermit, from his couch of straw freshly gathered that morning by Haïta's hands, "it is not like thee to weep for wolves—tell me what sorrow hath befallen thee, that age may minister to the hurts of youth with such balms as it hath of its wisdom."

Haïta told him all: how thrice he had met the radiant maid and thrice she had left him forlorn. He related minutely all that had passed between them, omitting no word of what had been said.

When he had ended, the holy hermit was a moment silent, then said: "My son, I have attended to thy story and I know the maiden. I have myself seen her, as have many. Know, then, that her name, which she would not even permit thee to inquire, is Happiness. Thou saidst well to her that she was capricious, for she imposes conditions that man cannot fulfill, and delinquency is punished by desertion. She cometh only when unsought, and will not be questioned. One manifestation of curiosity, one sign of doubt, one expression of misgiving, and she is away! How long didst thou have her at any time before she fled?

"Only a single instant," answered Haïta, blushing with shame at the confession. "Each time I drove her away in one moment."

"Unfortunate youth!" said the holy hermit, "but for thine indiscretion thou mightst have had her for two."

An Heiress from Redhorse.

Coronado, June 20.

I find myself more and more interested in him. It is not, I am sure, his—do you know any noun corresponding to the adjective "handsome"?—one does not like to say "beauty" when speaking of a man. He is beautiful enough, Heaven knows; I should not even care to trust you with him—faithfulest of all possible wives that you are—when he looks his best, as he always does. Nor do I think the fascination of his manners has much to do with it. You recollect that the charm of art inheres in that which is undefinable, and to you and me, my dear Irene, I fancy there is rather less of that in the branch of art under consideration than to girls in their first season. I fancy I know how my fine gentleman produces many of his effects and could perhaps instruct him how to heighten them. Nevertheless his manner is something truly delightful. I suppose what interests me chiefly is the man's brains. His conversation is the best I have ever heard and altogether unlike anyone else's. He seems to know *everything*, as indeed he ought, for he has been everywhere, read everything, seen all there is to see—sometimes I think rather more than is good for him—and had acquaintance with the *queerest* people! And then his voice—Irene, when I hear it I actually feel as if I ought to have *paid at the door*, though of course it is my own door.

July 3.

I fear my remarks about Dr. Barritz must have been, being thoughtless, very silly, or you would not have written of him with such levity, not to say disrespect. Believe me, dearest, he has more dignity and seriousness (of the kind, I mean, which is not inconsistent with a manner sometimes playful and always charming) than any of the men that you and I ever met. And young Raynor—you knew Raynor at Monterey—tells me that the men all like him and that he is treated with something like deference everywhere. There is a mystery, too—something about his connection with the Blavatsky people in

Northern India. Raynor either would not or could not tell me the particulars. I infer that Dr. Barritz is thought—don't you dare to laugh—a Magician! Could anything be finer than that? An ordinary mystery is not, of course, as good as a scandal, but when it relates to dark and dreadful practices—to the exercise of unearthly powers—could anything be more piquant? It explains, too, the singular influence the man has upon me. It is the undefinable in his art—black art! Seriously, dear, I quite tremble when he looks me full in the eyes with those unfathomable orbs of his, which I have already vainly attempted to describe to you. How dreadful if he have the power to make one fall in love! Do you know if the Blavatsky crowd have that power—outside of Sepoy?

July 16.

The strangest thing! Last evening while Aunty was attending one of the hotel hops (I hate them) Dr. Barritz called. It was scandalously late—I actually believe he had talked with Aunty in the ballroom and learned from her that I was alone. I had been all the evening contriving how to worm out of him the truth about his connection with the Thugs in Sepoy, and all of that black business, but the moment he fixed his eyes on me (for I admitted him, I'm ashamed to say) I was helpless. I trembled. I blushed. I—O, Irene, Irene, I love the man beyond expression, and you know how it is yourself!

Fancy! I, an ugly duckling from Redhorse—daughter (they say) of old "Calamity Jim"—certainly his heiress, with no living relation but an absurd old aunt who spoils me a thousand and fifty ways—absolutely destitute of everything but a million dollars and a hope in Paris,—I daring to love a god like Him! My dear, if I had you here I could tear your hair out with mortification.

I am convinced that he is aware of my feeling, for he stayed but a few moments, said nothing but what another man might have said half as well, and pretending that he had an engagement went away. I learned to-day (a little bird told me—the bell-bird) that he went straight to bed. How does that strike you as evidence of exemplary habits?

July 17.

That little wretch Raynor called yesterday and his babble set me almost wild. He never runs down—that is to say when he does run down a score of reputations more or less he does not pause between one reputation and the next. (By the way, he inquired about you, and his manifestations of interest in you had, I confess, a good deal of genuine *vraisemblance*.) Mr. Raynor observes no game laws; like Death (which he would inflict if slander were fatal) he has all seasons for his own. But I like him, for we knew one another at Redhorse when we were young. He was known in those far fair days as "Giggles" and

I—O, Irene, can you ever forgive me?—I was called "Gunny." God knows why; perhaps in allusion to the material of my pinafores; perhaps because the name is in alliteration with "Giggles"; for Gig and I were inseparable playmates and the miners may have thought it a delicate civility to recognize some kind of relationship between us.

Later, we took in a third—another of Adversity's brood, who, like Garrick between Tragedy and Comedy, had a chronic inability to adjudicate the rival claims (to himself) of Frost and Famine. Between him and the grave there was seldom anything more than a single suspender and the hope of a meal which would at the same time support life and make it insupportable. He literally picked up a precarious living for himself and an aged mother by "chloriding the dumps"; that is to say, the miners permitted him to search the heaps of waste rock for such pieces of "pay ore" as had been overlooked; and these he sacked up and sold at the Syndicate Mill. He became a member of our firm— "Gunny, Giggles and Dumps" thenceforth—through my favor; for I could not then, nor can I now, be indifferent to his courage and prowess in defending against Giggles the immemorial right of his sex to insult a strange and unprotected female—myself. After Old Jim struck it in the Calamity and I began to wear shoes and go to school, and in emulation Giggles took to washing his face and became Jack Raynor of Wells, Fargo & Co., and old Mrs. Barts was herself chlorided to her fathers, Dumps drifted over to San Juan Smith and turned stage driver and was killed by road agents and so forth.

Why do I tell you all this, dear? Because it is heavy on my heart. Because I walk the Valley of Humility. Because I am subduing myself to permanent consciousness of my unworthiness to unloose the latchet of Dr. Barritz's shoe. Because, O dear, O dear! there's a cousin of Dumps at this hotel! I haven't spoken to him. I never had any acquaintance with him, but—do you suppose he has recognized me? Do, please, give me in your next your candid, sure-enough opinion about it, and say you don't think so. Do you suppose He knows about me already, and that that is why He left me last evening when He saw that I blushed and trembled like a fool under His eyes? You know I can't bribe *all* the newspapers, and I can't go back on anybody who was good to Gunny at Redhorse—not if I'm pitched out of Society into the sea. So the skeleton sometimes rattles behind the door. I never cared much before, as you know, but now—*now* it is not the same. Jack Raynor I am sure of—he will not tell Him. He seems, indeed, to hold Him in such respect as hardly to dare speak to Him at all, and I'm a good deal that way myself. Dear, dear! I wish I had something besides a million dollars! If Jack were three inches taller I'd marry him alive and go back to Redhorse and wear sackcloth again to the end of my miserable days.

We had a perfectly splendid sunset last evening and I must tell you all about it. I ran away from Aunty and everybody and was walking alone on the beach. I expect you to believe, you infidel! that I had not looked out of my window on the seaward side of the hotel and seen Him walking alone on the beach. If you are not lost to every feeling of womanly delicacy you will accept my statement without question. I soon established myself under my sunshade and had for some time been gazing out dreamily over the sea, when he approached walking close to the edge of the water—it was ebb tide. I assure you the wet sand actually brightened about his feet! As he approached me he lifted his hat, saying: "Miss Dement, may I sit with you, or will you walk with me?"

The possibility that neither might be agreeable seems not to have occurred to him. Did you ever know such assurance? Assurance? My dear, it was gall, downright *gall!* Well, I didn't find it wormwood and replied, with my untutored Redhorse heart in my throat: "I—I shall be pleased to do *anything.*" Could words have been more stupid? There are depths of fatuity in me, friend o' my soul, which are simply bottomless!

He extended his hand, smiling, and I delivered mine into it without a moment's hesitation, and when his fingers closed about it to assist me to my feet the consciousness that it trembled made me blush worse than the red west. I got up, however, and after a while, observing that he had not let go my hand, I pulled on it a little, but unsuccessfully. He simply held on, saying nothing but looking down into my face with some kind of a smile—I didn't know—how could I?—whether it was affectionate, derisive or what, for I did not look at him. How beautiful he was!—with the red fires of the sunset burning in the depths of his eyes! Do you know, dear, if the Thugs of the Blavatsky region have any special kind of eyes? Ah, you should have seen his superb attitude, the godlike inclination of his head as he stood over me after I had got upon my feet! It was a noble picture but I soon destroyed it, for I began at once to sink again to the earth. There was only one thing for him to do and he did it: he supported me with an arm about my waist.

"Miss Dement, are you ill?" he said.

It was not an exclamation: there was neither alarm nor solicitude in it. If he had added: "I suppose that is about what I am expected to say," he would hardly have expressed his sense of the situation more clearly. His manner filled me with shame and indignation, for I was suffering acutely. I wrenched my hand out of his, grasped the arm supporting me and pushing myself free fell plump into the sand and sat helpless. My hat had come off in the struggle and my hair tumbled about my face and shoulders in the most mortifying way.

"Go away from me," I cried, half choking. "O, *please* go away, you—you Thug! How dare you think *that* when my leg is asleep?"

I actually said those identical words! And then I broke down and sobbed. Irene, I fear I *blubbered!*

His manner altered in an instant—I could see that much through my fingers and hair. He dropped on one knee beside me, parted the tangle of hair and said in the tenderest way: "My poor girl, God knows I have not intended to pain you. How should I?—I who love you—I who have loved you for—for years and years!"

He had pulled my wet hands away from my face and was covering them with kisses. My cheeks were like two coals, my whole face was flaming and, I think, steaming. What could I do? I hid it on his shoulder—there was no other place. And, O, my dear friend, how my leg tingled and thrilled, and how I wanted to kick!

We sat so for a long time. He had released one of my hands to pass his arm about me again and I possessed myself of my handkerchief and was drying my eyes and my nose. I would not look up until that was done; he tried in vain to push me a little away and gaze into my eyes. Presently, when all was right and it had grown a bit dark, I lifted my head, looked him straight in the eyes and smiled my best—my level best, dear.

"What do you mean," I said, "by 'years and years'?"

"Dearest," he replied, very gravely, very earnestly, "in the absence of the sunken cheeks, the hollow eyes, the lank hair, the slouching gait, the rags, dirt and youth, can you not—will you not understand? Gunny, I'm Dumps!"

In a moment I was upon my feet and he upon his. I seized him by the lapels of his coat and peered into his handsome face in the deepening darkness. I was breathless with excitement.

"And you are not dead?" I asked, hardly knowing what I said.

"Only dead in love, dear. I recovered from the road agent's bullet, but this, I fear, is fatal."

"But about Jack—Mr. Raynor? Don't you know—"

"I am ashamed to say, darling, that it was through that unworthy person's invitation that I came here from Vienna."

Irene, they have played it upon your affectionate friend,

Mary Jane Dement.

P. S.—The worst of it is that there is no mystery. That was an invention of Jack to arouse my curiosity and interest. James is not a Thug. He solemnly assures me that in all his wanderings he has never set foot in Sepoy.

Appendix

The following materials, consisting mainly of extracts from *Wasp* and *Examiner*-based "Prattle" columns and editorials but supplemented with materials drawn from other sources where applicable, are grouped under the various tales according to the order of the individual stories as they appear in *Tales of Soldiers and Civilians*. Items related to particular tales are ordered chronologically according to their publication dates. The selections are meant to provide a representative sampling of material that will allow readers of the present edition to better understand the milieu from which the nineteen stories themselves and the original collection as a whole emerged.

A few brief words about the two San Francisco newspapers most of these selections appeared in:

The San Francisco *Wasp* was an illustrated weekly journal which was remarkable for its brilliantly cynical and satirical editorial style, a style which, from early in 1881 through the summer of 1886, was personified by Bierce, the paper's editor, editorial writer, featured columnist ("Prattle"), and most important and prolific contributor of other material including essays, short stories, and poems. By the autumn of 1881, under Bierce's idiosyncratic editorial hand, the *Wasp* was already thriving: the editorial for October 7, 1881, proudly announced that the paper's circulation was "upwards of 11,000 copies," which the *Wasp* thought "the largest circulation ever obtained by a weekly paper in California."[1] According to the same editorial, the *Wasp* was

> the only cartoon paper printed in colors west of the Rocky Mountains, and combining, as we venture to think, both literary and artistic excellence, has a double claim to support, which is in process of full recognition. It is not a journal that is read and thrown away, as is amply shown by the constant demands made upon us for covers and bound volumes. In this form the back numbers are preserved and will be read for years concurrently with the weekly issues[. . . .] (228)

In mid-March of 1887, Bierce, having become famous throughout the region as the man behind the sting of the *Wasp*, was hired by William Randolph Hearst, who, after graduating from Harvard, had just taken over the reins of the San Francisco *Examiner*. It has been said that hiring Bierce was the first thing Hearst did as a newspaperman after acquiring the paper as a graduation gift from his father. At the *Examiner*, Bierce's main duty was to provide a weekly installment of "Prattle," which ran on the editorial page. A key part of the working arrangement Bierce had with Hearst was that the material Bierce submitted for "Prattle" would run unaltered by the editors of the paper. Bierce's stories also appeared in the paper as he saw fit.

1. "A Horseman in the Sky." First published in the *Examiner* on April 14, 1889, under the title "The Horseman in the Sky," but renamed "A Horseman in the Sky" by Bierce when revised for inclusion in his 1892 collection.

Wasp, January 23, 1886, "Prattle": "To be ignorant of anything about the civil war— not to know accurately how any considerable event occurred, *both ways*—would be ignorance indeed in these days when every old soldier is in his anecdotage."[2]

2. "An Occurrence at Owl Creek Bridge." First published in the *Examiner* on July 13, 1890.

Bierce's serious head wound received at Kenesaw Mountain on June 23, 1864, quite possibly provided firsthand experience of a useful kind. Carey McWilliams's 1929 biography of Bierce contains a passage that hints at what such fever-inspired waking dreams may have involved:

> He never forgot the journey of that hospital train back to Chattanooga. They [the wounded] were loaded on flat-cars, covered with tarpaulin and left alone for hours with only the moon to commiserate their agonies. He once told his daughter that he always retained a vivid and unforgettable picture of that trip. Would they never reach the hospital? The skies were overcast at times with clouds, but a turn in the road would reveal the moon shining down with its cold, ageless clarity. The train cautiously made its way over miles of doubtful tracks; it barely managed to keep in motion at times; its movement was almost imperceptible. The journey was made at night and the heavy summer humidity finally condensed in a drizzling rain. (55–56)

The Official Record of the War of Rebellion contains a command relayed by James B. Fry from the Headquarters of the Army of the Ohio in Huntsville, Alabama, to General Hazen, Bierce's commanding officer, on July 24, 1862:

The general directs that you make it your business to see that stockades are erected for the defense of every bridge between Athens [in northern Alabama, some twenty miles west of Huntsville] and Reynolds' Station [not located], and he wishes you to go at this immediately. The regiments at Reynolds' must of course make working details. Report your whereabouts from time to time. No wagon trains must leave Reynolds' without escort. Tell Colonel McCook. (*Official Record*, volume 16, chapter 28, page 208)

Wasp, October 7, 1881, "Prattle." Bierce, reacting to an incident involving a man who had recently attempted suicide or, as Bierce put it, "to experience the sensation of approaching death" by slitting his throat with a knife:

It is said that in such a supreme moment the events of one's whole life crowd into his memory; that a mighty but stilly rhythm pulsates in his ears; that flashes of intolerable light blind his closed eyes; that confused, fragmentary speech babbles all about, and giant whispers affright the sense; that all this is felt rather than seen or heard. By those who have had this terrible experience and been afterward resuscitated, it is affirmed that one lives centuries in an instant; that his hair is smitten white, his face furrowed and blasted as with age; that he gets a stoop; that his teeth come out, and his manly gait is debased to a doddering shuffle. If a fellow can get all that for nothing I call it dog-cheap.

Wasp, November 18, 1882, unsigned article, "How You Will Feel When Hanged," containing material extracted from a fifty-three-page article that had appeared in the September 1849 volume of the *Quarterly Review*, under the running header, "Fontenelle *on the Signs of Death*." The portion of the essay that the *Wasp* reproduced opened by asking "What are the sensations experienced during hanging," and noted the available evidence suggested "that, after one instant of pain, the chief sensation is that of a mass of brilliant colors filling the eye-balls." One survivor of a deliberate attempt at a partial hanging that went further than intended recalled a pleasant, painless encounter with "'fire before his eyes, which changed first to black and then to sky-blue.'" Another survivor, when rescued, was said to have "complained that, having lost all pain in an instant, he had been taken from a light of which the charm defied description." Similarly, a "criminal, who escaped through the breaking of the halter, said after a second or two of suffering a light appeared, and across it a most beautiful avenue of trees." The brief excerpt concluded with several lines that draw attention to the divergent experiences of spectators and those engaged in being hanged:

All agree that the uneasiness is quite momentary, that colors of various hues start up before the eyes, and that, these having been gazed at for a limited space, the rest is oblivion. The mind, averted from the reality of the situation, is engaged in scenes the most remote from that which fills the eyes of the spectator.

Wasp, March 31, 1883. Short story, presumably authored by Bierce, attributed only to "He Who Was Hanged":

ON THE TRAP.

From my cell to this place is exactly thirty-seven paces. I wonder why I counted them? God knows I've something else more important to think about. Thirty-seven! A three and a seven. It seems to me I've read somewhere that the figures three and seven have some kind of a mystic significance. Thirty-seven! What is he saying? "Oh Christ, have mercy on this poor sinner." Is there a Christ? Can his mercy benefit me? What is the use of prayer? How do they know that there is a God of Love—a Christ who died to save poor, weak, sinful mortals— murderers? Was I created to stand here to-day? Did my Creator, omniscient, all-powerful, merciful, thrust me into an existence for which I never sought? If this is true—if the great God who loveth all things knew, when he created me, that I should come to this, that I was destined to commit a crime against the laws of my fellow-man and suffer a million death agonies ere my final punishment, is he a just God—a good God? And will the prayers of my fellow-men, weak and uncertain in their knowledge as I am, avail me now, in this my final mortal extremity? I suppose that short crack in the platform at my feet is one edge of the trap. I wonder whether the hinges upon which this palpable door of death swings are in front of me or behind me. I wonder whether they are anything like the hinges of other doors. How silent they all are. I wonder what they are going to do now. Straps? What is the use of straps? Ah, now I understand. How quick they work. And the clicking of the buckles—how loud they sound. One could almost imagine them the clicking of the teeth of some hideous, ravenous monster. And they bind me in folds as tight and as deadly as the anaconda. Arms, knees, ankles—pinioned in a grip that only death shall loosen. It will soon be over now. A few, short, precious moments and I shall dangle at the end of the rope, a writhing, helpless thing of clay—a clod—a corpse. How pale they all are, those people down below. Some of them clench their hands and grit their teeth as they gaze upon me standing here on the crumbling edge of my grave. I wonder if any of them sympathize with me in my awful extremity? No. I see nothing but horror in their faces—horror braced by the memory of the murder I have done.

Yes, there is one group calm enough. Those young men at my right, in the corridor there, are as unmoved as if they were witnessing a simple drama—a comedy, perhaps, so poorly performed that they refuse to damn it with even a sarcastic smile. And I think I have seen some of them before. I am certain I have. They are newspaper reporters. That long-necked fellow with the sharp nose and the dirty shirt collar interviewed me in the City Prison, and because I refused to answer his questions, lied about me in his paper—said I had a villainous, hang-dog expression of countenance and a general appearance of beetle-browed brutality. No wonder *he* can contemplate my misery calmly. And that other young man, with the red hair and the bob-tailed coat, who writes half the time without looking at his paper—I've seen him too. He came to my cell here after I was condemned and asked me how I felt—whether I was going to make a written confession or reserve it for my dying speech on the scaffold. And then he wrote a lot of hogwash about what I had to eat and how soundly I slept, who were my death watch, and derided the kind young ladies who brought me flowers, and cake and wine. They're cold-blooded wretches, regarding human misery as so much provender for their ghoulish newspapers and their patrons. I suppose that while I am dying they will scramble to my side to hear the doctor count the beating of my pulse or the wild throbbing of my heart. Curses on them, curses on them! A dying man's curse go with them, and may they live to suffer the agonies I am suffering now, ten thousand times over. A curse—Ha! Take it off—horror! Light—light—oh cruel, relentless men! Mercy! One more glimpse of the bright sunshine, only one more—for God's sake give me light—air—I cannot die like this—too late—too late.

* * * * *

The sunshine has come at last. It bathes the flower spangled slopes of a beautiful landscape with a radiance as soft and mellow as the dream of a twilight in Eden. The linnets are singing their vesper hymns in the swaying branches of the beech trees and the blackbird pipes in the field of yellow corn by the dusty road side. There are subtle odors creeping up from the river below and a gentle wind rustles the clambering jasmine and honeysuckle beside the cottage door. Slowly the sun sinks behind the Western hills and a crimson glory flames to the zenith like the streaming banners floating about the battlements of Paradise. A filmy haze—a twilight veil, shrouding the face of nature at her loveliest Indian summer period—lies along the emerald slopes, and the shrill song of the cricket begins to greet the coming night. Then the flaming banners above the fading hills droop and disappear, and the stars came out in the clear sky above the vine-clad cottage. At the door of that cottage sits a grey-haired mother and her blue-eyed boy—a child scarcely in his teens. And the mother, in a voice as soft and low and melodious as the murmur of a woodland rill, tells her boy of his duty as a man. She warns him of the evils that lie in his path. She teaches him the golden rule of humanity—do unto others even as you would have them do unto you. And the boy, clasping his mother to his innocent heart, promises to keep her counsel—promises that when temptation shall spread her wiles to lure him from the path of virtue and rectitude her memory shall be his shield in the battle for the right. Sunshine at last—the blessed sunshine of a mother's love glimmering like a heaven-born flame even through the dread pall of death. Sunshine at last.

* * * * *

But alas, too late, too late!

HE WHO WAS HANGED.

Wasp, June 9, 1883, editorial:

A New York man has invented an electric chair for executing condemned criminals without pain, and many of our Eastern contemporaries are urging such a change in the law as will permit its adoption. It would be professional though not strictly civil to ascribe a selfish personal motive to the writers who clamor for painless execution. We will not be so unkind, though it does appear to our untutored mind a little singular that a man who does not expect to be hanged should so strenuously object to hanging, on the ground of its demoralizing effect on the spectator, while saying never a word about murder's demoralizing effect upon the witness. We certainly favor painless death, if death must be, but surely the first steps toward that desirable end should be taken by those who murder. If our assassins will consent ro [*sic*] employ nothing but the electric chair in their business it will be easy enough to persuade state legislatures to adopt it for the use of sheriffs in executing the death warrant. It is hoped that all murderers reading this suggestion will endeavor to give it practical effect by urging the advantages of the electric chair upon their fellow craftsmen. After the first four or five hundred painless murders have "thrown a pall of gloom upon the community" the people's softened mind will indubitably turn to thoughts of painless execution. For the punishment of a man like Wheeler, the strangler, the country would even now hail it with joy, as being infinitely less "demoralizing to the spectator" than a couch of roses and a diet of strawberries and cream.

Wasp, October 6, 1883. Short story, "Scar-Faced Jim," attributed to Jas. P. Slevin. A farcical account of an Indian's ill-fated attempt to murder two prospectors in their sleep, the story contains an element clearly related to "An Occurrence at Owl Creek Bridge," as the following brief excerpt reveals: "Oh, Heaven! lend thy aid to these doomed men. Will no guiding spirit awaken them and save their lives? One of them moves—he is awake!—no, he but dreams! Once more he is home. His wife and children greet him and welcome his safe return. Dream on—it will be your last vision of home!"

Wasp, November 28, 1885, "Prattle":

Affected with a great fatigue, Mr. Snyder, of Allentown, Pennsylvania, who wrought rock in a quarry, disposed his mortal part flatwise alongside a box of dynamite. [. . .] The dynamite thrilled through all its cartridges with a sense of reserved power, smiled and bided its time. Into the fancy of Mr. Snyder—for he slept—came a great wild dream. He thought there was no sun and no moon; the stars too were quenched and space was darkness all, wherein the huge earth wallowed with a brute satisfaction like a black whale in a sea of ink. Appeared then, away on the cold confines of the universe, a point of light which grew in magnitude and splendor year by year—no, for time was dead. Nearer and nearer, as he aged, came this baleful star, beaconing the universal night and luminating the vast sides of dead worlds bordering its course. [. . .] All things began to melt in the insufferable fervor, and the steaming dreamer screened his seared eyeballs with his arms. The shock!—what pen shall describe it? Shot from his footing by the monstrous impact, surrounded by earth's crushed and corruscating segments madly gyrating, Mr. Snyder thought his broken body was flying through unthinkable reaches of the fields of space. As in fact it was.

Examiner, September 4, 1887, "Prattle":

When a man is under sentence of death he has but one ambition left—to show his fellow creatures that he can "die like a man." To this hope he clings; it consoles and cheers him. In nine cases in ten he achieves it, passing through the valley of the shadow with an unfaltering step, a steady eye and a color unchanged. And then, poor devil, he is meanly denied the modest glory of the performance, by a dozen brainless boys who smirkingly describe him as visibly affected with such strong emotions as, in their unripe judgments, they deem "appropriate to the occasion." They say that at the first sight of the gallows he "faltered and shrank back;" that when he felt the rope about his neck "a sudden pallor overspread his features," and the rest of it. I never read a reporter's account of a hanging without feeling that the Sheriff got the rope around the wrong neck.

Examiner, January 7, 1888. "Almost Beheaded," news story, unsigned, apparently by Bierce: This article recounted at great length the execution of Nathan B. Sutton, in Oakland, California. According to the unnamed *Examiner* reporter's account, "The execution was a horrible sight, for, on account of the unusual length of the drop—eight feet—the throat of the unfortunate man was cut by the rope and the blood gushed forth in streams." After a paragraph describing Sutton's "remarkable coolness on the scaffold" and his "stoical indifference to his fate," and several paragraphs first describing Sutton's composition of his "farewell address" and then reprinting it, the *Examiner* reporter resumed narrating the execution moments before the drop, prefacing each paragraph of the story with an appropriate heading:

He Wanted the Necktie.

As Deputy Sheriff Woolsey took hold of the noose, Sutton grasped it in his right hand and pulled it towards him, smiling at Woolsey and saying at the same time, "Let me have the necktie;" but the Deputy shook his head and gently pulled the rope away from him. As the noose was passed around his neck he smiled again, and alluding to the straps with which his ankles were tightly bound, remarked: "I can't stand very well; these things are forcing me off my balance slightly. I left that collar off so as to give you a fair show, Mr. Woolsey." In the next moment the black cap was drawn over his face. Mr. Woolsey caught hold of the rope with his left hand at the doomed man's throat, and with his right pressing on the knot, slowly and steadily tightened the noose. Sutton moved his head as though to accommodate the motion of the rope, Woolsey stepped back, and at the same moment the trap fell and the body plunged downwards, the feet coming within six or eight inches of the ground.

A Horrible Sight.

Not a quiver of the body was perceived, and as the physicians were about to approach the blood gushed in torrents from Sutton's neck with a wheezy sound. The white shirtfront was instantly crimsoned, and the bright, red fluid was pumped over his shoulders down on his sleeves and rapidly formed a pool under the dead man's feet. Exclamations of horror arose from the spectators, and some of them were so much shocked that they rushed from the yard. The noose had cut the hanged man's throat, and the knot had slipped around to the back of his neck, raising the button of the cap and disclosing a strip of white flesh not more than three inches wide.

A Repulsive Exhibition.

Then occurred the most repulsive event of the execution. Drs. Woolsey, Crowley, Pratt, Simonton and Johnson stepped quickly forward.[3] Some of them felt at the wrists of the bleeding corpse while Dr. Woolsey raised the cap slightly and inserted his fingers into the wound. He removed several clots of blood and then proceeded to feel about in the gash until his fingers dripped blood. As he did so, a whispering whistling sound proceeded from the wound.

Said Dr. Woolsey to another physician who was feeling the right wrist of the corpse: "Put your finger in there," indicating some part in the inmost depths of the wound.

"There is some pulsation at his wrist yet," replied the physician addressed, as he complied with Dr. Woolsey's request.

In the mean time the Sheriff had ordered all the spectators, except the physicians and reporters, out of the yard.

The reporter's story ran for several more paragraphs, first addressing the haste shown in removing Sutton's body from the scaffold at Woolsey's announcement to the sheriff that Sutton's head was in danger of being torn off, and then including a cursory review of the coroner's inquest results. These remarks were followed by a review of the causes of the murder and a reprint of Sutton's diary entry that contained a detailed account of his actions. The reporter concluded his article with the news that Sutton's body, which Sutton himself had willed to the University of California's medical school, was not wanted because of the throat wound.

Examiner, July 29, 1888, "Prattle":

It is a fact having a cheerful significance that a brace of New York murderers sentenced to die by hanging, under the old law, have asked to be permitted to die by electricity, under the new. This appears to show that the reform is favored by the class to be reformed. Philanthropists and assassins have agreed upon a suitable punishment for the latter, it only remains to apply it to the former. If these two social powers hold a joint ratification meeting, let Mr. Elbridge Gerry take the electric chair.

There are valid objections to hanging, but it is observed that the strongest opposition has commonly come from those about to undergo it. It is probably as sure, painless and instantaneous as any other death, but it does not hit the imagination with so hard a horror as beheading—a method which more nearly than any other seems to fulfill all the requirements of the situation. Herein, as in most things, the logical mind of the Frenchman is in manifest superiority. The guillotine is an instrument of precision: it untops its rogue with a dextrous alacrity and without medical assistance. The physician with his needless ear and impertinent finger is unknown to it; the fact of its effectiveness is a corollary of the devolution of the pate. The precise moment of the victim's dissolution is unimportant; the termination of his mischievous activity dates from the moment when we make him two.

An advantage of decapitation is that it does not commend itself to devotees of the "rash act," whereas vast multitudes go to glory by way of the loopline. As to death by electricity, there can be no question of its popularity. It would long ago have superseded all other forms of suicide but that it requires some knowledge and a costly plant. Now that society has undertaken to administer it to all who qualify, it is not improbable that many of us will be summoned home from our business and homes to assist in the qualification. To secure a beautiful death, attended with all the comforts attainable by the skillful use of costly scientific apparatus, A will slaughter B with the first crude and unsuitable appliance that he can get his hands on. Clearly it is unfair for society to put B at this added disadvantage in a struggle for existence already beset with many obstacles to success. Execution by electricity should be the reward, not of hasty and perhaps unjust assassination, but of a long and blameless life devoted to the service of every high and noble aim.

Examiner, September 16, 1888, "Prattle." Opening this column by describing the scene where the condemned man's mother was watched over by six "deputy sheriffs, solicitous to prevent the old lady from passing poison from her mouth into his while kissing him," Bierce observed that "a more disagreeable exhibition of savage idiocy was never seen." Commenting that such a final embrace "which had to be hedged about with so indecent precautions should have been forbidden," Bierce asked next "what single incident of this whole Goldenson business (save only the cracking of the blackguard's neck) should *not* have been forbidden?":

This miserable "death-watch" custom should be abolished forthwith. That a man standing upon the very foreslope of eternity, his spiritual senses filled with the stir and murmur of its mysteries, its whispering silences and invisible glooms; his soul already half disembarrassed of its mortality for the awful venture—that a human being so solemnly circumstanced should be denied the boon of solitude and subjected to the cruel scrutiny of sleepless eyes and the fierce publicity of light unceasing, lest he step across the disparting [*sic*] line over which it is desired to push him—this is an outrage peculiarly barbarous and characteristic.
[. . .]

Dead Goldenson! Well, Heaven forbid
   That I should smile above him;
Though, truth to tell, I never did
   Exactly love him.

It can't be wrong, though, to rejoice
    That his unpleasing capers[4]
Are ended. Silent is his voice
    In all the papers.
No longer he's a show; no more,
    Bear-like, his den he's walking.
No longer can he hold the floor
    When I'd be talking.
The laws that govern jails are bad
    If such displays are lawful.
The fate of the assassin's sad,
    But ours is awful!
What! shall a wretch condemned to die
    In shame upon the gibbet
Be set before the public eye
    As an "exhibit"?—
His looks, his actions noted down,
    His words if light or solemn,
And all this hawked about the town—
    So much a column?
The press, of course, will publish news
    However it may get it,
But blast the Sheriff who'll abuse
    His powers to let it!
Nay, this is not ingratitude:
    I'm no reporter, truly,
Nor yet an editor. I'm rude
    Because unruly—
Because I burn with shame and rage
    Beyond my power of telling
To see assassins in a cage
    And keepers yelling.
"Walk up! Walk up!" the showman cries:
    "Observe the lion's poses,
His stormy mane, his fiery eyes,
    His—hold your noses!"
How long, O Lord, shall Law and Right
    Be mocked for gain or glory,
And angels weep as they recite
    The shameful story?
[. . .]

At the Goldenson hanging two physicians performed the customary "last sad rite" of eaves-dropping at the dying man's chest and monkeying with his pulse. Dr. Blach mounted a step-ladder, fingered the wrist and pitched the tent of his ear on the pectoral camping ground. Dr. Carpenter, standing below, unlaced the shoes and manipulated the ankles. And so, watch in hand, pride in heart and nothing in head, these twin relics showed themselves off to the worst advantage, keenly attentive to their own symptoms and conspicuously un-hanged. To what decent purpose? It is already known that in execution by hanging the pulse can be counted till the man is dead, and then it cannot. It is known that in no case can death ensue, in the medical sense, in much less than a quarter of an hour. What the devil would they be at with their earing and fingering before the late lamenting [sic] has had time to look about him, feel his ground and take in the situation? Is there not time enough to wait? What public interest would suffer if the worms'-meat should hang a needless five minutes? Bah! the doctor at a hanging wants to be a part of the performance. He wants the corpse to share its distinction with him. He craves the silent applause of the average man, who inly burns with admiration of the courage which is not afraid of a dead body. It is vanity all—vanity in its meanest form. I have had the happiness to see many of my fellow men hanged, though not enough of them, but I never yet saw a medico trying to stuff one of them, kicking, into his ear without feeling that the rope had got about the neck of the wrong man.

Examiner, December 1, 1888, excerpt from "Died Like a Coward." This un-signed news story, despite its claim that the drop killed the victim "instantly," graphically illustrated Bierce's claim about the length of time it took a hanged man to die. Describing the previous day's hanging in Placerville, California, of John Harry Meyer, one of three convicted murderers of John Lowell, a Sacramento man, the article reveals that Meyer, unlike Sutton, was not par-ticularly comfortable with his fate. In fact, several of Bierce's observations about such affairs were covered by this story. For example, the article ex-plains that Meyer had apparently attempted to cheat the hangman by over-dosing on a narcotic and was only with difficulty roused from his last night's slumber, claiming, fruitlessly, that he was too ill to be executed. In addition, while the sheriff had issued "some 300 invitations," according to the *Exam-iner* article "five times that number of people saw the punishment meted out, including a large number of women, boys, and even children of tender years, who pre-empted positions on the roofs, sheds and sides overlooking the new jail yard." Picking up the thread of the story more than a column into the description of Meyer's conduct, we find Meyer on the scaffold:

Struggling against the Death-Coil.

Meyer's bellowing was fairly frantic, and he attempted to twist his head out of the way of the fatal coil. The muscles refused to obey his behest, however, and the movement only resulted in the head lolling helplessly on his breast. The rope was thrown off and Napier had to make a second attempt. This time it was successful.

Meyer's sobs and groans grew a shade fainter, and a second later the black cap was drawn on and helped much to muffle them. His sobs came through the cloth in hoarse gurgles, and it was not until Napier drew the noose tight under his ear that they ceased.

There was a second or two of silence, but the convulsive heaves of the black-hooded figure showed that the murderer was still crying, though his sobs were choked back into his breast by the rope.

Meyer's knees were all right now, strange to say, and a steadying hand was all he required from the two men whose united strength was necessary to hold him up a moment before.

Down through the Trap.

Napier stepped off the trap and raised his signal to Winchell. Winchell released the lever holding the bolts supporting the trap, and the legal tragedy was over. The seven-foot drop killed Meyer instantly, dislocating his neck between the first and second cervical vertebræ, and there was not a struggle or a twitch to indicate that death was painful or agonizing. The body fell with a whirl that jerked the knot around from under the left to the right ear, and in its travels it tore the flesh from the lower part of the face and uplifted the right corner of the lower jaw so as to distort the mouth into a diagonal position. Some bloody froth and bubbles oozed from the rapidly purpling lips and a few drops of red fluid came from the chin, which was torn and cut by the rope's friction in shifting.

Noting the Pulse Beats.

Meyer's pulse beat 60 the first minute of suspension and 104 in the third. In the seventh it was down to 36, and then showed only an occasional beat until the thirteenth minute, during which there was a final pulse beat. Efforts at respiration ceased in the fourth minute, an unusually long time, and then faint muscular twitchings kept up at the rate of two or three a minute until the body had been hanging sixteen minutes. ("Died Like a Coward")

Examiner, August 7, 1890, excerpt from "How Kemmler Died." This news story recounted at length the execution of William Kemmler, a convicted murderer, in New York. It was the first execution by electricity in the world and the *Examiner* had been following Kemmler's story for months:

THE FATAL SHOCK.

The Warden turned and nodded his head to some one who stood in the secret room at the fatal switch. There was a quick convulsive start of the bound figure in the chair, a little squeaking sound of straining straps. The breathless watchers stood with every sense bent upon the motionless wretch bound head, hand and foot, and no sound, save the bird songs in the bright sunshine outside the window.

The bar of a heavy shade at one window was lifted by the straying breeze and fell back against the bars. The noise was slight, but to the tense and breathless watchers in the basement death chamber it seemed equal to the sound of clashing arms. Dr. Spitzka and Dr. Shady, drawn by deep interest almost unconsciously from their positions, moved on tip-toe to places by the chair. But all was still and no man spoke. Every faculty was contributing to that of vision.

Such a scene there was never on earth before. No man ever before had died thus by the deliberate purpose of his fellow man. After that convulsive start that marked the stroke of lighting [*sic*] upon Kemmler, there was no movement of muscle or twitch of nerve. The features, from the bridge of the nose to the chin, seemed to have been pursed up to those of one facing a sleetly storm, or of one breasting a powerful dust-bearing wind.

HOW DEATH CAME.

But was it death? Who should say? The law demanded that the current of electricity should be the [*sic*] sustained against his vitals until death should come, but who should tell when death had come?

The men of science believed that then the nerve-centers were being beaten as with heavy hammers in different directions at the rate of some 230 times each second. Their books, though they told of no case like this, led them to believe that the silent forces working in this man's body were disintegrating the nerve-cells, the tissues and the blood, too, by the divorce of oxygen from its corpuscles. They thought the blood was becoming, by mechanical or chemical change, fluidized and useless to sustain life, and so they watched and listened in the silent room, five————ten————fifteen————seventeen seconds.

"There, that's enough. Take off the current," said the Warden's chosen physicians—MacDonald and Spitzka—and the Warden passed the word within the adjoining room, where some one had let on the current and where the same some one cut it off. Then spoke the doctors:

Observing the Effect.

"Observe the lividity about the base of the nose and the entire nose itself. Note where the mask rests on the nose, the white appearance there." Thus spoke Dr. Spitzka, and other doctors came about and dented the flesh with their fingers and watched the play of white and red upon withdrawal. They saw an abrasion upon the right thumb. In that supreme shock the murderer's fist had become so clenched in the convulsion that the nail of the forefinger had dug into the base of the thumb.

Meantime, a button pressed in the secret room had signaled the stopping of the dynamo.

The happiest of all in the room was Dr. Southwick of Buffalo, the father of electricizing in capital cases and who has been studying and working upon the subject since 1881.

"There!" he exclaimed, as he strode away from the chair to a knot of witnesses at the other end of the room, "there is the culmination of ten years' work and study. We live in a higher civilization from this day."

But even while he spoke a quick, sharp cry went up from those yet closely watching about the silent figure in the chair. There had been a movement in the breast of the man whom all believed had died one minute and forty-seven seconds before. Soon there was another movement, accompanied by a sudden gasp, and then the breast began to heave with long, deep, stertorous respirations.

He Was Not Dead.

"Start the current, start the current again," shouted Dr. Spitzka.

All crowded about the chair and watched the laboring wretch, whose breast, despite the broad, tight bands about him, was rising and falling with strong force. Slightly foamy saliva was exuded from the mouth. The entire body racked [sic] in the efforts of the organs to resume their functions, and deep fear fell upon some lest consciousness should return.

The doctors declared, however, that the man was beyond consciousness, and some thought the action which startled all and sent the Warden away with a white face to order the current renewed, was only a reflex muscular action. Not so. One physician declared he would stake his name that he could bring Kemmler back to conscious life with brandy hypodermics. Meantime one of the witnesses, G. G. Bain of Washington, D.C., had fainted, and lay upon a bench where he was being fanned. This spectacle was continued from 6:45 until 6:47 o'clock; then there came again to the figure in the chair another shock under which the straps were strained again.

THE LUNGS FILLED AGAIN.

The lungs, however, filled again, and again, while the current was pouring through the unconscious body. At 6:51 another groan of dismay was heard near the chair, and smoke was observed curling up from Kemmler's back.

"He's burning," shouted one.

"Cut off the current," cried another.

"He's dead. There is no use keeping up the current longer," said some one else.

Again the Warden gave the signal to open the switch, and the body in the chair, surcharged with four distinct shocks that had been given it, developed no further movement.

Examiner, August 10, 1890, "Prattle":

It is not, I think, held by anybody that the late Mr. Kemmler is not dead enough: it is merely urged that he was not made dead quickly enough. That is to say, he was made dead so slowly that those who had the advantage of looking on could observe the various stages of the operation. Inasmuch as they were not compelled to experience them, I fail to apprehend the force of the objection. True, one of them is said to have incurred a cat-fit, but that probably did him no permanent injury, and the incident has no further significance than to emphasize the Warden's lack of judgment in selection of competent persons to witness the proceedings. Men have been known to faint at hangings—men who were not themselves in immediate peril of being hanged. There is nothing to show that Kemmler himself knew and felt that he was being made dead. Even if he did, the sense of discomfort could hardly have been so keen as that experienced by the late wife of his bosom when chopped in pieces with a dull hatchet. Possibly that is not a legitimate consideration. I am brute enough to feel that it is. In the adoption of comfortable methods of killing people I think the first step should be taken by those who murder.

Ought we, then, to revert to the discredited practices of our ancestors, who in some degree marked their sense of a criminal's desert by grading his pain to his offense, hanging the greater offender and burning at the stake his accomplice? (Women, too, were mercifully accorded what was considered the softer penalty of the fagot and the stake.) Should we restore physical torture to its old place in penology? I think not. At the same time, I find no ground of doubt that physical torment had a distinctly deterrent effect upon criminals. That the offense of "coining" (which was treason) was committed with a less light-hearted alacrity when, one hundred years ago, it was punished in England by roasting than at that time it would have been if the penalty had been imprisonment seems to me a proposition having a basis in the nature of things. When poisoners were boiled, as they were under a law of Henry VII, persons contemplating that sin had the advantage of a more powerful dissuadent than was given to Mrs. Maybrick. No doubt there was more crime in the old days than there is now. There were a denser ignorance, a keener poverty, a bitterer political discontent. The people—the "common people"—were a hard and heady lot: modern rosewater treatment would have fired them with inextinguishable laughter; to the preaching of your humane penologist they would have responded with yawps of derision and flung him a dead cat in the face, relieving him the while of trinkelage and habiliments. I do not say that he deserves anything of that now: the progress in public morality which has made him possible is in some sort his justification. But in his mad advocacy of dainty deaths for assassins he is going too fast and too far.

The ideal punishment for murder would inflict upon the murderer the exact amount of suffering which he inflicted upon his victim. That would be a powerful and intelligible incentive on the side of moderation. It would restrain many an assassin's fury and secure to his victim a gentler pang. The only objection to it is that it is impracticable. On the one hand, the victim's suffering cannot be calculated, nor, on the other, duplicated. For many reasons it is not desirable to make the death penalty more painful than it is, though its painfulness might with great advantage be shared by a vastly greater number of persons; but there is neither sense nor goodness in making the felon's end easy and honorable. None are so cruel as the merciful. They are "blessed," no doubt, for Christ has said so; but if they had a little world all to themselves to be blessed in, the rest of us would be safer in this. The baffling of their pernicious activity by the bungling of the Kemmler's executioners is a phenomenon which should be regarded with hope and satisfaction. That the distinguished widower perished miserably with a troupe of hot-footed pangs wire-walking his nerves and frolicking in the convolutions of his brain we are not permitted to know, but enough occurred to affect the intending murderer with a wholesome distaste of the electrical chair: like Guatimozin's coals, it is not a bed of roses—at least not obviously.[5] One feature of the affair I cannot conscientiously commend: as Mr. Kemmler (already dead) was not to be eaten, there was no real necessity for cooking him.

So dies, and so ought to die, this mischievous and ridiculous attempt to popularize capital punishment. It only remains to chuck Mr. Elbridge Gerry and his interminable tail of sugar-hearted cranks out of the temple of justice and throw their apparatus after them. Let us confess that they meant well, and not suffer them to mean well any more. If hanging is not good enough for them, let them go where it is not in fashion; it is good enough for the rest of us. We know that an essential element of its deterrent character is the possibility that it hurts like fun. Let him who thinks that this is not an important consideration in the mind of the rising young assassin ask himself whether it would not be an important consideration in his own. Let him fancy himself balancing the advantages and disadvantages of removing a needless neighbor—an engaging intellectual exercise. It is plain that his liability to physical torment at the hands of the public executioner would cut a figure in the problem. On the question of penal euthanasia the practicing cacanthrophile may confidently count upon a solid vote from the delegation of assassins. They are with him, to a scoundrel. By their leave, though, I venture to challenge the wisdom of doing anything to dissuade the unfortunate from the rocky road of suicide and enable them to reach the same goal by the flowery path of murder.

3. "Chickamauga." First published in the *Examiner* on January 20, 1889.

Wasp, January 23, 1886, "Prattle":

These battle yarns, indeed, are nursing a bably [*sic*] war, which now lies mouthing its fat knuckles and marking time with its pinky feet, in a cradle of young imaginations, but in another decade it will be striding through the land in seven-league boots, chewing soap.[6] Every generation must have its war; that is a law of nature; but if the younkers who are now tucking out their mental skins with the gingery comestible supplied by old soldiers do not kick up a shindy compared with which the late war was a season of religious tranquility you may have my share of the national debt.

Examiner, January 27, 1889, "Prattle":

Having found Samoa on the map and read something that was said about it in one of the newspapers the other day, I am ready to reply to the correspondent who asked me last week for my opinion on Samoan affairs. In the first place, I think the German Government is acting like a hog; not a wild boar, like the savage beast of the *Iliad*, which "harvests ravaged and great forests tore," and which Meleager stretched upon the plain—just an ordinary, plain, everyday hog. The essential hoggishness—or, as one may say, porcinity—of the Bismarckian policy in Samoa is, I take it, conceded by all: there remains, upon which to differ, the question only of what should be done about it. As to that let each be governed by his estimate of his power: *I* am going to stand it. I am not upon the warpath: there isn't any fight in me at all. If Bismarck wants Samoa he may have it, so far as I am concerned, with as many leagues of its enclosing sea as he may take a fancy to. I will throw into the bargain Hawaii and any other outlying regions where Americans have "interests." He can have them all and an indemnity for the trouble of accepting them if he wants it. I should be sorry to part with them. I am sorry he wants Samoa—sorry he prefers to act like a hog. But I respect his preference. The officers of the United States Navy say that in a contest with the German Navy they would not have the ghost of a chance. That is enough for me to know: that settles it. The question of right and wrong cuts no figure. When not heeled I give in. Writers who are better prepared for war may throw up their hats if they feel that way, but I throw up my hands. Don't shoot!

The most competent military authority states that a second-class German warship can lie outside the Heads and with a single Krupp gun working leisurely destroy more property in twenty-four hours than the entire value of Samoa. The loss, I am informed, would fall upon the just and the unjust—alike upon the patriot who with tongue and pen defended his country's rights, and the cowardly-traitor who, like me, was base enough to want to wait for better weapons. It seems needless to incur the loss of the islands and the city too. If we can save San Francisco by giving up Apia, and our reputation for common sense by giving up our "honor," that is the kind of a bargain that I am looking for; and if Bismarck will throw in New York, Boston, Philadelphia, Baltimore and Washington, or any one of them, I shall think it mighty good of him. I don't know why he has not burned them all to bed-rock long ago.

Bierce concluded his lesson in two final paragraphs where he dismissed the likelihood that England would "stand in with us" and criticized the saber rattlings of one midwestern politician and an assortment of the usual suspects in the local press before concluding that if war did come he would head for the safety of the hills to escape the shelling.

Examiner, February 3, 1889, "Prattle":

Study the history and literature of any vanquished people immediately before the war in which they were humbled and you will find that they held the strongest possible convictions of their invincibility. You will find that they grossly overstated their military resources and absurdly magnified their national prowess in the use of arms; that they relied with eager faith upon the most fanciful and extravagant statements concerning the disadvantages of the enemy, and flattered themselves with dreams of alliances between themselves and existing conditions, which eventually proved to be unfavorable or without effect upon the struggle. It almost seems as if defeat in war were a divinely appointed punishment for national conceit; so certainly is the stroke preceded by the boast.

[. . .]Who of us belonging to that elder generation which saw the Civil War has forgotten the confidence of the South in its ability to conquer twice its strength? Was not one Southron equal to ten Yankees? Would not the Northern Democrats make common cause with their Southern copartisans? Would England tolerate a blockade which would deprive her of cotton? Would the commercial-minded populations of Northern cities consent not only to be deprived of their Southern trade, but to pay extraordinary war taxes? Could not the seceding States build a more powerful navy than the Federal Government had, and was it not easy to defend the ports and rivers by torpedoes, without any ships at all? Had not the South a fertile soil, a clear sky, a climate genial to the native but deadly to the invader, and, above all, a martial and chivalric spirit? These are but a few of what that brave but infatuated people considered as decisive advantages; and when raised in solemn warning, the voice of reason was unheeded. The Southern patriot who, by presenting the most obvious truths and deducing the most natural inferences, endeavored to calm the storms of passion and spare his section the humiliation of inevitable defeat was hissed as a fool and silenced as a traitor. Even after the war, when from the wreck and ruin he raised his feeble "I told you so," he was execrated as an author of the doom which he had vainly endeavored to avert.

[...]

A nation is like an individual: when angry it is blind to the plainest considerations and most conspicuous facts. It forgets the values and relations of things; its whole intellectual world is suffused with a false light. The wildest and maddest fancies find acceptance, the soberest dictates of common sense are ignored. It is against this condition of things that the American people should be warned. They are angry with the German Government. Accepting as true the statements of this journal's correspondent—which I am bound to do— they appear to have good cause, though it is to be regretted that the quarrel should have been brought about by our abandonment of the wise policy of our fathers by extension of our "interests" in distant lands, by entrance into "entangling alliances" and precarious international "understandings" promising a problematical profit for an indubitable peril. It seems likely that we shall bitterly rue the day that we first heard of Samoa and its brutal savages who chop off the heads of their wounded enemies and drink one another's spittle.

[...]

I venture to admonish you, my countrymen, that you are going too fast. You are listening to war-talk from people who do not themselves mean to fight. You are believing assertions of our invincibility from men and journals who have heretofore taught you that we were at the mercy of any fourth-rate power that chose to make war upon us. You rely upon shadows and dreams no more substantial than the shadows and dreams that "fired the Southern heart" and lured France into a hopeless contest without a grievance. We have a grievance, apparently, but it is not true in military affairs that he is thrice armed who has a just quarrel. The justice of the quarrel makes no difference. Granting the justice of ours, whether war with Germany is desirable or not depends on our chance of winning. We have no chance of winning. Such a war will necessarily be fought upon the ocean, and despite the vaporings of such swashbucklers as Commander Leary and his O how gallant midshipmen it remains true, and every brave and sober-minded naval officer knows it is true, that the German navy can destroy ours in six months, or drive it off the high seas and herd it in neutral harbors. Our old ships are worthless, armed with worthless guns. Our new ones are incomplete and untried; to every one of them Germany has three superior ones, armed with guns of greater range and precision. Her ships are the swifter, and in a naval engagement the swifter ship chooses the distance. We are told that Germany, menaced at home, cannot send her great ships to fight ours. Another dream: German ports are not menaced, and are impregnably fortified. There is no prospect of a European war, nor has there been for ten years, outside the dispatches of press correspondents. Germany will send her great warships to sink ours and bombard our ports. The air along our seaboard will be full of iron!

Iron is tonic; it does a nation good sometimes. Heaven forbid that I should be affected by the grandmotherly doctrines of the Peace Society! I honestly think that the fat and fatuous prosperity of this country might advantageously be broken by a good, righteous foreign war to renew our manhood. But I want an even chance to win. To fight without hope of success is not soldierly; it is the act of a fool. A general who should bring on a decisive engagement with all the advantages on the side of the enemy would be dismissed, and should be shot. We are apparently endeavoring to force Secretary Bayard to commit the criminal folly of making war unprepared. It is time for somebody to speak a good word for him. He is sacrificing himself for his country. May he have the strength to endure.

It has all at once been discovered that San Francisco and our other seaboard cities are in no danger of bombardment. For a score of years their danger has not before been questioned; it has been used, and rightly used, by every American who has written or spoken on the subject, to damn successive Congresses for not providing means of national defense. But now, presto! all is changed; bombardment of cities is "contrary to the laws of war!" It is not contrary to the laws of war; it is customary, and no neutral nation intervenes with anything more than a perfunctory consular protest. We must count upon bombardment: we shall have shells, and enough of them. Thank Heaven, they are not as fiery, nor as loud, nor as hollow as the editors and politicians on our side!

If I were dictator and Bismarck wanted Samoa he would not need to ask for it but once. If he would not protect American interests there I would fetch away all the Americans and compensate them out of the national treasury. If he did not wish us to have the harbor of Pago Pago I would tell him we were about to give it up anyhow. But for every unjust demand that he made I would fortify a seaport. For every injury to this country I would lay the keels of a dozen war-ships. For every insult to the American flag I would establish a cannon foundry. And some fine morning early in the twentieth century I would put commander Leary on the retired list, hand the German Minister at Washington his passports, start a fleet from San Francisco, capture and annex Samoa, and drive every German subject off its islands. That is about my notion of a "statesmanlike policy" suitable to the present "crisis." The hither end of it does not show very brilliantly, I confess, but in the grand *finale* there would be some pretty lurid effects, sufficiently startling and picturesque to gratify such of the fiery patriots of to-day as might not by that time be utterly consumed by the fervency of their own courage.

Examiner, April 24, 1898, excerpts from autobiographical essay "Chickamauga" or "A Little of Chickamauga," not present in *Collected Works* version. The opening paragraph:

In choosing the Chickamauga National Park as a point of rendesvous [*sic*] for the army the Washington authorities probably had in mind only strategic considerations; yet the place can hardly fail to speak to the hearts of our soldiers in a most impressive way. On that historic ground occurred the fiercest and bloodiest of all the great conflicts of modern times—a conflict in which skill, valor, accident and fate played each its important part, the resultant a tactical victory for one side, a strategical one for the other. At the end of two days of tremendous fighting the Federal force retired from the field to the position at Chattanooga, which it had been the purpose of the campaign to gain and hold.

And the concluding paragraph:

To those of us who have survived the attacks of both Bragg and Time, and who keep in memory the dear dead comrades whom we left upon that fateful field, the place means much. May it mean something less to the younger men whose tents are now pitched where, with bended heads and clasped hands, God's great angels stood invisible among the heroes in blue and the heroes in gray sleeping their last sleep in the woods of Chickamauga.

4. "A Son of the Gods." First published in the *Examiner* on July 29, 1888.

Excerpt from "What I Saw of Shiloh." Included in volume 1 of Bierce's *Collected Works,* this essay had appeared in the *Wasp* in two installments, on December 23 and 30, 1881, and was subsequently reprinted in the *Examiner* on June 19 and 26, 1898:

It was plain that the enemy had retreated to Corinth. The arrival of our fresh troops, and their successful passage of the river had disheartened him. Three or four of his gray cavalry vedettes moving amongst the trees on the crest of a hill in our front, and galloping out of sight at the crack of our skirmishers' rifles, confirmed us in the belief; an army face to face with its enemy does not employ cavalry to watch its front. True, they may have been a general and his staff. Crowning this rise, we found a level field, a quarter of a mile in width; beyond it a gentle acclivity, covered with an undergrowth of young oaks, impervious to sight. We pushed on into the open, but the division halted at the edge. Having orders to conform to its movements, we halted too; but that did not suit; we received an intimation to proceed. I had seen this sort of ground before, and in the exercise of my discretion I deployed my platoon, pushing it forward at a run, with trailed arms, to strengthen the skirmish line, which I overtook some thirty or forty yards from the wood. Then—I can't describe it—the forest seemed all at once to flame up and disappear with a crash like that of a great wave upon the beach—a crash that expired in hot hissings, and the sickening "spat" of lead smashing into meat. A dozen of my brave fellows tumbled over like ten-pins. Some struggled to their feet, only to go down again, and yet again. Those who stood fired into the smoking brush and doggedly retired. We had expected to find, at most, a line of skirmishers similar to our own; it was with a view to overcoming them by a sudden *coup* at the moment of collision that I had thrown forward my little reserve. What we had found was a line of battle, coolly holding its fire till it could count our teeth. There was no more to be done but get back across the open ground, every superficial yard of which was throwing up its little jet of mud provoked by an impinging bullet. The field looked, indeed, something like one of those sluggish sputtering levels that lie below the steam of a crater. We got back, most of us, and I shall never forget the ludicrous incident of a young officer who had taken part in the affair walking up to his colonel, who had been a calm and impartial spectator, and gravely reporting: "The enemy is in force just beyond this field, sir."[7]

Wasp, July 14, 1883, "Prattle":

A line in last Tuesday's dispatches, to the effect that a French colony in Senegal has been attacked by typhus fever, recalls an incident of the civil war. After the battle of Nashville I happened to be serving on the staff of the illustrious General Sam Beatty, of Ohio. His command was at one time greatly scattered in pursuit of the enemy, who retired sullenly, and one brigade of it held a peculiarly exposed position some ten miles from General Sam's headquarters. There was a telegraph, however, and one day the commander of this brigade sent the general a dispatch which read thus: "Please relieve me; I am suffering from an attack of General Debility." "The ablest cavalry officer in the Confederate army," said my honored chief, showing me the telegram. "I served under him in Mexico." And he promptly prescribed three regiments of infantry and a battery of Rodman guns.

I was directed to pilot that expedition to the scene of the disaster to our arms. I never felt so brave in all my life. I rode a hundred yards in advance, prepared to expostulate single-handed with the victorious enemy at whatever point I might encounter him. I dashed forward through every open space into every suspicious looking wood and spurred to the crest of every hill, exposing myself recklessly to draw the Confederates' fire and disclose their position. I told the commander of the relief column that he need not throw out any advance guard as a precaution against an ambuscade—I would myself act in that perilous capacity, and by driving in the rebel skirmishers gain time for him to form his line of battle in case I should not be numerically strong enough to scoop up the entire opposition at one wild dash. I begged him, however, to recover my body if I fell.

There was no fighting: the forces of General Debility had conquered nobody but the brigade commander—his troops were holding their ground nobly, reading dime novels and playing draw poker pending the arrival of our succoring command. The official reports of this affair explained, a little obscurely, that there had been a misunderstanding; but my unusual gallantry elicited the highest commendation in general orders, and will never, I trust, be forgotten by a grateful country.

Wasp, October 31, 1885, "Prattle":

A man runs away from a death which we assume he ought to face. That is cowardice. A man deliberately embraces a death which we assume he ought to avoid. That is cowardice too. Between these two extremes lie deeds countless in number and infinite in kind, having relation to the danger of death. All must be cowardly, for in each the predominating motive allies it to one extreme or the other. *Ergo*, we all are cowards. Admirable conclusion, not altogether false.

Examiner, excerpt from "The Crime at Pickett's Mill," May 27, 1888. In this war essay Bierce describes the heroic actions of the brigade commanded by William B. Hazen, his commanding officer, in a particularly bloody engagement that took place in Georgia on May 27, 1864. Hazen's single brigade was sent out to engage the entire Confederate army under General Johnston:

It is seldom, indeed, that a subordinate officer knows anything about the disposition of the enemy's forces—except that it is unamiable—or precisely whom he is fighting. As for the rank and file they can know nothing more of the matter than the arms they carry.

Bierce's description of the brigade's advance reveals that on this particular occasion he was, as a subordinate officer, in a position to observe the disposition of the enemy's forces—and his own:

> We moved forward. In less than one minute the trim battalions had become simply a swarm of men struggling through the undergrowth of the forest, pushing and crowding. The front was irregularly serrated, the strongest and bravest in advance, the others following in fan-like formations, variable and inconstant, ever defining themselves anew. Our course for the first two hundred yards lay along the left bank of a small creek in a deep ravine, our left battalions sweeping along its steep slope. Then we came to the fork of the ravine. A part of us crossed below, the rest above, passing over both branches, the regiments inextricably intermingled rendering all military formation impossible. The color-bearers kept well to the front with their flags, closely furled, aslant backward over their shoulders. Displayed, they would have been torn to rags by the limbs of the trees. Horses were all sent to the rear; the General and staff and all the field officers toiled along on foot as best they could. "We shall halt and form when we get out of this," said an aid-de-camp [*sic*].[8]
>
> Suddenly there was a horrible ringing rattle of musketry, the familiar hissing of bullets, and before us, through the interspaces of the forest, all was blue with smoke. Hoarse fierce yells broke out of a thousand throats. The forward fringe of brave and hardy assailants was arrested in its mutable extensions; the edge of our swarm grew dense and clearly defined as the foremost halted, and the rest pressed forward to align themselves beside them, all firing. The uproar was deafening; the air was sibilant with streams and sheets of missiles. In the steady, unvarying roar of small-arms the frequent shock of the cannon was rather felt than heard, but the gusts of grape which they blew into that populous wood were audible enough, screaming among the trees and cracking against their stems and branches. We had, of course, no cannon to reply.
>
> Our brave color-bearers were now all in the forefront of battle in the open. They held their colors erect, shook out their glories, waved them forward and back to keep them spread, for there was no wind. From where I stood, at the right of the line—we had "halted and formed," indeed—I could see six at one time. Occasionally one would go down, only to be instantly raised again by other hands.

Bierce breaks off his personal narrative at this point to quote from General Johnston's narrative of the event:

> The fire is, of course, as deadly at twenty paces as at fifteen; at fifteen as at ten. Nevertheless, there is the "dead-line," with its well-defined edge of corpses—those of the bravest. Where both lines are fighting in the open without cover—as in a charge met by a counter-charge—each has its "dead-line," and between the two is a clear space—neutral ground, devoid of dead, for the living cannot reach it to fall there.

At Pickett's Mill the dead-line developed as Bierce watched:

> I observed this phenomenon at Pickett's Mills [*sic*]. Standing at the right of the line I had an unobstructed view of the narrow, open space across which the two lines fought. It was dim with smoke, but not greatly obscured: the smoke rose and spread in sheets among the branches of the trees. Most of our men fought prone upon the ground, many of them behind trees, stones and whatever cover they could get, but there were considerable groups that stood. Occasionally one of these groups, which had endured the storm of missiles for minutes without perceptible reduction, would push forward, moved by a common despair, and wholly detach itself from the line. In a second every man of the group would be down. There had been no visible movement of the enemy, no audible change in the awful, even roar of the firing—yet all were down. Frequently the dim figure of an individual soldier would be seen to spring away from his comrades, advancing alone into that fateful interspace, with leveled bayonet. He got no farther than the farthest of his predecessors. Of the "hundreds of corpses within twenty paces of the Confederate line," [Bierce is quoting here from General Johnston's report] I venture to say that a third were within fifteen paces, and not one within ten.

5. "One of the Missing." First published in the *Examiner* on March 11, 1888.

Examiner, June 26, 1898, "War Topics" (Bierce's column during the Spanish-American War):

> In order to persuade me of my unworth in having asserted that army Chaplains are not enamored of the battlefield some good Christian sends me a copy of a monthly publication called "U.S. Soldier"—a title which seems to attest a type-famine. An article in this pious periodical begins thus:
> "Chaplains in our army and navy always have had the incorrigible habit of keeping anywhere but in the rear. They have been the first on the field of battle

and the last to leave. A dozen Chaplains in the army gave up their lives, not by reason [*sic*] of being hit [*sic*] by chance shots, but in actual hand-to-hand fighting."

Merely remarking that nobody ever was "hit" by a chance shot, though many persons have been struck by them, I will proceed with the case of army Chaplains; for obviously those of the navy could not go to "the rear" without swimming. The writer says a dozen were killed, though he is able to name only ten. But is not a dozen a rather small number if they were really addicted to hand-to-hand fighting? Every regiment had one Chaplain, as it had one Colonel. How many regiments there were I have not the statistics by me to show; there were many hundreds—several thousands. And how many Colonels were killed in battle? That I cannot say either, but I can name off-hand more than a dozen whom I personally knew. I knew as many Chaplains as Colonels, but not one of them ever was struck even by a spent bullet.

Nearly every army corps had its "fighting parson," but not nearly as many of them were killed as might have been with distinct advantage to the service and to religion. The "fighting parson" was commonly a famous raconteur of the campfire, his own deeds being his sweetest theme. He usually had a beautiful, hair-triggered squirrel rifle and was partial to scouting, the "deeds" being performed in solitude beyond the outposts; on the battlefield he was indiscernible.

6. "Killed at Resaca." First published in the *Examiner* on June 5, 1887.

Wasp, December 26, 1885, "Prattle." "In all this world of sycophants I know no stupider sycophant than the man who is always abasing himself before [women], and actually believes them half divine."

Wasp, January 9, 1886, "Prattle." Bierce's pronouncement on the "warpapers" then being triumphantly published by *Century* magazine: "hardly one has been free from lying."

Wasp, January 23, 1886, "Prattle." Bierce railed against the proliferation of the market in old soldiers noting "its growth threatens to swallow up every other industry in the country" and adding of the old soldiers themselves that "most of them talk pretty well, and many didn't fight." Bierce then went on to forecast the imminent arrival of the next war:

These battle yarns, indeed, are nursing a bably [*sic*] war, which now lies mouthing its fat knuckles and marking time with its pinky feet, in a cradle of young imaginations, but in another decade it will be striding through the land in seven-league boots, chewing soap. Every generation must have its war; that is a law of nature; but if the younkers who are now tucking out their mental skins with the gingery comestible supplied by old soldiers do not kick up a shindy compared with which the late war was a season of religious tranquility you may have my share of the national debt.

Wasp, February 20, 1886, "Prattle." Writing about the looming gathering of Grand Army veterans which was to be held in San Francisco that August, Bierce envisioned a grim reality: "the period of their 'encampment' in San Francisco next August will be made hideous and odious by a cataclysm of bosh unthinkable and fudge lacking an end." Continuing in the same speculative vein, Bierce fleshed out his fears concerning the approaching reunion:

> The mortifying memory of her indiscretion with the "Knights Templar" may possibly save San Francisco from another scandal of similar magnitude,[9] but the giddy old girl will indubitably go again astray, to repent in burlaps and ashes; her local veterans themselves blushing through their scars for their part in the escapade. The reunion of the gallant old lads of the battle period is a subject that lends itself with fatal facility to the horrible purposes of the infestive sentimentaler, who will wreak himself upon it in the language of the heart a hundred and fifty ways, deboweling the mind of him to its ultimate intestine; for when afflict with a right entuzimuzy, your true sentimentaler will expose his in'ards with all the disquieting indelicacy of a skeleton clock. If the villain isn't already pigeon-holing abundance of screamy adjectives and rocketing adverbs in the various newspaper offices I'll eat my head.

Wasp, March 20, 1886, "Prattle." Bierce's observations on the overused phrase, "save the day" (he had noted this phrase was frequently employed by misguided historians): "I believe I am myself the only man who was present at the battle of Stone River who did not either 'save the day' or assist in its salvation by his brigade commander." After another paragraph devoted to setting the record straight about the particular saved day in question, Bierce absolved the implicated individual from blame:

> I am confident that General Miller never put forth any such ridiculous claims for himself as this person [the reporter and source of the story] puts forth for him—or rather against him. Among my other reasons for thinking so is this. A few weeks before he left for Washington the last time, he and I were speaking of that very battle and the bitter controversies that arose from it among the glory-grabbers, and he related with evident enjoyment how some of these gentlemen, immediately after the engagement, were heatedly debating their respective claims in the presence of General Thomas. Thomas listened with indifference for some time and then in a tone that was a verbal expectoration

exclaimed: "Bah! What's the use of blathering about a baaattle?" [*sic*] To the mind of that great soldier, who lost no fields and won no fame, a senseless discussion and a battle were equally trivial.

Bierce could not resist one last jab at the living who went about exaggerating the roles of individuals (and those usually officers) in the late war:

Apropos of day-savers, I beg to submit the subjoined lines as an epitaph (when occasion come)[10] for all the private soldiers of the great rebellion:
Their drums are stilled in all the South;
    They're sleeping, East and West,
With dust in every silent mouth—
    A worm in every breast.

Though mean their station, yet they served
    With willing heart therein:
Their friendly approbation nerved
    The generals to win.

Wasp, April 17, 1886, "Prattle." "He was a soldier, it seems—the good Dr. Munhall, revivaler":

He fought with material weapons in the civil war and "won distinguished honors" as a color-bearer. He says so himself. "His escape from death was simply a miracle," as appears from a transcript of his military record—as expounded by himself to a wondering reporter; though, for my part, I don't know which is the greater miracle, the narrowness of his escape or the breadth of his modesty. God, it is writ, exalteth the horn of His people; but Munhall exalts his own, and through that aspiring tube makes utterance of his merit and his valor. O, he is modesty itself. Let him be known as the Swaggering Violet.

Wasp, May 15, 1886, "Prattle":

A movement is afoot to organize another association for perpetuating the patriotic spirit, and conserving the blessed memories, of the war-time. It is to be called "The Rank and File," and its membership will consist solely of those who served as privates in the late lamented rebellion. Some difficulty has been experienced in getting them together, for one is bed-ridden and the other can't leave his work.

Wasp, June 26, 1886, editorial addressing a series of "some hundreds of private pension bills" awaiting presidential action:

Millions of dollars of the public money are being voted away every year in private pension bills, with a scoundrel disregard of reason, justice and honesty. If the rascality attain much greater magnitude the old soldiers of the civil war will have to spring to arms again to defend their country against its pensioners—of whom a full half on the regular rolls, and ninety-nine one-hundredths on the special, are men of peace, unaccustomed to arms, and could therefore be easily overcome. Their extermination would make a pretty wide gap in the Grand Army of the Republic, too.

Wasp, June 26, 1886, editorial. In this editorial bemoaning and mocking the plights of "[c]ertain ex-Confederates" then serving "as janitors" who were reduced to "purifying the cuspidores [*sic*] used by negro clerks," Bierce in particular mocked the fall from slave owner to servant that had befallen this group of men, headed by "a distinguished ex-major who doubtless owned niggers himself, sir, befo' the wah." While he coolly advised the ex-major that a simple solution could be found in "resigning" from the position that grieved him, Bierce was nevertheless disturbed by the situation: "the Southron of 1860 cleaning spittoons for the Nigger of 1876 is too startling a figure in the shifting panorama of human life to beget emotions altogether pleasurable in a generous bosom—*our* bosom." Bierce is apparently saying that while he takes pleasure in seeing the slave owner humbled, he is not entirely convinced the freed slaves merit an equally great reversal of fortune.[11]

Later in the same editorial of June 26, 1886:

President Cleveland's invitation to the encampment of the Grand Army is engraved on a sheet of gold presented by Colonel Andrews. The gallant Colonel took that unique way of testifying his warm attachment to his old companion in arms during the civil war—their substitutes served in the same regiment.

Wasp, July 10, 1886, editorial. Bierce reported that a drive was underway that sought government compensation for those men who paid substitutes to serve in their stead during the Civil War. Bierce continued his discussion with his tongue cynically in cheek:

The measure has a good chance of success, for nearly all the eminent statesmen of today have a personal interest in it—particularly those restless spirits who chafe under the restraints of peace and wish to refer all international disputes to the arbitrament [*sic*] of the sword. It ought to command the approval of both the great political parties, for it would be money in the pocket of both the white-plumed knight and his great white-feathered antagonist.

Wasp, July 24, 1886, editorial:

We are rather sorry to observe that the brave old boys of the Grand Army have begun to "blot" one another's "escutcheon" with a singularly civilian earnestness: hands which once leveled the deadly rifle or brandished the biting blade have in some recent instances impelled the mudball and generated the parabolic curve of the trajectory of a dead cat. Don't do this thing, comrades—it is most unpretty of you. The public is willing to believe you all equally brave and the "records" to which you "point with pride" similarly genuine. If any man attempts to haul down the fame of General Salomon we shall shoot him on the spot. The malefactor who would rape the laurels from the brow of General Backus should have them—and him—crammed down his throat. We will stand by you so long as you stand by one another; but when you go about intimating that Colonel Cutting was wooden-horsed for taking the last pig a poor Irish woman had in the house, and that General John McComb was not in command of the Federal forces at Vicksburg, and that General Frank Pixley was drummed out of camp for plundering the dead at Cold Harbor, we won't have it. If you fellows wear out your teeth on one another's backs how are you going to eat the bread of charity when the Democrats have turned you all out of office?

Several paragraphs further along:

I'm a gorgeous golden hero
    And my trade is taking life.
Hear the twittle-twittle-tweero
    Of my sibillating fife
And the rub-a-dub-a dum
Of my big bass drum!
I'm an escort strong and bold,
    The Grand Army to protect.
My countenance is cold
    And my attitude erect.
I'm a California Guard
    And my banner flies aloft.
But the stones are O, so hard!
    And my feet are O, so soft!

Also in the July 24, 1886, editorial:

After the annual encampment of the Grand Army of the Republic a movement will be made in favor of a change in the conditions of eligibility to membership. It is thought that actual service in the civil war ought not to be required in the case of an applicant who has faithfully "sat out" the various patriotic poems of Mr. Fred. Emerson Brooks. Such fortitude is justly considered a civic equivalent to all the military virtues of the war time.

Wasp, July 31, 1886, editorial:

> Well, comrades, I'm off now—good morning.
>   Your talk is as pleasant as pie,
> But—pardon me—one word of warning:
>   Speak little of self, say I.
>   That's *my* plan. God bless you, good-bye.

In so far as the Wasp may speak for the citizens of California, the delegates and individual members of the Grand Army are welcome. We hope all their proceedings in council will be harmonious and crowned with a satisfactory result, that the public festivities in their honor may be acceptable, the private hospitality warm and generous, the weather propitious, the whisky pretty good and the decorations endurable. We want the genuine old soldiers to have a good time, and are willing that the impostors among them—wolves in sheep's uniforms—shall enjoy themselves as much as their consciences will permit. Some of these latter sent substitutes into the field who did excellent service and died game. Others have a title to our compassion through pensionable wounds incurred in running away from the enemy. Some endured with soldierly fortitude the incredible hardships incident to a residence in Canada to escape the draft—hardships comparable only to the poetry of Mr. Fred. Emerson Brooks, which, also, they must endure. Most of them have ever in mind the awful dread of detection and exposure. The couch of imposture, like Guatimozin's fervent grill, is no bed of roses—*crede expertum;* we have never lain on it ourselves, but many of its most ingenious and thrilling discomforts are of our invention. The impostors in the Grand Army are a minority, but their representatives at the Annual Encampment are as fairly entitled to considerate treatment as was the deputation of thieves that petitioned Louis XI. for a reduction of the watch. We are not greatly addicted to gush in these columns, but we bespeak for all old soldiers of the late lukewarmness between the North and the South an earnest welcome from all "fair women and brave men"—several of whom are connected with this paper, the writer being particularly distinguished that way.

Examiner, March 27, 1887, "Prattle":

The tiresome procession of brutal and cowardly murders halted the other evening for as much as an hour in deference to the performance of an impromptu duel which had in it some of the elements of manliness. True, the combatants were of the criminal class, and one of them being an American naturally acted with the treachery of a blackguard. There is no such blackguard as your star-spangled native American blackguard; your blackguard of another birth may be firmly grounded in the principles of the art and variously accomplished in its graces, but in the scope of his powers and the colossal magnitude of his attainments, the strength, splendor and vivacity of his method, our compatriot blackguard (hoodumnus of the public school) is inaccessible to comparison, uniquely great. No blood was shed in the duel mentioned, but it was nevertheless interesting as marking a distinct, if transient, departure from the elder practice of shooting objectionables on sight without apprising them of the distinction intended for them. The abolition of dueling appears to me to have divided the males of the English-speaking races into two grand divisions—cowards and assassins. Many of us are sufficiently liberal to belong to both.

I am entirely serious. Dueling, as practiced among the highly civilized peoples of the European continent, is, in my judgment, a beneficent and humane institution which I should like to see established in America. [. . .]

[. . .] On the continent of Europe the studied civility characterizing the intercourse of the class of clean-shirted men is in marked contrast to the brusque and frequently offensive demeanor of the corresponding social element in England and the United States. I am convinced that the difference is almost altogether due to the duello's superiority as a peacekeeper to the abominable fist-fight, which a gentleman will rather endure insult than engage in, or the murderous "shooting scrape," that ultima ratio of a man maddened by wrongs for which he is denied redress. More men are shot down in the streets of San Francisco every year than fall in European duels in double the period; yet private assassination, unsupported by public opinion and unregualted by a "code," does nothing to soften manners—nothing to balm the wounds of self-respect—nothing, in short, to prevent bad blood and the shedding of it. For every drop drawn in formal combat all other drops in the entire community are held in their veins by a less precarious tenure.

Examiner, April 3, 1887, "Prattle":

John Long, Walter Turpin and John Hasty are, alas! no more. They were no mored the other evening with a double shotgun, supercharged with buckshot and operated through a knot-hole in a board fence. These gentlemen resided in Kentucky, and for vocation enforced law and order; also they assisted the moral sense of the community in pruning the liquor trade of its exuberances, and bore a hand, generally, in maintenance of the proprieties. In pursuance of their principles they deemed it expedient to tether a woman seventy years of age, and emboss the back of her with an intricate pattern of weals, traced with an implement usually, and perhaps preferably, employed in admonishment of the domestic mule—*calcitrator intolerabilis*. For this eminent crone, sinning against the light, had persisted in dissemination of blue ruin by trafficking in fervent spirits, known to the vocabulary of Messrs. Long, Turpin and Hasty as "liquid damnation." I have related this incident backward in order to obtain a truly artistic culmination: bloodshed, woman-whipping and Kentucky whisky. These are the successive steps in a climax of unspeakable terrors.

Examiner, May 15, 1887, "Prattle." Bierce related the story of a murder where a man had split "the head of his wife in clean halves with an ax" in a misguided pursuit of "domestic concord." While ostensibly sympathetic to the man's plight, Bierce condemned the man's choice of a solution as being excessive:

> The temptation to do so is no doubt very suasive; the straight, clean parting of a woman's hair, as commonly arranged, invites the ax; her private system of civility and heretical notions of allowable freedom in retort are powerful incentives to her removal by chopping. Nevertheless, moderation is the first law of nature, and endurance is a jewel.

7. "The Affair at Coulter's Notch." First published in the *Examiner* on October 20, 1889.

Examiner, December 23, 1888, "Prattle":

> One would think war horrible enough without the monstrous exaggerations that seem inseparable from the story of it. Nothing is more common than to hear and read about "mowing down" the enemy or being mown down by them, projectiles cutting "wide gaps" through charging columns, "heaps of slain" that clog the cannon wheels, "rivers of blood" and the rest of it. All this is absurd: nothing of the kind occurs—nothing, rather, of the degree. These are phenomena of the camp-fire, the hearth-stone, the "rostrum" and the writing-desk. They are subjective—deeds of memory in a frame of mind. They have a fine literary effect when skillfully employed, and in purely literary work are allowable, in the same way that it is allowable in landscape painting to aggrandize the mountains. Outside of literature their use is to humbug the

civilian, frighten the children and grapple the women's hearts with hooks of steel—all tending to the magnification of the narrator.

Examiner, March 1, 1891, "Prattle":

> When Stonewall Jackson was a young artillery officer in the Mexican war he was ordered by a superior to fire into a certain street of a city. He did so, killing at every discharge women and children. Later in life he was asked if his conscience approved the act. "Certainly," he replied; "your question should be addressed to the officer who gave me the order."

> In the confusion of the engagement at Shiloh the Captain of a Federal battery was commanded to stop the advance of a column of troops dimly seen through smoke and dust.
>   "General," he said, "those are our own reinforcements."
>   "You are mistaken, sir," said the general tartly; "do as I bid you."
> The captain promptly opened fire, smashing the head of the column and driving it to cover. He sighted one of the guns himself and did all the damage he could. He knew he was killing friends, but when obeying orders it was his habit to obey them in letter and in spirit. When he had stopped the column he seated himself comfortably on the trail of a gun and lit his pipe.

8. "A Tough Tussle." First published in the *Examiner* on September 30, 1888.

Wasp, May 5, 1883, "Prattle":

> Of all anachronisms and survivals, the love of the dog is the most reasonless. Because, some thousands of years ago, when we wore other skins than our own and sat enthroned upon our haunches, tearing tangles of tendons from raw bones with our teeth, the dog ministered purveyorwise to our savage needs, we go on cherishing him to this day, when his only function is to lie sunsoaken on a door mat and insult us [as] we pass in and out, enamored of his fat superfluity.

Wasp, March 1, 1884, "Prattle":

> There are those—mostly of military experience—who are imperfectly convinced that the sword is rightly entitled to the honorable place that it holds in literature and oratory as the emblem of destruction. I have myself carried a sword in many bitterly contested battles, but never have seen a man killed with a sword. (It was with the trusty fist, may Heaven forgive me, that I used

to load Southern fields with pyramids and cones of Confederate dead.) Confirming the famous dictum of the late lamented managing director of the Andersonville prison-corrals that the pen is mightier than the sword is the account of a double murder, telegraphed the other day from Chicago. A dead man and his widow, also deceased, were found, both shot, the male decedent having suffered the added disadvantage of nine broken ribs, the lady-corpse equally inconvenienced by the misadventure of a smashed head. The telegram explains that "a cane, a pair of tongs and an old sword were found near by and taken in charge."[12] Supposing, as is natural, that the shooting was done by the cane, the man's ribs broken by the tongs dancing upon his prostrate body and the woman's head crunched by a kick of the same agency, it is clear that the sword performed no service whatever. It never does perform any, and the difficulty of getting hurt by it is what makes the real heroism in Major-General Turnbull's soldierly resolve to fall by the sword if he dies for it.

Examiner, November 10, 1889, "Prattle":

That diligent student of human nature and profound philosopher, my good friend "Blunderbones," of the *Withered Weed*, has discovered that poor men are all superstitious. That, I suppose, is because they have to stay out of school to work. The most formidable enemy to superstition of every kind except the religious kind, which is invincible, is the primary school. One who has passed successfully through that and has still some traces of superstition of the "folk-lore" sort may justly boast himself a worthy descendant of the good arboreal ancestor who from his habit of hanging by his tail and seeing the world upside down came to regard that as its natural relation to him. The excellent though hairy fore-father's notions being all topsy-turvy, superstition was his customary mental state; and the man of to-day who believes in omens, signs, presentiments, charms, lucky and unlucky days, numbers and things, the influence of the moon's phases on weather and in affairs, etc., is intellectually but a short remove from the Great Progenitor.

Superstition has no other basis than ignorance, a fact of which the superstitious, naturally enough, are ignorant. I know many persons who count themselves intelligent; who would resent the imputation of ignorance with the heat and acerbity of a liar when called one; who wear clean linen, can walk on their hind legs and rise without disaster when sitting on their own coat-tails, who nevertheless are proud of their superstitions. They have evidently an undefined feeling that some stupid nonsense like the fear of the number thirteen at table, belief in unluckiness of the opal or reluctance to accept a knife from one whose friendship they value, gives them a picturesque personality; whereas it does not distinguish them at all, but is the mark of the beast, authenticating them as

Sons of Dullness. Some misguided souls even profess superstitions with which they are not afflicted—which is much as if one should falsely declare himself suffering from the itch. To that sort of deception women are most addicted: they think unreason becoming, and each has within the jurisdiction of her charms a multitude of mindless males to whom, in women who are not their wives, it is—though not more so than (in women who are not their wives) boils on the back of the neck would be.

Examiner, August 17, 1890, "Prattle":

If California has had a more humiliating experience than Warden McComb's campaign against three escaped convicts I have not had the joy to know about it. The three rascals, concealed in a jungle and well armed with Winchester rifles, were surrounded by some fifty guards, mounted and on foot, led by two Sheriffs and Warden McComb, who was once a Brigadier-General of the National Guard and has been a show-soldier the most of his worthless life. Yet this force of men, organized and maintained for just such duty, was held at bay by the three "desperadoes" for thirty hours, and finally accepted a conditional surrender, preceded by negotiation and followed by hand-shaking. The Warden himself actually shook hands with the fellows. And they put their pride in their pockets and shook hands with *him!*

Of that gang of cowards and incompetents any half-dozen could at any time during the siege have captured and killed the convicts. They had only to push boldly in, keeping tolerably well together, and when fired on make a rush. One or two might have been hit, possibly killed. Well, what do they suppose to be the nature of the risks which they are understood to incur in taking service as guards to more than a thousand criminals? For what purpose do they believe that they carry deadly weapons? These men are disgusting. To call them cowards is unjust to the cows. They are calfards.

It was once my fortune to command a company of soldiers—real soldiers. Not professional life-long fighters, the product of European militarism—just plain, ordinary, American volunteer soldiers, who loved their country and fought for it with never a thought of grabbing it for themselves; that is a trick which the survivors were taught later by gentlemen desiring their votes. I have no doubt that the few fellows of my company who came out of war alive, and may chance to be living still, have their arms as deep in the public treasury as they can get them; but that is another affair: when I had the honor to command them that last and highest lesson of patriotism was unlearned because untaught. Like the modest member of the G. A. R. who did not deem himself entitled to any of the higher honors of the organization, they didn't do anything in the war—they "only jest fit."

What I want to say is this: I wonder what those men of mine would have thought of me if I had posted them about a wood known to conceal three of the enemy, kept out of rifle range myself, ordered them to fire blindly into the brush when they heard anything, waited thirty mortal hours for the enemy to give in and finally negotiated a conditional surrender. [. . .]

9. "The Coup de Grâce." First identified publication in the *Examiner* on June 30, 1889.

Excerpt from autobiographical essay "What I Saw of Shiloh," drawn from the second installment of the original *Wasp*-based publication which ran on December 23 and 30, 1881: After describing the nonhuman casualties of the battle, including the bark of trees which, "from the root upward to a height of ten or twenty feet, was so thickly pierced with bullets and grape that one could not have laid a hand on it without covering several punctures," Bierce addressed the human toll:

Men? Oh, there were men enough; all dead, apparently, except one, who lay near where I had halted my platoon to await the slower movement of the line—a Federal sergeant, who had been a fine giant in his time. He lay face upward, taking in his breath in convulsive, rattling snores, and blowing it out in sputters of froth which crawled creamily down his cheeks, piling itself alongside his neck and ears. A bullet had clipped a groove in his skull, above the temple; from this the brain protruded in bosses, dropping off in flakes and strings. I had not previously known one could get on, even in this unsatisfactory fashion, with so little brain. One of my men, whom I knew for a womanish fellow, asked if he should put his bayonet through the sufferer. Inexpressibly shocked at the cold-blooded proposition, I told him I thought not; it was unusual, and too many were looking.

Examiner, June 3, 1888, "Prattle." Creed Haymond was a solicitor "of the Southern Pacific Company," part of the railroad empire controlled by the surviving members of the original "Big Four": Charles Crocker, Mark Hopkins, Collis P. Huntington, and Leland Stanford. Hopkins had died in 1878 and Crocker in 1888, but Huntington and Stanford endured and remained favorite targets for Bierce in "Prattle." Creed Haymond, given his connection to both men, was not far behind in Bierce's disaffections, and he was attacked at length in at least eight "Prattle" columns between June 3, 1888 and December 7, 1890:

Mr. Creed Haymond has a private system of determining the scope of an attorney's duty to his client. Pinnacled upon the mountain of his own esteem—

a sudden elevation due to some great convulsion of nature—Mr. Haymond has an uncommonly wide outlook, and while waiting for the devil to come and make him an offer has fallen into the habit of considering it already his own, and the legitimate domain of his activity. Nothing is done in that wide field that he would not himself be willing to do for the profit of the act, be it great or little. He sees no nut so bitter but if he were a monkey he would climb for it; no insect so offensive but if he were a bat he would pursue it; no toad so warty but if he were a snake he would swallow it; no puddle so odorous and green but if he were a pig he would root in it. Being neither monkey, nor bat, nor snake, nor pig, but a clean, high-minded and honorable gentleman, Creed Haymond is not compelled to subsist by ravaging the material universe: he makes his living by being a chattel. He is the property of Senator Stanford, and there is a mortgage on him. Among his duties, as he understands them, is that of being affected by whatever concerns the great man who owns him. When Senator Stanford is warm Creed Haymond perspires: when Senator Stanford is cold Creed Haymond puts on his overcoat. Is there work before the Senate Committee of which Stanford is Chairman? Creed Haymond in San Francisco rolls up his sleeves and spits on his hands. When there is ague at Palo Alto Creed Haymond puts his feet in hot water and rattles his teeth like castanets. [. . .] On Tuesday morning last Dr. Robinson, an old man, arguing his case against the railroad, [. .] asserted, needlessly enough, that Senator Stanford was guilty of falsehood. Creed Haymond promptly called Dr. Robinson a liar and an old rascal, and attempted to beat him with a walking-stick. Is it by such acts as these that this valorous man got his title of "Colonel"? Is this the kind of service that he is paid by the Southern Pacific Company to perform?

Bierce continued his attack on Haymond in the form of a five-stanza poem, the opening stanza of which is reproduced below:

> Creed Haymond, if you've resolutely set
> > Your mind (or what you call so) upon braining
> All men who love not Stanford, you should get
> > Yourself in form to do abundant caning.
> > Take my advice, brave soul: go into training:
> Drink blood until it floods you like a river—
> Try to incarnadine the lily of your liver.

Examiner, April 6, 1890, "Prattle." Bierce included another five stanzas of verse aimed at Haymond's military rank; the opening stanza is a sufficient example:

Creed Haymond, you're a Colonel—think of that!
    'Tis surely something such a rank to hold
And have the right to wear a feathered hat
        And coat-tails formidably striped with gold
        To terrify the enemy. I'm told
That when you turn your back upon them they
        Turn their's on you, all paralyzed with fear,
And let you run triumphantly away!
        The story, I confess, is rather queer,
        But you're a Colonel—that suffices here.

Examiner, September 1, 1889, "Prattle":

On Thursday last a woman who had attempted to drown herself was taken to the Receiving Hospital and subjected to physical torture by means of an electric battery. This was not done to resuscitate her, for her dip in the bay had done her no harm. It was not done in the way of "treatment" at all, but with a view to give her pain, so that she could not refrain from crying out; for she would not speak. The intolerable torment caused her to cry out, but not articulately; she uttered nothing intelligible. Whether she could have done so is nothing to the purpose: if the law permits Police Surgeon Foulkes to inflict torture in punishment of silence his exercise of that power was in this instance needless, ungentlemanly and brutal. [. . .] If I could have my way I would search every nerve and fiber of his own worthless carcass with a thrilling thunderbolt, and then hang him so high that the cherubs of heaven would nest in his hair.
[. . .]
    The woman not only would not speak; she would not eat. This did not suit Dr. Foulkes, who seems to have supposed himself charged by some mysterious mandate with the duty of directing, and, if necessary, compelling her appetite. Against her desperate struggles and regardless of the pain he was inflicting, he forced the tube of a stomach pump down her throat and loaded up her inside with beef tea. I hold heretical opinions on the right of one human being forcibly to keep another alive when the other prefers to be dead, but these are not pertinent to the matter in hand: the woman had been in custody but a few hours—not long enough to make it certain that she was hungry. Certainly she was in no peril of death from starvation. By what color of moral right did Dr. Foulkes commit this hideous assault upon her? Such misconceptions of duty can have but one origin: destitution of brains. It is of the nature of the mindless ass to fancy himself the custodian of his neighbor's welfare, and to determine what that welfare is by assumptions derived from

his own feelings and taking no account of anything else. Dr. Foulkes is the kind of man who would pursue and kill a wounded animal to "put it out of its misery" when it does not wish to be put out of its misery and keep in torment as long as possible a human being praying for death.

Examiner, July 5, 1891, "Prattle":

Out at the Pest-house is a Chinaman afflicted with that form of leprosy known as elephantiasis. He is miserable, incurable, hopeless—a horror to himself, a burden to the public, a constant and emphatic negative to doctrines held most precious by all the churches. The existence of this loathsome and suffering creature screams an emphatic "no" to every affirmation of an omnipotent and benevolent Deity—challenges the very fundamental faiths of all mankind. His death is demanded by every racial, national and individual interest directly or indirectly concerned. The world would be better off without him, the loss of his remnant of life and body would be a distinct advantage to himself. Why not put him to death?

I ask this in no flippant spirit, but in all seriousness; for in all seriousness I believe that the mercy which we extend to dumb animals, "putting them out of misery" when unable to relieve it, we are barbarians to withhold from our own kind. If it is kind and right to preserve as long as possible the life of a human being stricken with an agonizing and incurable disorder it is wrong and cruel to shoot a horse having a broken leg. Scores of times it has been my unhappy lot to deny the piteous appeals of helpless fellow creatures, comrades of the battle field, for that supreme and precious gift which by a simple move-ment of the arm I was able and willing to bestow—the simple gift of death. Every physician has had the same experience, and many (may blessings attend them!) have secretly given the relief implored. The Government has the right of intervention in this matter between a blameless citizen and an undeserved fate: if it has the right to take life at all it has the right to determine when and why. If it has the right to take a life that is perilous to the community it has the right to take one that is already a disaster to the individual. That it is immedi-ately expedient to set up a reform which public opinion has not demanded, and which the noisy declamation of cranks which passes for an utterance of public feeling might howl down, may well be doubted. Our present need is a discussion of the matter, by cranks and all, in a manner that is free (why should it be otherwise?) and fearless—there is nothing to fear. With a view to its proper debating, permit me to formulate the proposition in practical shape:

Resolved, That immediate death is a natural civil right of the citizen pain-fully and incurably afflicted.

I know the first move that will be made by the great body of those holding the negative: they will plant their controversial feet upon religious grounds: we are "placed" here and have no right to leave until taken away—even if that be done piecemeal. On this point I will only say that the world has for many centuries been trying to conform its laws, not to its own needs, but to the supposed wishes of some Power not affected by their action; to those observers who believe the result to have been satisfactory I have no argument in reply. Though you should bray them in a mortar yet would they not cease to do most of the braying.

It has been urged—for this question is as old as the Pyramids—that by putting the sufferer to death we cut off a part of the time in which he would otherwise prepare his soul for the other world. It is amazing how the pious disparage their Gods: to me it seems that a Deity of the ordinary intelligence would naturally make the appropriate allowance in favor of the deceased, crediting him with whatever sum and degree of penitence he would have felt if he had not been deprived of a part of his opportunity. A Deity who would not do that would be hardly fit for adoration.

10. "Parker Adderson, Philosopher and Wit." First published in the *Examiner* on February 22, 1891, as "James Adderson, Philosopher and Wit" and retitled "Parker Adderson, Philosopher" by Bierce for his 1892 collection.

First, a few apparent literary sources:

"It was a dark and stormy night" This infamous opening line, by Edward Bulwer-Lytton, appears in *Paul Clifford*, a story about a man spared from the gallows and redeemed from a life of crime:

> It was a dark and stormy night; the rain fell in torrents—except at occasional intervals, when it was checked by a violent gust of wind which swept up the streets (for it is in London that our scene lies), rattling along the housetops, and fiercely agitating the scanty flame of the lamps that struggled against the darkness.

Initially published in 1830, subsequent editions of *Paul Clifford* were brought out by Bulwer-Lytton in 1840 and 1848; both of these later editions contain prefaces authored by Bulwer-Lytton and it is with these prefaces that the links to "James Adderson, Philosopher and Wit" arguably draw tighter. In the 1840 preface, Bulwer-Lytton wrote, "this book is less of a picture of the king's highway [where crimes were committed] than the law's royal road to the gallows,—a satire on the short cut established between the House of Correction and the Condemned Cell." Arguably, Adderson's story was very much a similar satire with the focus on the path to the gallows or firing line or death and not on the criminal act of spying that landed Adderson on that path. More significant, the last paragraph of Bulwer-Lytton's 1848 preface appears to shed light on key elements of Bierce's story:

> With the completion of this work closed an era in the writer's self-education. From *Pelham* to *Paul Clifford* (four fictions, all written at a very early age), the Author rather observes than imagines; rather deals with the ordinary surface of human life than attempts, however humbly, to soar above it or to dive beneath. From depicting in *Paul Clifford* the errors of society, it was almost the natural progress of reflection to pass to those which swell to crime in the solitary human heart,—from the bold and open evils that spring from ignorance and example, to track those that lie coiled in the entanglements of refining knowledge and speculative pride. Looking back at this distance of years, I can see as clearly as if mapped before me, the paths which led across the boundary of invention from *Paul Clifford* to *Eugene Aram*. And, that last work done, no less clearly can I see where the first gleams from a fairer fancy broke upon my way, and rested on those more ideal images, which I sought, with a feeble hand, to transfer to the *Pilgrims of the Rhine*, and the *Last Days of Pompeii*. We authors, like the Children in the Fable, track our journey through the maze by the pebbles which we strew along the path. From others who wander after us, they may attract no notice, or, if noticed, seem to them but scattered by the caprice of chance. But we, when our memory would retrace out steps, review, in the humble stones, the witnesses of our progress—the landmarks of our way.

Clavering's peaceful death also harbors its own literary echoes. Beyond its similarity to John Donne's "Valediction: Forbidding Mourning" which opens by noting that "virtuous men pass mildly away," Clavering's passing more demonstrably draws on two numbers of the *Spectator* of Addison and Steele. The first, number 133, attributed to Richard Steele, contained a paragraph describing the noble death of a heroic general:

> Epaminondas, the Theban general, having received in fight a mortal stab with a sword, which was left in his body, lay in that posture till he had intelligence that his troops had obtained the victory, and then permitted it to be drawn out, at which instant he expressed himself in this manner. "This is not the end of my life my fellow-soldiers; it is now your Epaminondas is born, who dies in so much glory."

Addison, in issue number 289 of the *Spectator*, potentially provided Bierce with a general reason for writing about death:

The truth of it is, there is nothing in history which is so improving to the reader as those accounts which we meet with of the deaths of eminent persons, and of their behavior in that dreadful season. I may also add, that there are no parts in history which affect and please the reader in so sensible a manner. The reason I take to be this, because there is no other single circumstance in this story of any person, which can possibly be the case of every one who reads it. A battle or a triumph are conjunctures in which not one man in a million is likely to be engaged: but when we see a person at the point of death, we cannot forbear being attentive to every thing he says or does, because we are sure that some time or other we shall ourselves be in the same melancholy circumstances. The general, the statesman, or the philosopher, are perhaps characters which we may never act in; but the dying man is one whom, sooner or later, we shall certainly resemble.

The Official Record of the War of Rebellion on Shiloh: A battlefield report included in the Shiloh volume reveals that Bierce certainly may have heard of and perhaps even witnessed a particularly vivid scene involving a bowie knife. The report was submitted by Col. Walter C. Whitaker of the 6th Kentucky Infantry shortly after the Battle of Shiloh:

To Colonel Hazen, commanding Nineteenth Brigade United States forces, is respectfully submitted the report of Colonel W. C. Whitaker, of the Sixth Kentucky Volunteers, Nineteenth Brigade:

General Nelson's division, at the battle of Pittsburg Landing, on the Tennessee River, was put in advance on the night of the 6th of April, the Ninth Indiana on the left, and the Forty-first Ohio in reserve. At 5 o'clock on the morning of the 7th line of battle was formed, and the fight began at half past 5 between the skirmishers of the Sixth Kentucky and the Ninth Indiana and the pickets of the enemy. The enemy's pickets were driven back, and at about 6 the action began between the enemy and the Ninth Indiana, which was gallantly sustained by them. At 10 o'clock Mendenhall's battery, which had rendered efficient service, was assailed by a large force of the enemy. It was supported by three companies of the Sixth Kentucky, under command of Lieutenant-Colonel Cotton. They were severely pressed, and a charge was made by the remainder of the Sixth Regiment at the point of the bayonet, headed by Colonel Whitaker and Adjutant Shackelford. The acting brigadier-general, Colonel Hazen, most gallantry accompanied them in the charge. The enemy was routed from their cover behind logs and trees with terrific slaughter. The pursuit and fight were continued by Colonel Hazen's brigade (Ninth Indiana and Forty-first Ohio Volunteers) until the enemy was driven beyond his batteries. The action was most hotly and vigorously contested by six regiments—three from

Texas, the Eleventh Louisiana, one from Mississippi, and one from Kentucky—commanded by Colonel Thomas B. Monroe, who was killed in the action. In the charge the Sixth Kentucky took three pieces of cannon, two rifled and one smooth. One of the guns was spiked and abandoned, the other two held in possession. Colonel Whitaker cut down one of the cannoneers with a bowie-knife he had taken from a Texan he had captured. (343)

Examiner, January 17, 1897, letter signed "Yellow Back," and quite possibly authored by Bierce, appearing within an article addressing the question, "What Is Our Greatest Piece of Fiction?" The writer "is of the opinion that some few deserving writers have been overlooked" by the other respondents, and mentions several candidates in passing:

How about Mrs. E.D.E.N. Southworth and her wonderful heroines, with their coal black eyes and hair like fine-spun gold? How about Archibald Clavering Gunter, who has three great thrills in each chapter and whisks you from a foot-ball field to an Indian fight, to Labrador and to Patagonia, to Australia and "The Examiner's" manless isle in as many breaths? How about the Rives romancer who puts her heroines [*sic*] to sleep on the floor of her boudoir, with her red hair streaming out all about her like an aurora borealis? How about Buffalo Bill, who makes his heroines [*sic*] of the per-ary ride down che-hasms and up cle-iffs in her wild ride from the merciless men of the moccasin feet? How about Leatherstocking Cooper, who cooped so many wild tales of the border?

11. "A Watcher by the Dead." First published in the *Examiner* on December 29, 1889, as "The Watcher by the Dead" but renamed "A Watcher by the Dead" by Bierce for his 1892 collection.

Examiner, October 2, 1887, "Prattle": three mock "extracts" regarding certain individuals Bierce judged insane; the numbers only loosely conceal the identities of actual figures, "9302," for example, is most probably Frank Pixley, copublisher and editor of the *Argonaut:*

In the following extracts from the official record of the Commissioners in Lunacy, the patients' names have been omitted out of deference to the feelings of relatives and friends, and they are designated by their numbers only. The entries are transcribed from the volume entitled *Minutes of Examinations:*
    8981. _____. Banker. Believes himself a Commissioner of Police, but acts more like a knot on a log. Declares himself to have been Mayor of San Francisco and a good one. Was Mayor. Has two private keepers, named Hammond and Tobin, who chew his food for him and swallow it. Invincibly mad. Committed.

9302. _____. Journalist. Believes himself pursued by the Pope. Says he is a political party. Screams at sight of green flag. Cause of dementia—hereditary disappointed ambition and congenital chagrin. Kicks all round the compass. Steps gingerly, for fear of breaking through. Religion—atheist, except when he swears: very devout when he loses ten cents. Occupation of ancestors—digging postholes on Calvary. Has a tongue that will put a girdle round a rich man's foot in forty seconds. Harmless. Discharged.

9429. _____. Newspaper killer. Form of hallucination—egotism. Thinks he has his thumb and forefinger in the world's button-hole. Wears head high in hat. Declares neckwear is the root of all evil. Occupation when not at work—genius. Fancies he was sent upon earth to make it resemble Iowa. Ordered detained at the *Alta* office.

While inmate number 9429 is unidentified in this 1887 entry, in his "Prattle" column for December 8, 1889, two weeks prior to the publication of "The Watcher by the Dead," Bierce employed the same device with no attempt made to conceal the identities of his several targets, one of whom, John P. Irish, is probably the inspiration for the earlier 9429:

No. 432,348. Nov. 28, 1889. John P. Irish, nationality unknown. Believes himself an editor and orator. Makes speeches on the reclamation of an Oakland froggery, which he wishes to cover with cottages suitable for sale to the deserving poor. Wears his head uncommonly high in his hat and when he sees a shirt collar foams at the mouth. Has been known to fancy himself a Democratic nominating convention. Shows a singular antipathy to the name De Young, the pronunciation of which he abbreviates. Writes things. Addicted to running and revolving his arms and choo-chooing. If you pinch his ear at such times he emits a sharp hiss like the noise of steam escaping from a gauge. Committed to three Asylums.

Examiner, April 8, 1888, excerpt from a poem entitled "The Man Born Blind," which recounted what was seen by a man whose sight had been restored following "a painful operation." Bierce used the man's still "imperfect" vision to reveal, through the power of his "infant observation," the reality behind a series of figures, including a merchant, a patriot, a lawyer, a judge, and a doctor:

A doctor stood beside a bed
    And shook his head quite sadly.
"O see that foul assassin!" said
    The man who saw so badly.

Examiner, April 22, 1888, "Prattle." An accused murderer, Dr. Powell appeared in "Prattle" three times from April 1888 through September 1889:

> It is well for the interests of justice that Powell, the assassin of Ralph Smith, so far forgot the respect that is due to the dead as to fire a shot or two into the body after he had good reason to think that life was extinct: after his acquittal on the charge of murder he may perhaps be held for malicious mischief.

Examiner, August 26, 1888, "Prattle":

> It is clear now that Dr. Powell, who killed Ralph Smith, at Redwood City, was not born to be hanged; five vicious idiots were found who were willing to acquit him. If there is such a crime as willful and premeditated murder, his was that crime. If there is such an animal as a dangerous coward he is that kind of beast. May the good Lord who spares him for our sins deign to punish us otherwise. O thou great and mighty Satan, charged with the administration of divine justice here on earth, we level pious shins of entreaty and upturn palms of supplication. Remember not our virtues and good works against us, and forget not our wickedness. As thou wouldst that we should not do unto one another, do thou even so unto us. Betray, we beseech thee, thy trust, and let this villain come to grief. Afflict him with incalculable ills and smite him sore in all those organs wherein he liveth. Pang him hard with a serviceable multitude of evils so that he die and thou get the soul of him. Steal away the treasure thou art put to guard. Embezzle the scoundrel's immortal part and get thee to Redwood City beyond thy Master's jurisdiction. Do but this, Jack Satan, dear—commit this single breach of trust, and we will forgive thee a million fidelities.

Following this witty but vitriolic attack, Bierce next addressed to Powell a damning poem of fifty-nine lines which concluded with a harsh and formal rhymed condemnation:

> By your heritage of guilt;
> By the blood that you have spilt;
> By the Law that you have broken;
> By the terrible red token
>   That you bear upon your brow
> By the awful sentence spoken
>   And irrevocable vow
> Which consigns you to a living

Death and to the unforgiving
Furies who avenge your crime
Through the periods of time;
By that dread eternal doom
Hinted in your future's gloom,
    As the flames infernal tell
Of their power and perfection
In their wavering reflection
    On the battlements of Hell;
By the mercy you denied,
    I condemn your guilty soul
In your body to abide
    Like a serpent in a hole!

Examiner, September 16, 1888, "Prattle":

At the Goldenson hanging two physicians performed the customary "last sad rite" of eaves-dropping at the dying man's chest and monkeying with his pulse. Dr. Blach mounted a step-ladder, fingered the wrist and pitched the tent of his ear on the pectoral camping ground. Dr. Carpenter, standing below, unlaced the shoes and manipulated the ankles. And so, watch in hand, pride in heart and nothing in head, these twin relics showed themselves off to the worst advantage, keenly attentive to their own symptoms and conspicuously unhanged. To what decent purpose? [. . .] Bah! the doctor at a hanging wants to be a part of the performance. He wants the corpse to share its distinction with him. He craves the silent applause of the average man, who inly burns with admiration of the courage which is not afraid of a dead body.

Examiner, September 8, 1889, "Prattle":

In the Powell murder trial Dr. Stambaugh, the prisoner's brother-in-law, testified in that innocent's behalf, that for twenty years he had been afflicted with aphasia. One symptom of that disorder, according to the learned physician, is an inability to identify objects by their proper names. Then Powell has no such disease. If you speak the words "brute" and "coward" in his presence he will identify himself as the thing meant. He will never have aphasia: through all his life, be it short or long, he will know that the word "assassin" means him. And when the trumpet of shame blares abroad across the land the sound of "Stambaugh" he will be able to point out as unerringly as the finger of scorn the particular unfortunate to whom that opprobrious name justly applies.

12. "The Man and the Snake." First published in the *Examiner* on June 29, 1890.

Wasp, January 16, 1886, "Prattle":

> How we ever made shift to get on without the telegraph it is mournful to consider. One day last week it brought us a long account of President Cleveland's domestic habits, relating with special particularity how he recently stood at the top of the stairs, clothed in nothing but his night-shirt and the gray of the morning, shouting for a servant to come and find his collar-button which, with true American freedom, had abandoned its trust to roll under the bed.

Examiner, July 6, 1890, "Prattle": One week after the story's appearance in the *Examiner*, Bierce, apparently prompted by a query from "F. G.," clarified the status of the reference work he had purported to quote from in the opening of "The Man and the Snake": "F. G.—Morryster's *Marvells of Science* can certainly not be obtained in the 'book market.'"

13. "A Holy Terror." First published in the San Francisco *Wasp* on December 23, 1882.

Wasp, October 7, 1882, "Prattle":

> The *Sonoma Democrat* has a writer on its staff who is a holy terror. When he walks out, the houses and the trees strain back as hard as ever they can to get away from him. When he sleeps, all nature holds its breath lest he wake, and the stentorian cats are stilled along the ridge-poles. The earth bends like thin ice beneath his tread; the East observes his course, and says to the West, "Look out!" And his name is Schnabel.
>
> Cruel is the soul of Schnabel. The ghosts of his victims shriek upon the red streams of the tempest. He poises his pen and the widows of Sonoma weep. About that weapon cling like bats the disembodied souls of rival writers, a gloomy company, intent on its arrest. But strong is the hand of Schnabel, and his smile is like the lightning glimmering above the hills of Morven. His scowl depopulates a township. He toys with the locks of his enemy and dallies familiarly with the nose of him; explores curiously the dark corners of his visceral cavities, unkinking the reluctant entrail and readjusting the lobed liver. And then he writes: "Having dragged him from his obscurity, I will leave him there, blinking under the burning gaze of the multitude." Straightway the multitude ensues, shoveling fresh coals upon its eyes to singe the Schnabelian victim, and there is a smell of scorching meat. It is the biggest barbecue of the season.

Wasp, December 16, 1882, editorial:

Judge Hunt, of the Superior Court, has given a decision that appears to be applicable to other cases than the one before him: He has awarded damages to a man whose nerves were upset and his sleep disturbed by the noise of pounding clothes in a Chinese laundry. [. . .] In his decision he refers to another, by the Supreme Court of Massachusetts, in which it is stated that "noise which constitutes any annoyance to a person of ordinary sensibility to sound, such as to interfere with the ordinary comfort of life and impair the reasonable enjoyment of his habitation, is a nuisance to him." If that does not cover the clamor of church bells, strenuously pounded for the early Bridget at six o'clock in the morning, we do not know what application it has. The screaming church bell has, no doubt, a prime lot of holy associations connected with it, and derives a certain sanctity from the very fact of its finishing off so many of our loved ones with frail nerves; but in these days of three-dollar watches and four-dollar clocks, its mission is a purely destructive one. If the Chinese launderer spanking our soiled linen is a nuisance, the sexton punishing his howling bell is a holy terror.

Wasp, December 23, 1882, Christmas editorial:

In civil and customary recognition of Him upon whose natal day the angels— probably with a mental reservation—proclaimed peace on earth and goodwill to men, the *Wasp* permits itself to be pervaded by a truly Christian spirit for as much as a week. The editorial lightnings are decently blanketed, the editorial thunders hushed, the editorial gall and wormwood turned off; and above the heads of all mankind—our enemies alone excepted—we spread in benediction palms which have never been soiled by a dishonest dollar. This rite, we beg the good reader to observe, is a more gracious and impressive performance than the customary hollow and hackneyed ceremony of wishing him "a merry Christmas"—to the which meaningless salutation we have a sharp and lasting antipathy. In place of wishing our friends "a merry Christmas," we have endeavored to make them one by the publication of this present Christmas number—which we submit to them in the sure and certain hope that in the perusal of its pictures they may find a more tranquil and less expensive delight than we found in its making.

Some small measure of Christmas merriment we concede also to our enemies. Messrs. Stanford, Crocker and Huntington may ingest their respective birds in peace; we shall set up no skeleton at the feast, to rattle its reminding bones. Frank Pixley, under their table, shall eat of the children's crumbs, unterrified by the apparition of a lawless boot. Sammy Backus shall annoint [*sic*] his locks with fat, display his cuffs and, parting the coat-tails of his face, kick himself with a turkey-leg without let or hindrance. We might write him a saucy letter if the management of the Post-office were such as to encourage the hope that it would be delivered, but he shall have a week's rest from public censure. The militia shall go peacocking without fear that they may be attacked and routed by the boy in our office. The windows of the parson's mental heaven may be opened to pour a deluge of bosh upon the earth; we shall silently climb to the uplands of reason till the shower blows over. The Lily of the Valley shall bloom unmolested, and the ladies of the Palace Hotel pot him unafraid. Rogues, fools, impostors and disreputables of all sorts of kinds shall have a week of as perfect immunity from justice as if God were asleep.

This is a noble forbearance, for California has an opulence of persuasive backs inviting the cudgel. It is the land of the fool and the home of the rogue. Here the vulgarian runs riot; here the impostor flourishes luxuriant, and the knave plies his various prank [*sic*] upon the unguarded pocket. Male and female created He them: the vulgarienne is to the fore in quantity, the impostrix prevails, and from Siskiyou to San Diego, from the Sierra to the sea, the knavess performs sedulously her appointed function. Seated lordly atop of his social eminence, the parvenu chap floats in the sunshine of his accidental supremacy, with never a hand but ours to deliver him a loving stab for the liberation of the gasses of conceit wherewith he labors in the sides like a crocodile done to a turn on Nileside sands. His ears are stuffed with the music of adulation, his tense hide basted with literary butter. Billows of flattery beat upon and break against him; he pores them like a sucking sponge nor knows the luxury of the glad tidings "Thou fool!" Like a noxious fetish-tree in a burial-place, he has thrust his exacting tap-root down among the rich reverences that minister fatly to his preposterous growth. Circling about him in maddest of devotional can-can, the seraphim and cherubim of the sycophant press continually do cry. *Chapeau bas, Messieurs:* one thousand San Franciscan parvenu are worshipping themselves! But shall *we* blow the wild bugle and punish the mellow gong until the face of us is royally empurpled, adding our clamor to quell the still, small voice that whispers of the gilded villain's feet of clay? Nay, we know the wretch for what he is— a tallowy, hide-bound and unwholesome dolt whose longest reach of reason can grasp no higher truths than that he is great because rich, wise because successful and good because unhanged. This paper exists for his affliction, and if, in deference to the season, we forego that congenial function, we nevertheless debit him with the forbearance and shall exact an accounting.

We do not flatter ourselves that that incurious person, the general reader, is unduly interested in our own affairs to the neglect of his own. We have not the satisfaction of thinking that he cares much more for the details of our efforts to supply him with provend for his mental tooth than we for the means whereby he obtains the coal we buy of him (at an unkindly high price, we are sorry to say), or for his fashion of adulterating the food which it is our blessed privilege to procure at his corner grocery. It is our impression that when a newspaper talks very much about its internal affairs the motive is the same that inspires a man to lead a conversation round to the subject of his deceased liver—vanity. [. . .]

To the many thousands of readers who will this week see the *Wasp* for the first time, we beg to explain that this is not a "sample" number. While the *Wasp* is not in any sense a comic paper, it is perhaps overmuch given to the besetting sin of dealing with all human interest with a coldly unenthusiastic familiarity exceedingly distasteful to the optimist, whose unconsidering orbs persist in seeing things not as they are, but as they should be. We are not enamored of the world as it is. We find it is peopled with a thousand-and-odd millions of inhabitants, who are mostly fools, and it is our custom to set forth and illustrate this unsatisfactory state of affairs by instancing conspicuous examples. We also exercise the prerogative of superior virtue by admonishing men and making suggestions to God. In short, the *Wasp* is what is rather vaguely called a "satirical journal."

Wasp, January 6, 1883, editorial. Bierce opened with a denunciation of the practice of paying for newspaper reports about "private entertainments" which he claimed was fed by a "rage for social distinction" that had "assumed the character of a madness destructive alike to the social graces and the domestic virtues":

The field being open to any one who chooses to enter by the payment of money (and we cannot too often assure our readers that it is by direct payment of money that this kind of distinction is obtained) the vulgarians, upstarts and disreputables have naturally thronged through the gates and usurped all the commanding eminences of the wide domain. [. . .] As those who[se] tastes are low and whose lives are disreputable have most coin and least scruple; as it is they who most strongly believe that a shining mantle best hides a dirty skin— that social conspicuousness atones for obscure birth and faulty breeding, it follows that in the struggle for front place they are first.

Bierce went on to draw attention to a recent innovation in social depravity:

One of the latest and most outrageous developments of the "society reporter's" black art is the custom of printing on the last days of December a list of "ladies

who will receive" on New Year's Day. If only women who are otherwise decent made advertisement of themselves by this monstrous method it would be
bad enough to keep every well-bred gentleman from their doors; but the temptation to advertise also the *demi-monde* is too strong to be resisted, and sand-
wiched in among the other names are the "announcements" of notorious
courtezans who pay roundly for this annual privilege. We solemnly assure our
lady readers that this almost incredible statement is bald and frosty truth. [. . .]
Every woman who permits her name to be used in these lists of "ladies who will
receive," is made an accomplice in this immatchable crime against morality. (4)[13]

Wasp, January 13, 1883, unsigned story, apparently authored by Bierce:

FLOTSAM: A TALE OF THE PRODIGIOUS DAMPNESS OF 1852.
I presume most of my readers retain a tolerably wholesome recollection of the
annoyances they suffered at Jackass Flat in 1852. They remember how bad the
walking was, with eighteen or twenty feet of running water on the sidewalks;
and how cold the water was. They cannot have wholly forgotten the vexation
caused by their houses thumping against one another, lodging in the tops of
trees, and turning round so as to let the sun in on the carpets. Those of them
who lived in adobe cottages, it is true, escaped these latter evils by their habitations simply melting away and seeking the sea by natural outlets. Still, there
was a good deal of discomfort for all.

One of the greatest annoyances in those days was the unusual number of
dead bodies cruising about—privateers, steering hither and thither without any
definite destination, but aiming at making themselves generally disagreeable.
There were always some of the fellows sailing about in this desultory way; and
they were responsible, one way and another, for considerable profanity. I knew
quiet, peaceable citizens to get as angry as ever they could be when some waif
of this kind would lodge against their dining-room doors while the family were
at supper; and sometimes when you would throw up your second-story window to go out for an evening "at the office," one would come rocking gently in
amongst the children, and anchor on the hearth-rug. And the worst of it was
that if you did not feel hospitable, you might have to swim a mile or two to get
the coroner to deputize you to hold an inquest and eject the intruder. Otherwise, you were liable to shooting for removing a stranded body without authority. And if the coroner could not write (there were, I think, four coroners
during the time the water was laid on, and some could never be taught to hold
the pen right end up) you must take along a witness; or that official might "go
back on his word," and you would be at the trouble of killing him. All these
things made Jackass Flat practically untenable; but there was only one direc-

tion in which it was possible to leave; and that route led through several rivers, Suisun, San Pablo, and San Francisco bays, and so on out into the Pacific.

It was a wild black night in Bummer street.[14] The wind fairly howled! The rain scourged the roofs, twisting in wet sheets about the chimneys, and pulling them down, as the velvet train of a lady clings to the ankle of the unwary dancer, and upsets him in a minute. There was more water in Bummer street than you would have thought from merely looking at the surface; because, as rule, you can't see very far into water every cubic mile of which holds in solution a small range of mountains and two or three mining towns. The boarding house of Mrs. Hashagen presented, however you might look at it, a very dejected aspect. There was one tallow-candle burning dimly at an open upper window; and beside it sat, in anxious expectancy, the landlady's old mother-in-law, plying the busy needle. Her son, the man of the house, who was "having a little game with the boys" behind a dormer-window at Clawhammer Jake's, had promised to return at ten o'clock if he had "any kind o' luck"—which meant any kind excepting bad or indifferent luck—and it was now eleven. There was no knowing, either, how soon it might be necessary to take to the boats. Presently something bumped against the side of the house, there was a murmur of subdued swearing outside, a scow was pushed up to the window ledge, and Mr. Hashagen stepped into the room.

"How's business, Joseph?" was the laconic welcome from the aged mother.

"Disgustin'!" was the unamiable reply of her son, as he chained his barge to the shutter. "Never held such derned hands in my life. Beat the game, though. Ten or twenty dollars, I should say. But 'tain't no use fer me to keep up *that* lick. Fate's dead agin me—that's how *I* put it up."

"Quite true, Joseph," replied the old lady, mildly; "we have done better'n that to home."

"Did, hay?"

There was a long silence, broken only by the pounding and chafing of Mr. Hashagen's galley against the side of the house. The wind had died away, or moaned only at long intervals, like the warning wail of the Banshee. Some solemn and mysterious spell seemed to brood upon that household; a vague but ghostly presentment was at the heart of Mr. Hashagen—a subtle sense of helplessness and dread in the presence of some overshadowing Presence. He rose and looked out upon the moving waters.

"Mary Ann's got a customer, Joseph," said the old lady, with an air of forced cheerfulness, as if to dispel the gathering gloom by idle talk.

"What is he?" inquired her son, mechanically, not even withdrawing his eyes from the window—"roomer or mealer?"

"Only a bedder at present, Joseph."

"Pay in advance?"

"No, Joseph."

"Any traps?"

"Not even a carpet-bag."

"Know him?"

"We never none of us ever seen him afore."

There was another pause. The conversation had recalled Mr. Hashagen's faculties to the cares of the lodging-house business, and he was turning something over in his mind, but did not seem to get it right side up. Presently he spoke:

"Hang *me* ef I savvy! He didn't pungle, he ain't got no kit; and nobody don't know him! Now it's my opinion he's a dead beat—that's how I put *him* up! He lays out to get away with us—to play roots on the shebang. But I'll get the drop on *him*; I'll ring in a cold deck on him, or I'm a Chinaman; you just dot that down—that's *me!*"[15]

But all this time there was a chill fear creeping about Joseph's heart. He talked very bravely, but he felt, somehow, that it didn't help him. He didn't exactly connect this feeling with his mysterious lodger; but he thought he would rather have taken in some person he knew. The old lady made no further attempt to put him at his ease, but sat placidly sewing, with a face as impassive as that of the Sphinx.

"I say, mother, has he turned in?"

"Yes, Joseph, I belive [*sic*] he retired some hours ago."

"Then bust my crust ef I don't go for his duds!"

And seizing the candle this provident landlord strode into the hall, marched resolutely to the proper door, laid hold of the knob, and then, as he afterward described it, "you could have knocked him down with a one-dollar bill.["] However, he pushed open the door and entered.

And there, stretched out upon a bed and decently sheeted from sight, lay the motionless form of Mary Ann's lodger. Mr. Hashagen resolutely advanced and drawing off the covering exposed the whole figure, which was about ten inches long, and rosy as a summer sunset. The new bedder was as much as three hours of age and quite hearty.

Wasp, February 24, 1883, "Prattle":

One can't somehow quite get the hang of Mr. P. S. Dorney's poetry in the Sacramento *Bee*. Its sense is so subtle and its charm so elusive that it evades the understanding, and it mixes up the sensibilities worse that a pack of hounds after a jackass rabbit. This bard has a vocabulary that is a sealed book to mortals, and his private system of grammar is a holy terror to those who have not the clue. For example, in his great poem, "The Last Redoubt," he pushes out the soul of him as follows:

Bivouac forever—great dead—
Immortal, wooed and truly free:
Tho' cold your lips and still'd your tread—
Did not I love I'd envy thee;
I'd envy thee though wrap't in rout,
And stacked and stark in the last redoubt.

To the merely human intelligence this is altogether too entirely quite. If there were more than one of the mighty dead it is wicked to say "thee" instead of "ye"; if only one, how the other world could he be "stacked" in the last redoubt? And if there was only one there couldn't have been much of a fight, and Mr. Dorney might almost as well have set his muse yawping over the sainted result of a snake-bite.

The appalling conundrum suggested by Mr. Dorney in affirming that his "great dead" were (or was) "wrap't in rout" might perhaps be answered by an undertaker; but when he avers in the next stanza, as he grimly does, that they are (or he is) also "mantled in the victor's shout" he puts too severe a strain upon the imagination and it all goes to pieces in the effort to conceive the double swaddling. I suppose we must try to fancy the "great dead" clad in rout as its ordinary costume, and putting on the victor's shout as an overcoat when it feels itself growing uncumfortably [*sic*] cold.

14. "The Suitable Surroundings." First published in the *Examiner* on July 14, 1889.

Examiner, July 21, 1889, "Prattle":

Mrs. Florence Finch Kelley has published a book of fiction with the warning sub-title—adapted from the English of Edmund Yates: "A Story for Men and Women." That is honest of Mrs. Kelley, and I commend her forethought to Mesdames Ella Wheeler Wilcox, Laura Daintry, Amelia Rives Chanler, and Edgar Saltus. Mrs. Gertrude Atherton also might advantageously adopt the frank rattlesnake practice. I am not without a hope that the American novel of the future will be printed in two parts separated by a blank leaf, one part labeled "For Ladies," the other "For Gents."

15. "An Inhabitant of Carcosa." First published in the *San Francisco News Letter and California Advertiser* on December 25, 1886.

Wasp, February 28, 1885, "Devil's Dictionary" entry for "ghost": a noun that is an "outward and visible sign of an inward fear."

> He saw a ghost.
> It occupied—that dismal thing—
> The path that he was following.
> Before he'd time to stop and fly,
> An earthquake trifled with the eye
> That saw a ghost.
>
> He fell as fall the early good;
> Unmoved that awful spectre stood.
> The stars that danced before his ken
> He wildly brushed away, and then
> He saw a post.

Bierce concludes his definition by playing his trump card:

> There is one insuperable obstacle to a belief in ghosts. A ghost never comes naked: he appears either in a winding-sheet or "in his habit as he lived." To believe in him, then, is to believe that not only have the dead the power to make themselves visible after there is nothing left of them, but that the same extraordinary gift inheres in textile fabrics. Supposing the products of the loom to have this ability, what object would they have in exercising it? And why does not the apparition of a suit of clothes sometimes walk abroad without a ghost in it? These be riddles of significance. They reach away down and get a convulsive grip on the very tap-root of this flourishing faith. They are petards of logic, threatening to blow up the temple of ghostology and strew the entire intellectual landscape with a débris of fragmentary spook.

Wasp, March 28, 1885, "Devil's Dictionary" entry for "grave": "A place in which the dead are laid to await the coming of the medical student." Once again, Bierce included a poem:

> Beside a lonely grave I stood—
>   With brambles 'twas encumbered;
> The winds were moaning in the wood,
>   Unheard by him who slumbered.
>
> A rustic standing near, I said:
>   "He cannot hear it blowing!"

"Course not," said he: "the feller's dead—
    He can't hear nowt that's going."

"Too true," I said; "alas, too true—
    No sounds his sense can quicken!"
"Well, Mister, wot is that to you?—
    The deadster ain't a kickin'."

I knelt and prayed: "O Father smile
    On him, and mercy show him!"
That countryman looked on the while,
    And said: "Ye didn't know him."

Wasp, April 18, 1885, "Prattle":

The "astrologers," "fortune-tellers" and "mediums" who advertise in the news-papers are the most pernicious rascalry afflicting this felon-haunted commu-nity. The criminal depravity of these people is of unthinkable profundity. That fools and cranks whom they fleece are entitled to no sympathy is a truth im-perfectly justifying toleration; for, look you, these plundered simpletons are mostly sexed female-wise, and respectably husbanded and fathered. They visit the divining-dens with secrecy, close-veiled and circumspicious. It is not alone in pocket they are pillaged: your seventh son of a seventh son is commonly a girl-dealer, pursuing that crime under cloak of the other; your star-eyed seer-ess hath a nimble vision for eligible estrays. It is through these dens of dark-ness that the army of the sisterhood of sin is recruited, its dreadful procession wasted of its veterans at its head by age, debility and death, but ever reinforced at the hither end from the astrologer's awkward squad. My friends, it will not disprofit you to look to your wives, your sisters and your daughters. Retract your thinkers from your business long enough to consider your interests. No doubt, Mr. Hardhead, your wife is a very superior person, but I think I've had the pleasure of meeting her in the waiting-room of Professor Abracadabra, the Memphian Mystery, who used to wash dishes at the Berkshire Shoat res-taurant. If I rightly remember, she was alone; her daughters were in another slum, consulting the renowned Madame Aldrovanda, who was a queen in her own country but is now a Clairvoyant Revealer and arranges meetings be-tween young girls and the gallant gentlemen whom she sees in a vision. You need not concern yourself about the daughters—they will not squander any money in this kind of thing. It will cost them nothing but their souls.

Wasp, July 4, 1885, unsigned article, apparently by Bierce:

Dreams and Wakenings.

The relief of awakening from a dream of horror and oppression—the disappointment of awakening from one of transcendent bliss and rapture—which is the greater? To attempt to determine any such question as that were futile. But either kind of dream and awakening has its interest, and we propose to offer some illustrations from miscellaneous literature of both kinds—the sense of dejection at finding a beatific vision mere illusion—gone, as a dream, when one awaketh; and the same sense of tremulous delight at finding the terrors of sleep dispelled, and all the hideous shapes and spells and tortures of dreamland a bubble that has burst. Byron tells us that to dream of joy and wake to sorrow is doomed to all who love or live, and that, when conscious on the morrow, we scarce our fancy can forgive that cheated us in slumber only to leave the waking soul more lonely. The younger of his "Two Foscari," piteously deprecating exile from his too dearly loved Venice, talks of "dreaming a disturbed vision" of her glories, whence bitterly he "awoke and found them not." Equally doomed was Queen Katharine when roused from a rapturous vision to exclaim:

Spirits of peace, where are ye? Are ye all gone,
And leave me here in wretchedness behind ye?

Of the same style is the plaint of prisoner "Posthumus" in *Cymbeline:* "Gone! They went hence as soon as they were born. And so I am awake. Poor wretches that depend on greatness's favor dream as I have done—wake, and find nothing." "Caliban's" wild imagination found ecstasy in dreaming:

The clouds, methought, would open and show riches
Ready to drop upon me, that when I waked
I cried to dream again.

Has not the Hebrew prophet, in graver mood and higher strain, said much the same thing more than two thousand years ago? "It shall even be as when a hungry man dreameth, and, behold, he eateth; but he awaketh, and his soul is empty; or as when a thirsty man dreameth, and, behold, he drinketh; but he awaketh, and, behold, he is faint." So with visions of wealth; we wake, and the shining sovereigns and the rustling notes have turned into dry leaves, like the money paid by the magician in the *Arabian Nights.* So with visions of the old familiar faces, when the life-blood courses warmly through the old friendly hands and "dead babies crow and battle valorously in nurses arms," and dead sweethearts smile and blush, and dead boon companions crack the old jokes, sing the old songs, tell the old stories, till we wake into the "kingdom of the possible; and, ah me, the eye turns to a vacant chair, a faded miniature, a lock of soft hair in crumpled tissue paper, a broken toy; while the mind's vision recurs to a green mound and a half-effaced stone!" In the poet's land of dreams, the picture land of sleep, the bowers are fair, even as Eden fair:

All the beloved of my soul are there;
The forms my spirit most pines to see,
The eyes whose love has been life to me—
They are there; and each blessed voice I hear,
Kindly, and joyous, and silvery clear;
But undertones are in each, that say:
"It is but a dream; it will melt away."

One of Philip Bourke Marston's sonnets contains the telling simile:

Then am I as a man who sees in dreams
Some dead beloved face, and, seeing, deems
The past a dream, the dream reality.
But, oh! the bitter waking, when, alas!
He knows the mocking dream for what it was,
And gazes on a new day hopelessly!

Take, again, Campbell's "Exile of Erin," who, though sad and forsaken, in dreams can revisit her sea-beaten shore; "but, alas, in a far foreign land I awaken and sigh for the friends who can meet me no more!" His "Soldier's Dream," too, is a lyric to the purpose, dealing with a sweet vision the weary warrior has of household forms and faces, of children that cling to him and of a wife that implores him:

Stay, stay with us, rest—thou art weary and worn!
    And fain was their war-broken soldier to stay;
But sorrow returned with the dawning of morn,
    And the voice in my dreaming ear melted away.

The last letter to his wife, written during the night by Camille Desmoulins in prison, is called by Lamartine the final testament of his heart, which gave itself up to love before it was deprived of life at the hands of the executioner, and thus it begins: "A consoling sleep has suspended my sufferings. We are free when we sleep; we have no feeling of captivity. Heaven has had pity on me. But a moment since I saw you in my dreams, and in turns embraced you, your mother,

Horace—all! I awoke and found myself in my dungeon." As with the impris-
oned girl in Mrs. Norton's poem, who dreams of rescue by him she loves, dreams
of his overmastering her vile jailers and bearing her swiftly to a bower of bliss:

Safe in his sheltering arms one more she sleeps.
    Ah, happy dream! She wakes, amazed, afraid,
Like a young panther from her couch she leaps,
Gazes bewildered round, then madly shrieks and weeps.

For far above her head the prison bars
    Mock her with narrow sections of that sky
She knew so wide, and blue, and full of stars,
    When gazing upward through the branches high
Of the free forest.

In midnight slumbers Washington Irving's captive African holds sweet con-
verse with the tender objects of his affections; it is then the exile is restored to
his country; it is then the wide waste of waters that rolls between them disap-
pears, and he clasps to his bosom the companion of his youth. But, awaking, he
finds it is but a vision of the night; and then surge upwards *suspira de profundis*,
sighs from the depths, and tears of dejection steal down his cheeks. So again
with that seventy-second sonnet of Camoens's, when, wearied out with sorrows
still his theme, to sleep he yields his fancy prisoner; in dreams he then beholds
the shade of her who while in life to him was but a dream. "Spirit benign," he
calls, "oh, do not fly!" She turns on him a sweet and troubled glance:

Like one who says: "Alas, it cannot be!"
And hastens onward. "Dina" then I cry;
But, ere I can add, "mene," from my trance
I wake—for even illusion flies from me.

More than worthy of ranking with which Portuguese sonnet is that still
better known English one of Milton's, on the death of his second wife—dead
within the first year of their wedlock, and dying in childbed. "Methought," it
begins, "I saw my late espoused saint brought to me, like Alcestis, from the
grave;" and it ends with telling how she

Came vested all in white, pure as her mind;
Her face was veiled; yet to my fancied sight
Love, sweetness, goodness, in her person shined
So clear, as in no face with more delight.

But, oh, as to embrace me she inclined,
I waked; she fled; and day brought back my night!

The dying poet, Heinrich Heine, lay paralyzed, blind and bedridden in an obscure lodging of the rue d'Amsterdam, at Paris, where from morning to night he heard nothing but the rattle of wheels, the clatter of hammers, street brawls and the jingling of piano-fortes. But amid the turmoil of the city he was sometimes visited by sleep, "the balm of hurt minds," and then he dreamt of happier days,—dreamt that he was young once more and gaysome, and saw once again the cottage on the hill and raced along the well-known pathway with Ottilie, hand in hand, or lingered with her in love's dalliance, as wondrously her being thrilled his being:

I think that at the last I culled a flower,
    And gave it her, and then spoke loud and free;
"Yes, be my wife, Ottilie, from this hour,
    That I, like thee, may pure and happy be."

What she replied I never may remember,
    For suddenly I woke; and I lay here,
Once more the sick man, who in this sick chamber
    Disconsolate has lain full many a year.

We have all of us, sooner or later, and with more or less of frequency, and more or less of intensity, experiences of this kind in our dreams of the night— the illusory joys, the like disappointments in waking. And then fain would we rehearse anew the beatific vision and recall the dispersed phantoms of peace and sweetness and light, as with Southey's "Kailyal" in the *Curse of Kehama*, when

Soon she let fall her lids,
As one who, from a blissful dream,
Waking to thoughts of pain,
Fain would return to sleep and dream again.

Wasp, August 29, 1885, "Prattle":

Sleep fell upon my senses and I dreamed
    Long years had circled since my life had fled.
The world was different and all things seemed
    Remote and strange, like noises to the dead.
    And one great Voice there was, and something said:

"Posterity is speaking—rightly deemed
Infallible;" and so I gave attention.
Hoping Posterity my name would mention.

"Illustrious Spirit," said the Voice, "appear!
    Ere we confirm eternally thy fame,
Before our dread tribunal answer, here,
        Why do no statues celebrate thy name,
        No monuments thy services proclaim?
Why did not thy contemporaries rear
At least some school-house or memorial college?
It looks almighty queer, you must acknowledge."

Up spake I, hotly: "That is where you err!"
    But some one thundered in my ear: "You shan't
Be interrupting these proceedings, sir;
        The question was addressed to General Grant."
    Some other things were spoken which I can't
Distinctly now recall, but I infer,
By certain flushings of my cheeks and forehead,
Posterity's environment is torrid.

Then heard I (this was in a dream, remark)
    Another Voice, clear, comfortable, strong,
And Grant's great shade, replying from the dark,
        Said in a tone that rang the earth along
        And thrilled the senses of the Judges' throng:
"I'd rather you would question why, in park
And plot, my monuments were not erected
Than why they were." Then, waking, I reflected.

Wasp, December 12, 1885, "Prattle":

I know not if I was awake or dreamed,
    But somewhere once I came into a land
Where something strangely unfamiliar seemed,
    But what it was I could not understand,
    For all things were, to observation, planned
In such fair order as is most esteemed.
Men all were busy in their various manners;
Some cultivated skins and some were tanners.

But as I pondered 'twas revealed to me
    Wherein these people differed from my own.
When any man or boy of them would see
    A woman he was silent as a stone;
    And if perchance he found himself alone
With one, he would in mighty terror flee.
Such strange aversion to the sex exceeded
Even *my* coy diffidence when they have pleaded.

I asked why this was so. A man replied:
    "Why, surely, sir, I think that you must know
(Unless, indeed, you're from the other side
    The bay—arrived not half an hour ago)
    About poor Buck and t'other medico,
Who, scorning prudence, perished in their pride,
And many more who've joined the long procession
Of gentlemen who wail their indiscretion.

Wasp, February 27, 1886, "Prattle":

I mentioned last week the *Chronicle's* surprising astronomical diagram representing the moon's occultation of the star Aldebaran, and ventured to point out that the moon was in the felonious act of obscuring the wrong star. That extraordinary chart is worse than I had then observed; it is the very worst thing in the world. Men have died and great trees have grown up from their graves, matured, became well stricken in centuries, decayed and fallen since anything so immaculately vile, so divinely erroneous, so sweetly and superbly incorrect has blushed at its own wild beauty. It records the high-water mark of modern ignorance; it is the point XII on the dial of illiteracy. It is the offspring of a criminal relation between congenital incapacity and endemic stultifaction. It was drawn by a disobedient hand guided by a blind eye in a head full of quarreling vacuities.

Wasp, April 17, 1886, poem, unsigned but by Bierce:

THE DOCTRINE OF TEMPORARY ANNIHILATION.
I flung me down upon the earth and wept,
And then ensued a darkness. As I leapt
    Upon my feet again and looked about,
I said, bewildered: "Surely I have slept."

All things were unfamiliar. Round my feet
The grass grew and the flowers all were sweet,
　　But some dread spell was over all, and all
The place appeared unholy and unmeet.

Beneath the reaching hands of trees unknown,
With moss and lichen thickly overgrown,
　　Erect or prone upon the leafy earth
Was many an ancient monumental stone.

The walks, with brambles bordered now instead
Of flowers (though the roses still were red)
　　Drawing their devious ways beneath the weeds,
Started from nowhere and nowhither lead.

A voice assailed my ear—a passing swain
Sang with a jocund heart a villain strain.
　　I said, confronting him beside his way:
"Pray guide me out of this accurst domain."

Singing he passed as he had neither heard
Nor seen, and all so strangely it occurred
　　I trembled to conjecture what might be
The meaning, and my heart with terror stirred.

While striving with the dread of the unknown,
My eyes mechanically sought a stone,
　　The oldest in that awful field—all stained
By weather, worn with time, decaying, prone.

And there in letters half-effaced I read
My name and age!—a date. "How strange," I said—
　　"That is to-day!" Alas, Time's tell-tale work
Upon the stone!—I'd been for ages dead!

"Meantime where was I?" I demanded in
Hot curiosity. "You filled the skin,"
　　An angel, now made visible, replied,
"Of Dr. Bartlett of the *Bulletin.*"

San Francisco News Letter and California Advertiser, November 27, 1886, "Town Crier":

> I dreamed that I was dead. The years went by:
> The world forgot that such a man as I
>   Had ever lived and written: other names
> Were hailed with homage, in their turn to die.
>
> Out of my grave a giant beech upgrew.
> Its roots transpierced my body, through and through:
>   My substance fed its growth. From many lands
> Men came in troops that giant tree to view.
>
> It was my work, my monument: its fame
> Was mine, immortally—ambitious flame
>   Was slaked. Alas! The poet Welcker passed,
> And carved upon that tree his hated name!

San Francisco News Letter and California Advertiser, December 4, 1886, "Town Crier":

> What wrecked the Roman Empire? One says vice,
> Another indolence, another dice.
> Emascle says polygamy. "Not so,"
> Says Impycu—"'twas luxury and show."
> The parson, lifting up a brow of brass,
> Swears superstition gave the *coup de grâce*,
> Great Alison, historian, affirms
> 'Twas lack of coins (croaks Medico: "'Twas worms")
> And J. P. Jones, the scribe's suggestion collars,
> Averring the no coins were silver dollars.
> And now Pierre Lorillard, the millionaire,
> Stands forth his own opinion to declare,
> And shouts, with fine effrontery, that great
> Possessions paralyzed the Roman State.
> Thus, through the ages, each presuming quack
> Turns the poor corpse upon its rotten back,
> Holds a new "autopsy" and finds that death
> Resulted partly from the want of breath,
> But chiefly, though, from some disorder sad

That points his argument or serves his fad.
They're all in error—never human mind
The cause of the disaster has divined.
What slew the Roman Empire? Well, provided
You'll keep the secret I will tell you. I did.

San Francisco News Letter and California Advertiser, December 18, 1886, "Town Crier." After drawing attention to an *Argonaut*-based story about a costly new stained-glass window, imported from Italy by a Mr. Charles Main and currently on exhibit prior to being installed in Main's tomb, Bierce included the following poem:

Charles Main, I told you—'twas some moons ago—
How profitless the labor you bestow
    Upon a dwelling whose magnificence
The tenant neither can admire nor know.

Build high, build deep, build massive as you can,
The wanton grass-roots shall defeat the plan
    By shouldering asunder all the stones
In what to you will be a moment's span.

Time to the dead so all unreckoned flies
That when your marble all is dust—arise
    (If wakened), stretch your limbs and yawn—
You'll think you scarcely can have closed your eyes,

Take your fine window, when the foolish pride
That prompted its display is gratified,
    And fit it in your future lodging; but
Its light will scarcely warm the Thing inside.

A window in a tomb may be, no doubt,
Appropriately painted with devout
    Designs—impervious to sight: no eye
Cares curiously to look in—or out.

What though of all man's works your tomb
Should stand till Time himself be overthrown? alone
    Would it advantage you to dwell therein
Forever as a stain upon a stone?

San Francisco News Letter and California Advertiser, December 25 1886, "Town Crier." This column opened with remarks appropriate to the day, conferring a series of facetious gifts or blessings on prominent city officials, divines, competing journalists, educators, and the Devil. The paragraph's concluding line set up what followed, including the remainder of the editorial and "An Inhabitant of Carcosa": "To every strong man, the patience with which I endure the hollow, meaningless and maddening salutation of 'Merry Christmas,' in order that on that day the social domain may be a field of unthinkable carnage, rivered with flowing gore." In the next paragraph of the column, Bierce elaborated on his stance:

> For, look you, this is become an affliction and a bore. In it inheres precious little of lucent sense and wholesome sentiment. Christmas rites and ceremonies, traditions and observances are an insane jumble of early Christianity and earlier idolatry. They have a mingled odor of the monkery and the forest. Many of them are ailing survivals of old German and British superstitions, and have no more natural connection with Christianity than they have with algebra: Santa Claus is distinctly German, despite the Latinity of his title, and a clumsy conception the villain is—almost as hateful in his way as that distasteful creation of the Southern fancy in its decadence, known as Cupid and detested in all his forms and intrusions by every lover of art, graphic, plastic or literary. The utility of the Santa Claus yarn consists in this—it enables parents with sluggish imaginations to lie to their children without the mental throes of evolving a falsehood "by main strength and awkwardness." The ready-made lie, roughly adapted to the meanest capacity, hath ever a broad vogue and remaineth for centuries in steady demand.

Bierce next suggested that the trappings of Christmas derived from foreign superstitions should give way to native traditions:

> In describing Christmas observances as largely foreign, I am conscious of a base and reprehensible motive. I wish to array against them the sentiment of patriotism—a sentiment which also I regard with iron disfavor, and to whose alliance herein I have therefore no acceptable claim. But one half-brick is as good as another to heave at a dog out of range; and truly it is not expected that this present reprobation of Christmas will effect that hoary festival's immediate extinction. In course of time—in the process of the suns—when Mr. Pixley's American party shall hold the reigns of power and tool the nation along the road leading from the Joppa of political depravity to the Jerusalem of general perfection, we may hope to see every foreign element of Christmas sternly deported whence it came, and one thousand millions of freemen proudly celebrating the

distinctively American remainder, namely, the small boy, crossing his legs, orbing his cheeks and burying his eyes in the execution of instrumental halleluiahs [*sic*] and tin hosannas on a toot-horn.

The remaining material of interest appearing in the "Town Crier" column of December 25 includes two poems. The first is a poem about the apparently dreadful death poetry of Loring Pickering; it also happens to mention the resurrected corpse of a spouse:

Death-poet Pickering sat at his desk,
    Wrapped in appropriate gloom;
His posture was pensive and picturesque,
    Like a raven charming a tomb.

Enter a party a-drinking the cup
    Of sorrow—and likewise of woe;
"Some harrowing poetry, Mister, whack up,
    All wrote in the key of O.

"For the angels has called my old woman hence
    From the strife (where she fit mighty free)
It's a nickel a line; cond—n the expense!
    For wealth is now little to me."

The Bard of Mortality looked him through
    In the piercingest sort of a way:
"It is much to me though it's little to you—
    I've *taken* a wife to-day."

So he twisted the tail of his mental cow
    And made her give down her flow.
The grief of that bard was long-winded, somehow—
    There was reams and reamses of woe.

The widower man which had buried his wife
    Grew lily-like round each gill,
Till she turned in her grave and come back to life—
    Then he cruel ignored the bill!

Then Sorrow she opened her gates a-wide,
    As likewise did also Woe.

And the death-poet's song as is heard inside,
    Is sang in the key of O.

The second poem, despite its focus on the labor movement, contains themes
and images that also surface in "An Inhabitant of Carcosa":

I had a dream. The whole world seemed to be
    A desolation and a darksome curse;
And some one said: "The changes that you see
    In the fair frame of things, from bad to worse,
Are wrought by strikes. The sun withdrew his shimmer
Because the moon assisted with her glimmer.

"Then, when poor Luna, straining very hard,
    Doubled her light to serve a darkling world,
He called her 'scab,' and meanly would retard
    Her rising: and at last the villain hurled
A heavy beam which knocked her o'er the Lion
Into the nebula of great O'Ryan.

"The planets all had struck some time before,
    Demanding what they said were equal rights:
Some pointing out that others had far more
    Than a fair dividend of satellites.
So all went out—though those the best provided,
If they had dared, would rather have abided.

"The stars struck too—I think it was because
    The comets had more liberty than they
And were not bound by any hampering laws,
    While *they* were fixed; and there are those who say
The comets' tresses nettled Aldebaran,
An aged orb that hasn't any hair on.

"The earth's the only one that isn't in
    The movement—I suppose because she'd watched
With horror and disgust how her fair skin
    Her miserable parasites have blotched
With blood and grease in every kind of riot
When they can find a purse or throat to fly at."

Examiner, June 26, 1887, "Prattle":

How well I remember that grim and ghastly spot, the old Yerba Buena Cemetery. It was somewhat aside from the city's growth, but I sometimes made a long detour in order to pass through it in some of my nocturnal prowls. It was a little wilderness of prostrate headstones, gaping graves, decayed picket-fences, sandhills, lupine and scrub oaks. Here and there a yellow skull showed through the sand, as if a man had sprouted and was coming up. You would expect to see the whole skeleton in a few weeks rooted by the toes and growing vigorously. Other bones lay about—bits of blackened rib and unfamiliar vertebræ—but you had no confident fellowship with them, for dead dogs, too, had a habit of coming there, and during the winter rains ailing goats "tried the waters" with the customary result. People who had buried their friends there could never afterward find the graves. By some mysterious agency, inscriptions on tombstones were altered in a night and became sacred to the memory of persons with uncanny names. Murders were done there which never would out. Once in broad daylight a young man entered who never was seen again; a moment later an old man came out who never had been seen before. The senses here played pranks and performed one another's office: you could not distinguish the odor of the burial-vault from the tolling of a bell; the touch of the night wind upon your cheek made you cover your eyes to shut out the apparition.[16]

"O'er all there hung the shadow of a fear,
    A sense of mystery the spirit daunted,
And said as plain as whisper in the ear:
    The place is haunted."

In short, then, as in the day of Dennis Kearney and now, the site of the Sandlot and the new City Hall was a spot accursed of God and man.

I had a singular experience in the Yerba Buena cemetery. As I said above, I used sometimes to go into it at night. It is a way I have. I love the dead, and their companionship is infinitely agreeable. It was one of those half-dark nights of the winter time. There was a moon somewhere—I am uncertain if I saw it or heard it. Great banks of black cloud drove rapidly across the sky, extinguishing whole constellations, which unexpectedly flamed out again, looking strangely unfamiliar, as if their stars had been rearranged. The place was full of shadows, and some of them when merged in the broader gloom thrown from the clouds reappeared in another place. Many of them had no corresponding substances: they were foot-loose and could go where they would. I lay on a flat granite slab, supporting myself on my elbow. Suddenly—so suddenly as to startle—a man stood before me, within a pace. I had not seen him approach, did not know from what direction he had come. He was hatless and wore, I think, neither coat nor waistcoat. He seemed unaware of my presence. I lay in the shadow of a low oak, he stood in the light. His side was toward me and his face averted. Aside from the little "start" he gave me by his sudden appearance, I was not conscious of any feeling akin to fright. I thought him drunk—that ever ready and useful explanation of masculine eccentricity—and lay still to see what he would do. He did not turn his head; he did not move—not for a period that seemed to me some ten minutes. Then he looked at me over his shoulder and said: "Who the devil are *you?*" for my life I could not have replied, for the voice sounded exactly like my own, and I was now thoroughly frightened. As if I had answered, and asked a similar question, he added—but in a wholly different voice: "I am Josh Silsby." Then with a slight bow and an upward and outward motion of the hand—a gesture like that with which an actor sometimes withdraws from the stage—he was gone. I remained some time longer, but had not the happiness to meet him again.

To this day I am unable to say what there was in all this aside from my fancy about the voice, that was odd. The sudden appearance and disappearance could have been managed by stepping out of, and back into, a contiguous clump of bushes. I believe a little in the supernatural, but the name Josh Silsby—if I have rightly recalled it—seems ludicrously unghostlike; it resembles the invention of a humorist. Certainly I had never heard it before, and have never heard it since. That I was not asleep is also very certain. I kept a conscience in those days, or rather those nights, and having been sinning again it was hopeless insomnia that had driven me to the distractions of the graveyard.

Examiner, March 24, 1889, "Prattle":

They are a pretty pair—Boruck, the Roaring Violet, disclaiming the crown with a revolver in each hand, and Waterman, the Climbing Squid. Men have died and great trees have grown up from their graves since we have had two such holy shows rolled into one and exhibiting under a single canvas. [. . .] There are two ways of clarifying liquids—ebullition and precipitation; one forces the impurities to the surface as scum, the other sends them to the bottom as dregs. The former is the more offensive, and that seems to be our way; but neither is useful if the impurities are merely separated but not removed. We are told with tiresome iteration that our social and political systems are clarifying; but when is the skimmer to appear? [. . .] If the purpose of free institutions is good Government where is the good Government?—when may it be expected to begin?—how is it to come about? I humbly submit that it is no answer to say that I am not a patriot—nor is it true. Patriotism is love of one's country, not love of any particular plan for conducting its affairs. [. . .]

Systems of Government have no sanctity; they are practical means to a simple end—the public welfare; worthy of no respect if they fail of its accomplishment. The tree is known by its fruit. Ours is breaking down under its burden of Borucks, its weight of Watermans.

The remedy, why, truly, good friends, I have not to propose. [. . .] If the body politic is constitutionally diseased, as I verily believe; if the disorder inheres in the system; there is no remedy. The fever must burn itself out, and then nature will do the rest. One does not prescribe what time alone can administer. [. . .]

In that moment of time which is covered by historical records we have abundant evidence that each generation has believed itself wiser and better than any of its predecessors; that each people has believed itself to have the secret of national perpetuity. In support of this universal delusion there is nothing to be said; the desolate places of the earth cry out against it. Vestiges of obliterated civilizations cover the earth; no savage but has camped upon the sites of proud and populous cities; no desert but has heard the statesman's boast of national stability. Our nation, our laws, our history—all shall go down to everlasting oblivion with the others, and by the same road. But I submit that we are traveling it with needless haste.

After supplementing his argument by reproducing Shelley's "Ozymandias," "from memory and imperfectly, it may well be," Bierce concluded his lecture with a final damning paragraph:

My, friends, we are pigmies and barbarians. We have hardly the rudiments of a true civilization; compared with the splendors of which we catch dim glimpses in the fading past, ours are as an illumination of tallow candles. We know no more than the ancients; we only know other things; but nothing in which is an assurance of perpetuity, and nothing which is truly wisdom. Our vaunted *elixir vitæ* is the art of printing with movable types. What good will those do when posterity, struck by the inevitable intellectual blight, shall have ceased to read what is printed? Our libraries will become their stables, our books their fuel. Did—bah! the subject is grown out of reason.

16. "The Boarded Window." First published in the *Examiner* on April 12, 1891.

Examiner, March 29, 1891 (Easter Sunday), unsigned news article, "A Preacher Goes Daft":

Little Rock (Ark.), March 28.—A decided sensation was caused in this city to-day by the arrest on a charge of insanity of the Rev. T. J. Shelton, a prominent divine of this city and editor of the *Arkansas Christian*, the organ of the Christian Church of this State.

About two weeks ago he announced in his paper and from his pulpit that he was the Messiah and was endowed with all the powers of God. He also said that he was ordered to go to Kansas City, Mo., with the wife of a prominent merchant, who was a member of his church.

These statements caused the members of his flock to wonder, and the latter assertion concerning his proposed trip caused the husband of the lady spoken of to raise a rumpus that ended in an open row in the church.

This afternoon his acts reached the culminating point, when he was discovered in Oakland Cemetery hard at work resurrecting the body of a young lady member of his congregation who died a few weeks ago. As an explanation of his act he said he wished to raise the young lady from the dead.

The cemetery authorities placed him under arrest, and to-night he is in jail awaiting an investigation as to his sanity. His acts and his arrest are the talk of the city to-night.

Examiner, April 19, 1891, unsigned article, "Buried but Not Dead." A good example of the kind of material about death to which *Examiner* readers were regularly exposed, this article contains material that caters to the differing tastes of the incredulous and the skeptical where the question of the likelihood of premature burial is concerned. Judging by its content and timely publication, "Buried but Not Dead" may have been quickly and deliberately worked up from another source or even multiple sources for the *Examiner* by Bierce or someone acting with his previous week's story in mind:[17]

BURIED BUT NOT DEAD.
Grim and Ghastly Tales Told by Undertakers.
A PHYSICIAN'S STRANGE PROMISE.
How an Assistant Made Sure That the People He Laid Out Were Not Alive—A Rather Unpleasant Vow to Fulfill.

Several gentlemen well known in Chicago were seated in the rotunda of the Leland Hotel after supper the other evening, and some one brought up the subject of persons being buried alive. Two of the men were well-known undertakers and one a physician.

"It's all 'bosh' about people being buried alive," said one. "You read in the newspapers once in a while of such a case, but I never yet saw a man who had ever seen such a case. I think the changes in the position of the body, as is frequently described after a resurrection, are brought about by the careless

handling of the coffin, which causes the body to be rolled around and disar-
ranged."

"Never will any of the bodies buried by me come to life," remarked one of
the undertakers. "I have a perfect horror of such an idea. I always fix them so
that there is no danger of such an occurrence. No one will ever say that I buried
a live person. I started in business in a little town in Minnesota, and one night I
was called to arrange a body for burial. The body was that of a young girl. We
fixed everything up nicely and I went home to bed. The funeral was to occur the
next day, because it was during warm weather and they wanted to get the body
under ground," says the Chicago *Herald* [*sic*]. "At about 3 o'clock in the morning
I was called again, and what I saw made me creep. The girl had come back to life
and was the liveliest dead person I ever saw. She was a very nervous person and
had gone into a trance, during which she seemed to be dead.

"The body had looked exactly as though in death, and the attending physician had declared that life was extinct. The girl completely recovered, and the
last I heard of her she was married and the mother of a large family. I shudder
when I think of the consequences if she had been buried and afterward came
to life. To think of her agony and her suffering in finding herself confined in a
narrow box with several feet of earth and the solid box cover between her and
continued life. How she would have endeavored to free herself from the place
only to find her efforts unavailing.

"Now, whenever I have a body to prepare for burial I arrange it in the
proper manner and embalm it. After a body is embalmed there is no danger of
its ever coming to life again. I do this for the sake of the dead person, its
relatives and my own personal feeling in the matter. The embalming process
is very simple. An incision is made in the body, generally in the abdomen, and
the fluids are drawn off. The arteries of the heart are opened in some cases and
all the blood drawn off. This is done with a suction pump. Then the embalming fluid is injected into the veins and this preserves the body. The embalming
fluid is composed principally of arsenical properties: arsenic, you know, acting
as a preservative of the body."

"Yes, in case of a man dying from the effects of arsenic the body lasts longer
and is found in a better state of preservation if resurrected after some time. In
post-mortem examinations we find this always to be the case," said the doctor.

"Well, I don't believe that people are buried alive," said the other undertaker. "I never yet heard anything definite of such a case. But I used to have a
man work for me when I was in business in New York who had a horror of
such an occurrence. He was a Spaniard, and was one of the best men I ever
had work for me. One day he was arranging a body for burial when I noticed
a queer movement which he made. It was as though he were striking the body.

"When he left the room for a moment I turned the sheet down from the body, and right over the heart was a tiny round red spot. I examined it closely, and saw that an incision had been made with some instrument. We dressed another body that night, and I watched him very closely to see what he did. Finally I saw him draw something from his breast pocket, and, with a thrust, press it against the breast of the corpse. I sprang and seized his arm, which startled him so that he dropped what he had in his hand. It was a dagger, the blade being no larger than a needle. It was about five inches long and had a beautifully jeweled handle. I asked him what he did that for, and he replied that he always pierced the hearts of the bodies he prepared for burial.

"When in Madrid, where he learned his trade of undertaker, he had become involved in trouble, as one of the persons whom he had prepared for burial had been proved by a later disinterment to have been buried alive. The authorities made trouble over the matter, and he nearly lost his life as the result. He made a vow that he would never again run such a risk, and he made it a point ever afterward to pierce the heart of any body he prepared for burial. It had come to be a second nature to him, and he always carried it out as a part of the business. It may have been the proper thing in Spain, but it was too cold-blooded for me, and I had to let him go."

"I had patient [sic] once who had a great terror of being buried alive," said the doctor, "and one day he made me promise that after his body was ready for burial I would plunge a knife into his heart, so that he would not run the risk of waking up in his coffin. The poor old fellow nearly had a fit over the idea, and I promised to do as he requested. The day for the funeral came, and I was present to carry out the last wish of the old man. Several members of the family entered the room with me to watch the commission of the deed. I had a slender dagger which I had used as a paperknife. It was a relic which I had picked up in the East. I opened the clothing on the corpse, put the point of the knife over the place where the heart was and struck the handle of the dagger with the palm of my hand.

"My hair stood right up on end, and I felt as faint as though I had received a sunstroke. I pulled the knife out, arranged the clothing and we left the room. When I got outside I found that I was wet with perspiration."

"Didn't you feel like a murderer?" asked the undertaker.

"Why should I?" was the reply. "The man was as dead as a nail. He was a man no longer. I felt just as though I were handling a piece of lifeless clay. That is all it was anyhow."

17. "The Middle Toe of the Right Foot." First published in the *Examiner* on August 17, 1890.

Examiner, November 14, 1888, "A Desperate Combat." A front-page story about an improbable duel with bowie knives in a suitably darkened room:

A DESPERATE COMBAT.
Two Men Fight With Knives in a Darkened Room.
SLASHED AND STABBED.
One Cut to Pieces, the Other Is Killed in a Subsequent Encounter.

BIRMINGHAM (Ala.). November 13.—Two funerals took place here to-day which were largely attended and formed the climax of an extraordinary tragedy.

Robert Nabors was a prominent physician of Montevalle, in this State, and W. W. Shortridge was a successful lawyer in the same village. Both were young men. Some time ago Nabors employed Shortridge to collect a few claims against delinquent patients. The returns were not satisfactory, and the men quarreled, but parted without coming to blows.

Last Saturday Nabors called at Shortridge's office, and the old trouble broke out afresh. They finally agreed to fight with bowie-knives in a darkened room just off the office. Removing their coats and shoes, the men entered the room and fought blindly but desperately for nearly ten minutes.

FOUGHT TO THE DEATH.

The duel was one of the most vicious ever reported in Alabama. The men plunged their knives into each other until both looked as though they had been slaughtering beeves. Everything in the room was bespattered with blood.

Some persons living in the lower story heard the noise of the duelists as they rolled upon the floor and ran upstairs to separate the combatants.

When the door was broken open Nabors staggered into the office with the blood streaming from a dozen gashes in his face and breast. Without saying a word, he rushed down the stairs, still clasping a gory knife in his hand.

Lying upon the floor of the room was Shortridge. His head had been slashed in a most dreadful manner. The arteries of his neck had been severed, one eye had been gouged out and his hands were cut so terribly that the fingers hung only by the tendons. The man was dead.

MEETS HIS FATE.

Nabors, after leaving the office, ran out on the street, where his bleeding face and gory garments spread consternation among the negroes. He seemed to be crazed with pain and staggered wildly along the street until he reached a store where Albert Keenan, a negro, stood in the doorway. Without saying a word,

Nabors rushed at Keenan and struck him with the knife. The negro ran into the store, when the now thoroughly insane man made another desperate lunge at him.

Keenan seized a gun, which was lying upon the counter, and then turned to face the madman, who was in the act of making another lunge with his knife. The two men clinched, but Nabors, who was weak from loss of blood, was no match for his antagonist, and was quickly thrown upon the floor. Before Nabors could get upon his feet again, Keenan dealt him a terrible blow upon the head with the stock of the gun, and then, leaping over his body, ran into the street and out of town.

Nabors never regained consciousness. His skull had been fractured. He died at midnight. Keenan cannot be found.

Examiner, November 18, 1888, "Prattle":

One incident of the recent dark-room duel with bowie-knives, in Birmingham, Alabama, was of a character tending, it is to be feared, to bring such contests into undeserved discredit. The survivor and victor on being released from the room of honor ran furiously down the street, covered with gore as he was, to a store kept by an inoffensive negro and attacked him with all his remaining ferocity. In self-defense the negro was compelled to kill him. No doubt the sight of an antagonist clearly visible, and even conspicuous by reason of his color, constituted a powerful temptation after the events of the preceding half hour—a consideration to which, doubtless, the negro was insufficiently sensible—but forbearance is a virtue which should accompany valor, and if the victor in an affair of honor cannot abstain from attacks upon non-combatants, he proves himself to have been unfit to fight at all. The deceased was clearly no gentleman, and if the other deceased had known in time the character of him to whom he was invited to give satisfaction he would have been almost justified in refusing it. If the deplorable occurrence have the effect of surrounding the duel *in camera obscura* with more stringent regulations for the safety of outsiders the party to the third part will not have saved his own life in vain.

Examiner, January 1, 1888, "Prattle":

It is hoped that with further practice the good people of Scott City, which appears to be in Missouri, may acquire greater skill in extracting small children from well-tubes. The plan of letting down a hook when the child is at the depth of eighty feet and fits the tube like a cartridge in a gun was tried the other day and was only partially successful. The hook took hold very well,

under the chin, and a strong pull by willing hands hoisted the small unfortunate a considerable part of the distance to the surface, where its anxious mother
and friends (including the blacksmith who made the hook) awaited it: the
screams became more audible every moment, carrying joy to every heart. But
the friction and consequent fatigue were very great and the men at the rope
ceased work for a moment to rest. By some mischance the rope was permitted
to slacken and the hook, having unluckily been made without a barb, disen-
gaged itself by its weight, and as the child settled slowly past it refused to take
hold again. The whole work now had to be done over again, but these brave
hearts never faltered in their humane efforts, although a spectator whose suggestion of baiting the hook had been received with contumelious inhospitality
coldly remarked: "I told you so"—which was not accurately true. Further attempts, however, were unavailing: the hook would not take a firm hold, though
an occasional timely scream as the rope drew taut inspired a momentary hope
which speedily proved fallacious. The hook, repeatedly drawn up and examined, showed each time enough new and crimson evidence of its partial efficacy
to raise the spirits of all except the mother; but finally this method of rescue
was reluctantly abandoned and the child got out by digging. Unfortunately it
had in the mean time died. The tube-wells of Scott City are now closed, pending the blacksmith's production of a more effective appliance for saving life—
something, preferably, acting on the principle of the corkscrew.[18]

Examiner, February 24, 1889, "Prattle." Bierce criticized what he saw as an
alarming development, "[t]he custom of fathers killing all the females of their
families," explaining that it was "not in accordance with modern ethics." Although it was an outbreak of the practice in the East which had brought
Bierce's concern to the fore, he noted that "[i]t is admitted that the Eastern
woman is in many respects distinctly inferior to the admirable creature whom
it is our happiness to know on the Pacific Coast." Still, Bierce admonished it
was "the duty of the husband and father to love, cherish and obey her in the
hope of effecting her reformation." Later in his discussion, Bierce cited two
examples of the crimes he had in mind. The first occurred in Tecumseh,
Michigan, and was perpetrated by "the late Mr. Silvers":

Mr. Silvers, it appears, was a horsebreeder of some eminence—a fact which
seems to confirm the theory that there is an immoral emanation from the
horse, which, sooner or later, destroys all the best instincts of those who have
to do with its rearing, care and keep. Certainly something must seriously have
impaired Mr. Silvers' sense of right and wrong, for although he was "in pros-
perous circumstances and his relations with his family were pleasant," he shot
them all—wife and two daughters. At this point Mr. Silvers seems to have

realized the compromising nature of his act, or possibly was overwhelmed with a sudden sense of loneliness, for "on the quarry of these murdered deer" he added the death of himself.

The second crime:

> Mr. Elsmer being highly incensed—whether justly or not is not stated—by the tardiness with which his supper was served, brained his wife and two daughters with a fire-poker. Unlike Silvers, he did not crown the work by dispatching himself—perhaps the character of his weapon would not permit—but hunted down the servant girl and sent her over to the great majority instead.

Examiner, December 25, 1887, Christmas editorial, presumably by Bierce. This first Christmas editorial published in the *Examiner* during William Randolph Hearst's tenure at the helm, running alongside Bierce's "Prattle" column, is beyond a reasonable doubt the work of Bierce's pen: After a series of paragraphs on topics ranging from the violence-prone "pious ruffian of the Middle Ages," who "consecrated half of each week to a holy peace" only to make sure that the peaceful interlude was "balanced by half a week of hell," to a commentary on a recent achievement of the "Railroad King" W. K. Vanderbilt, who had "found that dreamland paradise of disaffected millionaires—the place where wealth is respected for its own sake," the Christmas editorial shifted gears to include a series of paragraphs under the subheading "Concerning Ghosts":

> The belief in ghosts is natural, universal and comforting. In many minds it is cherished as a good working substitute for religion; in others it appears to take the place of morality. It is rather more convenient than either, for it may be disavowed and even reviled without exposing oneself to suspicion and reproach. As an intellectual conviction it is, in fact, not a very common phenomenon among people of thought and education; nevertheless the number of civilized and enlightened human beings who can pass through a graveyard at midnight without whistling is not notably greater than the number who are unable to whistle.
>
> It may be noted here as a distinction with a difference that belief in ghosts is not the same thing as faith in them. Men—many men—believe in the adversary of souls, but comparatively few, and they not among our best citizens, have any faith in him. Similarly, the belief in ghosts has reference only to their existence, not to their good intentions. They are, indeed, commonly thought to harbor the most evil designs against the continuity of peaceful thoughts and the integrity of sleep. Their malevolence has in it a random and wanton quality which invests it with a peculiarly lively interest: there is no calculating

upon whom it will fall: the just and the unjust alike are embraced in its baleful jurisdiction and subjected to the humiliating indignity of displaying the white feather. And this leads us directly back to the incident by which these remarks had the honor to be suggested.

A woman living near Sedalia, Missouri, who had recently been married alive to a widower, was passing along a "lonely road" which had been thoughtfully laid out near her residence. It was late in the evening, and the lady was, naturally, somewhat apprehensive in a land known to be infested by Missourians of the deepest dye. She was, therefore, not in a suitable frame of mind for an interview with an inhabitant of the other world, and it was with no slight trepidation that she suddenly discovered in the gloom a tall figure, clad all in white, standing silent and menacing in the road before her. She endeavored to fly, but terror fastened her feet to the earth; to shriek, but her lungs refused their office—the first time that an office was ever refused in that sovereign commonwealth. In short, to use a neat and graphic locution of the vicinity, she was utterly "guv out." The ghost was a tremendous success. Unluckily it could not

curb the lust of war,
Nor learn that tempted fate will leave the loftiest star.[19]

It advanced upon its helpless victim and said in hollow accents: "I am the spirit of your husband's first wife: beware, beware!"

Nothing could have been more imprudent. The cowering lady effected a vertical attitude, grew tall and visibly expanded. Her terror gave place to an intrepidity of the most military character, and she moved at once to the attack. A moment later all that was mortal of that immortal part—divested of its funereal habiliments, hair, teeth and whatever was removable—battered, lacerated, gory and unconscious—lay by the roadside awaiting identification. When the husband arrived upon the scene with a horrible misgiving and a lantern, his worst fears were *not* realized: the grave had bravely held its own. The object by the roadside was what was left of his deceased wife's sister. On learning that her victim was not what she had incautiously represented herself to be, the victorious lady expressed the deepest regret.

Such incidents as this go far to account for that strong current of human testimony to the existence of ghosts which Dr. Johnson found running through all the ages; and at the same time they throw a new and significant light upon Heine's suggestion that ghosts are as much afraid of us as we of them. It would appear that some of the less judicious of them have pretty good cause.

Examiner, June 19, 1890, excerpt from "To Expiate Their Crime." This unsigned front-page article about a soon-to-be-hanged husband and wife murder duo, Josiah and Elizabeth Potts, revealed that the body of the murder victim, Miles Fawcett, was discovered after "the house formerly occupied by the Potts was rented to a family named Brewer":

> In January, 1889, the house formerly occupied by the Potts was rented to a family named Brewer. The house had two dug-out cellars. The roof caved in, and in removing the debris in one of them the Brewers found the body of Miles Fawcett buried about a foot deep in the top of the side wall, next the roof, the new and loose earth being covered over with straw. The body was horribly mutilated, the skull being crushed and partly burned, as were other portions of the body, and the limbs were severed from the trunk.

18. "Haïta, the Shepherd." First published in the *Wave*, a San Francisco weekly edited at the time by Bierce's friend Hugh Hume, on January 24, 1891.

Carey McWilliams in his 1929 biography of Bierce briefly addressed a failed wartime romance Bierce appears to have had. In a later article, published in 1932 ("Ambrose Bierce and his First Love: An Idyll of the Civil War," *The Bookman* 75, 254–59), McWilliams reprinted a recently surfaced letter from Bierce to the sister of his fickle lover and fleshes out the story of what, if in the main true, must have been a sad romantic Civil War interlude. Bierce, on furlough from active duty while recuperating from a serious head wound, apparently returned to Indiana only to discover that his girl was no longer interested in him. The letter expresses Bierce's willingness to transfer his affections from one sister to the other.

McWilliams in his biography also related a story Bierce's daughter, Helen, told him about Bierce from the time he spent near St. Helena, one of the various rural retreats he lived in while seeking respite from recurrent bouts of asthma in the late 1880s:

> He would take his daughter, Helen, for long walks through the mountains. She remembers that he would have her wait while he strode forward into the center of a glade or clearing. There he would stand perfectly still and erect, the sunlight touching his hair into a blaze of gold, while he called wild animals. It was a soft call, half a whisper and half a cry, and birds would come and light upon his uplifted arms, perch on his shoulders, and jump about on his hands. (190–91)

Examiner, July 27, 1889, "Stung to the Heart": This front-page news story reported the death of Day Bierce, Bierce's son (because Mrs. Barney, the apparent source of the account, is implicated in the affair, we need to be skeptical about the details):

Yesterday's Tragic Sequel to a Recent Chico Elopement.

A LOVER'S DESPERATION.

Shooting of Young Hubbs and His Bride by the Man They Had Deceived.

SUICIDE ENDS THE TRAGEDY.

[*Special to the* EXAMINER.]

Chico, July 26.—The Hubbs-Adkins elopement case culminated in a horrible tragedy this afternoon.

The causes which led to the shooting are as follows: Miss Eva Adkins, daughter of Mrs. C. Barney of this city, is a well-developed and handsome young lady of about seventeen years of age. Last May she met at a picnic here a young man by the name of Raymond Bierce, commonly called "Day" by his associates. Young Bierce had been sojourning in Red Bluff, and was commissioned by a paper of that place to furnish an account of the picnic, which was given by the A. O. U. W. While here he was introduced to Miss Adkins and became very much infatuated with the young lady. On his return to the Bluff he threw up his situation there and returned to Chico, where he has been employed in various capacities ever since.

Both he and Miss Adkins for a while were working together in the cannery and he was her devoted suitor. It was soon whispered that the couple were engaged, as Bierce was her constant attendant.

About two months ago a young man about twenty-three or twenty-four years of age, by the name of Neil Hubbs, arrived here from Stockton, where his parents now reside. Hubbs secured employment of the livery stable of Weed & Barnard. While around with the young men he met Bierce, and they soon became fast friends. Bierce had never cared to associate with the other young men here and held himself aloof from them.

QUICK TEMPERED.

Bierce was rather odd in some of his actions, but quick to resent an insult, as he promptly challenged a "tough" to fight him one evening for making insulting remarks while he was passing with Miss Adkins, and the "tough" was handsomely knocked out.

Hubbs, on the invitation of Bierce, met Miss Adkins, and frequently saw her at the Elliott House, where she was employed after leaving the cannery.

About two weeks ago young Bierce took up his residence at the house of Mrs. Barney, as Barney had failed to provide for his family, and Bierce's board bill helped to keep the wolf away from the door.

Barney, who had been in the country, returned here and at once objected to Bierce's being about the house, saying he did not want any one running his house but himself, as Bierce seemed to be doing. They had a row, and Barney, who is the step-father of the girl, attempted to throw Bierce out. He was put out himself, and had Bierce arrested for assault. Hubbs went Bierce's bail for $20, and at the trial both the mother and daughter testified that Barney was the aggressor, and Bierce was acquitted.

The couple were engaged to be married two years hence. The affair with the father, however, determined the young people to have the marriage take place on Monday night, the 22d. A license was secured, a minister engaged, the neighbors invited and full preparations made for a wedding that evening. Hubbs was to be the "best man" at the ceremony.

The Elopement and Marriage.

On Sunday night Miss Adkins informed her mother that she would like to spend the evening with the young lady who was to be bridesmaid. The mother consented and Miss Adkins left. She came up town and, in company with Hubbs and a young lady, remained in proximity to the depot, and when the south-bound Oregon express train reached here they boarded the train without any one seeing them, purchasing tickets on the train. They went direct to Stockton, to Hubbs' parents' house, and were married.

Bierce on Sunday heard of the elopement and rushed frantically around, searching for the couple and threatening dire revenge. He cooled down later on and seemed to take the matter calmly. On Tuesday evening Hubbs and his wife returned and took up quarters at the Central Hotel.

When Bierce heard of their return he tried to have them arrested for living together without being married. On being informed that the marriage had been performed he seemed to be satisfied, and expressed his determination to go to San Francisco, where his father had secured a situation for him in the Stock Exchange.

He accordingly left on Wednesday night but returned again last evening. He stayed up town until this morning, when he went to see Mrs. Barney, Mr. Barney being away in the mountains.

Mrs. Barney expressed surprise at seeing him, and when asked why he had returned he said he had changed his mind and would remain a week longer in Chico. Mrs. Barney informed him that she had heard he had made threats against Hubbs and his wife, and that she did not want him to raise any row. Bierce said he thought as much of Eva as he did of a sister, and would not harm a hair of her head.

Mrs. Barney told him that she had been to see Hubbs and his wife the night before, and had freely forgiven them, and had invited them to call this afternoon and take dinner with her; also, that she intended having the couple make that place their future home, and that Bierce would have to leave. To all this he assented and left the house.

Waiting for Them.

About half-past 1 o'clock a knock was heard at the door, and Mrs. Barney opened it. Bierce stood there, pale and trembling, and said:

"Mrs. Barney, I'm sick and can hardly stand. Won't you let me come in and lie down?"

Mrs. Barney told him she expected her daughter and her husband there in a few minutes, and she would not have any trouble for the world.

"I'll promise faithfully to remain in the bedroom, if you'll let me in," said Bierce, "and I'll not come out while the folks are here."

Mrs. Barney then let him in the bedroom, just off the parlor. Bierce closed the door and lay down on the bed.

Hubbs and his wife arrived in a few minutes. After about fifteen minutes' conversation the bedroom door opened and Bierce strode into the room. He spoke to the couple and said, "You're a happy, lucky married couple, ain't you?" They replied they were as happy as could be.

After a few minutes' general conversation Bierce suddenly began to upbraid the girl for her conduct. She told him that was past and not to refer to it again. He talked for a while longer, and then again began to call her names. Hubbs and his wife got up and said they would leave. Mrs. Barney told Bierce he would have to be quiet or leave. He turned around and ran into the bedroom.

A Desperate Fight.

While he was out Hubbs drew a revolver and stood with it by his side. Bierce threw open the door and, and leveling a pistol at Hubbs fired, the bullet striking Hubbs in the side. Hubbs fell to the floor, and while lying there returned the fire, shooting five shots to Bierce's four. Hubbs struggled to his feet and ran out of the front door, closing it after him.

Bierce then sprang to the side of Mrs. Hubbs and caught her, throwing her to the floor with the remark, "I'll now finish you." He placed the pistol to her head, but just as he fired Mrs. Barney grabbed him by the arm, saying, "You coward, you shall not kill my child."

Bierce pulled the trigger, but Mrs. Barney jerked his arm, and the bullet passed through Mrs. Hubbs' right ear, glancing along her skull, inflicting a severe scalp wound.

When Hubbs went out Bierce locked the door, and when he grasped Mrs. Hubbs she screamed for her husband.

He ran back on the porch and tried to get in the door, but could not. He began bursting it in, and succeeded in breaking out a panel, through which he crawled. He rushed upon Bierce and caught him by the throat, and the two men had a deadly struggle for about five minutes. Hubbs beat Bierce over the head with the butt of his revolver until Bierce fell to the floor, exhausted.

Hubbs was preparing to make short work of the man when he saw he could no longer defend himself, and got up from the prostrate body. Bierce said to him:

"My God, Neil, what have I done? Just put a cartridge in your revolver and kill me—kill me; I'm not fit to live."

Then, a few seconds afterward, Bierce begged Hubbs not to kill him.

A Shocking Scene.

Hubbs picked up his wife, who had fainted, and ran out of the house with her, followed by Mrs. Barney. Bierce staggered to his feet and followed them to the porch. He was bleeding from twenty different scalp wounds and presented a terrible picture. He called out to Mrs. Barney to return, as he wanted to see her. She told him she was afraid he would kill her. He promised that if she would come back he would not harm her at all and started toward them. Hubbs continued running with his wife and ran through the residence of Judge Leaman into that of Mrs. Keyes, where he fell exhausted. Mrs. Barney returned to the house and Bierce said to her: "My God, Mrs. Barney, this is horrible. I will kill myself. Help me into the bedroom." Mrs. Barney said: "Go in, if you want to; I'm going to take care of my child."

Bierce then said: "Telegraph my father, won't you? Tell him all about it, and if anything else happens to me, let him know. Poor father!"

A Suicidal Shot.

He then went into the room. Mrs. Hubbs [sic} hurried out, and just as she reached the corner she heard another pistol shot.

Marshal Mansfield reached the house just at this moment, and ran in. Bierce was lying on the bed, with a ghastly wound in the right temple, having reloaded the revolver, placed a cloth containing chloroform over his face and fired. The bullet passed clear through the skull from temple to temple, the brains oozing out on the pillow.

Dr. Bodley had been summoned and quickly had Hubbs and his wife under his care. Hubbs had been shot in the bowels, the bullet penetrating the spleen. The doctor probed for the missile, but could not find it. The wound, he states, will probably result fatally. Mrs. Hubbs will recover.

Bierce died at 4:15 o'clock, and his body was removed by Coroner Bay to the morgue, where an inquest will be held at 10 A.M. to-morrow.

Hubbs' parents in Stockton have been telegraphed for and message has also been sent to Bierce's father. Young Bierce was about twenty-two years old.

The town is in a terrible state of excitement over the affair, and considerable feeling is expressed against Mrs. Barney for allowing the persons to meet. She was placed under arrest by the Marshal to await the finding of the Coroner's jury.

It now transpires that Bierce left here Wednesday night, going as far as Sacramento and returning last night. It is said he had made threats to shoot Mr. and Mrs. Hubbs if they returned to Mrs. Barney's. On their way down they were met by a friend who, when informed where they were going, told them not to go on, as Bierce was there and would make trouble for them.

Dr. Bodley has probed three times for the bullet in Hubbs' body, but has failed to locate it. He says his chances for recovery are one in ten.

Examiner, January 25, 1891, "Prattle":

The expulsion of the patriotic ass from journalism is incomplete. For example, a morning paper of this city published last Sunday a telegram from Berlin, beginning thus: "The Berliners have been very busy skating in the Thiergarten." It goes on to say that "among the fashionable skaters" are Miss Soandso, Miss Thisandthat and Miss Tother, Americans. That is all that is said of them, but the lover of his country who prepared the dispatch for the compositor headed it: "Skating on the Ice. Several American Girls Attract Attention by Their Skill." He was born in Squedunk, is a self-made man and has been "prominently mentioned" for the Inspectorship of Light-blue Bodies at the Morgue. [. . .]

Brother Moffitt, of the Oakland Times, wants the police patrol wagon covered, and intimates with considerable breadth that his recommendation is in the interest of the City Councilmen of to-day who may be riding in it next year. He is thought, though, to have in mind his esteemed contemporary, Senator Dargie. If so, his recommendation takes high rank among the rare and shining examples of fraternal consideration known to the annals of the press. Brother Moffitt cannot fail to reflect deeply on the vicissitudes of public life and the transitory nature of earthly honors for he was once himself a Senator. But now, looking upon his fellow-editor in the very noon and midway of his glory, the set sun of the session that is gone before is heard to murmur: *"Deposuit potentes de sede, et exaltavit humiles"*—which means, in Oaklandese: "He has pulled down the mighty and set up the mighty small."

A "friend at my elbow" (Mr. Sad Experience) suggests that for advantage of those worthy persons imperfectly familiar with my style of humor I ought to explain that the foregoing paragraph is devoid of malice, meaning and sense. But what would you have? What can one say of editors who lead blameless lives, like Homer's Ethiopians, and whose readers send them to the State Senate? What can be done with two rival journalists who deny to one another the title, "Our Loathsome Contemporary"? These things paralyse [*sic*] the understanding and confuse the judgment. Evidently the conditions of journalism in Oakland are exceptional and peculiar. To the outsider they are as inscrutable as the laws of chance. Of Oakland newspapers and Oakland newspaper men he must write unearthly nonsense or hold his peace—which is not to be thought of.

O the Oakland newspaper, the Oakland newspaper!—spring of surprises, river of mysteries and ocean of delights! I pass a considering eye along its lines and the World of Unthinkable Things is about me. I hear the far moan of the Sea of Sleep. A flash of domestic infelicity lights up for an instant the realm of consciousness, followed by the thunder of the captains and the shooting. Coil upon coil, the *Boulevard constrictor* wraps itself about the helpless Lake; shrieks an adverse interest in vain protestation, its voice drowned in the superior shriek of a pedestrian in course of bepulping by the local train. Striking through the moan of the Sea of Sleep, I hear the clang of cymbals and the boom of a punished drum—the skirl of a tormentina: the Salvation Army is abroad in the streets. A fragment of orthodox theology, like a flung flame "ruinining [*sic*] along the illimitable inane," corruscates [*sic*] the situation "and leaves the world to darkness and to me." From the editorial column, in the faint phorescence [*sic*] of a dead issue, reeks slowly upward the visible and audible fragrance of the marsh near the Sixteenth-street station, swirled by the dispelling breath of John Irish. I remove my eyes from the printed page in vain: the spirit and essence of Oakland and the Oakland newspaper have invaded me at every pore, thronging all the avenues of the senses. I taste the Oakland water. I hear the Oakland crank expounding his fad on the curbstone and the footfalls of doomsealers fleeing to the hills. The Oakland dog—a distinct species, *Maxillator Quercuterrensis*—howls in the mental desolation; the melancholy, mild-eyed cow passes like a memory and the street squirrel squeaks unafraid. Murder red-handed stalks by, dragging the body of the wrong man, and Innocence is hanged for the offense. The Judges put one another in jail before my face. Lo! yonder portentous shadow is Dr. Bartlett; it passes swiftly by, borne on the breeze from the woods. Lower and more confused are the ghosts of sounds of village life, the visions fleeter and dimmer. I nod; the lids drop slowly over my eyes, shutting out the big black letters; the paper slips from my knees with a crisp rustle and I spring awake. It is midnight and the cats of Oakland are calling to the cats of San Jose. I am at San Jose.

19. "An Heiress from Redhorse." First published in the *Examiner* on March 15, 1891, under this title but renamed "A Lady from Redhorse" in the 1898 Putnam's collection.

Examiner, unsigned news article, FROM WANT TO WEALTH, subtitled "A Pomona Lady Falls Heir to Several Million Dollars," May 2, 1889:

POMONA, May 1.—Mrs. Phoebe Sawyer of this place has received authoritative information that her claim to one-half of the estate of Thomas C. Bean, the Texas cattle king, who died in Grayson county, Tex., in 1887, will be recognized in the courts. This information has naturally caused an unusual sensation in Pomona. [. . .]

Examiner, "Prattle," May 5, 1889:

A poor woman in Pomona has "fallen heir" to several million dollars. This will prove of great advantage to her: it will enable her to withdraw herself from contact with those who were her friends in adversity and associate on equal terms with those who despised her.

Notes

INTRODUCTION

1. The title page of the book bears the date 1891, and Bierce had distributed some copies to his friends in December of that year, but its official U.S. publication was delayed until January 28, 1892, in order to facilitate its simultaneous publication in Great Britain. Mary E. Grenander, "Ambrose Bierce and *In the Midst of Life*," *Book Collector* 20, no. 3 (Autumn 1971): 324–25.

2. "Prattle," February 17, 1883.

3. It has been occasionally argued that "The Monk and the Hangman's Daughter" merits this designation, but it is more properly a novella; moreover, its pedigree is weak as it was translated from a German source by Bierce's then-friend Adolf Danziger and then subsequently edited and expanded upon by Bierce.

4. Grenander, "Ambrose Bierce and *In the Midst of Life*," 321–31.

5. In a letter to Neale of September 1, 1909, Bierce discussed a recent reviewer's attempt "to prove me an imitator of Poe" and after objecting to a pair of claims put forward by the reviewer conceded the obvious: "But I *am* an imitator of Poe. Poe wrote tragic tales of the supernatural; so do I. This immortal ass evidently does not know that anybody else ever did, and thinks nobody else should have dared. Well, if I had left out the tragedy and the supernatural I would still have been an imitator, not only of Poe, but of others, for my stories would still have been tales."

6. I have not been able to identify the "book of fiction" in question, but Florence Finch Kelley was primarily a writer of social tracts advocating the reform of labor laws and similar issues and thus Bierce's description is almost certainly satirical.

7. As Grenander explains, "G. H. Putnam, a former major in the Union army, felt that the civilian stories bore 'no connection' with the others" (322–23).

APPENDIX

1. On May 26, 1883, the *Wasp*, claiming to reach "every part of the Pacific Coast," reported that its circulation was "nearly 14,000" and that it had added "1,107" new subscriptions since March 1, 1883 ("Ourselves" 3).

2. Bierce's italicized phrase "*both ways*" refers to the fact that Union and Confederate forces and veterans typically interpreted the same events in dramatically different

fashions. This situation can arguably be said to still exist today among the different descendants and inheritors of the two traditions.

3. The earlier references to "Dr. Woolsey" appear to be in error.

4. Although this line can be taken to refer to the actions that precipitated Goldenson's arrest, the remainder of the poem reveals that Bierce is particularly referring to the postsentencing actions of Goldenson where he performs from his jail cell for his audience like a dancing bear.

5. Guatimozin, or Guatemotsin, was the last Aztec emperor of Mexico. Captured by Hernando Cortés, Guatemotsin was eventually tortured to death by the Spanish in a futile attempt to force him to reveal the location of the Aztec treasury.

6. Chewing soap being Bierce's substitution for foaming at the mouth like a mad dog.

7. This passage is reproduced from the second installment of the essay's *Wasp*-based publication.

8. The aide-de-camp was most probably Bierce himself.

9. With great and, from Bierce's point of view, embarrassing hoopla, the Knights Templar had descended en masse on San Francisco in 1883. To Bierce's perceptive eye, despite their elaborate rituals and oft-repeated claims, these knights lacked even a tenuous connection to their long dead namesakes. The grammatical and spelling liberties found in this passage reflect Bierce's ebullient mood. One might say he is spoiling for a fight.

10. The occasion had still not come when Americans could honor all the fallen dead of the Civil War with equality. The Union and Confederate dead were still treated separately by the living at the discretion of some unforgiving members of the victorious North, a practice that Bierce disparaged.

11. Bierce's reference to 1876 is apparently a reference to that year's bitterly contested national elections where a racist backlash against Reconstruction policies and laws played a pivotal role in allowing the Democratic party under Samuel J. Tilden to win the popular presidential vote and just barely lose the contested electoral vote to Rutherford B. Hayes and the Republicans.

12. Bierce is perhaps playing with the notion that the "pair of tongs" were members of a Chinese secret society.

13. Bierce went on in the following paragraph of the editorial to cite the San Francisco *Chronicle* as "the foulest hand addicted to this sordid practice of using the vanity of respectable women to advertise the business of prostitutes" (Editorial, *Wasp*, January 6, 1883, 4).

14. "Bummer" was the name of a dog owned by Emperor Norton, a famous Gold Rush–era resident of San Francisco. See Franklin D. Walker, *San Francisco's Literary Frontier* (New York: Knopf, 1939), 134, and index, iii.

15. Beyond hinting broadly at Bret Harte's "Plain Language from Truthful James," the dialect of this passage, while similar to that used by Barney Bree, is reminiscent of that spoken by a character named "Dummie" who appears in the opening chapter of Bulwer-Lytton's *Paul Clifford.*

16. That Bierce describes synesthesia so succinctly suggests he, like Poe, experienced its manifestations.

17. The clearest evidence of both haste and a third-party source is found in the article's third paragraph, which contains the phrase "says the Chicago *Herald,*" where "said the undertaker" should logically appear.

18. Originating in the *Kansas City Times*, the *Examiner* ran the story Bierce is referring to on December 17, 1887, a full month after the events described had happened; Jessie's body was finally recovered from the well tube on November 19, 1887 ("Jessie Died in the Tube").

19. Bierce had used this same quotation, referring to Napoleon's tragic flaw, drawn from Byron's *Don Juan*, in "Chickamauga."

Bibliography

Many of the supplementary documents I have drawn on in preparing this new edition of Ambrose Bierce's *Tales of Soldiers and Civilians* are reproduced or partially extracted in the appendix. They are also discussed at length in my study, *Ambrose Bierce's Civilians and Soldiers in Context: A Critical Study*, also published by the Kent State University Press. Thus, rather than repeat the bibliographic citations that appear in part in the appendix here and in full in the bibliography of the other, I have elected to restrict this bibliography to the three typescript/manuscripts and the three books that bear most directly on the present edition.

Bierce, Ambrose. *Can Such Things Be?* ts/ms for vol. 3 of *The Collected Works of Ambrose Bierce.* Huntington Library, San Marino, California.

———. *In the Midst of Life: Tales of Soldiers and Civilians.* New York: Putnam's, 1898.

———. *In the Midst of Life (Tales of Soldiers and Civilians).* New York: Neale, 1909. Vol. 2 of *The Collected Works of Ambrose Bierce.* 12 vols. 1909–12.

———. *In the Midst of Life (Tales of Soldiers and Civilians).* ts/ms for vol. 2 of *The Collected Works of Ambrose Bierce.* Huntington Library, San Marino, California.

———. *Tales of Soldiers and Civilians.* San Francisco: Steele, 1892.

———. *Tales of Soldiers and Civilians.* Paste-up ts/ms. 5992. Univ. of Virginia Library, Charlottesville.